FIREFLY EFFECT

FIREFLY EFFECT

USA TODAY BESTSELLING AUTHOR

K.K. ALLEN

COPYRIGHT

To those brave enough to blaze trails, lighting paths for others to see. You are an inspiration. Ignore the haters. LET THEM.

PROLOGUE

EVELYN

14 YEARS AGO

Wild flames from the campfire danced between us, the bright-orange glow resembling a bald cypress tree bowing and rustling with the wind. If only the imagery was enough to shield my view from *him*—Foster Pruitt, the cute older boy with the thick chestnut hair and intense focus on everything but me.

Not even his lack of acknowledgment was enough to stop the pitter-patter running rampant in my chest when I caught a glimpse of him.

"Tell us the story," Kyle, a boy my age sitting near Foster, asked my Uncle Patrick. "The one about the Firefly Man."

The wide eyes of every kid there fixed on my uncle, who sat beside me. Uncle Patrick had been forced to retell the same spooky story every night since we'd arrived at Deep Creek Campground.

Meanwhile, Foster's natural pout deepened. "Again?"

His gaze shifted around the fire, as if to see if anyone would object, but he seemed to be the only one with a problem, and I didn't know why. Not even I was sick of hearing this folklore for the fifth night in a row.

Just then, Lilith, a girl Foster's age, sat down on the log between Foster and Kyle. She was wearing a short black skirt and tight black tank top that revealed a hint of cleavage. Jealousy swirled in my heart—Lilith had a far better chance of getting Foster's attention than I ever could.

From my other side, Carley, Foster's younger sister, elbowed me gently. "Lilith needs to get a clue. Foster hasn't spoken a word to her all week."

Her words soothed the daggers of envy swirling through me, and I smiled back at her, amused. "Really? She's so pretty."

Carley rolled her eyes. "She's annoying. That's what she is."

Stifling a laugh, I watched Foster as Lilith whispered to him, his frown deepening by the second. As cute as Foster was, I couldn't miss the constant glower on his beautiful face, like he lived beneath a cloud of gloom and doom. All I wanted to do was make him smile—but I was running out of time.

"You want the Firefly Man story again? Are you sure?" Uncle Patrick teased the lot of us.

"Yes!" several of us called simultaneously.

"Please, Patrick," Carley added.

"It's the last night. You have to," said Kyle.

"It's tradition," Janessa reminded him.

Janessa was right. Every night, before we went out to watch the synchronous fireflies ceremoniously select their mates, Uncle Patrick would retell the story of a mysterious hiker who stalked the woods every year around this time. The Firefly Man's mission was to scare away anyone who attempted to disturb his precious fireflies or their mating ritual that illuminated the woods.

Patrick cleared his throat and began to speak. Just like every other night, my friends and I huddled around the fire and giggled at the story. Meanwhile, I kept sneaking glances at the boy scowling from across the fire. I couldn't look away.

"Daydreaming will get you nowhere, my dear," my mother would often taunt when she caught me in a similar trance. I could hear those words rushing through my mind now as if she were here. While I hated admitting when my mother was right, Foster had clearly stolen my attention ever since Uncle Patrick and I had arrived here last week.

Not that I could help it.

At first glance, I saw that they didn't make boys like Foster back in Raleigh. At least, not that I'd ever noticed. He was different—quietly observant, oblivious to my family's wealth, and seemingly fascinated by the nature that surrounded us.

I desperately wanted him to be just as fascinated with me.

He was just so… *interesting*. Especially when compared to Carley. The siblings were opposites in most cases, but I loved how he watched out for his little sister.

I wondered if anyone else looked out for her like he did. Carley was a wild child, a rebel, but with the sweetest heart of anyone I had ever met. She had a curiosity that craved adventure, and I adored the way she often dragged me along for the ride. I felt like we'd known each other our whole lives rather than just the five days we'd spent together this week.

"Evelyn Beatrice Vaughn, did you hear me?" Carley asked.

My head whipped in Carley's direction. The girl had an amazing memory, given she'd just asked me what my middle name was while swimming earlier in the day.

"Yes," I said automatically, realizing Patrick had already finished telling the Firefly Man story.

She grinned. "Well, are you just going to sit there and stare at my brother all night, or are you coming with us?"

Heat blazed in my cheeks like a wildfire. Luckily, daylight was fading, making my blush difficult to see. I couldn't believe Carley had practically caught me drooling while staring at her brother.

"What?" I laughed. "I was just thinking about that story," I lied, covering my shame with a smile.

Carley's giggle came with a wave of her hand, telling me she didn't care if I was gawking at her brother. "You mean the same firefly tale your uncle has told us every single night this week? Has he always had such a wild imagination?"

I nodded. My eyes were wide as I tried to select my words in a way that would paint her a picture. "You should see his book collection. He has so many that he started building bookshelves in his bar. They take up practically every single wall from the floor to the ceiling."

Beside the outdoors, my uncle's bar was my favorite place to be when I got to stay with him. He even named the bar Firefly thanks to my love for the tiny creatures.

"Wow," she said in a dreamlike state. "I'd love to see that. I have to beg my parents to take me to the library."

Her eyes dimmed with sadness. "We can't afford to have bookshelves like that."

Guilt pelted me in the gut. "You should come by Firefly on your way out of town." I grinned. "I'll have Patrick find a way to convince your parents."

Carley perked up and squeezed my hand. "That would be the coolest."

I smiled, unable to control my overwhelming sense of hope at the thought getting to spend a day with her among my uncle's bookshelves.

"We should go." Carley seemed barely able to contain her joy as she tugged me forward. "Everyone's already heading into the woods. Last one to the creek jumps in."

My enthusiasm mirrored hers, even though she couldn't see it. I'd learned at a young age to hide my emotions at all costs. Vulnerability was a window into the soul—a weakness my mother could never bear to witness.

Still, excitement compounded in my chest just thinking about the entire reason I begged my parents to continue letting me come to Bryson City, North Carolina, for the summers—the synchronous firefly show. When I was younger, nothing was more magical than watching the entire woods erupt with blue and green sparkling lights.

I looked over to the nature trailhead where our peers were walking into the woods, chanting, "Run, run, as fast as you can—you can't catch me, I'm the Firefly Man," followed by hysterical laughter.

"Evie!" my uncle called.

I halted and looked over my shoulder at Uncle Patrick, who stood with all the other parents and a few more of his friends. They all held red Solo cups filled with some alcohol mixture that seemed to be endless in its supply.

"Remember to stay on the path," he warned. "And don't stay out too late. We'll be playing cards at Jimmy's campsite. Find me there when you're done."

"Okay!" I said, more than happy to oblige. Who would want a detour into the freakishly scary woods in the dark, anyway?

Patrick smiled. "Have fun, Evie girl."

With another tug of Carley's hand, I followed her, astutely aware that Foster was right beside us.

Once we were around the first bend of the trail, Carley stopped, a wicked look flashing across her face. She pulled something out of the inside pocket of her jean jacket. As soon as I saw the glass mason jar, unease filtered through me.

"Carley, no…" Panic beat at my chest like a warning cry.

Her eyes twinkled. "Why not? It's our last night."

My disbelieving gaze bounced between Carley and Foster. Shock and confusion flowed through me like a tidal wave. Until that night, we'd never tried to trap the fireflies. No one broke that rule. After all, the moral of the Firefly Man tale was to let nature be. "W-what about the Firefly Man?"

Carley's laughter made my cheeks flame. I hadn't thought through my question before asking, but after it slipped out, I realized how immature I sounded.

Foster's reaction was different, his downturned mouth creating yet another frown that did little to alleviate the intensity of my attraction.

Carley stepped toward me, her freckled features mischievous. "That's just a silly campfire tale, Evelyn." Her smile was warm and reassuring—she must have sensed my panic. "Besides, it's not like we'll keep them in the jar to die. We'll let them go."

Relief eased my tension. How bad could it be if no harm came to the innocent creatures?

"Here," Foster said, revealing his own jar and holding it out to me. Just the sound of his voice had my heart tripling its beat. "You can use mine."

My eyes locked in on the round top and metal latch of the jar before I looked back up at him. My heart caught in my chest as I stared back into a sea of green. Gold specks swam within them, distracting me momentarily from my shame. I was caught between fear of the Firefly Man and attraction to the boy I had been crushing on all week.

I didn't even have time to return the jar before Carley clutched my arm and started to pull me in the direction of the woods, my heart practically kicking out of my ribs. Guilt knotted inside at the thought of disobeying the one person who had ever truly taken care of me.

Patrick told that story before the mating ritual began for a reason. Fireflies were becoming endangered, thanks to light pollution and the destruction of their natural habitat. I didn't want a part in any of that, yet I couldn't say no to Carley and her brother.

The three of us were the last ones to enter the woods. We followed a dirt trail that wound through the trees and veered off in various directions like a spiderweb. In daylight, the trails were easy to navigate, the tree cover sparse enough to see far in the distance. As nightfall descended and the sounds of woodland creatures filled the air, the world around us began to alter into something I didn't recognize.

Maybe my fifteen-year-old imagination was at play or

my senses had gone completely out of whack in the presence of a cute boy, but it felt like I'd just stepped out of my boring life and straight into one of my mystery novels. I didn't know what would be waiting for me when I turned the page.

A squeal split the air, and Carley's fingers slipped from mine and pointed straight ahead. "Look! It's starting."

My head turned to find nothing but a faint outline of the trees, but I knew in mere seconds my eyes would adjust to the heartbeat of the marsh. That was what my uncle called the entire mating phenomenon, when male fireflies flashed their light to attract a mate and the females flashed back if they liked what they saw.

That night, it took a bit of focus for my eyes to adjust to the tiny sparkles and streaks that flickered in the distance, but as they did, I became mesmerized like I was seeing it all for the first time. The trees simply disappeared and were replaced by a bioluminescent light show I would never get enough of, while cicadas, crickets, and who-knows-what-else provided the soundtrack for the night.

A blueish-white streak crossed my vision, and my eyes followed it into the distance. "Wow, the blue ghosts look so pretty tonight."

Carley's jaw dropped—she'd just noticed the rare species of fireflies too. "I've never seen so many of them mix with the synchronous ones." She turned to her brother, eyes wide with delight. "Have you, Foster?"

He shrugged. "Don't think so."

She laughed at his disinterest and grabbed his hand. "Did you know the blue-ghost ones can light up for almost a minute? That's why you see those streaks through the air."

Again, he didn't react to the fun facts Carley was spitting out, but she didn't seem to care. Instead, she took the lead, charging ahead and venturing farther down the path. Once Carley got ready to capture the tiny insects, I copied everything she did. How she unlocked the metal clasp of her jar then held it snugly in the palm of her hand. How she slowed her pace while her captivated eyes locked on the lights flickering around her. And how, with a twist of her palm, she captured her first firefly, catching and trapping it in one quick motion.

My breath came fast as I watched the light dance around her jar. Instinctively, I turned to find Foster, expecting to see him wearing one of his deep frowns or contemplative looks. This time was different—a hint of a smile tugged at his lips as he watched his sister's joy.

That was all it took for me to open the lid of my jar. One by one, the glass wall brightened with the glow of a dozen tiny fireflies—innocent beings, their lifespans a blip in comparison to humans. But I couldn't get over the magic created in their combined light.

I hadn't even noticed that the others in our group had veered off in different directions until Carley darted away from the path and farther into the woods, something my uncle had told me not to do under any circumstances. I was to stay on the trail, and I had promised that I would.

My feet halted, the thought of disobeying Uncle Patrick an invisible collar around my neck, pulling me back.

"Carley, we need to stay on the trail," I called, unable to contain my alarm.

She didn't stop. Instead, she tossed me a grin over her shoulder then ran even faster. "Run, run as fast as you can, Evelyn! They'll be easier to catch out here!"

"Carley, wait up!" Foster yelled. He took a step off the trail toward his sister but stopped to look back at me. "I have to follow her. Come with us." He gestured to the flashlight he carried, which he had covered with red cellophane to allow night vision. "I have light."

In true stubborn-Evie fashion, I held up my mason jar. "So do I." But when I looked at the jar, I frowned. While I had some light, the jar full of fireflies I'd collected didn't provide enough to help me actually see my way through the darkened woods.

Meanwhile, I couldn't get my uncle's warning out of my head. I looked around for a path that veered in the same direction Carley had gone. "I'll stay on the path. You should find Carley."

Foster frowned and seemed to hesitate for a second. "Suit yourself." Then he paused and looked back at me with a sarcastic rise of his brows before following his sister. "Just don't make any sudden movements. You know, in case the Firefly Man is watching."

My jaw dropped as I watched him turn and dart into the woods. Suddenly, Foster Pruitt wasn't so attractive anymore. He looked the opposite of cute, and I glared at his back, hoping he could feel my irritation, until he completely faded from view. A moment later, I continued down the path, trying my best to not think about the fact that I was all alone.

Insides rattling with fear, I walked for what felt like the next hour. Time slowed in the worst possible way. My ears became tuned into any small noise, but that backfired—the slightest rustle of a tree or crunch of a leaf sent me into an anxiety tailspin. If I could just find any of the dozen others who had gone into the woods, I would have felt so much better.

Eventually, I arrived at an intersection. One way pointed back to camp, and the other led to the creek. But I needed to find Carley, at least, if not her stupid brother. With a low growl, I stomped down the path that led to the creek.

"Run, run as fast as you can." The words were just a whispering hiss, slithering through the woods.

My heart leapt into my throat as I spun around. "It's not funny if I can't see you," I growled angrily.

A low chuckle followed the haunting rhyme, then I heard feet pounding, charging toward me. A scream ripped from my throat as a figure jumped forward, arms raised and ready to attack.

The moment the figure landed, I held up my jar for light to find Gabe bursting into boisterous and annoying laughter. My fist flew out, socking him in the chest. "You asshole. I almost murdered you with my jar of fireflies."

He laughed even harder, clearly enjoying himself. "Oh, come on, Evelyn. You had it coming walking out here alone."

"Yeah, well." I punched him again, this time making him wince. "That's how I like it. Go away, Gabe."

He raised his hands and backed up. "Geez. Fine. Don't cry to me if you get lost out here."

I rolled my eyes. "How could I possibly get lost on this trail?"

He shrugged, then winked and turned to head back the way he came. "See ya."

I only made it another few steps when I heard someone hiss, "Psst," from nearby.

My heart lurched into my throat, and I whipped around to survey my surroundings. *Not again.* No one was visible, thanks to the darkened sky. I was a beat away from taking off in a sprint toward camp when a branch cracked loudly.

"Evie," a deep voice called. "Are you okay?"

I snapped my head toward the sound, this time finding Foster heading toward me. He looked worried, like he cared. My insides flipped and flopped in ridiculous fashion. I had never before wanted to murder a boy and kiss him at the same time.

"I didn't realize I was so close to the path, then I saw you." He searched my face, his brow wrinkling. "You okay?"

No, I was not okay, but I wasn't about to tell him that he'd just scared the shit out of me.

"I still haven't found Carley," he said. "She must be down by the creek where we're supposed to meet everyone. I didn't get that far before I heard you scream."

"I'm sorry," I said automatically, as I always did when someone around me was disappointed. At least that was what Patrick said. He said I needed to stop blaming myself for things that were out of my control. "I screamed because Gabe was being an asshole."

Foster scrunched his nose, seemingly disgusted with my friend. "What's new? We should stick together now."

A sigh of relief relaxed me. Then I noticed how out of breath Foster was from his search. He'd removed his black hoodie, too, revealing a white shirt that must have gotten snagged on some branches because the arm was torn.

"Come on. We can get to the creek quicker this way." He gave it a few moments before apparently realizing I wasn't going anywhere. "Come *on*," he said again, sounding angry. "I'm not leaving you out here alone again."

This time, my feet jolted from their spot and took me into the woods until I was right by his side. I hated that I was ignoring the promise I'd made to my uncle in order to follow a boy into the deep, dark marsh, but what else was I supposed to do?

"You're such a jerk," I said once my heartbeat began to steady.

Foster shrugged. "You don't even know me, Evie girl."

Something about the way he used Uncle Patrick's nickname for me warmed my chest. But Foster was right. I knew nothing about him or Carley other than that they were visiting the area with their family from Murphy, North Carolina.

We reached a clearing that opened to the water, but at first glance, Carley was nowhere to be found.

"Dammit," Foster muttered, frustration coating his tone. "Where the hell is she?" He looked around, aiming his flashlight in several different directions, and called, "Carley, where are you?"

We both got quiet, waiting for her to respond.

I tried next, sticking close to Foster's side. "Carley! Come out, come out, wherever you are." I laughed lightly, trying to mask my nerves.

Still, no answer.

Foster sighed. "This isn't funny, Carley. C'mon."

I frowned, unease compounding in my chest. "Carley, answer us."

Together, we continued hollering her name, getting nowhere.

Foster's entire body looked as tense as his words. Then

realization illuminated his features. "Isn't there a clearing to the creek down that way?" He nodded in the direction we were walking then swiveled around, flashing a light on the waterfront. "Yes, this way." Excitement coated his tone now. He took off running. "Come on!" he shouted back to me.

This time, I didn't need him to beg me to follow. As I ran to catch him, I wanted to comfort him. To tell him Carley could handle herself. She was a tough girl. Besides, the woods were full of our fellow campers, and she would surely be with some of them. But before I could say any of that, a violent, horrific scream ripped through the night.

Gabe again. That was my first thought, figuring he was getting some sick pleasure in terrifying girls in the woods at night. Still, Foster and I stopped dead in our tracks. We listened closely, and I was sure I would hear someone berating Gabe for his antics, but that never came. In fact, the woods were too quiet.

The fright in my chest was no match for what I saw in Foster's reaction. All color left his face as his eyes flared wide, and the way he took off into a sprint could have rivaled an Olympic athlete.

I had no choice but to follow him—follow Carley's scream. Because while I had only known the Pruitts for the week, I realized that voice belonged to my new friend. Foster recognized it, too, and by the look on his face, he was about to pummel Gabe one hundred times harder than I already had.

When Foster slowed, his head swiveling left then right like he was lost, I said, "That way." I pointed. "It came from near the water."

Foster's head snapped to me, his eyes narrowed into a

glare I knew came directly from stress. "How do you know?"

I couldn't explain it—I just knew. And we had no time for a leisurely chat. So I darted past him, toward the phantom echoes of Carley's scream, running faster than the wind. Weeds cut across my legs, branches whipped against my cheeks, and marsh water soaked the lower half of my body, but I didn't care. I didn't stop until we entered the clearing that led to the lake.

That was when I saw it—a jar with a metal lid, lying on the ground, a dozen fireflies escaping from where the glass was cracked.

And then I saw her.

Carley Pruitt, my new friend.

Unmoving at the water's edge.

Wearing Foster's black sweatshirt.

Blood soaking the back of her head.

Campfire tale becomes reality in a string

of Appalachian serial murders.

Published May 21, 2024

In June 2010, at Deep Creek Campground in Bryson City, North Carolina, Carley Pruitt, a fifteen-year-old female, became the first victim in a string of murders that have since been linked to a single unidentified suspect some claim to be the Firefly Man.

The Firefly Man got his infamous nickname from the campfire story of the same name. As the story goes, the Firefly Man hunts those who cause harm to fireflies during their mating rituals. Pruitt was found near a broken mason jar filled with several dead fireflies.

Despite the nickname, there has been no evidence found to suggest the killer is male or female. All eleven victims were found alone at various campgrounds in the Great Smoky Mountains and died from blunt force trauma to the skull. Thus far, Pruitt is the only female victim connected to the killings.

Swirling red-and-blue lights accompany the brief, steady yelps of a police cruiser, forcing a little red sports car to pull over against the Main Street curb. I set an empty beer mug beneath the tap before pausing to take in the action through the long rectangular window framed with alphabetized books directly across the dimly lit bar.

My curiosity gets the best of me. Another Firefly Man murder was discovered last month, this one several towns away. Before that, it had been two years. But it doesn't truly matter when they happen, or where. The small town of Bryson City becomes anxious in waiting, praying that this is the time the killer will finally get caught. That time never seems to come.

I watch as Gabe steps out of his cruiser and begins an agonizingly slow and steady walk toward the sports car. He wears an overly confident expression on his perfectly clean-shaven face, one that gives way to the truth of the matter this is the most exciting thing that's happened to him in weeks.

Downtown Bryson City has its perks, quiet streets being one. Events like these are few and far between—especially from where I'm standing. One would think the most popular bar in town would invite the most action on an early Friday evening, but the opposite is true. Regulars come here for the quiet ambiance, made possible by the low lighting, the wall-to-wall shelves holding used books organized by genre, and the indie soul music streaming from the speakers.

"Looks like Gabe is having some fun tonight," Uncle Patrick mutters with a grin as he walks from his office to the long bar to stand across from me.

Tearing my eyes from the scene outside the window, I shrug and flip the nozzle to the beer tap. "Seems a bit anticlimactic to me." I'm careful to tilt the glass to prevent getting too much foam. "A car chase, a drug bust... Anything would be more thrilling than the same old traffic stop."

Uncle Patrick gives me his famous I-don't-believe-you side-eye. "That why it didn't work out between you and Gabe? He wasn't thrilling enough?" When I don't immediately respond, he chuckles. "The guy's a cop, Evie. Following the rules is the man's job."

My entire body cringes at my uncle's teasing words. He means no harm, but I can't give him an explanation that will make him understand that Gabe isn't the problem— nor is any other man I've attempted a relationship with. According to my therapist, it's me. I'm the problem. And until I'm ready to move past being starved of love by my parents while growing up, I may never experience it at all.

"Gabe's a great guy," I say while sliding the full beer glass to him. "He's just not for me." Grabbing hold of the tie on the back of my apron, I tug it loose and whip it over to where his waiting hands catch it. "If you think he's so great, maybe *you* should date him." I wink.

My uncle glares, and I manage to dodge his playful nudge as I walk by him. "He's a little young for me, smart ass. Hey," he calls out behind me, holding the beer. "Where is this going?"

Without looking back, I point to a woman sitting cozily on a couch in the corner of the room. "She just started a tab." After a quick wave, I push through the green double doors and say over my shoulder, "I'll be back in a couple hours to close."

A warm breeze wraps me in a hug the moment I enter the sidewalk. There's nothing better than stepping out from the frigid temperature of the bar to the perfect summer air. While most people dread the humidity, especially during these peak months, I live for it. There's nothing better than throwing on my signature outfit—a mid-length fitted skirt with a single slit running up one thigh and a retro T-shirt that reaches a millimeter above the top of my waist.

Luckily, Gabe is too busy talking to the driver of the red car to notice me when I walk by. Thank goodness. Ever since I ghosted him last month—his term, not mine—our encounters have been awkward at best. In my defense, we both agreed to keep things casual in the beginning. His attention was flattering, the sex was a good distraction, but no matter how persistently Gabe worked to transition the relationship into something more serious, I just couldn't get there. He didn't take the news well.

After I quickly round the corner, darkness engulfs me

between the shadows of the buildings on either side. Not much scares me anymore, not after finding Carley in such a brutal way that night long ago, but I've never been able to erase the chilling fear that someone is watching me. Not always, but from time to time, like now, when I'm most vulnerable—a woman alone at night without a single witness to vouch for her whereabouts.

Clutching the pocketknife I carry with me wherever I go, I pick up the pace, determined to make it to my appointment on time for once. Yeah, I might be numb to a lot these days, but I'm not stupid.

After a scolding last week, I realized how desensitized I've become to my weekly sessions with J.D. Wright, an old childhood friend of my uncle's and the only therapist in town. It's hard to believe there was a time when sitting on J.D.'s worn leather couch at Calm Waters felt critical to my survival—when I clung to routine visits like they were a safety net. But it's been twelve years, and until recently, quitting therapy has simply never been an option.

The two-story, red brick building that overlooks the Tuckasegee River is a statement as much as it is a historical landmark for the town. Structured much like a townhome, there's a comfort it brings just stepping foot inside its double doors. I was a teenager the first time I entered this spacious foyer, and save for a few art pieces, nothing has changed. Well, except for Doreen, the Calm Waters receptionist, whose usual warm expression is nowhere to be found as she talks on the phone with her head down like she's in a serious conversation.

Not wanting to disturb her, I make my way through the waiting room and around her desk to my therapist's office. Twelve years of coming here has made me comfortable enough to walk straight through the open door to take a seat on J.D.'s burgundy couch. There isn't much to the narrow gray office, just a window that takes up one long wall, a gray bookshelf that takes up the other, and a matching desk against the back wall.

Sinking into my favorite corner of the leather couch, an instant calm washes over me. I used to joke that this place was my home away from home, but at one point in time, I didn't even know where home was. After I got kicked out by my parents at seventeen, my uncle was right there to take me in, insisting I stay in the extra bedroom above the bar. His only conditions were that I talk to a professional and help around the bar as much as I could, being underage at the time.

A click of the door as it closes alerts me of my therapist's presence, and I wait to hear the sophisticated drone of J.D.'s voice. He walks by as my gaze is lowered, and I take in an unfamiliar scent. For as long as I've known my uncle's friend, he's carried a musky scent with subtle tones of vanilla. So when the smell of rich cedar, mint, and green apple intensifies, my eyes shoot open to find a man who is most certainly not J.D. Wright taking a final step to reach the desk before turning around to face me.

"Hello, Ms. Vaughn." The deep voice that greets me so warmly is as foreign as it is shocking.

I'm at a loss for words, my confusion making it difficult to process the tall stranger with a full beard standing in front of me.

A piercingly handsome stranger.

A stranger who knows my name and who just walked into my therapy session.

The man wears a white button-down shirt, a fitted gray

suit jacket, and matching slacks that do nothing to hide the muscular form of his thighs. His dark-rimmed spectacles cover his eyes, making it difficult to make out exactly how he's assessing me now.

"Who are you?" I sweep a glance around the room, like maybe I missed J.D. entering the room along with the mysterious man. When there's no sign of him, I look back at the stranger now leaning against the front of the desk, seemingly far more comfortable in this space than he should be, considering it's not even his. "Where is J.D.?"

Lines form across the man's brow. "I'm sorry?" He looks just as confused as I feel.

"J.D.," I say again before realizing the problem. Referring to a therapist by his initials is not exactly standard. "Jenkins," I correct. "Jenkins Douglas Wright—J.D."

His mouth opens like he finally understands. "Oh." Another uncomfortable pause. "Doreen assured me she contacted everyone. I'll be filling in for Mr. Wright."

Filling in for J.D.?

My mind spins, trying to make sense of this news.

The man hesitates for a second then picks up a folder from the desk and places it in his lap. "I'm giving all of Mr. Wright's patients a free consultation so we can get to know each other and to ensure I'm the best fit for your sessions moving forward. No obligation. You don't sign a thing unless you want to. We can just take this time to get to know each other." The man searches my eyes as if uncertain how to phrase his words. "I'm so sorry you weren't informed ahead of time."

Tension radiates through my body, tightening my muscles while my blood pulses wildly through my veins. Panic, discomfort... curiosity. This doesn't make sense.

Certainly, if something happened to my therapist of twelve years, Doreen would have told me about it.

I slowly sit up, straightening my back and shoulders. "I still don't understand. Why are you filling in for J.D.? Where is he?"

Before he can respond, I push off from the couch.

"You know what?" Shaking my head, I head toward the door. "I need to go."

"Ms. Vaughn. I know this must feel sudden. I would very much like the chance to…"

I ignore him, not able to hear another word as I throw open the door so hard that it bangs against the wall. *Oops.*

Doreen jumps and spins in her chair to face the noise. She sighs with relief when she sees it's me. "Oh, Evie. You scared me. I didn't see you come in."

"You were busy, so I let myself in." The words are rushed as I get to more important matters. "Where is J.D.?" I look over my shoulder to find the mystery man slowly lifting himself from the desk and taking a step in my direction. Lowering my voice and leaning forward, I ask, "And who is *that*?"

Her eyes flash wider and blood drains from her face. "Oh my. Didn't I call you? That's Doctor Reed, dear. He's filling in for J.D."

I give the sweet old woman a bewildered stare. "But why?"

She shakes her head, clearly filled with as much concern as I would expect, given the unexpected circumstances. "I'm afraid I don't know the details. Gena called last week and said that J.D. would be taking an unexpected leave and that the Care Group would be sending a replacement therapist in his absence."

Well, that explains how a stranger could just walk into my session… I think… but I have so many questions.

"An unexpected leave?" What a strange thing for J.D.'s wife to say without explanation. "For how long?" I'm trying not to become too angry with the sudden turn of events.

Doreen blinks like she's still trying to process the information herself. "Indefinitely, I suppose."

I squeeze my eyes shut, as if somehow the darkness will help stop the feeling of the ground opening up below me. "None of this makes any sense. Why wouldn't he reach out to me himself?"

She opens her mouth like she wants to reassure me, but I see the conflict that flickers through her expression. "Whatever is going on with J.D. must be very personal. All we can do is wish him and Gena the best and hope we hear from him soon."

My heart clenches for the poor old man—a man who has always felt like more of a friend than a professional hired by my uncle during a dark time in my life. I hope he's okay. I hope his family is okay. But how am I supposed to start seeing someone new *now*, especially when I've been questioning if I should still be coming here at all? Surely after all these years I should be able to kick away the crutch and walk on my own, but this turn of events has thrown me into a tailspin.

Doreen begins muttering something about being so organized and forgetful which is why she probably never left me a voicemail, but I can't listen anymore. I look around the reception area instead. I've never understood why J.D. filled it with so many plush leather chairs when there's only one office. Maybe guests wait there every now and then for their loved ones in sessions or arrive early for appointments of their own, but I've never seen anyone else sit there.

Still reeling from the news, I turn at the sound of someone approaching. For a brief second, I forgot anyone was behind me. My eyes connect with the new therapist's, and shame washes over me as I replay my reaction to seeing him.

"Maybe we should try this again." The man's deep voice rumbles when he speaks. He holds his hand out. "Dr. Lincoln Reed. It's nice to meet you, Ms. Vaughn."

Swallowing, I reach out to take the offered hand. His firm grip engulfs mine. "Just Evelyn," I say, blushing at my own correction. "Ms. Vaughn is too formal and reserved only for my mother, whom I haven't spoken to in years."

A glint of humor sparks in his eyes, and I'm afraid I've led the gorgeous man to believe that I'll actually sit back down on that couch and spill my guts. It's not going to happen, though I do allow myself to shake his hand.

"In that case," he says, still holding my hand. "I'm just Lincoln. No need for formalities here."

For the first time, I really look at him. Just on physicality, I would have never pegged him as a therapist—or a doctor of any sort. Maybe I would place him at a construction site or wielding an ax in the middle of the woods, preferably shirtless. Then again, what else do I have to compare to other than J.D., a sixty-something man who never goes anywhere without his gold cane?

Green eyes stare back at me beneath the reflection of his glasses. His full beard somehow makes him more of a mystery up close—and that scent. Now that I'm taking it in again, I realize how much the cedar and citrus tones remind me of an apple orchard my uncle and I once went to in Asheville during one of my summer visits. I was eight and remember it being one of the most magical days of my life, exploring endless rows of trees, climbing small ladders to pluck my favorite fruit from the branches, dancing to live music, seeing happy faces, and eating from food trucks. My uncle bought me my first caramel apple that day, and nothing had ever tasted better.

When I finally pull my hand away from his, I can feel some of the tension roll off my body. "Do you mind if I have a private word with Doreen? Just to work out some scheduling conflicts?"

Lincoln nods and takes a step back. "Of course. You know where to find me when you're done." He gives the smallest of smiles before turning away and retreating into J.D.'s—well, *his* office.

"Oh." Doreen perks up slightly, bringing my attention back to her. She hands me a dark-gray business card with the name Dr. Lincoln Reed and contact info in gold script. "You'll probably want one of these. And I'm happy to look at your scheduling conflicts." She turns to her computer and begins clicking around to get to the right screen.

"Thanks, Doreen." I look down at her, feeling a tinge of guilt for what I'm about to say. "But I don't think I'll need any more appointments."

Doreen's crystal-blue eyes widen on me. "At least take the consultation, Evie. He came with glowing recommendations from the Durham branch office." She leans in, lowering her voice even further. "And he's a real doctor. A psychologist with a slew of degrees and certifications. The cost to you won't go up a single penny." She searches my expression with visible concern. "Give him a chance."

I shake my head, committed to my decision—a decision

I think I made even before coming here. "No offense to Doctor Reed. This has been on my mind for quite some time. J.D. leaving just makes it easier, I guess." I give Doreen a warm smile, hoping she won't take this personally. "I'm ready to end my sessions. Permanently."

With those final words and a goodbye hug to Doreen, I head straight for the exit. And as I pass a little red sports car in the parking lot, I take a long deep breath and smile. Because for the first time in over twelve years, I feel okay— like I can let go of the crutches that have helped hold me up for so damn long and just *live*.

I t's nearly nine o'clock by the time I get back into town from my afternoon trip to Durham. After several back-and-forth trips over the past few days tying up loose ends, I've become exhausted, not to mention overworked from trying to keep up with the free therapy consultations.

Helping patients gain trust with a new therapist is anything but easy. It takes time—sometimes months—to build that relationship. All I can do is hope that some of Jenkins Douglas Wright's clients will at least give me that chance.

I frown, thinking of a certain someone from earlier this week who most certainly won't. Evie Vaughn, with her wavy blonde hair, perfect fair skin, big blue doe eyes, and undeniable beauty. The one who couldn't run away fast enough.

Her rejection stings extra-deep knowing that she had been a patient of Wright's for twelve years. I couldn't even get her to stay five minutes.

Sighing, I make my way up the steps and turn over my wrist to glance at my watch. Eight-thirty. I'm too late for bedtime. There's an ache in my chest as I turn the doorknob and twist to push it open.

Francine is sitting in a chair in the great room near the front window, my sleeping daughter in her arms. They've probably been there for a while, waiting for me to come home.

"Shhh," Francine warns quietly as I walk toward her.

Every ounce of stress from the past week melts away at the sight of Lucy. Instinct takes over as I reach out to hold her. Lucy moves steadily from her grandmother's arms to mine without waking up, and just like that, my little girl pulls my immediate focus. With her, I'm centered, alert, and present in all the best ways. Nothing else matters.

It's just like how it felt the first day I got to hold her. Nothing had ever made me feel so complete. My life finally had purpose, and maybe, just maybe, I did one small, good deed in the world to deserve it.

I take in the sight of my almost-four-year-old. Her blonde hair is a nest of tangled ringlets, her mouth hangs open as she sleeps, and she wears her favorite pink Barbie pajama set.

"Hi, sweet girl," I whisper, bringing my nose to her tanned cheek. Clearly, she'll only continue to get more adorable by the second. "Daddy missed you today."

"She missed you, too, Lincoln," Francine says gently.

As grateful as I am that Lucy's grandmother agreed to move to Bryson City with us, her presence in our lives doesn't alleviate the guilt that consumes me knowing that I can never bring Lucy's mother, Francine's daughter, back.

It's just Lucy and me—and Francine, for as long as she decides to stick around.

My chest aches. "I should have been here to put her to bed."

Francine tilts her head, looking sympathetic. "It's one night. Don't beat yourself up. Lucy is lucky to have a father who cares so deeply. You have a great job in a small, beautiful city, and you found the perfect rental with more than enough room for all of us."

"I know." The words come out with a sigh. No matter what I do, it never feels like enough. I can't steal back lost time. Unfortunately, I've had to learn that lesson the hardest way possible.

Between getting the offer to work at Calm Waters, moving Lucy and me out of our old house, and Francine from her townhome in Durham, to then settling into my new office here, I haven't had a chance to stop and breathe. That all changes now.

"Speaking of this rental," I tell Francine, more than ready to change the subject, "I have a few more loose ends to tie up with my landlord, then we can focus on settling in." I know I'm not the only one sick of living amongst stacks of boxes.

Francine nods. "Good. And how's work going? You winning 'em over with each consultation?"

It's hard not to smile at Francine's faithful words. She knows the pride I put into my work and how I feel about the people I get to help. Just knowing I have someone on my side, believing in me and supporting me through so much change, is something to marvel over.

"Ah, I don't know." I shrug. "Time will tell, I guess."

I rock Lucy for a few more minutes before walking her

to the only decorated room in the house. After laying her down in her bed, I sit on the floor beside her and adjust the blue-and-pink blankets that match the painted closet door.

My heart melts just looking at her. Loving Lucy has been the easiest thing in the world compared to the shit I've been through in my life. There's nothing I wouldn't do for her. Not a single thing. The proof of that is in the fact that I'm here right now, in the one town I swore I would never return to.

My phone lets out a loud ding, and I quickly mute it before checking to make sure Lucy is still fast asleep. She is, of course—when my girl is out for the night, she's out for exactly twelve hours like clockwork.

I look back down at the screen to find a message from my landlord.

Patrick: Still swinging by tonight?

Fuck. The curse word rings loudly in my head. I pick myself off the floor and step out of Lucy's room. Leaving the door open just a crack, I walk back into the kitchen.

"Have you eaten?" Francine asks as soon as she sees me. She knows me so well.

"Not in a while, but I forgot I need to run back to Main Street. The landlord has some stuff for us—extra keys for the house and shed in the back, and an extra garage door opener for you. I guess he's leaving town for a couple of months, so tonight is my last chance to grab it."

Francine narrows her eyes and gestures for me to sit down. "Eat first. I made lasagna."

As much as I want to get this final meeting with my

landlord over with, I can't deny Francine or my rumbling stomach. I shoot Patrick a quick response.

Lincoln: Be there soon.

After shoveling down my food, I head back into the night, feeling comforted by the knowledge that this trip will take no time at all. Soon, I'll be home and in bed, ready for the full night's sleep I desperately need.

The green-and-blue neon sign reads Firefly when I pass the bar to find a place to park. The last time I parked near this place, I was getting pulled over. That asshole cop, Officer Gabe, cited me for speeding, saying I was doing thirty in a fifteen. He wasn't wrong, but I hadn't seen any speed limit signs. I profusely apologized, but it didn't matter. The guy had something to prove and an ego to inflate.

I find a spot in the small parking lot behind the bar then follow the sidewalk around the building. The open entrance sits below the buzzing neon sign on Main Street. Before I even step a foot inside, I spot the wall-to-wall bookshelves on both floors of the main room. If I hadn't seen the long bar on the wall across from the door, I would have thought I'd just stepped into an upscale private library. The ones that don't bother with alphabetized labels on the spines because everything is a first edition. The ones that add value the more dust they collect. The ones that feel more like a museum than an actual library.

Walking into the space, I'm even more in awe, looking at the red-leather seating, the oversized chairs in front of a grand fireplace surrounded by shelves of books, long red-oak tables, and a spiral aluminum staircase that reaches a second floor of more books. I've never seen anything like it in my life.

Well, maybe I have. But not with a bar sitting prominently across the back wall.

"Lincoln," a voice calls.

Turning toward the back of the bar, I see my landlord, Patrick, waving as he heads in my direction. He's wearing an apron and a black shirt that promotes the name of the establishment. Given the fact that the man also has a well-established real estate portfolio, I'm going to assume he owns this place too.

Patrick smiles as he closes in and holds out his fist.

I bump it with mine. "Hey there, Patrick. Cool bar name."

Patrick grins proudly. "Got the idea from my niece, actually. She was eight when she saw her first firefly and became obsessed. I bought this place the same year."

Unease spreads through me. With what I know about this town, the bar name is a strange one for the history attached to it. Everyone has heard about the Firefly Man, the serial murderer rumored to find his victims at campgrounds in the Smoky Mountains, especially those who disturb the peace of the fireflies during mating season. While the moniker stems from an old campfire tale rather than having anything to do with the actual motivation behind the killings, one would think the name would carry more weight in this area.

I nod and let myself scan the two-story structure again, genuinely impressed with its design. "At first, I thought maybe the name had something to do with that girl dying years ago."

Patrick's entire body seems to sag. "In a way, it does. We

decided to keep the name after that incident. My niece insisted on it to honor those who have passed. 'As long as that neon sign is lit, their lights will never die.' That's how she likes to put it."

When I settle my focus back on him, I manage a smile. The sentiment is sweet but isn't one I want to dwell on. "Thanks again for the rental. It's a great piece of property. The guesthouse is perfect for us too."

Patrick nods, appearing pleased. "I know it's not right to have favorites, but you definitely scored the best of my rentals. I lived in that one for ten years until I was finally ready to downsize but had a tough time letting it go."

I tilt my head, curious. "Why did you?"

He shrugs. "Too big for me now. My niece doesn't live with us anymore and my ex-partner just left me, so setting off to do some traveling to mend my broken heart." He clutches his chest dramatically. "Hence, why I'm heading out of town tomorrow." He slides a large manila envelope across the bar to me. "That should be everything you'll need while I'm out. Left some phone numbers in there, too, just in case there's an emergency. My niece can handle anything in my absence."

Without thinking twice, I pull myself onto the stool and pat the envelope. "Appreciate you pulling this together for me."

"Not a problem at all. Now," he says, pointing to a chalkboard of listed drink specials above his head. "What's your poison?"

"Nah, I don't need anything. I just want to go home and get to bed. It's been a long couple of weeks."

Patrick grins, exposing a perfectly white set of teeth. "Isn't that why people drink?" He leans forward, eyes confident like he's not taking no for an answer. "This one's on me."

Temptation lures me in. A nice glass of liquor wouldn't hurt. "All right, you win. Something spicy. Your choice."

Patrick finds a bottle of Tennessee Fire from the top shelf and pours until the glass is a quarter full then slides it to me. "Give that a try."

I put the glass to my lips when he walks away to check on other customers. In the same moment he's leaving the bar, another figure steps into view behind it. The elusive Evelyn Vaughn. I recognize her instantly, if not for that thick mane of blonde hair than for the pout of perfectly pink lips that rests on her naturally downturned mouth.

She wears a red-velvet skirt with a slit up her thigh and a tight graphic tee that ends at the small of her waist, just below her navel. When my eyes slide up to her chest, I look away immediately. Her outfit reminds me of what she wore the day I found her in my office, save for this shirt's V-neck, which brings my focus exactly where it shouldn't be.

Fuck me.

It goes against everything in my professional nature to be drawn to one of my potential patients like this. That was never part of the plan. I'm not even sure that it's all sexual —maybe I was stung by her rejection when she stormed out of my office. There's just something about her that plays on my curiosity like a bow to a fiddle. I want to know more.

She's slowly making her way in my direction while scanning the customers at the bar, pulling empty cups and dirty napkins from the counter, and asking each person if there's anything else they need. She doesn't even look in my direction until she's a few feet away.

When she does, she appears frozen with shock. Kind of like how my nerves feel right now.

Evelyn only pauses for a few seconds before she seems to snap out of it and continue her trek toward me. Her eyes slip to my lips, where I'm still holding my glass. "Need another?"

For a moment, I'm confused, until I realize that I've already downed my entire drink. I set the glass on the bar and shake my head. "No. I should get going." I stand, internally screaming at myself to just walk away, but something holds me to the spot. Then I blurt, "I'd like to see you again."

Her eyes flash wide with surprise, and I can feel my cheeks heat from the recklessness of my words.

"On my couch," I add stupidly. I'm making it worse, throwing gas on an already blazing fire, and I don't know how to stop. "Jesus, I just meant…"

She holds up a hand, seemingly unfazed now that the initial shock is over. "I get it, Dr. Re—"

"Lincoln," I cut in, reminding her.

"All right, Lincoln. No offense. I'm sure you're amazing, but I'm not looking for a new therapist. I'm not even sure why I continued seeing J.D. as long as I did." She shrugs. "Habit, I guess."

I have to bite my tongue to stop myself from launching into a diatribe about how caring for your own mental health doesn't have an end date and can be beneficial in all phases of life. Instead, I say the only thing that comes to my mind next. "Twelve years is a long time." I search her stunning blue eyes, hoping to catch any reactions. "I'm sorry about Jenkins."

There's a flicker of something I can't totally identify.

Disappointment, sadness, fear? Maybe it's a subtle combination of the three, and something about it tells me I shouldn't give up on her.

"If you change your mind, I'd still like to give you that free consultation. No commitments." I attempt a smile. "After that, you can determine if I'm a good match for you or not. And vice versa."

She reaches forward and wraps her hand around the glass tumbler. "You said it yourself. Twelve years is a long time. You think you can just read my file and pick up with me where J.D. left off?"

This nugget of hope gets my heart going like a kick drum. "Of course not. We would establish something new. We'd start a new file."

Evelyn shakes her head like I've completely missed the point, and I know that somehow, I have. "It took me a long time to feel comfortable with J.D. I don't want to start over. I don't want to go back…"

Something about the way the words die on her lips squeezes my heart. "Understood." It's a knee-jerk response —fight or flight—because the last thing I want is for her to be upset with me. That would completely dismantle any chance I have of gaining her trust.

I'm just starting to wonder if there's any chance at all.

I take the envelope from the bar top and push out a smile. "Well, it has been good to see you again, Ms. Vaughn."

"Evelyn," she corrects with a stern look.

"That's right," I say, delighting in the fact that just the way I say her name gets a little bit under her skin.

As I start to back away, not wanting to leave but

knowing I must, Patrick makes his way back in our direction.

"Hey, Lincoln. Before you go." He slides up behind the bar so he's directly beside his niece. "I know you said you only needed the house temporarily, but there's some information in the envelope about renting-to-own, if you're interested. A portion of your rent would go toward paying down the costs to close. Just think about it and let me know if you're interested."

I don't want to tell him that Bryson City isn't a place I'll ever consider home, no matter how great a deal he cuts me. I'm simply here for a job opportunity I couldn't ignore. It's all temporary—but just like so much about me and my reasons for being here, no one can ever know.

Instead, I nod. "Thanks, Patrick."

"No problem," he says. Evelyn looks between us with obvious confusion but says nothing as Patrick wraps an arm around her shoulders. "I see you've already met my niece. Evie here will be looking after things for me while I'm gone. I left her contact information in that envelope, but if you can't reach her, you know where to find her." He gestures around the bar with his free hand.

This information feels like an unexpected treasure. Smiling for real, I back farther away from the bar, my eyes landing on Evelyn's. "Then I guess I'll be in touch… Evie."

She pins me with a glare that leaves me with a sick sense of satisfaction before I turn around and exit the bar.

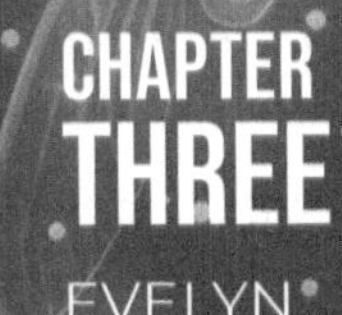

CHAPTER THREE

EVELYN

I t's late on Saturday afternoon when I make my way to the festival at Livingston Farms. Every weekend, the owners put together a full family event with live music, local food and craft booths, activities for kids, and an epic U-Pick experience that benefits them all year round. While I'd happily attended the event with Uncle Patrick when I was a kid, it's one I've tried to avoid in my adult life. The festival involves too many people and too many opportunities to be socially awkward.

On the other hand, it's great for Patrick's bar since he's the exclusive beer and wine vendor every year. He's out of town this year, though, so I'm the one running Firefly's tent along with two of our employees—my childhood friend, Janessa, and her husband, Armando. Luckily, I always feel comfortable behind the bar, no matter the size of the crowd.

"I'm going to take a break and do some shopping for the bar," I tell Armando as I slip off my apron. He's ringing up a customer while Janessa helps another, so he simply gives me a nod to acknowledge he heard me.

After a pit stop in the bathroom, I make my way through the Livingston Farms market like I normally do every Saturday morning when there isn't an event. If I'm not shopping for my personal kitchen, I'm grabbing fresh ingredients for the bar—fruits and herbs for the garnishes, cheese and nuts for the complimentary snacks, and fresh vegetables for all the bloody marys I know I'll be making tomorrow afternoon with the brunch crowd.

While Beth, the cashier, is ringing me up, a figure catches my eye outside the window, someone who doesn't belong here. That much was certain from the moment Lincoln walked into J.D.'s office. It's not every day that the town of Bryson City acquires a new resident, most certainly none in my age range, not to mention a doctor—a psychologist, even. But there he is now, in my neighborhood market, standing six-foot-something with his ruggedly handsome beard, dressed in dark shorts and a sleeveless athletic shirt that reveals a well-sculpted body.

The man is gorgeous. Strikingly so. And I can't even see his pine-green eyes from this distance. But just because Dr. Reed has stock in the looks department means nothing for my mental health. In fact, the anxiety I felt over the possibility of seeing a new therapist—of divulging my complete history filled with trauma, heartbreak, and abandonment all over again—brought me to a level of anxiety that I haven't felt since I was a teenager. I can't go back there.

Shaking off those intrusive thoughts, I hand my reusable grocery bag to the manager for her to store it for me while I wrap up things at the bar's booth. Then I get back to work, handing out samples, pouring drinks, and taking money. Time flies as the three of us work like a well-oiled machine, just like we do back at Firefly.

As I work, the town's gossip inundates me as they loiter around our tent. Usually, I try to ignore it all, but when I hear J.D.'s name, my ears perk up. The man was popular in our small town, with a full client list and a great reputation. So when he disappeared, naturally, the rumors began. Still, no one has any concrete idea of what happened to him.

"I heard he and Gena are getting a divorce," one woman mutters to another as they sip their beers.

The other woman gasps in response. "Really? Jenny thought maybe he was dying of cancer."

I can't listen to this anymore. "Armando, you've got the register," I say. "I'm going to pour."

He takes over for me while I move to the side of the tent to pour the drink orders and hand them to customers.

At some point, I hear a deep voice rumble, "Don't worry. I come in peace."

Chills shoot through every inch of my body. I pivot, my eyes slow to connect with his. The number of times I've thought about standing face-to-face with Lincoln Reed since seeing him at the bar last week has been far too many to admit, even to myself. Until him, I've never wondered what a beard would feel like nestled between my legs, tickling my thighs while I'm lapped by a devilishly warm tongue, leaving my skin tender with whisker burns long after a mind-blowing release.

Holy shit, I need a cold shower.

In all fairness, with a man like Lincoln, how could an orgasm be anything but mind-blowing?

Despite my nerves, I manage a smile, figuring I've been hard enough on the man. "What'll it be"—the temptation to continue calling him "Doctor" is too strong, but I correct myself before I can make that mistake again—"Lincoln?"

His eyes narrow playfully, like he can read my exact thoughts, then he nods to the tap behind me. "What do you recommend?"

"I don't drink beer."

He gives me a second glance before focusing back on the selection of drinks. "In that case, the seasonal lager sounds right up my alley."

As I turn to pour his drink, I'm painfully aware of his view of me, in the pair of black shorts that recently started riding an inch higher than when I purchased them three summers ago and the short black tank top that cuts into the smallest portion of my waist, accentuating every curve of my body. Normally, I wouldn't think twice about the clothes I wear, let alone anyone's opinion of them, but I've never had a Lincoln Reed watching me before.

My paranoid self can practically feel his eyes burning a hole as he scans my figure. But that's probably just ridiculous wishful thinking. I take a deep breath to settle my nerves and turn back to face him, handing him his drink. "Seven dollars," I say, avoiding eye contact this time for the sake of my sanity.

He whips a bill from his wallet, hands it to me, and takes the drink. When I start to grab change from the till, he waves his hand. "Keep it."

I stare down at the twenty, baffled, then blink up at him. "It's too much."

He shrugs. "Maybe I'll want another one later."

Laughing, I shake my head and shove the till closed. "Then you'll be out of luck, because my shift is almost over and they," I say, pointing to my two co-workers, "don't know you."

Lincoln grins. "I didn't say I'd want another *today*."

An older, petite, white-haired woman approaches, her hand attached to that of a small child stumble-walking behind her. "Oh, thank heavens," the woman says.

To my surprise, she steals the beer out of Lincoln's hand before he's even taken a sip and starts to gulp it down. But that's not even the most surprising part. Lincoln doesn't even flinch when the drink leaves his hand. Instead, he instantly reaches for the little blonde girl, who's wearing a red-and-white-checked jean dress with white tennis shoes, and lifts her into his arms.

"Hey, Lucy," he greets the girl fondly. "Do you want to meet a friend of Daddy's?"

Something flutters in my chest, and I'm not sure if it's because he just referred to me as his friend or because he called himself Daddy. At the same time, there's a sense of panic that Lincoln has a daughter, which means he probably has a wife, and that wife is most likely nearby.

My eyes dart to the thick fingers securing Lucy's waist. *No ring.* Then I shake my head at my own thoughts. He could have just forgotten to put it on this morning.

Lucy smashes her cheek into Lincoln's chest shyly like she wants to burrow into him. "Okay," she says in a quiet voice.

My smile is instant when I focus on the sweet girl. She's beautiful, with big blue eyes that seem to be taking in everything going on around her and perfect ringlet curls that bounce with every slight movement she makes.

"This is Evie," Lincoln tells her, refocusing her attention. "She used to live in our house."

With that, Lucy picks her head up from Lincoln's chest, eyes growing wide. "Did you sleep in my bedroom too?"

I let out a light laugh. "I don't know. Does your bedroom closet have blue, pink, and purple flowers all over it?"

Lucy squeals and claps her hands together. "Yes! Daddy put glow-in-the-dark stars on the ceiling too."

"Did he? That was so nice of him."

"What can I say?" Lincoln grins. "I'm a nice guy after all."

I bite down on my smile. "I never said you weren't."

"Fooled me."

He's teasing, but I can't help but feel a pang of guilt for giving him a hard time at J.D.'s office. All he had done was offer a free consultation to give me a chance to work with him if he was the right fit. And I turned him down without even hearing him out.

Before I can say another word, he turns to the woman who's chugged nearly half of the beer he bought. "This is Lucy's grandmother, Francine."

The way he phrases it feels odd. Why wouldn't he just say his mother-in-law?

I smile at the woman. "It's nice to meet you, Francine."

She nods without cracking a smile, but her eyes are friendly in a way that tells me she's still assessing me. "Nice to meet you as well." She squints at Lincoln as if to remind him that he didn't finish introducing us.

He startles a little as he realizes it then says, "This is Evelyn Vaughn, Patrick's niece. Evie manages the Firefly bar on Main Street and is handling things for Patrick at his rental properties while he's away."

Francine perks up slightly. "Hi, Evelyn. Would you

happen to know how to get the furnace to turn on in the guesthouse? Linc's been trying to figure it out for days with no luck."

Lincoln visibly cringes, causing me to smile.

I turn to Lincoln, amused. "There's a trick to it. Can I stop by Monday morning to show you?" Then I smile. "It's an old furnace. Don't feel bad."

When Lincoln doesn't answer, Francine steps in. "Of course you can stop by when you can," she says, shooting a glare at Lincoln. "Thank you, Evie."

Lucy grips Lincoln's shirt, distracting us all from the conversation. "I wanna look at the sunflowers, Daddy."

"You do? Well then, let's get to it." He touches his nose to hers before setting her back on her feet and turning to me. "Thank you for th—"

Before he can finish, a little voice chimes in. "Come with us to look at the flowers, Evie."

"Me?" I ask before having time to think.

Lucy nods emphatically while her father and grand-mother stare back at me, waiting.

If anyone else had asked, I would have declined the invite easily. But it's Lucy, and the way she's staring up at me eliminates all possible answers but one. "I'd love to."

Another squeal from her lights up my insides as I try hard to ignore Lincoln's intense stare.

"Come on." Lucy takes off, dragging Francine along with her.

I say goodbye to Armando and Janessa then walk around the bar. Lincoln and I fall into step, following close behind Francine and Lucy.

"I couldn't say no," I admit, feeling sheepish.

"Trust me—I know the feeling." He glances over at me.

"She's got me wrapped around her little finger. Francine calls me a sucker daily."

"That just means you're a good father."

He pauses, a hesitation I don't quite understand. "I hope that's true."

One moment passes then another. I don't know what to say or how to phrase all the questions I want to ask. Where is your wife? Why aren't you wearing a wedding ring? Why are you renting my uncle's house instead of purchasing your own?

"Lucy's mom died almost two years ago," Lincoln says.

His abrupt words stop my heart. In fact, it might take me a few seconds to remember how to breathe. But even as I begin to collect myself, words don't form quickly. I'm not sure I can form any words at all.

His eyes dart between mine. "I just had to get that out of the way. I knew the question was coming, and it's not an entirely comfortable one for Francine or me."

"I… I'm sorry." That's all I can think to say, though I still haven't completely comprehended what he just told me.

"Don't be." He's quick to respond, then his brow dents in the center. "I mean, thank you for saying that, but Lucy and I are happy. Francine too." He smiles at the sight of Francine lifting Lucy up so the girl's nose touches giant sunflower petals. "Lucy was still a baby when she lost her mother, so she doesn't remember her well."

Again, I have so many questions, but I'm not sure if any of them are appropriate to ask, so I steer clear from questions completely. "That must have been extremely difficult for you all."

Discomfort is written all over his face. "To say the

least." He hesitates another few seconds. "Lucy's mom and I weren't..." He lets the words trail off.

"Married?"

"No, we weren't married." He lets out a deep sigh. "We weren't even dating." His eyes catch on mine nervously, then he clears his throat. "We were a one-night thing. I didn't know about Lucy until after her mom died."

"Oh." The word rushes out with my breath. "How old was Lucy when you met her?"

"Thirteen months. But I didn't get to add my name to her birth certificate until many months later. Francine was her primary caretaker after Becca died, but she made sure Lucy and I got to spend as much time together as we could." He smiles a little. "She's been incredible. To both of us."

My head spins so fast that I can't put together my response quick enough before Lucy comes barreling into Lincoln.

"Daddy, chase me!" she shouts.

The next thing I know, Lucy is squealing as she takes off into the field, and Lincoln doesn't even hesitate to chase after her.

I laugh and slow down to match Francine's steps. "Lucy is an endless ball of fun, isn't she?"

Francine gives me a wide-eyed nod that tells me I have no clue how right I am. "She's also the sweetest, smartest, and funniest little girl you've ever met in your life. That fire in her will take her to great places one day."

My heart warms, and I'm not entirely sure why. Sure, the way Francine speaks about her granddaughter is sweet, but there's got to be something deeper there, maybe something that comes with Lucy not having a mother.

Again, I have so many questions, but I'm not sure what's appropriate, so I keep the conversation light. "How does she like Bryson City so far?"

Francine gestures to Lincoln and Lucy, who've stopped their chase to look at another sunflower. "As long as her daddy is here, she's happy. He's her home and vice versa."

Lucy reaches for the bright-yellow flower in total admiration before Lincoln plucks it from its stem and hands it to her. When Lucy's face lights up at the gesture, my heart goes liquid right there in my chest.

"I loved it here when I was Lucy's age," I say, not that Francine needs any comfort. "My parents used to ship me off to stay with Uncle Patrick every summer and every spring break. This place had so much to explore, so much to do."

Francine seems to take in what I'm saying, nodding slowly. "I think it will grow on all of us, Lincoln especially. There's certainly no drought in all that inspiration required for him to get words on the page."

It takes a second for her meaning to click. "He's a writer?"

Francine shrugs. "He wouldn't call himself one, but the man spends every extra hour of his day pounding away at his computer lately."

A few seconds later, Lucy comes rushing back, the arm holding the sunflower extended to Francine. "For you, Gammy."

Francine gasps and leans down to kiss Lucy on the cheek. "Thank you, sweet girl. Now I need to find one for you."

Just as Lucy pulls Francine back to the flowers, Lincoln

is by my side again. "She'll keep you on your toes, that's for sure," he says, watching them.

There's something about Lucy and her carefree nature that brings me back to my own childhood, running around this same sunflower field with Uncle Patrick, daring him to keep up with me. My own parents would have never dreamed of allowing me to have so much fun.

Just the thought of my parents pulls a dark cloud over the otherwise sunny day. No matter the time, no matter the distance, that resentment lives deep in my soul. I can't escape it. I can't release it. It's just there, a relentless scar that never quite fades and remains sensitive to the slightest touch.

Before I can stop myself, I ask him, "Did you mean what you said the other night?" I pause, thinking for a second. "You know… about starting something new with me? In therapy," I add quickly, because who knows how he could have taken my question otherwise.

Lincoln's eyes pivot to mine with surprise. "Of course I meant it. And you would have to sign your medical records over for me to gain access to your file, Evie. That's completely optional."

The way he uses my nickname, so casually, warms my chest. My eyes search his. "It is?"

"It is." He's so matter-of-fact, but he must see my confusion, because he continues. "Whatever I'd find in that file is from the past, anyway. I don't want to start there. I want to start with who Evelyn Vaughn is today."

His gaze explores mine so surely, so intensely, that it's like I'm in a deep well I have no chance of escaping. For a second, I forget he's talking about therapy.

"I want to know about your hopes and dreams, your

goals," he says. "I want to know about your job, your hobbies, and your family. I don't want to know what brought you to therapy twelve years ago. I want to know what has kept you coming back week after week. There's a comfort there for you that I'm not even sure you've explored."

He pauses. "And maybe, just maybe, you'll come to the realization that you already have the tools to detach from your weekly sessions. And if that's the case, if you're truly ready and happy, then at least you know you're not quitting because of me." He shrugs like all the things he mentioned are simple goals. "That's all."

My nerves get the better of me, and a laugh floats past my throat. "That's all," he says, like his job isn't dependent on all the things about myself that *don't* make me happy.

He frowns. "I'm not here to criticize the relationship you had with your therapist before me, and I can promise that I'm not here to profit from your unhappiness. The way I work is just different, that's all."

"What makes it different?"

His piercing gaze meets mine again, the green-and-gold backdrop of the sunflower field making his eyes even more stunning. "My goal isn't to get you to stay, Evie."

I let out a nervous chuckle. "Then what is your goal?"

He shrugs. "To set you free."

More giggles rise in my throat, an instinctual reaction that seems to stem from confusion more than anything else. I certainly don't find what he said funny, just unexpected. "I'm sorry," I say, calming myself a bit. "Didn't I free myself by quitting therapy already?"

Lincoln's lips twist, bringing all my attention to his beautiful mouth. "Yes, but didn't you only quit because you were afraid to start over with a new therapist?" He raises his brows as if in challenge. "The next time you quit, it should be for you. Because you feel a sense of closure."

I squeeze my eyes together then open them again to regain control over my emotions. The way this man flusters me. "Quitting had been on my mind for some time," I say. "I just…"

He waits patiently while I'm still thinking of how to finish.

Finally, raising my chin, I stare boldly back at him. "I just hadn't decided yet."

His smile is wide, filled with far too much charm and a perfect set of white teeth. "You just made my point."

I open my mouth again to continue the argument—he needs to realize that he's not right about that—but Lucy steals our attention.

"More flowers, Daddy!" Lucy stands between us, staring up at her dad with a half-dozen giant sunflowers in her hands.

"Wow," Lincoln says, bending down to examine her bouquet. "You picked some great ones."

Lucy leans toward Lincoln's ear and whispers something. When she pulls back, he puts his lips to her ear and murmurs something in return. It's the cutest exchange, and even as flustered as I was moments ago, I have nothing but warm and fuzzy feels watching them together now.

After their whispered conversation, Lucy swivels around, a sweet smile on her face as she tilts her head and looks up at me. She extends a hand, holding out one of the sunflowers.

I gasp, a genuine reaction to her most innocent gesture. "For me?"

Lucy nods. "Isn't it pretty?"

Nodding, I accept the flower, taking it into both hands and smiling back at her. "The prettiest flower I've ever received. Thank you very much, Lucy. You just made my whole day."

Lucy beams, her radiant smile lighting up her entire body, before she throws herself into her dad's arms. At that moment, it's painfully clear that Dr. Lincoln Reed is the least of my concerns. It's his daughter who has the potential to steal my heart.

CHAPTER FOUR

LINCOLN

Join the five o'clock club, they said. You'll be wealthy, they said. You'll run the world, they said.

What a joke.

While waking at this insane hour of the morning used to be inspired by my drive to earn my degree at the fastest rate possible, it's now an essential part of my life if I have any hope of getting shit done. I've quickly learned that any type of productivity goes out the window the moment Lucy's feet hit the floor each morning. That's when daddy duties begin, then work priorities take over, and after all that, I'm too exhausted in the evenings to do anything but eat dinner and cuddle up with Lucy to watch one of her favorite shows.

As soon as my head lifts from the pillow that Monday morning, I slip into my den to beat on my keyboard, filling the Word document with all the inspiration I've been acquiring since moving here.

Once my alarm goes off, I gather laundry baskets and

start the wash, then I clean the kitchen from the mess I was too tired to clean the night before, check work emails, and pay bills. Then I'm finally ready to dress for my morning run.

Now this, I actually enjoy. I start at a slow pace, beginning to create my mental checklist as I go.

- ☐ *Shower and get dressed*
- ☐ *Wake and dress Lucy*
- ☐ *Make breakfast*
- ☐ *Pack Lucy's daycare bag*
- ☐ *Drop Lucy off downtown*
- ☐ *Grab dry cleaning*
- ☐ *Run by post office*
- ☐ *Coffee and donuts for the office*
- ☐ *Client appointments*

Before I realize it, I'm on my fifth and final mile, and sweat has completely drenched my shirt. With a quick tug, I yank it from my body and tuck it into the waistband of my black shorts. As soon as I'm back in the house, I head straight to the kitchen and down a large glass of water then pour another. One might think I would be used to humid summer mornings after a lifetime spent in North Carolina, but that will never happen.

There's a knock at the front door, and before I can run through the list of possible visitors, Francine is opening the door.

"Evie," she says, "thank you for coming."

I freeze, water glass still cold against my lips as my eyes catch on my fill-in landlord. Her hair is curled with half twisted up into a thick bun and loose pieces framing her heart-shaped face. She's wearing another mid-length skirt slit to the thigh, this one burgundy. Again, she's sporting another vintage black T-shirt, but this one appears to be a couple inches shorter than the others.

She's beautiful—phenomenally so—and in the simplest of ways. Her hard-shelled demeanor only adds a level of mystery, reminding me of all the parts of her I still don't know.

"It's no problem," Evie says. "The furnace will only take a minute to fix."

I completely forgot Evie said she would be over in the morning to help Francine in the guesthouse. But Francine should have mentioned the time. Maybe then I would have been prepared to deal with my unfiltered thoughts.

Francine steps back. "Come inside, please."

Evie takes a step into the foyer at the same time her eyes find mine—or, rather, my bare chest. I'm not sure even she knows she's doing it, but her gaze glides over every inch of me before finally flickering to meet my gaze.

Her cheeks darken when she realizes she's been caught staring.

I'm no better. I don't know why words are failing me so miserably, but we don't exchange a single word before Francine leads Evie out the back door of the main house. I watch as they follow the stone trail to the small guest cottage that gives Francine her own space and makes this house perfect to rent from Patrick.

Once they disappear inside the cottage, I rush to the master bathroom to shower. I'm already off schedule, and Lucy will be waking up soon.

As if on cue, as soon as I'm dried and dressed, I hear

the pitter-patter of little feet in the hallway. I swing open my door and scoop up Lucy, smiling back at my sleepy-eyed, pouty-faced little girl. "Morning, sunshine." I plant a kiss on her cheek, which earns me a grumpy groan.

Chuckling, I carry Lucy back into my bathroom while I finish getting ready. After setting her on the counter, I apply deodorant and trim my beard just enough to keep it tidy. I don't mess with my hair, other than to smear in some gel and rough it up a bit. Lucy reaches her hands up, her fingers apparently itching to do the same to my hair. I laugh and lean down so she can slide her fingers in there.

"Eww, Daddy." She wrinkles her nose and looks at her hands like they've turned into aliens. "Sticky-icky."

Letting out a dinosaur roar, I scoop her up. "Who are you calling sticky-icky?"

I give her a quick bop on the nose, making her giggle, then I take her back into her bedroom to get her dressed for the day. I lay out three of her favorite outfits, all dresses with leggings, and she instantly goes for the yellow one with white flowers on them.

"Great choice."

After Lucy's all dressed with her hair brushed, we race into the kitchen. I pick her up to set her in her booster seat then turn on the speaker to play her favorite playlist, filled with kids singing the hottest current hits. Pulling down three different cereal boxes from the pantry, I set them on the table. "Take your pick, Lucy Goosey."

She giggles, just like she does any time I call her any one of her nicknames. "You're a silly goose, Daddy."

I gasp and lean over to tickle her side. "I'm a what?"

She squeals out her laughter. "A silly goose!" she tries to say between giggles.

Releasing her, I reach for a box of cereal, pull out the plastic bag inside, then stretch the box over my head to wear it like a hat. "What about now? Am I still a silly goose?"

Lucy explodes into the type of infectious belly laughter I find myself living for these days. In an effort to keep Lucy fully entertained, I do a ridiculous dance around the kitchen while I grab a bowl and the milk before finally placing it all in front of Lucy.

But instead of eating, she reaches her hands in the air. "Dance with me, Daddy!"

Pulling her out of her seat, I take her little hands in mine and spin her around the room, complimenting her intricate stomp-like dance moves as she tries to keep up with the beat. On the final note of the song, I support Lucy's back while I dip her, nearly forgetting that she was an all-star in gymnastics last year. She bends back so far that her hair sweeps the ground, causing me to laugh.

Someone clears her throat, causing me to look over to the back door of the kitchen. Francine has a joyful expression on her face as she stares adoringly at her granddaughter, while Evie looks like she's trying to hold back a smile—and failing.

Lucy runs up to Francine and pulls her into the kitchen. "Gammy, dance!"

As the two of them start bopping around the kitchen, I take the opportunity to step over to Evie and say what I should have said when she initially arrived. "Hi."

Evie smiles fully, a twinkle of amusement never leaving her eyes. "Hi." Her focus rises to my head while mine drops to her mouth.

She gently licks her bottom lip before biting down on it. "My favorite."

There's a kick in my chest at her words, and for a second, I think she's somehow referring to me being her favorite.

Then her arms raise to lift the cereal box off my head. "Lucky Charms," she adds, confirming that I'm an absolute idiot. "Lucy has good taste."

"Actually," I say, taking the box. "Those are *my* favorite. Lucy happens to like Cheerios better."

Evie's jaw drops in mock astonishment. "Nobody likes Cheerios better than Lucky Charms."

"She's three." I wink. "Give her time." We share a grin, brief but memorable all the same. "I happen to have enough Lucky Charms to share if you'd like to stay for breakfast." As soon as the invite leaves my mouth, I worry it's too much too soon. "Unless you have to be somewhere."

Evie opens and then closes her mouth, clearly conflicted. "Actually, I should go. It's our monthly staff meeting at Firefly, and with Patrick gone, it's mine to lead."

"So, you're running the show, huh? Between the bar and the rental properties, you're a busy woman."

She shrugs. "Nothing I'm not used to. Patrick loves his vacations, and I basically run the bar as it is already. Eventually, he'll hand it over to me, but the Firefly's been his baby for nearly twenty years. He's not ready to let it go just yet."

"Is that what you want?" My eyes search hers. "To own the bar?"

Her wistful smile catches me off guard. I get glimpses of depth in Evelyn Vaughn with each conversation, but it's a depth I'm not sure she's explored yet.

"It's always been more about the books for me than it is the bar," she says, and somehow it feels like she just confessed one of her deepest, darkest secrets. Like she's never said those same words aloud to anyone else.

Or maybe that's just wishful thinking—me hoping there's some part of her that feels comfortable to open up just a little bit more.

Before I can ponder that thought further, Evie excuses herself from the kitchen, saying goodbye to Lucy, Francine, then me and heads toward the front door like she's in some kind of hurry. I'm drawn to her like the opposite pole of a magnet, following her to the front drive, searching for something to say as if I don't want her to leave.

That's just the thing, I realize. I *don't* want her to leave, and it's not because I want her as a client.

I've been attracted to many women in my life, dated a handful when I felt like we could eventually become something more, but I've never felt an attraction quite this strong to someone I barely know. Since the moment I laid eyes on her in my office, I've been fighting an obsession to know more about Evie. I know it's not healthy or normal— and from a professional standpoint, it's wrong in every way.

But as I look at Evie, I'm just not sure how much I'm willing to listen to that bird chirping away inside my head about what's right and wrong.

"Thank you again for helping Francine with the furnace issue," I say.

Evie's lips curve up. "Not a problem, really. I lived in that guesthouse for a few years, so I know all the tricks. It's just a broken nozzle. You have to remove the plastic cover and turn the actual metal piece itself." She sighs. "Patrick tried ordering a new piece years ago, but it's so old that they don't make replacements anymore."

"Well, you're a lifesaver."

Evie shakes her head and chuckles. "You're giving me way too much credit."

I shrug, craving more laughs from her just like that one. "Get used to it. I'm sure your assistance will be needed again soon."

She smiles. "You know where to find me."

When she turns and begins to stroll down the driveway, I realize she isn't heading toward a car. "How did you get here?"

She tilts her head. "I walked."

Mortification rips through me. "You walked all the way here?"

Evie lets out another laugh. "You say that like it's far."

My mental calculation of time and distance isn't adding up fast enough, so she takes pity on me.

"It took ten minutes," she says. "It's fine. Really."

"Let me drive you." I didn't mean to blurt out the words like that, so I try again. "We're heading in the same direction," I say, this time making a conscious effort to slow down my words. "I just need to get Lucy fed, then—"

"It's okay, really." Evie starts to back away. "It's my choice to walk rather than drive."

I move toward her, not ready to give up. "You're telling me you have a car?"

"I don't, but Patrick has plenty. I can always borrow one of his if I really want."

"But you don't want." It's not a question. I just can't believe what I'm hearing.

Evie shakes her head then swivels around to walk away.

She raises one hand and waves without looking back. "See you around, Doc."

And as I watch her reach the end of the driveway and turn the corner, I wonder how many other excuses I can find to get her to come back to my house soon.

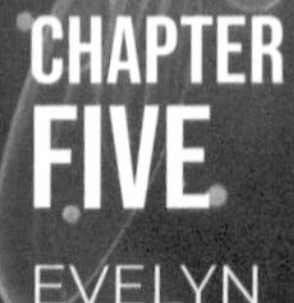

Golden, foamy liquid splatters onto the red-oak surface of the bar, thanks to the beer mug someone just slammed onto it.

What the fuck? My head whips up to see one of my regulars.

"What's the problem, Jimmy?" I ask, holding back my temper as I wipe up the spilled drink with my rag. "Spot that ex-wife of yours again?"

Jimmy's still scowling as he swivels his neck back to face me. "Fuck her, that cheating whore."

The man has been divorced for four years, but that doesn't stop him from reminding the town that his then-wife's infidelity ruined his life. Can't say any of us were surprised about the affair, seeing as his ex-wife is Lilith's mom. The woman has had more marriages in a lifetime than should be legal.

I take a slow, deep breath, hating the way his words trigger me. I despise hearing men speak about women with such a bitter, disrespectful tone, yet I hear it constantly when I'm working here.

"Maybe you should try dating," I suggest. "Take your mind off her."

He coughs out a laugh before gulping down a quarter of what's left of his beer before slamming it down again. "And maybe you should mind your fucking business."

The words are muttered almost under his breath, but I hear them loud and clear.

I glare at the man who's used up my last ounce of patience. "That's it, Jimmy. Time to go home." I grab the nearly empty mug. "You're cut off."

Rage illuminates the drunk man's face. "The fuck I am." He lunges toward me, the top half of his body leaning over the bar. He swipes at his beer mug, wraps his fingers around the handle, and manages to yank it from my hands, but his intoxicated grip falters, causing the glass to fall to the floor and shatter all around my feet.

"Hey!" Armando booms, stepping in front of me. "Outta here, man. You know we don't put up with that shit here."

I want to tell Armando it's not a big deal—that Jimmy doesn't mean any harm—but Patrick wouldn't stand for that type of behavior either, even though he and Jimmy were longtime friends. Their relationship isn't as close as it used to be, but it's a friendship nonetheless.

Armando comes around the bar, and Jimmy's face turns beet red as he fights hard against the younger man, but while their lanky builds are evenly matched, Armando clearly has the advantage against the drunk patron.

"I've got it from here," booms an authoritative voice.

Officer Gabe stands directly behind Jimmy, one hand

on his police baton like he wants everyone to see he's prepared for battle. I hadn't even noticed Gabe walk in, but there he is, ready to save the day.

It takes everything in my power to refrain from rolling my eyes. Armando shoots me a look of annoyance—he knows this is exactly the type of power trip Gabe gets off on.

"C'mon, Jimmy, let's go," Gabe commands. "You don't want to make this worse for yourself."

As much as I hate to admit it, Gabe's presence has a positive effect on the situation, as Jimmy seems to listen. He raises his hands and backs away from the bar, although he eyes me like he's not done with me yet. And I'm sure he's not. Jimmy's one of those men who works to get shit-faced at the Firefly, even if that means living paycheck to paycheck—or worse, in debt.

I shiver, thinking about the drunken camping trips Uncle Patrick and his friends used to take me on when I was younger. Every summer for years, Uncle Patrick would take me and a group of other folks to Deep Creek Campsite to see the fireflies. Some of his friends had kids my age, but we always found other kids there that we didn't know. I was always making friends.

One in particular was my favorite.

Frowning, I try to push memories of Carley Pruitt away. I've never been able to escape her completely, haunted beyond repair by the deep regret and sorrow I felt for years after her death and the guilt I still feel when I think of how we got separated that night. In only minutes, we lost Carley to something dark. Something sinister.

Her death was ruled a homicide, her murderer never found.

To top it off, I'll never forget the boy who was arrested that night—Foster Pruitt, Carley's brother. Not even my statement had been able to help support his alibi, since we got separated at some point in our jaunt through the woods even though we were together when we heard Carley scream. Foster remained the number one suspect for months before the authorities finally released him due to insufficient evidence.

Outside of us hearing Carley's scream in the woods that night, no one else came forth as a witness, and while Foster's prints were all over his sister from him trying to find a pulse, the rock that had been used to bludgeon her showed no trace of his DNA. That lack of evidence ultimately saved him, but it wasn't enough to prevent the rumors that circulated for years to come.

The residents of Bryson City were convinced Foster had to have done it. "Just look at him," they would whisper. "He must have been wearing gloves."

But they weren't there to see the fear in Foster's eyes when he discovered his sister. They didn't hear his anguished scream as he raced to her and tried to find any sign of life. They didn't witness the utter heartbreak of a brother realizing his baby sister was gone forever.

Maybe I shouldn't have raced back to the campsite right then. Maybe I should have never left Foster alone with Carley's dead body. Maybe I should have tried to help find her pulse too. If I had stayed, maybe then Foster wouldn't have looked so guilty when the authorities followed me to the crime scene and saw the teenager cradling Carley's lifeless body. Maybe he could have mourned his sister with friends and family instead of alone behind a set of cold steel bars.

And maybe, just maybe, Foster wouldn't have disappeared as soon as he was cleared from all charges. The only evidence I've found that he is still alive is a single published poem in an online journal, written by none other than Foster Pruitt.

A Flicker of Light
By Foster Pruitt

What happens when a light burns out?
Does it spark back to life or die?
That night, I heard a terrified shout
When a flicker lit up her cries

She died under a pale-blue moon
Bioluminescence bled her path
With blood-soaked hair and lake-shone shoes
Weapon placed in a moonlit bath

A final breath squeezed between bones
Her small body, so limp, now serene
A moment too late, her light flown
Yet somehow, I knew she was free

"Evie, you okay?"

My entire chest feels like it's wrapped in the coils of a giant snake squeezing the life out of me as I stand there, not even trying to free myself—an all-too-familiar feeling that hits me like a hammer, reminding me why twelve years of therapy will never be enough. Not when memories like this can paralyze my psyche at any time. One mental image and it's like I'm right back at that campground, chasing after fireflies in the woods one minute and losing my friend to murder the next.

"Evie," the voice says again, this time more firmly, lifting me a bit further from my trance.

I look over to find Janessa staring at me, her forehead dented in the center, as her hands shake my shoulders gently.

"I'm… I'm fine." I suck in a slow breath, wanting the words to be true. My shoulders straighten against her hold, and I back away.

When I step down, a sharp pain stabs the bottom of my foot. "Ow!" Looking down, I realize a shard of glass just went through my sole and into the arch of my foot. Fuck me for wearing slippers in the bar. One day, I'll actually listen to my uncle's warnings.

I lift my foot then pluck the piece of glass out and discard it into the nearest trash can. Next, I look around for the broom only to find that Armando already has it in his hands and is walking toward us.

"We'll clean this up, Evie," Janessa says. "Why don't you take the rest of the night off? Armando and I can close."

Looking into Janessa's serene eyes, I find myself wondering why we haven't become better friends. We've known each other since I started visiting my uncle. We're the same age. She's nice. We already spend so much time together at work, and we seem to share the same love for EDM pop and classic literature. But Janessa was always super popular in town, and when I came to visit my uncle growing up, I felt like such a third wheel to all the established friendships in town. Which is probably why I gravitated toward Carley so easily. She was an outsider too.

But wondering is pointless, considering I know the exact reason I haven't bonded with her at a deeper level. Relationships aren't my thing. Boyfriends, friendships—they're all commitments that will inevitably lead to disappointment, abandonment, heartbreak, and sometimes even tragedy. Nothing lasts, so why even try?

"Thank you," I tell her, taking her up on her suggestion. "I'm going to bandage my foot, then I think I need to go for a walk or something."

"Take your time." She squeezes my arm. "If you're not back, we'll lock up."

I look around the full bar. It's one of the busiest weeknights we've had in a while. Patrick would be elated to see the crowd. "I owe you."

Janessa tilts her head. "Evie, we get paid for this." She jerks her head toward the door. "Get out of here."

I back away, hesitating for only a moment before removing my apron. After a quick stop at the first-aid kit, I head for the door.

The moment I step outside into the night air, I pull a deep breath into my chest, but it's not enough. Instinctively, I reach for my phone and use speed dial to call the one person who knows how to calm me in these dark moments.

But three rings in, reality hits me. J.D. isn't going to answer. He may never answer again.

Tears are blinding me by the time I round the first corner, just as his generic voicemail answers and prompts me to leave a message.

"Um, hi, J.D. It's me—um—Evie. I just..." I clear my

throat. "I had one of those days, you know? The bad ones where I remember so much."

I squeeze my eyes shut before opening them again to blurry surroundings. "Jimmy was drunk again at the bar, and then I just started thinking about all those nights you and Patrick would get drunk at Deep Creek Campground."

My chest tightens as I smile sadly. "Then I started to remember Carley and I panicked a little." I take in a shaky breath. "Anyway, I'm sorry I called. For a second, I forgot you quit. Or retired." I let out an awkward laugh. "Or went on leave. To be honest, no one knows why you left or where you are."

I frown, realizing just how strange it all sounds to say out loud. Patrick doesn't even know where J.D. is, and they've been friends forever. Why doesn't anyone know what's going on with him? Why hasn't J.D. called to explain why he had to leave so suddenly? And why do I abruptly feel so incredibly lost?

"I hope you're okay," I say then add, feeling desperate, "If you are and you get this, can you call me? I would really like to talk to someone and you're the only one who knows everything I've been through." I pause. "Doreen wants me to see this replacement guy. He's a psychologist. I guess he's nice and stuff, but the last thing I want to do is explain my life story to someone new."

I'm just rambling now, but it's almost as therapeutic as an actual therapy session.

At the same moment I hang up the phone, I am halted at the crosswalk as cars whizz by at their green light. I've paid no attention to where I was going, but it seems that instinct played me once again. Directly across the street from where I stand is a familiar building with a large rectangular window. The lights are on, and Lincoln Reed sits at his desk, typing as he focuses on the screen of a laptop.

Desire hits me. Not lust or sexual desire, but a sensation so strong that I can't even begin to explain it.

I want to talk to someone. I miss talking to someone. And if that someone can't be J.D. Wright, then perhaps I should take Lincoln up on his offer.

After a final deep breath and a slow exhale, I cross the intersection, walk up the steps of Calm Waters, and step straight up to Doreen's desk.

"Evie." She practically gasps my name. "It's so nice to see you again."

My pulse is racing. "I need to talk to Doctor Reed."

Doreen's eyes flash wide. "Oh. I'm afraid he's done with his appointments for the night, but I can—"

Just then, the office door swings open, the sound causing Doreen to spin around in her chair. Lincoln's gaze settles on my face like he'd been expecting me. Like he knew I would need him at this very moment.

"It's all right, Doreen," he says. "I have time for one free consultation before I go home."

Her face falls. "Oh, I was just about to leave for the night. Do you need me to stay?"

He shakes his head. "No, no. You're fine to head out. I'll see you tomorrow."

Doreen's entire body seems to let out a sigh, then she smiles at me. "Excellent. Have a great session, you two." She immediately begins to gather her things.

Lincoln's focus turns back to me, and for a moment, I imagine something else sizzling beneath the surface of his professional demeanor. "I'm ready for you now, Ms. Vaughn."

CHAPTER
SIX

LINCOLN

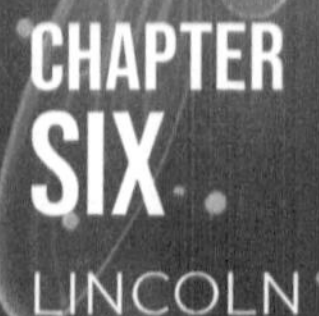

"It's Evie," she corrects me as soon as I've shut the door to my office behind her.

I chuckle silently but stop as soon as she swivels to face me. "I hope you don't take my formalities in front of Doreen as a sign of disrespect. It's quite the opposite."

She blinks and her mouth falls open, drawing my attention to the perfect form of its natural pink pout. "Every time someone calls me Ms. Vaughn, I think of my mother. Let's just say I've made it my life goal to be nothing like her."

A tinge of excitement lights me up from inside at this new piece of information. Even if I had guessed that she had difficulties with her mother, the confirmation from Evie is oh-so-satisfying. "Then I apologize, Evie. Can we start again?"

Her frown begins to smooth. "Sure."

"Why don't we start with why you decided to come in tonight?" I try not to let concern break through my features and tone. I've only known Evie for the past two weeks, but there's no denying she's a strong, smart woman who lives her life by comfort and habit. While I couldn't know for sure, I had thought she might come back to the office.

The why—what triggered her—is what I want to find out.

Instead of answering my question, her eyes shift from mine and begin to roam around the office. She takes one step forward, then another, until she's slowly perusing my diplomas and the personal photos on my wall.

"Your decor is so much different than J.D.'s."

"Artistic tastes are cultivated over time and with experience. From what I know about Jenkins, he was a homebody. Perhaps that has something to do with it."

She pauses while tracing a slow finger over a piece of art I collected during my studies in Athens, Greece. "Plato's Academy," I tell her, in case she isn't aware. "The world's first university. What I would give to be among such a brilliant cast of philosophical minds."

Evie glances over her shoulder, her expression one of curiosity and confusion, like she's trying to piece together a puzzle just by looking at the image on the box. "I thought you majored in psychology."

"Psychology and philosophy share the same roots, I suppose. What the human condition is versus how and why the human mind functions the ways it does." I shrug. "I studied both, but psychology was the clear career path for me."

Evie moves on from the painting and approaches the bookshelf that wraps the side and back walls behind my desk. This time, I follow her, staying several feet behind. She looks over the books, stopping every now and then to pull something from the shelf and examine it.

I just watch her, intrigued by her shifting focus as she moves around my office. I almost forgot that she's here for a free consultation, but none of that matters. This is her time. Her session. And if she wants to spend it familiarizing herself with my office, then so be it.

"Certified sex therapist? That's a thing?"

I almost choke. There's a reason I keep that certification on the back of my bookshelf. "Uh, yeah. That's a thing." My urge to change the subject takes control. "Um, so you didn't mention what brought you back here today."

She raises one shoulder and continues past the bookshelf, around my desk, her focus centered on the single photo of Lucy and me that sits there before her eyes flit to mine. "I had a bad day."

"I'm sorry to hear that." And I truly am. "Do you want to talk about it?"

Evie shakes her head, her eyes leaving mine. "Not particularly." She continues her path around my desk and over to the long window that overlooks the road parallel to the Tuckasegee River. "I would normally call J.D. on days like this. I tried."

A pang hits my chest. Is that guilt I feel for replacing the one man she trusted? Or jealousy for not being the one she trusts? "You can talk to me, Evie. I know I'm not Jenkins Wright, but I'm here for you in the same way."

Doubt casts a clear shadow on her expression, moving like a dark cloud, as she walks over to the couch. "What made you want to study psychology?" she asks as she sits in a careful motion.

I reach the front of my desk and lean against it, crossing my ankles in front of me. "As a child, I always had an insatiable thirst for knowledge that only grew stronger as I aged.

Books and nature were all I had to satisfy my palate until I was old enough to be on my own. At eighteen, I spent every waking minute in the library at Duke University. One of the professors there took notice of me, and we got to talking. He took me under his wing."

Her eyes widen in surprise. "Just like that?"

I cock my head. "There's a bit more to the story, but we don't need to get into the details now. This is your time, Evie. What do *you* want to talk about?"

She folds her arms across her chest. "What makes you think we're not already talking about it?"

Chuckling, I realize I might have underestimated the woman. "You'd like to know more about the professor who mentored me and helped me become who I am today?"

Her eyes sparkle as she nods. "Very much."

Accepting that response, I sort through the many answers I could possibly give before I walk to my bookshelf to pull out the short story that changed my life. After I hand it to her, I walk back to my desk and wait.

She reads the title aloud. "*Waterfall Effect.*" Her brow creases as she turns to the back of the book to read the description only to find none there. "What is this?"

"An allegory." I give her a small smile. "Written by Dr. Phillip Rohls, a philosophy professor, also known as my mentor. 'Waterfall effect' refers to a philosophical approach to memory and how simply existing in nature affects our memory over time. The way we bend and alter our past experiences based on our surroundings. The way we hold onto some things and forget others."

I point to the book she's flipping through. "That was the book my mentor found me reading in the library when he first approached me. I had no idea he was the author until we started diving into the meaning behind the work. Apparently, one of Dr. Rohls's patients had gone through trauma that resulted in a form of amnesia. She was a victim in a string of mysterious murders in Balsam Grove, not too far from here—the only victim lucky enough to make it out alive."

"I heard about that," Evie says, her eyes wide with what looks like fear. "That poor girl. They say the person who did it found victims all over the Appalachians. What he did to them was…" She trails off, shuddering.

I nod, remembering it too. "It changed her forever. Well, Dr. Rohls dedicated his allegory after her. In fact," I add, surprised at myself for wanting to tell her this next bit, "I'm writing a little something of my own."

Evie relaxes into the back of the couch, a smile tilting her lips. "Tell me more."

My own smile widens in response. "I think I've already overshared. Should we turn the tables back around to you?"

"Not yet," she says. "I have one more question."

I raise my eyebrows in anticipation.

"Why do you have so many certifications that have nothing to do with your practice?" she finally asks.

Tilting my head, I try to search her eyes, but the twelve feet of distance between us makes it hard. "I use them all in some way or another."

Her eyes narrow, but a small smile still plays on her lips. "Certified sex therapist? Explain that one."

"Okay." I chuckle. "A couple of years ago, I had a long-time patient I'd been seeing for her commitment issues. When she finally met the right person, she couldn't live up to his expectations in bed. I was only able to explore so much with her and ended up losing her as a client. That was when I took up the additional studies, so that would never happen again."

"And what exactly is sex therapy?"

I shouldn't find her questions as intriguing as I do, but I try to appease her with a simple answer. "It's getting to the root cause of sexual anxiety and adopting a positive relationship with sex." When she doesn't respond, I decide to ask the question I'm not sure if I should. "Is sex something you'd like to talk about?"

She balks at my question, a short, sharp laugh bursting from her. "With you?" She shakes her head. "No."

"Is that something you and Jenkins would talk about?"

Laughter bubbles up from deep in her belly. "Are you insane? There is no way in hell I would ever talk to J.D. about my sex life."

Her reaction throws me for a loop. "You said he knew you better than anyone."

"He does," she says, eyes wide. "He knows my past, he knows my fears, and he knows all about my family drama. Those things combined are more than anyone else knows. I don't see what sex has to do with any of that."

"Maybe nothing," I say, nodding. "Or maybe everything." My eyes linger on hers. "That's for you to answer. Either way, sex is generally a big part of life." I hesitate, wondering if I should keep going about this after she said she didn't want to talk about it with me. "Sex benefits our health in so many ways. It relieves stress, promotes happiness, provides exercise—"

"I know all that." She sighs. "I just mean, what does sex have to do with my fears, hopes, and dreams?"

To me, the answer is fairly obvious, but I'm not sure if Evie is ready to hear it—and I can't ask her more questions to explore this topic with her, considering she already told me no.

"Then let's leave sex out of it. How about we talk about your relationships, instead? Friendships, boyfriends, ex-boyfriends."

She stares back at me, and I swear I see a challenge in her eyes. "I got out of a casual relationship a few months ago." The way she scans me now makes me wonder if she's looking for a reaction. "The sex was terrible."

My internal fist pump is yet another indicator that we should not be anywhere near this subject. *What is wrong with me?* I clear my throat and ask, "How so?"

"Isn't it obvious?"

I frown. "Not really. What was terrible about it? Was it painful?"

She lets out an uncomfortable laugh. "No."

"Okay, then, was it the guy? Was he selfish with his needs?"

"No, he definitely *tried* to…" She pauses like she's not sure how to phrase what she wants to say.

"But he couldn't take care of you." I shouldn't make that kind of statement. It's not for me to speak to what she needs to say. She should be entirely sorting it out for herself.

"You're talking about orgasms," she says.

I nod. "Of course."

Her cheeks pinken slightly. "Then no. He couldn't."

Aha. "Well, you mentioned this was a casual relationship. Perhaps you were craving an emotional connection?"

Her headshake comes too quickly. "Sex is sex. It doesn't have to be emotional. There doesn't have to be a cosmic shift in the tides for me to get off every single time."

She's not wrong. "But you couldn't get off?"

She squirms in her seat. "No."

"So, what do you think the problem was?"

Evie frowns, and the way she looks down, like she's ashamed, tells me the answer before she even speaks. "He wanted more than a casual thing." She runs her palms down the front of her skirt. "He wanted the emotional connection, and I didn't." Realization flickers across her features. "I guess it all fucked with my head. It's my own fault."

"Why are you so quick to put that blame on yourself?"

"Because I'm the problem. I've always been the problem." She shrugs. "Casual sex is so much easier with men I haven't known since childhood. I should have never entertained a fling with Gabe."

Gabe. The name triggers annoyance in the back of my mind, but I can't be sure she's talking about the cop. I push the thought away. "Sometimes when a person feels guilty for their actions, they self-sabotage. Do you think that's why the sex was terrible?"

She thinks about it then nods.

"Can I ask why you didn't want to explore an emotional connection with this Gabe guy?"

The way she looks into my eyes before responding makes me realize just how intensely I'm anticipating her question. She shakes her head firmly. "I guess it's the same reason I don't explore emotional connections with any guy. It has nothing to do with Gabe in particular."

"And why do you think that is?"

Her mouth opens then closes.

"I'm not judging you, Evie," I say to clarify. "I'm only trying to help you understand."

She shifts in her chair, indicating discomfort. "I don't know."

The quick, dismissive answer tells me she might have some inkling about why she avoids attachment, but I let it go. Clearly, she's not ready to explore those reasons why yet.

"Okay," I say. "Then why sex? What do you get out of it?"

Her cheeks burn with color again, this time a darker red. "I... I don't know. I suppose it's something I can get lost in."

Narrowing my eyes at this answer, I try again. "Close your eyes, Evie."

They flutter closed.

"Why is sex something you want to get lost in?"

She visibly swallows.

"Take your time," I say. "Think back on your experiences."

Her breathing goes shallow, and her palms rest in her lap. "It's like... an out-of-body experience. In a weird way, I can be someone completely different. Someone confident. I feel... powerful and in control."

She takes in a deep breath then lets it out slowly as if she's finally relaxing. "There's something about the feel of a man between my thighs while I'm riding him, slipping up and down his erection while gradually quickening my pace." Her thighs part slightly, and her chest heaves a bit. "The contact of our bodies. The sensation of it all building and building. The orgasm that brings me crashing down." Her breath hitches with her words, like she's experiencing it all right there in the office. "It's all so freeing. So addicting." She inhales deeply and opens her eyes to meet mine. "And none of that requires an emotional connection."

Fuck me. For the first time in my entire career as a therapist, I question just how much of a professional I am. I'm hard—so fucking hard—and all I can do is squeeze my hands together above my lap to try to hide it.

Evie doesn't seem to notice. Instead, she stands up, straightens her skirt, and flushes intensely. If I had to guess, I would say her pussy was soaked after the mental picture she just worked up. I imagine this is how she would look after fucking me in the exact way she just described.

"I should get home. Thank you for seeing me."

I want to leap to her from where I'm leaning on my desk, but she's sure to notice the way my pants have tented in reaction to her words. "You're welcome anytime, Evie. I'll have Doreen call you tomorrow to book your next session."

Evie's eyes widen, and she shakes her head. "That's not necessary. This was a one-time thing. I'm not sure I should come back."

Disappointment crushes me. "Wait. What?"

She turns away to walk toward the door. A growl roars inside me, stemming from frustration that surpasses my greater instincts. Why does this woman have to be so infuriating?

I step forward, doubling the stride of my steps to catch up with her just as she's opened the door. "Evie, please. Just wait a second."

She swivels around, catching me off guard since she's standing so close. Her eyes burn into mine. "Coming here was a bad idea."

"It was a great idea," I argue, confusion swirling through me. Talk about whiplash.

Her eyes slip down my body to where my hard-on is

finally deflating. Her lips turn up in a smirk as her gaze fixes back on mine, and she tilts her head as if in challenge. "You sure about that?"

I don't have an answer. I can't defend myself. I can't explain my way out of this one. So I let her go, still somehow confident that no matter what she's saying now… she'll be back.

I mages of Lincoln Reed appear on my phone screen with one tap of my finger. He was easy to research, with scholarly articles and interviews all featured on Duke's website and his biography the same in every place it pops up, full of the boring info he's already shared. Nothing new. Nothing exciting. Nothing… real.

He seems to have no social media, and I find no trace of him on any local dating groups, nor do I find a drop of information about his daughter's mother or details about his childhood. The man's past is a giant mystery, and as much as I know I shouldn't care, I'm far too curious to pretend I don't.

I flip to a new photo—this one of Lincoln at a casual dinner with fellow classmates in Durham. He's wearing a red polo shirt and tan slacks, his beard is much shorter, and he looks far separated from the seemingly pretentious group he's surrounded by.

If there's one thing I've learned about Lincoln Reed, it's that the man is anything but stereotypical. Every time I think I have him figured out, he throws me for a loop, making me second-guess everything.

Sighing, I lay my phone down on the mattress and stare up at the yellow popcorn ceiling of my studio apartment. My thoughts slip back to the last time I saw Lincoln, before I ran out of his office, before I knew one of us had crossed a line. I wasn't sure who'd caused it, and I wasn't precisely sure what the line was, but I knew the session had to end.

Lincoln almost had me.

He got me talking, telling him things I'd never told another soul. What I can't figure out is what possessed me to confess such dirty details about myself.

Then again, I have no reason to feel shameful for my confessions. He's supposed to be the professional one. I'm the one who needs help. Clearly.

My core aches, remembering the slow rise in the crotch of his slacks when he thought my eyes were completely closed. He thought he could hide it, but I knew the truth—he wanted me.

My breathing goes shallow as I reach between my thighs, into my underwear, to feed the desire I've tried my darndest to stifle, the needs that have been growing ever since I laid eyes on Dr. Lincoln Reed, with his thick beard, dark-rimmed reading glasses, incredible body, and insanely gorgeous eyes that always seem to be following me.

Two fingers move from my clit to my slick opening before slipping inside. I tilt my hips to deepen my reach, and a moan escapes me as my eyes flutter closed. All I see is him. My fingers are soaked, my hips working double-time as I imagine Dr. Reed's cock driving me to infinite bliss. In that moment, there's no guilt, no timidity, no regret—just my most erotic fantasies firing off an intense series of orgasms that blast through my body and send me floating on a puffy cloud of happiness.

I'm not sure how long it takes me to come down from that high, but I eventually manage to get out of bed and be somewhat productive. I throw a load of laundry in and tidy up, which isn't hard considering I have one room, save for the bathroom and single closet. I get ready for work by early afternoon and spend the next couple of hours in my uncle's office, working on next week's schedule and preparing an inventory list for my upcoming shopping trip.

My shift at the bar starts at four in the afternoon, and as soon as I walk into Firefly, I can see it's going to be a slow night. There's only one customer, a man with a black hoodie zipped up with the hood covering his head. He's sitting in the back corner of the bar, buried in a book and giving off the vibe that he does not want to be disturbed.

My co-worker for the night, Kyle, is currently typing fast and furious on his phone—most likely texting his girl-friend, who hates that he's working in a bar. They've only been dating for a few months, but he's completely smitten to the point that he almost comes off as a standoffish asshole to the women who sit down to be served by him. He won't flirt. Hell, he won't even make eye contact, and it drives them completely mad.

Chuckling to myself, I sidle up to him and start to clean the dirty glasses he's left in the sink. "Trouble in paradise?"

He doesn't even look up, just continues to text. "No. Making plans for this weekend."

I raise my brows. I don't usually ask about such plans, but curiosity wins out. "What's going on this weekend?"

He slides his phone into his back pocket and knocks his hip into mine, bumping me aside so he can take over at the sink. "Janessa's putting together a birthday party for Armando at our picnic spot on Saturday. Live music, swimming, tubing. You know the drill." He gives me some side-eye. "You should come."

Instinct has me shaking my head. As much as I love my co-workers, I've never felt the need to spend more time with any of them—not to mention, the picnic spot he's referring to is far too close to the campground I try to stay away from at all costs. Living in such a small town, that's nearly impossible. Deep Creek is the hub of entertainment around here, so I've been back there on occasion but *never* to camp. That's where I draw the line.

"I have to get to the market to stock up and then work a double since you all took the day off," I remind him playfully.

Kyle rolls his eyes. "Whatever, boss. The market opens at six on Saturday and the party will be going on into the wee hours of the night. You can close for a few hours—Armando will be bummed if you don't at least stop by."

Somehow I doubt that, but I try not to play into self-deprecating feelings. And he's not wrong about the possibility of closing down for a few hours. Since we run on such a skeleton crew, we've had situations in the past when no one can work, even on a Saturday. "I'll see what I can do."

Kyle's smug smile nearly makes me regret agreeing to even the possibility. Instead of giving into my inclination to take it all back, I swipe the cleaning rag from beside the sink and leave the bar area so I can wipe down the tables. Even if they look clean, I have to Clorox them at the beginning of every shift. Patrick calls this unnecessary and obnoxious. I just call it sanitary.

I've only finished three tables when two figures walk

through the entrance. "Francine," I say, surprised to see the older woman here. And then my focus shifts to the little girl beside her. "And Lucy." My smile goes wide when I see the adorable toddler in her sparkling-pink dress.

"Evie!" Lucy exclaims with a giant wave.

I wave back then toss the rag onto the table I just wiped down and walk over to greet them both. "What brings you two by?"

Francine shrugs, her eyes wide as she examines the bar in one long sweep. "I just picked Lucy up from daycare, and we thought we'd go on a stroll around town. She saw the books in the window and wanted to check it out."

Looking back at Lucy, I kneel to match her height. "Do you like books, Lucy?"

Her big blue eyes shine brilliantly as she nods.

"What kind of books?"

She just stares at me as if she isn't sure how to answer.

"Can I show you some of my favorites? I think you might love them."

Again, she nods but doesn't say a word, her eyes fixed on mine. I stand and hold my hand out. Lucy takes it without an ounce of hesitation, melting my heart with one touch.

Francine gestures for us to go on without her. "I think I'll take a look at your menu."

I make eye contact with Kyle and send him a silent message—*take care of my friend*. He nods in return, an understanding and a promise.

Then I turn my full attention back to Lucy and grin. "All right, let's go."

The girl follows me to the other end of the room to a nook with bench seating and a corner bookshelf behind it. I pull out a handful of classic fairytale books and scatter them on the table for Lucy to see. She immediately grabs *Sleeping Beauty* then pushes it into my hands.

"Read, please." She tilts her head sweetly, like she knows exactly how irresistible the move is.

I smile. "My pleasure."

Lucy curls up next to me while I read the book to her, playing up the accents and voices like I'm in my own theater production and Lucy is the only audience member. She seems riveted, her eyes glued to the illustrations as I turn each page.

We're halfway through the next story when Lucy's little voice squeals with delight.

"Daddy!"

I look up to find Lincoln approaching our table and sinking down beside his daughter so she's sandwiched between us.

"Hey there, sweetie." He wraps an arm around her small body and kisses the top of her head. "Whatcha reading?"

Lucy steals the book from my hands, causing Lincoln and me to laugh. "This one, Daddy. Ariel the mermaid and Eric the prince!"

Lincoln's amused eyes meet mine and linger. "Who would have known you had kids' books tucked away in this small corner?"

I smile back into his deep-emerald gaze. "You wouldn't know it by the looks of it, but Firefly is a family establishment. All ages are welcome."

"Well," Lincoln says, taking the book in both hands. "Thank you for helping Lucy find her happy place. She loves books."

"My motive was entirely selfish, I assure you. Books are my happy place too."

"Good to know."

The way he says those three words, like he's keeping a mental note for later, creates a fluttering effect in my chest. I push my way out of the booth to give the father and daughter some privacy and make my way to where Francine was mingling with Kyle at the bar.

"Did you know your friend here was a burlesque dancer back in Chicago?" Kyle asks as I approach.

Francine waves a hand like he's giving her too much credit. "In the seventies, darling. It's been a lifetime since then."

Kyle points at her as he starts toward the other side of the bar, where one of our regulars just sat down. "I bet you've still got it, Francine." He pretends to tip an invisible hat as he grins.

"Hardly," Francine mutters, but she smiles at me. "My daughter was a much better performer than me. Unfortunately, North Carolina wasn't the best place to develop talent like hers. She gave up on theater after high school graduation, then she always wondered—what if?"

I lean my elbows against the counter, heart heavy after hearing the story. "That's so sad."

"You're telling me." Her eyes flicker from her hot tea to the bottle of Tennessee Fire on the counter. "Can I try some of that?"

Something tells me the subject of her daughter weighs on Francine. I can't help but wonder if her daughter's death plays into that depth of sorrow too.

"Of course." I smile and fill a glass with ice before

topping it with two shots of the thick, sweet honey-colored liquor. "You struck me as a martini girl."

Francine takes the glass and swirls it slowly, watching as the liquid coats the inside of the glass. "That was the old me. The married me." She meets my eyes then narrows hers playfully. "Always so predictable." When the glass's rim hits her lips, she tips her head back, gulping down half the liquor in one swift swallow. Afterward, she sets the glass down and grins. "Not anymore, baby girl."

Laughing, I shake my head. "Maybe your daughter was just intimidated by your talents. It's a tough job living up to our parents' expectations, you know?"

Francine shakes her head. "I wish that was the reason—that would mean there might have been a chance of saving her from the dark path she went down. No, my Becca was a night owl, partying until all hours, hanging out at the wrong clubs. Eventually, she just stopped coming home." She takes another sip of her whiskey. "Until years later when she turned up three months pregnant." Francine's tone shifts. "I finally had my baby girl back. Well, until Lucy was born, anyway."

I frown, curiosity about all the small details I'm missing eating away at me. "She left Lucy after she was born?"

Her face ashen, Francine nods. "Said she was going to the grocery store and never came home. Lucy had just turned one." She takes another sip of her whiskey. "After I found out Becca died, I got her phone back and started to put together clues as to who the father was."

"Geez. That's—a lot." I have no other words for what I'm hearing, for what Francine and Lincoln went through to become a family for Lucy. As much sense as it makes now in context, there's nothing normal about it. "I'm sorry"—and I hate that I'm even about to ask this question, but I have to—"can I ask how Becca died?"

"An overdose. A mixture of things I couldn't even begin to name for you. It's a miracle Lucy is as healthy as she is. God knows what Becca was doing before she knew she was pregnant."

I reach across the bar and cover her hand with mine. "Lucy is perfect because your daughter, for twelve whole months, was her very best self. In her own way, she loved Lucy very much. She cared enough to make sure her baby was healthy, even if she was struggling."

Francine nods, her eyes meeting mine. "Thank you for saying that, dear."

"I mean it." I squeeze her hand.

A noise from the back corner of the bar steals my attention. Turning back to the nook, I see Lucy fussing in Lincoln's lap. He stays calm through it all, talking to her gently, kissing her cheek, and then carrying her over to where Francine sits.

"This baby goose is hungry," he says.

The adorable nickname makes me smile, even though I don't understand the meaning behind it.

"I should get Lucy home," Lincoln says to Francine first before looking at me. "Thanks again for showing her your books. I'm sure she'll be begging to come back sometime soon."

Lucy buries her face in his armpit, and I have to bite the inside of my lip to not laugh.

"Anytime," I say. "Thanks for swinging by."

"Next time, I'll be a paying customer," Lincoln adds. "I promise."

I wave my hand to dismiss his thoughtful comment. "Don't worry about it. Have a good night."

After Lincoln walks out with Lucy, Francine pushes her unfinished glass toward me and leans into the counter like she wants to be sure I can hear when she says, "He's a good man." Something about her tone tells me she's acknowledging this for herself as well as for me. "A handsome man, too. Also, very single." She winks and hops off the stool. "Anyway, do what you want with that unsolicited information."

Gratitude fills me up. Francine might be completely overstepping, but it's nice to feel like someone is on my side. I can't help but smile long after Lincoln, Lucy, and Francine depart, floating around the establishment while tending to customers and ignoring Kyle's amused glances.

When it's closing time, I shut the blinds while Kyle sweeps, then he begins to mop while I count the till. We're a well-oiled machine. All the while, a late-night news program blares from the flatscreen behind the bar. Usually I can tune out the noise and stay focused on the mission at hand, and I do a good job of that... until something the broadcaster says makes my head turn to face the screen.

A reporter is standing in the middle of the woods at Deep Creek Campground, her face filled with bewilderment as fireflies flash their synchronous lights all around her.

"And there you have it, folks," she says. "Firefly season is at its peak. You won't want to miss this natural phenomenon in action." She points a finger sternly at the camera. "Remember the rules. You can look, but don't touch."

A chuckle comes from the other side of the bar where

Kyle is removing his apron. "That's right," he mutters to no one in particular, "or the Firefly Man will come and getcha." Then he locks eyes with me and flinches, like he forgot who was in the room. He offers me an apologetic smile. "See you tomorrow?"

Sometimes it blows my mind how my childhood playmates can speak of the Firefly Man like he's still just a campfire tale when there's an actual serial killer on the loose who has earned that name. He's still out there, claiming victims throughout the Appalachians.

Then again, my peers hadn't been close to Carley like me. And they weren't the ones who had stumbled upon her dead body.

For a second, I almost forget to answer his question. Janessa's party. My stomach knots in a way it hasn't for years. *Get ahold of yourself, Evie.* I can go to the picnic area. I can stay for a short time to celebrate Armando. It's not like I have to go anywhere near the campground.

Sucking in a slow, deep breath, I try to hide my anxiety behind a smile. "Of course. Tomorrow."

Kyle nods and heads out the front door. "See ya, boss!"

CHAPTER EIGHT

LINCOLN

Lucy erupts into a fit of giggles as I pretend to race her to the water's edge. She slows at the rocky shore and throws out a hand to me. I help her over the small rocks, thankful I thought to buy her water shoes before coming here. She's adorable in her blue bathing suit with its ruffled skirt and the pink floaties wrapped around her arms and waist. There will never be enough bubble wrap to protect my little girl.

We stay near the rocks, splashing around and waving at the tubers who float by. Every now and then, I dart glances at the gathering in the pavilion that has been bursting with activity since the moment we arrived. A guitarist plays to a group of people who are celebrating Armando's birthday.

It was Francine who slipped me the information that there would be a party here today—Kyle had mentioned it to her at Firefly. The possibility of running into Evie was too enticing to pass up.

"Did you see your friend?" Francine asks with a giant smile as she sets up her folding chair by the water's edge.

I cock my head, playing dumb. Friends are not something I have in this town, nor do I plan to ever have friends. Still, I know exactly who she's referring to. It's the same gorgeous blonde I've been trying hard not to stare at since we arrived.

I allow myself to look at Evie now. She's wearing a white bathing suit cover-up and is lounging on a large blue towel in the picnic area, reading. There's something angelic about the way her long blonde hair splays out behind her head that makes me smile.

An internal groan sneaks up on me. I haven't stopped thinking about the last time we were alone together, when she walked out of my office. She had every right to leave. Every right to tell me she was never coming back to therapy. And I, in turn, have absolutely no right to hope she would ever want to have a session with me again. My reaction to her confession was unprofessional, to say the least. I wanted her to trust me with her thoughts and feelings, not feel preyed on because of them.

Just then, Evie pushes herself to a sitting position and tucks a strand of hair behind her ear. She lays her book down and begins to roll her neck like she's been stuck in the same position for too long.

"Look, Daddy." Lucy brings a rock up from under the water and pushes her hand close toward my face so that I can get a good view of the shiny white stone. "Gems!"

I gasp and take her hand to pull it closer. "Wow, goose. That looks like real treasure to me."

She giggles and pulls her hand back to look at it again. The pride that lights up her entire body makes me smile.

"Go show Gammy your new treasure," I tell her. "I need to go say hello to a friend."

Lucy nods and climbs back onto the shore. I step out of the water behind her to make sure she stays safe on the rocky terrain then make my way to Evie.

It's like Evie senses me coming—she looks up when I'm several feet away, her eyes quickly finding my bare chest before flicking back to my face.

"Look at that. We meet again." I smile, unable to help the way I react to this woman, the way I desperately need her to want to be around me too. "What a small world."

She slips her sunglasses up onto her head and squints up at me. "You mean what a small *town*. Not exactly a ton of options around here."

I shrug. "You're probably right. Though Lucy might argue with you. The options were swimming here, gem mining, or petting the goats. The girl had a tough decision to make."

Evie's lips curl up on the sides. "Poor thing. However did she choose?"

Grinning, I sit on the ground beside her, careful not to get her or her towel damp. "I might have had some influence."

Evie glares playfully. "How selfish of you."

Chuckling, I shake my head. "What can I say? I'd rather swim in a creek than feed smelly goats." I pause. "Looks like you made the same decision."

She seems to ponder what I said. "I might be on Lucy's side here. Goats are much more enjoyable in my opinion. Unfortunately, I came for a birthday party."

I look at the group of people around the guitarist. "Then why aren't you over there?"

"I put in my time with them. Now, I want to read."

Something about her matter-of-fact attitude impresses

me. Evie's not forcing herself to be anywhere she doesn't want to be, even if that means separating herself from her peers.

"What are you reading?" I ask, changing the subject.

She flips the book over so I can see the cover. "An oldie but goodie."

I squint at the tattered hardback, wishing I recognized anything other than psychology-reference material. "*Anne of Green Gables*? What's that about?"

Her mouth widens in a smile, and she runs a gentle finger across the cover. "It's a children's classic about an orphan girl with a wild imagination. She goes through a terrible experience with foster families but is eventually adopted by a brother and sister who live on a farm." She lets out a small laugh. "However, when she shows up to live with them, they realize she's a girl and not the boy they had asked for."

At my frown, she rushes to continue. "They end up keeping her," she explains. "And she has a crush on this boy, Gilbert Blythe." She flushes with that last statement. "Anyway, it's just a great tale that spans a lifetime when you continue reading the series. They even made it into a miniseries. It's my favorite story."

My eyes still search every inch of her face, delighting in how animated she's become. "I can see that."

She shrugs. "It's inspiring. Anne doesn't let her past determine her future. She observes the world with wide-open eyes and believes anything is possible."

"Do *you* believe anything is possible?"

Her smile fades, and she tenses a bit. "I'd like to, but… in the real world, there's so much out of our control."

I'm not sure how much deeper we should get into this

conversation, but I guess I can test how much she's comfortable sharing. "Like what?"

She hesitates for a second, seeming to think of about she wants to respond. "Well, for instance, when I was younger, I would hear about my parents' lavish vacations. I dreamed of them taking me one day, but they never did. Instead, I always came here to stay with Uncle Patrick."

A piece of the mysterious puzzle that is Evie begins to slowly snap into place. "That explains why you had a bedroom at his house."

"He wanted me to feel like his house was mine too. By the time I was a teen, Bryson City felt more like home than where I lived in Raleigh with my parents."

There's a pang in my chest. "What was your life like in Raleigh?"

She gives me a knowing smile. "Is this one of your incognito therapy sessions?"

I frown. "No, Evie. I'm asking because I'm curious how you ended up here."

She studies me for a few more seconds before her shoulders relax a bit. "Raleigh was… prestigious, pretentious, and lonely. Very lonely." She takes a deep breath. "My parents were very much into the social scene, and children weren't allowed. By the time I got old enough for my parents to allow me into society, I was too much of a disappointment to them. My classmates were assholes who followed in their parents' footsteps, and we just didn't get along."

A sigh escapes her. "After graduation, my parents threatened to cut me off if I didn't go to college. So I packed my overnight bag and took the first train to Bryson City to live with Patrick permanently, and he welcomed me with open arms. All before my eighteenth birthday."

"Sounds like Patrick was more of a parent to you than your own."

"That's an understatement." She lets out a sarcastic laugh. "When I moved in, his only stipulation was that I had to go to therapy, and that's when I started my sessions with J.D." Her eyes dart to mine, like she's said too much. "Patrick was worried over what detaching myself from my parents might mean for me."

There's clearly much more to the story there, but it's not my place to push the conversation any more than I already have. With perfect timing, Francine and Lucy walk toward us. Lucy is wrapped in a big towel, her pigtails wet and tangled on top of her head, but she looks very happy.

"Hey, you two!" Francine grins.

"Hi, Francine. Hi, Lucy," Evie says, giving Lucy a big smile that Lucy returns tenfold.

"Lucy here keeps talking about those darn goats," Francine says. "I think I'm going to take her. Do you two want to come?"

I look at Evie, hopeful she'll say yes.

Just then, another person calls out to her from behind us. "Evie! We're going tubing. You coming?"

I look over my shoulder to see her co-worker Armando waving her over.

"Bring your friends," he adds with a nod to me.

By now, I assume I'm a familiar face in this small town, so I smile and nod back.

Evie looks torn between Lucy and her friends, but Francine jumps in.

"You two go tubing," she says to me and Evie. "I'll take

Lucy in the car to see the goats, and then I'll pick you up whenever you're done."

I glance at Evie, trying to assess if it's okay for me to crash the party.

She starts to gather her things but makes sure to make eye contact when she tells me, "Tubing sounds fun, actually. You should come."

That's the only confirmation I need. After giving Lucy a quick hug and kiss on the cheek, I smile at the way she waves a shy goodbye to Evie, then I follow Evie to a pile of tubes at one of the picnic tables. She reaches for a hot-pink one while I grab a blue one, but before we follow the others, she sets her tube down and removes her white sundress to reveal the sexiest yellow bikini I've ever seen.

Holy fuck.

If that day in my office was too much for my dick, this is most certainly worse. The triangles on top reveal the not-so-subtle swells of her breasts and the drastic dip of her waist compared to her thick, sexy hips and thighs.

Evie doesn't acknowledge my avid gaze. Instead, she wraps one arm around her tube and turns to follow the others, giving me a front-row view of her perfect ass as she walks.

I scramble to follow, forcing my thoughts back into the safe zone, as difficult as that feels in the moment. "So, uh," I begin, rushing to say anything that will distract me from her body, "do you still talk to your parents at all?"

She shakes her head and doesn't look at me. "Not anymore. At first, my mom tried to get me to change my mind by calling and sending me texts—encouraging me to look at my future and how not going to college would limit my opportunities. My dad would come visit under the guise of seeing his brother, but he wasn't fooling Patrick or me. He wanted to see if I'd changed my mind. Eventually, he realized I never would."

I ponder this information, which feels like a lot to take in. "Patrick and your father seem nothing alike, from what you're telling me."

Evie chuckles lightly. "Polar opposites. Night and day. Patrick was the rebel in that family, always going against everyone's wishes, like me." She cocks her head like that status is something she's proud of. "He wanted a simple life, and that's what he got by moving here. He took his inheritance and built his dream bar then invested the rest in the properties he still manages today. Now he's living like a nomad, traveling the Appalachians in his camper. He's happy."

"And what about you? Are you happy?"

Evie finally looks at me, her eyes locking on mine, and I think I can see the answer there before she can say anything. "I never know how to answer that question. I mean"—her eyes dart ahead of her again—"happiness comes and goes, doesn't it? No one is in a permanent state of bliss. There are bad days and good days." She pauses. "What about you? Are you happy?"

I'm almost surprised to be asked the question in return. I usually ask it in a therapy session with a patient, and they would never think to reciprocate.

"I am." I nod. "It helps to have Lucy around. Seeing the world through her eyes is everything I need in this lifetime. She helps me find gratitude in all the moments— good, bad, and in between. She makes me want to be the best person I can possibly be every day, to set an example of myself for her to see. So, yeah. I'd say I'm pretty damn happy."

Then a darker cloud thickens over my head. "That's not to say I'm in a constant state of bliss, though, as you pointed out. I have my bad days. The good, however, far outweighs them."

She blinks at me, and for a moment I think I might have offended her until her eyes begin to fill and a smile tugs at her lips. "That was beautiful, Lincoln. You really do have a special little girl."

My heart squeezes. "Thank you, Evie."

In the pause that follows, we share a single glance, but it's a moment that feels bigger than any we've had so far. There's so much about Evelyn Vaughn that I haven't been able to get out of my head, and every minute I spend with her draws me in deeper, like an addiction that I'm trying to justify however I can. I want to believe this particular addiction is healthy, but I know in the depths of my soul that it's most definitely not.

CHAPTER NINE

EVELYN

I'm not oblivious to the attention Lincoln gives my body as we wade into the water then climb into our tubes. I didn't exactly choose the most family-friendly attire for the day—not that I own any other options. In all fairness, I thought I was going to be sunbathing by the creek with a good book in my hand, but Lincoln Reed changed my plans, although I won't dare tell him that.

Still, I would never have agreed to float down Deep Creek if it weren't for the small glimmer of hope that he would come too.

Once we're both secured in our tubes, we let the slow current take us around the bend. I'm in no hurry to catch up with the rest of the group, so I resist paddling at all, content to drift in the calmer waters. Our speed will pick up once we get to the rockier sections that'll take us down and around the campground, so for now, I lie back, relax, and enjoy the view.

Lincoln follows my lead and lounges with his hands behind his head, arm muscles flexed and revealing his thick biceps. Clearly, the man has an entire fitness routine that includes more than just taking morning runs, which is obvious from his sculpted chest and abs. Even his muscular thighs look like they could squash a big juicy watermelon.

"Tell me about your best friends," he says. "They seem like a lot of fun."

I assume he's referencing Armando, Janessa, and the gang. "I wouldn't call them my best friends." The words come out carefully. I don't mean any disrespect. "We're friends, but they're also my co-workers. I'm their bar manager. I've known most of them for a long time and I do care about them—hence, me shutting down the bar to stop by and wish Armando a happy birthday." I sense that more questions will follow, so I try to get ahead of them. "I've just never formed deeper relationships with them."

He turns his head to look at me, though sunglasses cover his green eyes. "Really? I thought establishments like Firefly encourage close friendships."

"There's no rule against it," I admit. "But I'm still the owner's niece, and one day Patrick will hand the bar completely over to me. I just think drawing the line between manager and co-worker is safer."

"Safer." Lincoln repeats the word thoughtfully. "But you came to the birthday party today. How is that safe but forming a deeper friendship isn't?"

I squirm a little in my tube, suddenly uncomfortable. "I'm not heartless, Lincoln, but I set boundaries. I brought a gift and was only planning to stay a short time."

Heat that crawls up my neck much the same way my defenses have shot up like a rocket. I was okay talking about my parents and even part of the reason why I ended up here under Patrick's care—and J.D.'s—but talking about friendships crosses into territory I don't like to step into. With anyone.

Just as I begin thinking of ways to end the conversation, the first familiar sign of Deep Creek Campground comes into view—a small wooden deck and a rope swing, upgraded from the one I'd been on hundreds of times as a kid. And then come the waterfront tent sites.

My stomach knots as my mind begins to replay images from my childhood. Every familiar landmark triggers new memories, some older than others, but the haunting ones include Carley and the fast friendship we'd made in that short week. The way we clicked like we'd known each other our whole lives was something I had never experienced before. I felt… happy when I was with her.

"Evie, what's wrong?"

Lincoln's voice comes through faintly compared to the vivid memories. Roasting s'mores. Running from one side of the creek to the next. Skipping rocks. Guitars and off-tune vocalists, tree swings, hide-and-seek, fishing, canoe races.

The list goes on and on and on. My chest is heavy with sadness, and the ache only intensifies as we clear the camp-sites and reach the thicket of woods where our firefly chasing began. Guilt follows in its wake, telling me I should have stayed close to Carley that night. And I should have never let Foster go off to find her alone either.

Fear paralyzed me on that damn trail like a deer in headlights—until it was too late. Until Carley was dead and her brother was arrested. After that, the rest of my teenage years ended up in complete shambles.

My tube stops at the same time the site of Carley's murder comes into view—a small inlet to the lake paved with tiny rocks from the shore. Just beyond it is where we found her dead. I kick my feet to get my tube moving again, but I'm stuck for some reason.

Panic rips through my body, a guttural cry erupting from deep within as I struggle against the unknown force.

"Evie, stop!"

That voice—deep and familiar—snaps me back to the present. I whip my head to find its source, locking eyes with Lincoln. Relief floods my body, *whoosh*, and suddenly, for the first time in fourteen years, I feel safe.

There's no explanation for it. Lincoln hasn't done anything, yet, to deserve such a place in my breakthrough.

"Are you okay?" He grips his tube with one hand while his other hand secures mine in place, locking me to this spot like a prisoner.

"No," I finally say, wiggling my tube to get him to release it. "I… I thought I was caught on something."

His forehead dents in the middle as if he's confused, then he follows my gaze over his shoulder to the dreaded spot of my friend's murder. If I didn't know better, I might think Lincoln knows exactly why I desperately need to get away.

He releases my tube instantly and even gives me a little push in the right direction, then he flips over on his tube so he can breaststroke toward me, catching up in no time.

My next deep breath comes as soon as we round the next bend, when a waterfall comes into view. Dozens of colored tubes lay discarded on nearby rocks or float in the pool of calm water. I dare a glance at Lincoln, but he seems to be caught up in his own thoughts, probably ones of deep regret for following me down this creek.

"I'm going to stop here," I say. "You can keep going, if you want."

There, I gave him an out, one he'll surely take after my freak-out.

But the look he gives me now is one of utter disbelief. "What? No, I'll stop here too."

Still embarrassed, I launch myself into the water and swim the rest of the way to shore, haul my tube out to the nearest rock, and sit beside it. Lincoln is right behind me, following my every move.

In silence, we watch people swim as close as they can to the falls, laughing and chatting as they go. It's oddly peaceful here, even among the herd of people sharing the community waters. As much as I can, I bask in the simplicity of it all.

"Hey," Lincoln rasps, his voice gentle but enough to get my attention.

I turn to stare into his apologetic eyes.

"Whatever happened back there," he says. "Whatever I did. I'm so sorry."

My body shudders out a sigh, and suddenly I'm overcome with the need to make sure he's okay. "You didn't do anything, Lincoln. I just… freaked out."

His gaze searches mine. "Can I ask why?"

This is where I should say no. This is where I should enforce the line I've been so good at drawing all these years. I don't talk about Carley. What happened to her was a lifetime ago, and while I will never forget those gruesome details, I certainly don't need to remind the town of it.

Instead, I tell him, "I don't like to go back there."

He squints like he's truly puzzled. "Back where?"

"To the campground. Something terrible happened

there years ago, when I was a teen. Anyway, passing by that spot was hard enough, but when you stopped my tube…"

"I'm so sorry," he says again, his ashen expression convincing me his contrition is genuine. "I only stopped you to make sure you were okay. You went pale, and it seemed like you couldn't hear a word I was saying."

I nod slowly. "Yeah, um, Patrick and I used to go camping out there all the time. The last time we were there, a girl was murdered." My eyes shift back to his, feeling peace in his gaze. "She was my friend, and…"

A rough, calloused hand covers mine, causing me to take a deep breath that seems to reach every tense muscle in my body. I clear my throat and open my mouth, not sure what is about to come out. I never had to explain the details to J.D. during our therapy sessions. He was there that night too. He knew the details as well as anyone.

"I didn't see… the act… but I was one of the ones to find her after it happened. And she…" I immediately begin to tremble, and even Lincoln squeezing my hand doesn't quell my nerves this time.

"You don't need to explain if you don't want to, Evie."

I suck in a fortifying breath anyway. "It all happened so fast. I heard her scream, and I just knew something terrible was happening, but… we couldn't get to her fast enough."

Lincoln scoots toward me on the rock, his arm sliding around my body until I'm wrapped in a firm, warm hug. "We?" he asks gently.

Our eyes connect again, and I swear the color of his irises matches the wooded environment behind him, mossy green with speckles of gold-like glints from the sun. Those eyes are hypnotic—or at least, they steady me in a way I've never felt before.

"The girl who died, Carley, had an older brother." I debate using his name. It's not like that really matters, but somehow it feels important. "Foster. He was with me when we found her."

Lincoln blinks and takes in a long breath. "You're talking about the Firefly Man murder." His brow crinkles as he searches my eyes. "The first one."

The blood seems to drain from my face in utter shock. "You know about it?"

He nods, looking disturbed. "All too well. They made us study all that shit in my criminology class. The Firefly Man has his own section in the *Serial Murder* handbook. That was one of our course texts." He pauses. "Anyway, I figured everyone in the Appalachians knew the story. I even talked to your uncle about it a little bit because of the name of your bar."

My mouth forms an O, as I already know why that topic would have come up. "Fireflies have always been my favorite creatures. They were Carley's too. I refuse to let a psychotic freak change that. So I took back the word. People can call him the Firefly Man all they want, but that won't change the fact that Carley's light will never die. I won't let it."

He gives my shoulders a squeeze. "That's beautiful. I'll bet Carley would love that sentiment."

My heart swells at the emotion behind his words. "I hope so."

Silence passes between us for a few more beats until Lincoln lets out another sigh. "It's awful that the killer is still out there after all these years."

My mouth opens on a sharp breath. "And to think they all thought Foster did it."

Lincoln's hold tightens slightly. "They?"

"The cops at first, but rumors spread throughout the town and even beyond." I stare off into the distance, seeing nothing save for the blue and red lights that bounced around the darkness that night for what seemed like hours while Patrick held my shivering body close. "They took Foster and interrogated him. They even threw him behind bars for months—said he had all kinds of DNA all over him. Her hair, her blood." I shiver as my eyes pool with tears. "Her blood was all over his clothes and on his skin from holding her body, trying to wake her." I wipe a tear from my cheek. "He had just found his sister bludgeoned— what did they expect?"

Lincoln's mouth presses against my cheek, and his other arm wraps around me. He's so much closer. "You don't need to do this now. It's okay. You're okay."

I raise my head to face him, angered by the insinuation that there will ever be an "okay" time. "And when would a better time be? When I'm in your office?" My eyes narrow. "On your couch?"

His arms fall away, but he doesn't put any distance between us. Instead, he glares right back at me. "What the fuck, Evie?"

Guilt instantly crowds my chest. *Yeah, what the fuck, Evie?* "I'm sorry." Every ounce of my being feels apologetic for something I don't even understand. "I wasn't trying to snap at you. I just don't want anyone else to be burdened with what I've been through."

His expression immediately relaxes, and what I see next recharges me completely. "I think you forget what I do for a living."

The bad-timed joke makes me smile, and my face heats. "Clearly not, since I just referred to your couch."

He shifts so he's facing me, his hands inappropriate, but not at all unwelcome, on my thighs. "I could never feel burdened by anything you have to say. This is difficult for you. I can see that. I just didn't want you to feel pressured."

I mirror his movement, facing him and trying not to feel the buzz of electricity between us as his hands shift, one on each leg. "I'm sorry," I tell him. "I haven't talked about any of this to anyone for a very long time. I've just kind of bottled it up in my own firefly jar, trying to keep Carley's memory alive while suffering through the loss of her. Sometimes, it's hard to breathe." I can hardly believe the words even as I say them.

"Maybe it's time to open the jar."

I cringe at the implications behind his words. "I don't know if I can. Not until her killer is found."

He frowns. "What did Jenkins say about all this? And your friends who were with you that night?"

I hesitate to explain the reasons behind our silence, especially mine. "J.D. and I never talked about that night specifically. He was there, too, so it's not like he needed the gritty details."

Lincoln's eyebrows bunch together. "You never talked about what happened that night? Even if he was there, it was a significant time in *your* life. It altered your future, your relationship with your parents, your view on friendships."

I lean back to squint at him, wondering why he stopped there when I could list off a few dozen other ways that night changed my life. "We might not have rehashed those events, but he helped me learn how to deal with my insomnia and the nightmares. His job as my therapist was to help me stop carrying the weight of the tragedy, to *not* rehash it all. He gave me a safe space to just… breathe."

Lincoln stays quiet for another beat. "What did your parents think of what happened that night?"

I shudder at the memory of how cruel they were when I got home, like I was the one who'd killed somebody. Turned out, they were afraid for their reputations and what would happen when their friends found out that I was there that night.

"My parents." I laugh a little. "They didn't care to hear any of it. They wouldn't even let me go visit Foster in jail."

Lincoln's frown deepens. "That's awful, Evie. I'm so sorry. That had to have been rough."

I shake my head, feeling numb inside. "Honestly, I can't remember how it made me feel. There's a lot about that night and the events afterward that I just don't remember."

Lincoln nods. "Sometimes we subconsciously suppress memories that are harmful to our psyche. It's possible you were so hurt by your parents' reaction—and anything else around that time—that you just blocked it out." He chews on his bottom lip like he's debating something internally. "That's not entirely healthy in the long run, but I understand that everyone needs to cope with tragedy differently."

What he's saying makes absolutely no sense to me. "Why would I want to remember any of that?" I grimace. "I remember enough as it is."

Lincoln's eyes squeeze shut, then he opens them again with full attention on me. "I understand. It's just… Not talking about the trauma that changed your entire life can be dangerous, Evie. If you're not dealing with it, you're just suppressing it."

"Lincoln…" I pause, not sure how to get through this

conversation without exposing the absolute worst sides of myself. "When I first saw J.D., I'd been dealing with that night for two years all on my own. My nightmares were constant, my anxious thoughts debilitating. I thought about every moment of that night on repeat. I *wanted* to suppress it." It's the truth.

Lincoln appears to consider my words then nods slowly. "I understand."

I take a deep breath, waiting for him to say more. When he doesn't, I realize exactly why he went quiet and ask, "How would you have approached it if you were my therapist back then?"

"Without going through it all with you, I can't quite be sure," he says. "What I can tell you is what I believe in, which is while therapy is a tool—a helping hand through life—trauma complicates that. I strongly feel that trauma should never be ignored or suppressed. You might have built a strategy to cope for a long period of time, but trauma is like water building up against the dam. One day, you might get triggered and explode."

My heart has begun beating fast. Suddenly, I'm questioning the last twelve years of my life. It's no secret, even to myself, that I live on a routine. Nothing new, nothing too exciting. I'm just... living. Surviving. I guess I always thought that was the most important part.

Until the day Lincoln Reed came into my life.

"Then again," he says, and I can already feel him backtracking, "if what Jenkins did for you helped you heal in any way, then it was the right thing to do."

I'm not sure how to respond to that, so I say nothing.

Lincoln looks toward the water and leans back onto his elbows, letting silence linger between us for an oddly comfortable minute. "No wonder you reacted like that when we passed that place," he murmurs. "I'm surprised you can go near there at all."

I sigh. "I chose to live here with Uncle Patrick. But living here meant facing the constant memories of losing Carley. I had to make a choice to accept that. I had to learn how to deal with the pain as it came. I had a difficult time at first, seeing as no one can exactly escape Deep Creek when living here, but I think I've managed it pretty well."

Lincoln looks at me again, this time with eyes that express so many things. Compassion, sympathy, pride, sadness. It's a storm that reflects my own feelings, and I don't understand how someone who's known me for no time at all can see me so clearly.

"I'm sorry for putting all that on you." My chest tightens as I wonder if, even with how understanding he's been, my story has been too much.

He sits up and leans closer. "You never have to apologize for the things that weigh on your heart, Evie. You've been carrying this for such a long time. Let me help you."

The words trigger a gut reaction of panic and disappointment. "Help me? Please don't tell me you're saying that as a therapist."

He shakes his head adamantly. "Of course not, Evie. I was offering as a friend."

I let out a sigh of relief. "Good. But isn't this… unethical or something?" I point between him and me. "Divulging all these personal details outside of a therapy session?"

He gives me a slight smile. "I think we're past the point of you becoming my patient. We're talking now as friends."

Something kickstarts in my chest, and I wonder if this

means we could be anything more than friends. Do I even want that? The way my body reacts to him confuses the hell out of me. I've never wanted that kind of relationship before—with anyone. Why Lincoln? Why now?

"Maybe I was a little desperate for clients when I first met you." His lips quirk. "Pursuing you the way I did isn't something I'm exactly proud of."

I tilt my head, curiously. "Then why did you do it?"

He seems to consider his response. "Maybe I wanted to see you again for reasons that had nothing to do with your mental health."

My heart skips a beat. "That is most definitely not ethical."

He shakes his head, looking frustrated with himself and maybe some of his decisions. "Not at fucking all. But if you haven't noticed, I haven't asked you to come back to my office since the last time. If you did, it would strictly be as a friend." The way his eyes burn through mine at the word "friend" tells me he most definitely means something more.

My eyes widen and my breath goes shallow. "Are you saying you don't want to be my therapist, Doctor Reed?"

The way he pins me with his stare—desperate, hungry, and insatiable with need—makes my entire body come alive.

"I want to be whatever you'll let me be, Evelyn Vaughn." His eyes roam over my body, coming back to my lips. "I'm just not sure you're ready for it."

God, the way Evie makes me insane for absolutely no reason at all. My confession doesn't make it anything easier. "I want to be whatever you'll let me be, Evelyn Vaughn. I'm just not sure you're ready for it."

What the fuck was I thinking, saying that? I'm lucky that Evie finally trusts me enough to divulge any details of her tragic past. Me telling her I'm into her will only complicate how much information she's willing to share. I didn't move Lucy to Bryson City for nothing. I have work to do. This is where I need to be.

Evie stands. Her ass checks, bare beneath the cloth of her bikini, stare me in the face. *Fuck me.* If she were mine, I would drag her down onto my lap and kiss her senseless. Maybe then she would feel my truth, my need, my desire for her.

Instead, I stand, too, following her back down to the water.

"We're falling behind the others," she says, sounding breathless.

I would love to know if her lack of breath has anything to do with me, but she picks up her tube and moves to the water so fast, I have trouble keeping up. I stumble over every rock until I'm practically tripping into the water with my tube in hand.

Meanwhile, she's sitting pretty in her tube, giving me a confused look. "Are you okay?" she asks, sounding amused.

I try to make my belly flop onto my tube more graceful, but that's nearly impossible as my face lands on the hot rubber before I can reposition myself. "Yup," I call out anyway. Once I'm finally onboard, I flip my body around until I'm facing the sky. I take a series of slow, deep breaths to calm my heart rate and refocus on the mission at hand.

Then I turn back around and paddle to close the distance to Evie. She's got her head leaned back as if she's completely relaxed, her eyes closed as she basks in the sun.

She must sense my presence because she opens one eye. "How does Lucy like Bryson City?"

Her question makes me smile. "She loves it." I nod, thinking about just how much that statement is true. "She's even already made a list of friends she wants to invite to her birthday party. The question is where on earth am I going to host ten little kids and their parents?"

Evie laughs. "Your house. Or somewhere like this."

I don't want to give Evie all the nitty-gritty details about how I would *never* celebrate my daughter's birthday in the woods. "My house would be fine—I just have no clue how to entertain her friends. Are piñatas still cool? Do I need to come up with a bunch of games? Oh, and do I have to entertain and feed the parents too?"

Evie does that cute head-tilt thing, a signal that she wants to let me know I'm being too hard on myself. "I think whatever you do will be perfect. Focus on Lucy. On what Lucy wants. What will make her happy? The rest will fall into place."

That's it. One simple, honest statement, and I already feel better. Perspective is everything when you're a parent. Just spending time with my little girl has shown me how fragile life can be and how futile it is to sweat the small stuff. Evie's right. All that matters is that Lucy's day is filled with love and friendship. Nothing else matters.

I nod. "Maybe I should hire you to help me plan it."

She smiles. "I'm sure you've got this, Lincoln. But you know where to find me if you need me."

I need you, I want to say. Instead, I keep the focus on my daughter. "I didn't expect for her to make so many friends in daycare already. Back home, she just stayed with Francine while I worked. I wasn't sure if I was ready to give her days to strangers, but she's adapted so well here. I'm afraid…" I falter, questioning how much information is too much.

"You're afraid of what?"

The inquisitive look Evie gives me launches a rocket of guilt straight into my chest.

"I'm afraid I don't have what it takes to be a long-term therapist here," I tell her. "I've failed to convince more than half of Jenkins's patients to give me a chance, and the only new patients booking consultations with me are…" Again, I stop myself.

Evie narrows her eyes. "Why are you hesitating so much? I just poured my guts to you earlier. What are you hiding from me?"

Panic kicks me in the gut. "Nothing. I was just going to say that the only new consultations I've been booking are with married women around my age. Mothers. Specifically, Lucy's friends' moms."

Evie looks like she's trying to hold back a smile. "You're telling me the married women in town have the hots for the new doctor?" She widens her eyes in mock disbelief. "No."

I roll my eyes and lean my head back to face the sky again. "Ha ha. I'm glad you find this funny because it's been causing me some severe anxiety."

Evie turns over onto her stomach and arranges her tube so she's floating backward to face me. "Have they made advances toward you? Like, are you certain they're booking these consultations for reasons that have nothing to do with their mental health?"

I frown. "My consultations are confidential."

She tilts her head and purses her lips. "I'm not asking you to out any women in particular. I'm just asking, in general, if any of them have come onto you."

Against my better judgment, I tell her the truth. "Yes."

Her face darkens a shade, and I swear I see a new emotion on her face. Jealousy? Annoyance? I'm not quite sure, but something dark and devious inside me loves it all the same.

I reach for the handle of her tube to pull hers toward mine. "I'm not interested in any of those women, Evie."

Her cheeks flush even darker. "I wasn't suggesting that you were."

I bite down on the inside of my cheek. "But you were thinking it."

Her mouth opens and closes, then she frowns. "I mean, sure. I've seen the women in this town. Plenty of them are rich and beautiful. Certainly, you must find at least one of them attractive. I can see why you're afraid. You might slip."

Desire roars inside me like a wild beast. "There's only one woman in this town I find attractive. I think you know that."

She averts her eyes, doubt cascading over her features. "A bold statement."

I reach out, cup her chin, and turn her to look me in the eyes. "It is. And it's true. Why do you think I dragged my family out here today?"

Her eyes widen like she's taken aback. "What do you mean?"

"I mean," I start slowly, not wanting her to miss a single syllable, "that Kyle mentioned to Francine that he'd invited you here today." Evie still doesn't seem to be taking my meaning. "At the bar last night."

Her eyes flash, telling me my point has finally clicked.

I finished with, "So I made a family day out of it, hoping that you would be here."

"Oh," she whispers.

My heart is practically in my throat as I wait for her to say more, but before she can, I hear the roar of the water and look over Evie's shoulder. "Shit."

Evie reacts quickly, snapping her head to look behind her then flipping around in her tube so her butt is back in the center. "You're going to want to get in your tube, Lincoln."

I scramble to follow her lead, planting my ass in the tube just in time for the first downhill plunge of the trip. Large rocks protrude from the water as the water becomes more turbulent. We're jerked like Ping-Pong balls from one side of the creek to the other as our tubes take on a mind of their own. Evie shrieks then laughs so hard I can't help but do the same.

It's a wild ride for the next several minutes but so worth it once we take the final bend that deposits us into another stream of calm waters.

"Damn, that was intense," I gasp, still shocked after the unexpected thrill.

Evie is giggling with her head tossed back and sunshine beaming down on her beautiful features. "The look on your face when you saw those rocks." She laughs even harder, the kind of hilarity that bubbles up straight from the belly.

"It wasn't that funny," I say with a glance heavenward.

She's still got the uncontrollable giggles and begins wiping tears from her eyes. Retaliation is the only thing on my mind when I slide free of my tube and reach for hers. She squeals and starts to flip onto her stomach to begin paddling away, but she slips off her tube instead.

"Where do you think you're going?" I wrap one arm around her waist and pull her close until she's right where I want her—inches away from our lips meeting. I can't fucking wait to kiss this woman.

Her sapphire eyes lock on mine while my heart hums like a hammer drill. All I have to do is lean in.

She sucks in a breath, that quick inhale the admission I need to continue my advances. Her tongue darts out to wet her lips before her teeth drag over them, showing me she wants this just as much as I do. And after what she confessed to me in my office, she might even *need* this.

My voice is rough when I speak. "Give me one reason I shouldn't kiss you right now." There it is—her out, if she chooses to use it.

Small fingers feather over my waist before digging in to grip me just slightly. One side of her mouth curls up. "Is that a threat?"

I resist the urge to growl out my need and instead lean in so my lips glide against her ear. "Yes. It's only fair, given that you've consumed my mind since the moment I met you. Say it's not just me."

She shivers in my arms. "It's not just you, Lincoln." One of her legs wraps around my waist, then the other leg follows. My hands move to support her ass, adjusting her enough so we fit together, so she can feel how hard I am for her.

My mouth moves to the crook of her neck. She smells sweet like pineapple and cherries, a unique combination I would love to devour. My tongue darts out, desperate for a taste of her, famished for a decent meal after nearly three years of fasting.

It doesn't help that her heels dig into the backs of my legs while she grinds her center against me, as if my cock is a tree trunk and she's using it to scratch an itch.

I pull my head up again, my focus on her lips, anticipating what they might feel like against mine. I start to close the gap until I'm right there, lip to lip, just barely grazing the surface, when a voice calls to us from up on the hill near the road.

"Evie! Lincoln!" It's Kyle. "Where are your tubes?"

Evie scrambles in a mad dash to separate our bodies, then she looks around frantically, on a mission to find her tube and possibly mine. But they're nowhere to be seen.

"Oops," I say.

Evie cringes and looks up the hill at Kyle. "Guess they floated away. I can pay you back for them, Kyle."

He grins and looks between us, definitely onto our little charade. "Don't sweat it, boss. This one's on me." He chuckles while Evie's cheeks flame red. "You two need a lift back to the picnic area?"

Evie immediately begins to move out of the water. "Yes, thank you, Kyle."

I follow closely, begrudgingly, behind. That's the buzzkill needed to ruin a perfectly good first kiss. I guess that just means we'll need a second chance at it.

R ain pelts my apartment window at a slow and steady pace, matching the speed with which my thoughts roll frame by frame, the events of yesterday playing out again and again. I slap the poetry book I'm trying to read closed, unable to focus on its words.

I keep remembering the moment I spotted Lincoln running toward the creek with Lucy and pretended not to notice. Him finally seeing me and approaching. Our adventure in the tubes, my panic attack, and the conversation that followed. Finally, the most intense almost-kiss I could have ever imagined.

A moan hums through me as I think about the way my legs wrapped around him, giving in to my own insatiable desire. I've never felt like this with a man before—desperate for his attention, aching for his hands on every inch of my body, ready to take him however he'll let me have him.

I no longer need to question Lincoln's desire for me. He made that abundantly clear yesterday, leaving little room for doubt, when his thick cock pressed into the thin fabric of my bikini bottoms, desperate for entry. I heard the guttural groan that came from deep in his chest as he pulled me closer. I saw the need in his eyes as I rubbed against him and felt the heady undertone of sex when his lips met my ear. And I recognized his deep sense of disappointment when we were interrupted before our lips could completely meet, because I felt it too.

In my mind, it's no longer "if we have sex." It's "when." And I'm anxiously awaiting that opportunity.

Just like every other morning when thoughts of Lincoln Reed spiral through my brain and trigger my sexual hunger, I'm wet and eager for relief. But rubbing my clit isn't enough this morning when I'm imagining his hard cock inside me. If we'd only had more time, I would have let him take me right there in the creek. If he had slipped my bikini from my skin and slid me down his shaft, I would have fucked him without a single ounce of regret.

Two fingers slip into my entrance, and I push them inside until I'm fucking myself, imagining it's Lincoln slipping, sliding, groaning, deepening. Imagining his thick beard scratching and teasing my skin.

Relief erupts from me in a wave of orgasm that leaves me floating for the rest of the morning. Clearly, it's been too long since I've had sex, but I've gone months before and the need has never hit me like this—like I can't function without getting myself off. It's the Lincoln Reed effect, one I'm not sure I'll ever get over.

I go through my morning routine at the bar, making sure I unpack everything I bought at the market yesterday, cutting fresh fruit and garnishes, sweeping and mopping the floors, and going over paperwork in the office. I continue working even when Janessa comes in with shades over her eyes, clearly hung over.

"You going to be okay today?" I smile, knowing Armando's birthday party continued long after I left.

Janessa groans. "That's debatable."

Chuckling, I take a seat at the bar and watch her struggle with her apron as she walks to the register to clock in. "If you give me one hour to run an errand, I can cover your shift," I offer.

She frowns, sunglasses still covering her eyes. "You're closing tonight. I can't let you do that—and believe it or not, Armando is worse off than me."

"Maybe Kyle can—"

She cuts me off, shaking her head. "Trust me. I'm the best you've got today."

Laughing again, I slap the counter. "It's fine, babe. I'll take the double. I'll even pay you for the day off. Just get me back another time."

Janessa doesn't have to express her relief with words. It's written all over her body. "Okay, deal. Go run your errand, and I'll try not to vomit while you're gone."

She flashes me a smile as if to assure me she's kidding, and I give her a smile in return. Then I hop off the bar stool.

"Wait, I meant to ask you something," she says.

I turn to face her. "Ask me what?"

Instant regret hits me when I turn around and see the teasing smile on her lips. My cheeks immediately get hot—I know what's coming.

"What's going on with you and the new doctor in town?" she asks, still grinning. "Kyle said he caught you two in a lip-lock."

Shit. "We were not in a lip-lock. We were…" I don't know how to get myself out of this. "He was saving me from drowning." There. A lie, and a shitty one, but who's going to question me?

Janessa folds her arms across her chest. "You almost drowned? You're the best swimmer I know."

I shrug. "You must know a lot of drowners."

A laugh bursts from her throat, but she's not ready to let up. "So he was, what, giving you CPR while your legs were wrapped around his waist?"

Double shit. Instead of admitting a single thing or explaining that Kyle's terrible timing ruined the damn kiss, I raise my shoulders again. "He's the doctor, not me." Before she can question me any further, I turn around. "See you in an hour."

I step out of the rideshare at J.D.'s house as the driver promises to wait for me. Walking most places in town is fairly simple, but not when it comes to where J.D. resides by the lake with his wife, three dogs, and two horses.

A shiver runs up my spine. The last time I paid a visit to J.D.'s personal residence was right after my uncle agreed that I would live with him. Patrick brought me to meet with J.D. in his home, rather than at his office downtown. I didn't think anything of it at the time—Patrick and J.D. were friends, and I was the quiet, troubled teen who had gotten out from under her parents' control and was finally able to make choices for herself.

But now that I look at the quaint one-story house on the lake, I can't help but wonder why it started here.

Shaking off the thought, I focus on the mission at hand. I'm here to find out what the hell happened to my friend and therapist.

The tubing adventure of the day before had sent my thoughts into a memory spiral after I got home. Seeing the campground again and remembering that night in such vivid detail triggered me, ultimately leading me to confess too much to Lincoln. And before work, unable to help myself, I'd tried calling J.D. again, which only resulted in his voicemail.

Now I'm determined to get answers, even if that means taking matters into my own hands. I'm going to find J.D. myself and ask him directly. Selfish or not, I need to know.

At the door, I ball my hand into a fist and raise it to knock, taking a deep breath before I do. It's close to a minute before I hear the latch on the other side of the door, followed by the sound of the knob turning. When the door opens, Gena, J.D.'s wife, appears on the other side of the screen. She doesn't seem surprised to see me, but she also wears a guarded expression that makes me reel back a step.

"Hello, Evelyn." So formal. So cold. Not at all like the woman I knew who often accompanied J.D. into town for dinner and events.

"Hi, Gena. I'm sorry to bother you." My eyes dart to the open staircase and hallway behind her, unsure what I'm expecting to find. J.D., perhaps? "I was hoping to speak to your husband for a moment."

She frowns, clearly displeased. "I'm afraid he's unavailable."

That same confusing answer. "Like, forever? Or just today?"

"Indefinitely, as far as I know."

Shock stings me. I hadn't expected a warm welcome, but I certainly didn't anticipate my visit warranted such a cold response. "It's just… He didn't leave word for me. I guess I just wanted to see him, see if he's okay." My heart beats loudly in my chest.

Her eyes narrow into a glare. "Excuse my bluntness, Ms. Vaughn, but my husband's whereabouts are none of your business." Something flickers in her eyes, and she tilts her head to the side. "I was told you and his other patients were taken care of. Doreen assured me you've all been appointed someone new to oversee your mental health goals."

Still stunned, I manage a nod. "Y-yes, someone has been appointed, and he's nice, but—" I pause before I blurt out that Lincoln Reed cannot become my therapist, not with eyes and lips like his. "I've been in J.D.'s care for twelve years." There. That should get her to understand why I'm so curious and concerned that I came all the way out here to check on him. "The change caught me off guard. It all felt so unexpected."

Her face softens slightly. "I apologize for that, Evelyn, but you really shouldn't be here."

Her eyes shift to something behind me for just a millisecond before they're back on mine, and I turn to see what caught her attention. At first glance, I notice nothing of importance, until I realize a black car with tinted shades is parked at the curb across the street.

A chill shoots up my spine. "Who's that?" I demand.

Gena blinks, appearing startled by my question. "Who's who?"

I make a dramatic show of pointing at the car. "There."

"I have no idea." The discomfort in her voice, her mirthless little laugh at the end, tells me she's lying.

Confusion begins to melt into frustration. Dropping the subject of the car, I focus back on trying to get through to her. "I… I don't understand. Even if J.D. is no longer my therapist, he's still my friend."

Gena flinches—maybe at my boldness? "You should leave." She begins to shut the door.

Not ready to give up, I take one more desperate look around the outside of the house. Not a single light appears to be on, and the shades all seem to be drawn. I can't conclude if any of that is out of the norm for J.D. and Gena, but something feels… off.

"Tell me he's okay," I beg as the door closes.

Gena pauses and stares back at me, one eye hidden behind the door, then she nods slowly. "He's perfectly fine. Now, good day, Ms. Vaughn."

The door closes completely, and I hear the lock click, signifying my opportunity is over.

But I got what I came for. Didn't I? I got confirmation that J.D. is okay, straight from his wife. I may never find out why he chose to leave or why he left the way he did, but at the end of the day, that isn't what matters.

And Gena is right—it's none of my business.

I walk back to my rideshare flooded with disappointment, but I try to force myself to think about what's next with my therapy, wondering if it's something I still want. I just hate that all these memories I thought I'd finally drowned have been triggered again after one tubing adventure down Deep Creek. I've gone years without visualizing the sordid details of that night. Now, I can't seem to stop retracing my steps through those woods. Asleep or awake, they continue to come.

Unfortunately, even if I did want to drown the dark memories like before, I know that's impossible now. Not with Lincoln's seeming obsession with wanting to know every detail about me, including my tragic past. He thinks releasing my suppressed memories will free me from the tethers that hold me to that awful night.

Maybe he's right—maybe that's exactly what I need to do.

I just don't know how.

CHAPTER
TWELVE

EVELYN

After thanking my driver, I hop out onto the Main Street sidewalk and dash back into Firefly. Janessa is still sporting her shades as she stares up at the television, pale as a ghost.

"Just call me your knight in shining armor and get the hell out of here before you get sick in my bar," I tell her, my tone teasing.

She doesn't even acknowledge my presence. Her eyes are still glued to the television, her mouth open. I look up to see what's gripped her attention then have to squint to make sure I'm seeing what I think I'm seeing on the local news.

It's a scene much like the one we were part of nearly fourteen years ago. Swirling red and blue lights reflect off a campground that, at first glance, looks just like Deep Creek. Crime scene tape cordons off the surrounding areas, and a white tent sits propped within the tape's border. I shouldn't be aware of what goes on under that white tent, but I know all too well. When there's a dead body, that's where the collected evidence is taken for review before it's photographed, bagged, and taken to a facility for testing.

It takes me a while to tune into what the reporter is saying, but even then, I only catch bits and pieces.

Another man found deceased in the woods.

No witnesses.

Last seen hiking alone just the day before.

Police are investigating a homicide.

Suddenly, I'm hanging on every word.

"Spectators are already asking if there's a connection to any of the other rumored Firefly Man murders that have taken place in the Great Smoky Mountains, beginning with fifteen-year-old Carley Pruitt," the reporter says. "Pruitt's murder took place at Deep Creek Campground in Bryson City, fourteen years ago. Police will certainly be looking into all similarities of the crimes."

"What campground is that?" I ask, my body shaking. "Why is our local news reporting it?" I have to force the words from my throat.

Janessa frowns. "I don't know." Our eyes stay glued to the screen until we both see it at once.

Backcountry Camp 60, reads the ticker. It takes me a few seconds to place that location on my mental map. Several camps like that are available for wilderness hikers who venture through the Appalachians, and they are often used by backpackers who are making their way past Bryson City.

"That's like five miles from here." I say the words out loud, but Janessa knows the backcountry far better than I do.

"I know," she croaks. "I've camped there."

We look at each other, the panic in Janessa's glazed-over features matching how I feel inside. If it's only five miles from here, that means it's even closer to Deep Creek Campground. And if the news report is true, and this crime is possibly connected to the Firefly Man, that means the killer is closer to Bryson City than he's been in fourteen years.

That's too close.

Why? Why, after all these years, would he come so close to the scene of his first crime?

I don't even hesitate to send Janessa home to shut down the bar. I leave a note on the door, letting our customers know that Firefly management is reserving this time to grieve for another life lost.

Once the bar doors are locked and the shades are drawn, I sit back down and turn up the volume on the television, listening for more updates. Whoever did this must pay. All I can hope is that whatever evidence the police are gathering leads them straight to the piece of shit responsible. I don't think I can handle another unsolved murder in this area.

I'm buzzing from four green tea shots when there's a knock on the Firefly door. At this hour of the afternoon, I'm not surprised. The locals would normally start trickling in by now, and Patrick would never allow his bar to shut down during regular operating hours. Then again, this place hasn't seen a homicide in fourteen years, so I feel justified in calling the shots with this one.

I make my way to the entrance and open the shades, planning to let whoever it is know that the locked door isn't a mistake. But when I see Lincoln staring back at me, a worried frown creasing his forehead, I immediately unlock the door.

The moment I open the door, he rushes in, enveloping me in a hug like he knows it's exactly what I need.

He holds me close. "Are you okay?"

I squeeze my eyes shut, a flood of emotions pouring through me, and I bury my face in his shoulder to keep the tears at bay. I'm not okay, but I'm not sure I can speak quite yet. Instead, I shake my head and cling to him a little tighter while he shuts and locks the door behind us. He even redraws the shade before fully engulfing me in an embrace so real, so powerful, I almost forget why I needed it in the first place.

Finally, I manage to say, "I couldn't keep the bar open after hearing about that man."

He holds me tighter. "I'm so sorry. As soon as I heard the news, I couldn't help thinking about that story you told me about your friend Carley. They even mentioned her on the news."

"I know. I've been watching for updates all day. Well, after I found out. I ran out for an hour to go see J.D., and when I came back, the news must have just broke."

Lincoln looks completely taken aback. "Wait. You what?"

I search his face, trying to understand his reaction. "I went to J.D.'s house." When Lincoln's expression doesn't change, I sigh. "Look, he wasn't just my therapist. He was my friend. Doreen didn't know why he suddenly up and left the business he'd spent his life building, so I paid him a visit. I wanted to make sure he was all right."

Lincoln's eyes dart between mine. "And? Did you talk to him?"

Disappointment engulfs me at the memory. "No. His wife wouldn't give me any information. Just that he's unavailable, whatever that means."

Lincoln's entire demeanor seems to relax a bit. "Then

he must be fine. She would know if something was seriously wrong. Evie, the man is well past the average age of retirement. Maybe he was just ready to say goodbye."

"That's the thing, Lincoln. He didn't say goodbye. He disappeared without a single word, giving us no reason. On top of that, the rumors that are starting to swirl around town are making me crazy. I just need to see him."

Lincoln's shoulders sag. "You don't believe Gena?"

I hesitate for a second before shaking my head. "No, I don't. She's hiding something. I can feel it."

He purses his lips and frowns like he finally understands. "I wish I knew—I would have come sooner. Maybe then I would have avoided getting questioned by your friend Gabe." Lincoln rolls his eyes.

"What do you mean, questioned?"

"Gabe and some other cops stopped by the house earlier. I guess Kyle told him we were at Deep Creek together yesterday." Lincoln looks completely perturbed. "Since that backcountry campsite isn't too far away, they're probably questioning everyone who was in the area."

I frown. "Really? No one has spoken to me."

"They probably stopped by and saw your sign, but they're making their rounds." His expression goes grim again. "Did you know the man who died?"

I shake my head. "They haven't identified him yet, but rumor is that it's someone from out of town, so I don't think I know him." I struggle to frame my thoughts through a tempest of emotions. "They're saying it could be the Firefly Man. But why come back to this area?"

While I know Lincoln doesn't have the same connection to this murder as I do, the look on his face tells me he's haunted just the same. "I don't know, Evie, but I trust they're going to catch whoever this monster is."

Anger bubbles up inside me. "How can you be so sure? Do you know how many murders go unsolved in the Appalachians every year? Eleven are linked to the Firefly Man alone. Maybe twelve now. They were lucky they caught the Balsam Grove killer. That murderer ran free for far too long."

A muscle in Lincoln's jaw ticks, and then his eyes soften on me. "Try to have faith, Evie, for Carley."

The way his voice catches as he speaks my friend's name causes tears to well in my eyes. "I'll have faith when justice is served to this monster. Did Gabe or the other cops give you any details about the crime?"

He seems to think about this for a moment. "Not too many. They mostly asked questions to establish a timeline on me. When was I at the picnic area? When did I go tubing? Who was I with? When did I get home? Who took me home? Did I notice anything suspicious when I passed by the campground? That kind of stuff." His eyes flicker to mine like he has something else on the tip of his tongue.

Something twists in my chest. "What?"

He looks away, like he's nervous, before he says, "I mentioned you were with me, and Gabe's attitude changed in a major way. He immediately went on the attack and started probing me harder, almost interrogating me like I had something to do with that man's death."

Uneasiness settles in my chest. "I'm so sorry. I'm sure his interrogation had nothing to do with the murder at all. He has no reason to question you like that." I chew on my bottom lip. "I told you about Gabe and me. We weren't serious, but he's having a hard time believing that."

Lincoln's palms begin to rub my back in a gentle caress. "I fucking hate that you slept with that guy. He's such a creep."

Despite the circumstances, I have to bite back a smile. "You hate that I slept with Gabe because he's a creep? Or because he's not you?"

That earns me a glare and a tightened hold. "Both."

A fluttering starts in my chest, something I'm beginning to get used to when I'm around Lincoln. "Don't let him bother you. He's just jealous."

Lincoln's gaze darts to my lips then back to my eyes. "Does he have a reason to be?"

My cheeks heat like twin blow torches. "I'd say so."

The small smile that curves Lincoln's lips make my entire chest take flight. He slides one hand from the small of my back to my cheek. There's a seriousness in his gaze that lights up every nerve ending in my body. The effect this man has over me is unreal.

"In that case," Lincoln says, his raspy tone igniting something deep in my core, "let me take you home."

Now it's my turn to smile. Sometimes I forget that he doesn't know every single thing about me. "I'm already home."

Lincoln's head tilts with confusion. "I'm not following."

"I live here." I point up to indicate the second story. "In the apartment behind that bookshelf. I moved out of Patrick's house at twenty-one and came here to help manage the bar. It's been the perfect little home for me over the years."

Intrigue is written all over his face. "Do you have a secret entrance and everything?"

I shrug and smile. "Yup, but don't ask me which book

you have to pull to enter. You'll need top-secret clearance for that."

His eyes narrow. "How does one apply?"

"Well," I tease with a little purse of my lips, "if one meets the strict criteria, I suppose a verbal request would suffice."

He nods, his eyes searching my face. I wonder what he's expecting to find. "I'm afraid to ask if I meet the criteria or not."

Laughing lightly, I raise my chin. "You most definitely meet the criteria." Then my mood dims, just thinking about this shit show of a day. "I just don't think I'm up to reviewing applications tonight."

He squeezes my hand. "That's okay, Evie. I need to get home to Lucy, anyway." He smiles softly. "I really was just going to take you home."

I give him a mock glare, letting him know I'm not sure I believe him.

"You have my number," he says. "You know, in case you need to get ahold of me. To talk… or if you need anything at all."

He releases me, triggering an ache of disappointment. He's right to go, but it doesn't mean I want him to.

"Thank you, Lincoln."

He takes a step back, our eyes still locked together. There's a charge in the air, a connection I've never felt to another human, and I know Lincoln feels it too. His eyes light up, and he moves back to me, his arms wrapping around me in one confident swoop before he pulls me close. His mouth lands softly on my cheek then glides to my ear, leaving goosebumps in its wake. His beard is rough yet intoxicating all the same.

"So you know," he rasps, "refraining from kissing you is the equivalent of holding my breath for too long. For now, I'll starve myself of air, but that won't be the case the next time we're together." He takes my earlobe gently between his teeth. "Consider it a warning."

He steps back, leaving a chasm of space between us. So close, yet so far. The buzz of electricity radiates through the air, the current so strong that I can't deny it. Finally, he makes his way back into the night, and the door shuts between us, clicking once I secure the lock.

Suddenly, I'm starved of air too—trapped like a tiny firefly in a jar, desperate to get to the man who just signaled his interest with a blink of his light. All I need to do is return his call with a flash of my own.

If only it were that easy.

CHAPTER
THIRTEEN
LINCOLN

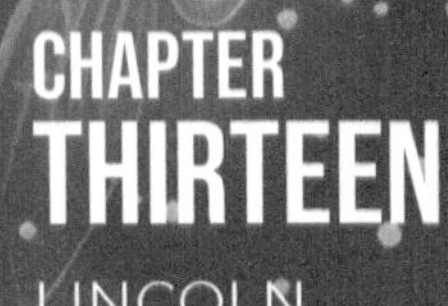

Since the moment I left Evie, I've resisted the urge to check in with her as often as I'd like, in person and over text. Toting the fine line between worrying about her after the latest murder and wanting to see her for purely selfish reasons is a more difficult feat than one would imagine. Save for the breakfast deliveries to her door every morning from a local Main Street business, the casual texts throughout the day, and the happy hour drink I allow myself after work at Firefly before getting home to Lucy and Francine, I try to give her space to process the latest events.

The news is already proclaiming the kill to be the work of the Firefly Man. Which is mind-blowing, considering whoever is responsible has left no clues behind, as far as the public knows.

My eyes skim the morning paper's front-page story.

Body of Firefly Man's suspected twelfth victim

found miles away from original kill site

Published June 21st, 2024

Robert McClain, 31, male, was found late in the evening of May 20th at Backcountry Camp 60. McClain was traveling alone on a backpacking trip through the Appalachians and was reported missing two weeks earlier by his wife after he stopped responding to her calls and messages.

McClain is the suspected twelfth victim in a string of linked serial murders across the Great Smoky Mountains. Due to the nature of his injuries as well as the collected evidence, McClain's murder is suspected to be linked to the infamous Firefly Man. Backcountry Camp 60 is just over three miles from Deep Creek Campground, the site of the first Firefly Man murder.

I close the paper and set it aside, hating that this is the world my daughter is forced to live in.

"Hey, Lucy," I say, pouring her out more cereal. "What do you think about inviting your daycare friends here for your birthday? We can get a bounce house with a slide and make the backyard a fun waterpark."

Lucy's eyes grow wide. "Yesss!" She pounds the handle of her spoon into the table. "Can I invite all my friends?"

Francine gives me a look of utter concern, but I shrug. *What could possibly go wrong with a bunch of kids playing at our house?* "Of course you can, sweetie. I'll fill out the invitations now, and you can hand them out today."

I walk over to the kitchen counter where the pile of invitations sits.

Francine is right there by my side. "Maybe limit the invites, Linc. Ten, tops. There are twenty kids in her daycare class."

"It will be fine," I assure her. "There's no way every kid will make it to the party with such short notice. You'll see."

Francine scoffs. "Do you even know if there's a bounce house available to rent?"

I make a face. "Of course one will be available. I'll take care of all the details. I mean, I don't know of a better plan."

"A better plan is to limit the invites to her closest friends and avoid promising things like bounce houses when you don't even know yet if you can rent one." Francine crosses her arms. "Lucy would be perfectly fine with a few friends and a tea party."

I can't help but laugh. Francine means well, but she doesn't understand what these milestones mean to me. If Lucy wants a giant party with five bounce houses and a tea party in the sky, I'm going to make it happen. "Do you mind making sure Lucy remembers to hand these out today? Better yet, could you hand them directly to parents if you see them at pick-up or drop-off?"

Francine sighs before shaking her head, apparently giving up. "You got it, but I warned you." She points a finger in the direction of the dining table. "I got you a printout of the names of the daycare kids. Maybe just leave out that boy AJ." She leans in and drops her voice to a whisper. "He's a little asshole."

I swipe the invitations off the counter and lean in to plant a kiss on Francine's cheek. "You're the best."

"I know, I know."

Smiling, I sit down beside Lucy with a pen in hand. As I start to fill out the blank lines of the invitation, I peer over at my daughter. "Are you excited to invite your friends to your birthday, Lucy Goosey?"

She nods, eyes wide and shining bright. "Mm-hmm," she says around a mouthful of food. Then she swallows and points at me. "You get one too, Daddy." She grins at Francine. "You, too, Gammy." She takes another bite of her cereal and chews for a bit before her eyes light up again. She can't swallow fast enough before she shouts, "Evie! Can I invite Evie, Daddy?"

I chuckle at her excitement. "Of course you can. Anyone else?"

Lucy scrunches her nose and shakes her head, her blonde hair wildly whipping around, which effectively ends the conversation until another thought pops into my head.

"How about I pick you up from daycare today and take you to Firefly, and you can hand Evie the invitation yourself? Would you like that?"

Lucy claps her hands together and nods eagerly, just like I knew she would, and I give her a wink. She's my precious little girl and I would do anything for her, but she's also my secret wingwoman.

It's four o'clock on the dot when I walk into Firefly with Lucy on my shoulders. I spot Evie immediately at the entrance to her office. Her back is turned and she's wearing another one of her skirts that stretches nicely around her curves, this one navy and paired with a simple white tank top. At closer inspection, she seems to be having a heated conversation with someone inside the room.

Lucy must see her, too, because she's squirming in an attempt to climb off my shoulders. "Evie!" Lucy yells.

Evie's head snaps toward us, her face flushed and weighed down with stress. Her eyes connect with mine first then slide up to Lucy. Suddenly, her entire face changes, illuminating with the most beautiful smile I've ever seen from her. For a moment, she's relaxed, happy, and free. All because of my little girl.

Unfortunately, that peace only lasts a moment.

As I'm helping Lucy off my shoulders and setting her down, another figure appears in the doorway.

Officer fucking Gabe.

My blood boils, and my hands ball into tight fists. Evie takes two steps away from Gabe then turns to face him. I wish I could hear their conversation. If only I knew exactly what he had done to make her lovely light fade into the depths of her own shadows. I could end him.

Lucy runs to Evie, her messy ringlets flying in the wind. She launches herself at Evie, who's ready with open arms. She scoops Lucy up like it's the most natural thing in the world, and I swear my heart leaps like it just bounced off a fucking trampoline in my chest. Despite Gabe's presence looming behind them both like an annoying cloud, I grin when Lucy hands Evie the invitation.

Evie reads the card, her smile growing with every second. Then she looks straight at Lucy, nodding as she says something, and wraps her in a hug. Something about the way Evie's eyes close during the embrace tells me she needed that hug.

For a second, Evie's eyes find mine. No words are needed. She's grateful—for what exactly, I'm not sure, but specifics don't matter when the woman you've come to admire connects with your daughter on a level like this.

When Lucy comes running back to me, she has the sweetest smile on her face. I pick her up, my eyes wide to demonstrate the suspense she's put me under. "Well, what did she say?"

Lucy's face is alight with excitement. "She said yes!" she squeals.

I can't help but laugh. "Of course she did, silly. Who could say no to you?"

The pride on my little girl's face says it all. I look back over to Evie and mouth the words, "Thank you."

Despite our eyes locked in silent exchange, I'm not oblivious to the man in uniform standing beside Evie, a heated scowl radiating on his face. If Lucy weren't here, I wouldn't even hesitate to put my body between them and ask him to leave. It doesn't matter that he's probably here on police business—surely he's asked all his questions by now. It's time for him to go.

Evie must sense my reluctance to leave her there with Gabe because she gives me an encouraging smile and mouths the words, "It's okay," before nodding to the entrance, releasing me from whatever need I might feel to protect her.

With a rush of disappointment that I didn't get to even speak to her, I respect her wishes and carry Lucy back to the sidewalk.

"Evie is pretty, Daddy."

Just like that, my foul mood dissipates, and a smile curves my lips. "She is, isn't she?"

Lucy nods. "You should kiss her."

She says those words so innocently, having no idea that kissing Evelyn Vaughn has been a fantasy of mine since I first laid eyes on the woman.

"Maybe I will, goose."

Light fades to darkness as Lincoln and Lucy walk out of sight. It only makes me despise Gabe more. I whip around to face him, furious at the way he came in here to question me "off the record," as he put it. His questions have all been nothing but a pathetic attempt to be the one who solves the Firefly Man serial murders.

Gabe is a traffic cop—and a bad one, at that. His arrogance constantly gets him into trouble. Lucky for him, there isn't exactly competition in his profession, especially in a small town like this one, so he gets away with it.

"Come back into the office," he demands. At least he has the decency to keep his voice low in front of my customers.

Thank goodness I'm not the only one working tonight. For a weekday, we're surprisingly busy. Janessa is covering the bar while Armando handles the floor, so I've been available for Gabe's interrogation.

"No," I tell him firmly, facing him. "I need to get back

to work, and you shouldn't be talking to me like this. If you have questions for me, I'll come to the station."

"Why do you have to be so damn difficult, Evie? I'm just trying to do my job."

The way this man enrages me. "You already have my timeline, my alibi, my fucking DNA. Investigate me all you want."

Gabe lets out a frustrated sigh. "It's not *you* I'm trying to investigate." He looks around to make sure no one else is listening then glares at me. "You think it's a coincidence that J.D. retires, Lincoln Reed moves to town, and suddenly there's a homicide linked to the Firefly Man near Deep Creek? You know I don't believe in coincidences."

I shake my head. "I don't really care what you believe. I've already told you everything."

Gabe's jaw clenches. "Yet, you won't tell me the details of your relationship with the good doctor."

Rolling my eyes, I try my best to hold onto my composure, but my temper is thinning by the second. "There are no details. He's not my therapist, if that's what you're getting at."

Gabe tilts his head in obvious disbelief. "C'mon, Evie. Do you think I'm not going to talk to Doreen?"

I groan. "I went for a free consultation. That's it."

His accusing stare only gains intensity. "I've seen him at this bar more than the drunk locals."

Matching his stare, I raise my chin. "Maybe he's thirsty."

"His daughter just handed you an invitation to her birthday party."

I nod, a small smile teasing my lips. "And I accepted."

He heaves out a heavy, exasperated exhale. "So, there's nothing suspicious about this guy to you? You don't think the timing is at all weird?"

I grit my teeth and force myself to pause before responding to him. My anger is mounting too fast and too hot. "Not any more suspicious than my ex-boyfriend coming here to interrogate me 'off the record' about a man who has been nothing but kind to me."

Gabe looks like he's just been slapped. He reels, taking a step back, his eyes searching mine like he's suddenly looking at a stranger. "Jesus, Evie. A man was just murdered nearby. That doesn't burn you to the core after what we went through with Carley?"

My body begins to quiver. "What *we* went through? You weren't the one who found her bludgeoned corpse."

"No, but I saw her." He scowls. "After *you* ran off." He blows out an angry breath. "And I saw her guilty-as-sin brother holding her bloodied body. You think that shit didn't fuck me up? Why do you think I became a cop?"

For the first time since Gabe got here, I empathize with him. He's right about how Carley's death affected us all. We're broken by it as much as we are connected. "I'm sorry. I shouldn't have compared your pain to mine. Of course what happened to that man tears me up inside. I haven't stopped thinking about the murder, about Carley." I swallow against the lump in my throat. "But I have nothing else to tell you that can help your investigation. I'm sorry."

"What about where you went that night after you ran off?"

The accusation in his tone causes my breath to hitch sharply into my throat.

"W-what?"

His eyes narrow. "You know what I'm asking, Evie. I read all your interviews and watched your deposition about your side of the story. Something doesn't add up."

I shake my head, eyes squeezing shut. "Stop it, Gabe. I'm not going to do this."

I can practically feel the anger rolling off him in waves. "You conveniently blacked out between the time you left Carley's body until the police arrived," he says. "An entire hour went by before you found someone to call the cops. Why'd it take you so damn long, Evie?"

Panic whips through my body and steals my breath. My hand flies to my chest as I try to calm myself. I can't even begin to think of how to answer that question. "Stop," I try to say, but this time, my word is barely a whisper.

I open my eyes to see his expression beginning to soften.

"I'm not accusing you of anything," he says, his tone gentler than before. "But whatever you can remember will help me find whoever keeps doing this to keep him from doing it again."

The way he uses the word "me" like he wants to be the one to crack this major case. It's not even his case to solve—it's been linked to the Firefly Man, and the FBI took over that case after Carley's murder.

"I. Don't. Remember." I unclench my teeth and inhale deeply.

Finally, Gabe sighs. "Fine." He takes a step away. "Thank you for your time, Evie. If you think of anything, please call the station." His formal demeanor cracks as worry covers his features. "And please be careful with Lincoln." Genuine concern beams from his eyes. "There's something off about the guy, and it has nothing to do with you developing feelings for him even if it does drive me insane. Just… be careful."

He doesn't wait for me to agree. He doesn't look for a reaction. Instead, he bows his head, lets out another sigh, and walks away.

Luckily, I choose that moment to grab my phone in the office, hoping for a quick distraction, because a message from Lincoln lights up my screen.

Lincoln: You made Lucy's whole day.
Thanks for saying yes.

My heart warms, and I can feel my deep frown smoothing into a smile.

Evie: And what would I have done instead?
Break a little girl's heart? I think not.

Lincoln: Nah, Lucy's resilient. She would have been okay. The only heart you would have broken was mine.

Biting back a laugh, I type my response.

Evie: You put her up to that, didn't you?

Lincoln: No way. That was all Lucy. Well, I might have suggested dropping it off tonight, but she thought to invite you.

Evie: Impressive.

Lincoln: Which part?

Evie: All the parts.

He doesn't write back again for a few minutes, so I

make my way out to the bar area to check on things before settling into a cozy chair near the main window.

Lincoln: Looked like we interrupted something when we walked in earlier. Sorry about that.

My frown returns, and the heaviness that weighed down my heart during my altercation with Gabe returns like a slow drip into my veins.

Evie: Gabe was questioning me about my whereabouts the other day.

Lincoln: You okay? I didn't like leaving you there with him.

Evie: I'm okay. Gabe means well. He just gets on these power trips sometimes.

Lincoln: *Sounds like you know him pretty well.*

There's a pang in my chest—I sense Lincoln's jealousy.

Evie: We've known each other since we were kids. He's always been protective over me.

I nibble on my bottom lip, wondering if I should divulge additional details. Maybe then he'll understand why the two of us have a deeper connection than we should, considering we've been broken up for months.

> Evie: Gabe was there the night of Carley's death. Carley's the reason he became a cop. He wants to protect the town from tragedies like that. This recent killing hit him pretty hard.

When no reply comes until well into closing down the bar and locking the doors, I begin to worry that I've made too many excuses for Gabe. That might not sit well with Lincoln, considering the two of them don't get along. Finally, my phone lights up when I'm alone in the empty bar.

> Lincoln: Sorry, had to feed Lucy and then help Francine put together the new dresser she bought. Lucy just went to sleep. I'm sorry if I was being insensitive about Gabe.

I rush to type a reply.

> Evie: You weren't. It's okay.

> Lincoln: Well, now that I feel like a jackass...

> Evie: Please don't feel like that. You're not a jackass. You just didn't know.

A few beats of silence go by before I try again.

> Evie: See you Saturday?

This time, I don't have to wait long for a response.

> Lincoln: How about now?

There's a light rapping at the entrance to Firefly, causing my heart to leap into my throat. I rush to the door and pull down the blinds to see Lincoln standing there, rain coating his dark hair and glistening from his beard. Under the neon lights of the Firefly sign, his eyes appear a brighter tone of green than normal, and they affect my core like he's just undressed me with them.

Pulling open the door, I take a step back, allowing him room to walk through. "Hi." It's all I'm able to say. I'm too shocked. Too curious. Too… happy.

"Hi," he says, giving nothing away in his expression. Instead, he closes the door behind him then focuses back on me. "I hope it's okay that I'm here. Lucy slept in the guest-house with Gammy, and I wanted to see you."

I smile at Lucy's nickname for her grandmother and at his admission. "That's twice in one day, Doctor Reed. I might start getting the wrong idea."

His gaze darkens, and he takes another step, closing the gap between us. "You really need to stop calling me that."

I bite down on the inside of my cheek in an attempt to keep my composure. "What if I like it too much?"

"Then you'll need to ask permission." He wraps an arm around my waist and pulls me closer, nuzzling into my hair. "I think permission could be granted—on one condition."

Heat flames in my cheeks. I can only imagine what this condition might be. "I'm listening."

Lincoln's strong fingers slide through my hair before he grips the back of my neck. "You see," he says softly as his mouth closes in, "there's something I've been desperate for. Something only you can give me."

A thrill runs through me. "Is that so?"

He nods and his lips brush mine. "Mm-hmm."

My eyes flutter closed, ready for the kiss we've both been yearning for. So far, my imagination has set it all up for nothing but failure considering how intensely the possibilities play out in my mind.

"Well," I say, my head buzzing from the electricity between us. "What are you waiting for?"

A smile curls his mouth briefly before his lips press to mine—his warm, firm, commanding lips—eliciting a moan from me. My heart beats firmly at the sensation, a steady acceleration in my chest.

All these weeks, so many electric moments, a handful of whispered teases, a million secret wishes. So much anticipation. It has all been building to this lip-lock that trumps every single dream of what kissing him could have, should have, would have felt like.

Holy fuck, only our lips are touching, but my entire body is quivering, aching, desperate for more. He feels it too. I can tell in the way he presses against me, his arm tightening around my waist and securing me to him.

My back arches and my arms slip around his neck so I can hold on for dear life. It's the only way to survive this kiss, which is everything I hoped it would be and so much more. As if by magic, the song "Lovely" by my favorite band, Fly By Midnight, begins playing through the bar's sound system—a perfect soundtrack for a perfect moment.

He pulls my bottom lip between his, his teeth scraping me gently as I moan into his mouth. Then he kisses me again, righting me so that I'm standing straight as his palms smooth against my back. I'm completely drawn in, my senses on fire with overstimulation. This is the only heaven I want to know.

"Damn," he murmurs against my lips. "Permission granted, I suppose."

I feel a slow smile spread across my face as I pull back to look at him with an evil glimmer of my own. "Good. Because I think that kiss was just what the doctor prescribed."

His mock glower sends shivers up my spine before he leans back into me, his mouth so close. "Damn straight he did." His lips curl before they meet mine again. "With infinite refills."

My nerves buzz and crackle to life the moment I step onto the gravel driveway of the home where I once lived with Uncle Patrick. I can't believe I'm about to walk into a four-year-old's birthday party. Only Lucy Reed could pull me so far outside my comfort zone like this—the adorable spitfire of a little girl who clearly takes after her father. In fact, if Lincoln hadn't mentioned inviting me was her idea, I would have assumed he put his daughter up to the whole thing.

I pause for a moment halfway up the drive as a rush of memories hit me, thanks to the log-home architecture that's not changed since I lived there. It makes me happy knowing a little girl is making happy memories here, just as I once did.

The relief and elation that consume me the moment I stepped foot on the property are unmatched. Patrick's place has always been my home away from home—a place where I was given the freedom to just be a kid, play with friends, go on adventures, and get dirty without being reprimanded.

My true home, as I always thought of it. My mom hated when I would say that out loud. Everything started an argument with her, but that kind of comment would get me the tongue-lashing of a lifetime.

"You ungrateful brat." She would practically spit the words in my face. "After everything your father has done to continue the Vaughn legacy here in Raleigh, you'd rather live in that *swamp?*"

No matter how visceral her attacks would get, I found myself incapable of backing down. If I inherited any characteristics from my mother, they had to be my stubborn nature, my fierce stance in whatever I believed in, and my bravery to stand against anyone who dared oppose me. Between my mother and me, neither of us ever won a match, and in the end, we both walked away losers. She lost a daughter, and I got completely cut off from my parents. Still, I would choose this life any day of the week over the one they tried to groom me into.

Taking another few steps up Lincoln's drive, I begin to hear more from my surroundings, almost like layers of an audio track. Music streams from somewhere nearby, bouncing off the trees in nature's surround sound. Shrieks of laughter, happy chatter, and joyful screams ebb and flow in waves. There's a splash of water, and I smile—Lincoln must have decided on a waterpark theme. The scent of something on the grill adds to the entire vibe of the day.

I skip the front entrance and walk around the house, following the stone walkway I helped Uncle Patrick create when I was eight years old. Why he decided to leave such a project for the hottest day of that summer is still beyond me, but it's a small piece of history I'm proud to be part of.

My stomach rumbles at the strong scent of cooking

meat, reminding me just how late I am. Kyle had a car appointment that ran an hour into his shift, so I covered for him until he could get back to the bar. If there's anything more uncomfortable than going to a party, it's arriving late and having all eyes shift to you. Which is exactly what happens when I round the corner to the backyard.

I'm not sure what I expected, but it certainly wasn't such a large gathering for a four-year-old's birthday. There must be twenty kids, all accompanied by parents. The yard is packed with a long pink Slip 'N Slide, a splash pad, a rectangular inflatable pool, and a bounce house with a water slide.

Smoke plumes from the open grill where Lincoln is already serving hamburgers and hot dogs.

Francine is the first to greet me, her giant eye-roll saying it all. She is completely and utterly annoyed. "I warned him," she complains. "He insisted on letting Lucy invite whomever she wanted. Look at this circus. It's insane."

I turn to take in the entire scene again. A smile tugs at my face. "It's incredible."

Francine scoffs while folding her arms across her chest and surveying the party with me. "My daughter would throw ragers that stressed me out less than this."

Her sarcasm makes me laugh.

"He spoils Lucy rotten," Francine adds then sighs. "But she is one happy girl."

My smile widens when I finally spot Lucy stomping around the splash pad with her friends, a look of pure glee on her face. "Sorry I couldn't get here on time," I say. "I had to cover for someone at the bar." I scan the crowd, trying to ignore the stares of disapproval aimed in my direction from bikini-clad moms who clearly have no idea why I would be at this party. I'm not sure I can blame them.

Francine takes my wrapped present for Lucy from my hands. "Well, you're here now. Feel free to get to work." She winks. "Or just enjoy yourself. There are adult drinks in the red cooler, hot food on the grill, and snacks everywhere. Help yourself." She adds my present to the picnic table with all the others.

I take a hesitant step forward, not knowing where to go first. I'm so obviously out of place. Lincoln is at the grill, focused on flipping a section of burgers while Lilith Thornefield, now a widowed single mom, talks animatedly by his side. The entire town knows how unfaithful she was to her husband before he died—she barely grieved before she was onto her next lover.

Now it seems Lincoln is her new target.

Jealousy stings me like a pesky bee—fast and sharp, the venom soaking into my veins. It's one thing to have a crush on a man like Lincoln Reed, a sexy doctor with the body of a Greek god. It's another to enter a space among a dozen other women, married or single, who all want to fuck him. And let's be honest—these women here have something in common with Lincoln that I don't. They are all parents.

I'm almost surprised when Lincoln finally looks up from the grill and spots me. His eyes widen, and he says something to Lilith before handing her the spatula and walking away. Her confused expression becomes layered with anger as she watches him head toward me.

I turn my eyes away from her and focus on Lincoln just in time.

He smiles at me. "You made it."

I lift my hands and drop them by my sides, his proximity a welcome relief. "I did." I make a sweeping look around. "Looks like a success so far."

He runs a hand through his hair, not looking convinced. "You think? There are so many people here—it's hard to make sure everyone is doing okay."

"Trust me," I tell him with a smile, "as someone who runs a bar, it's not your job to make sure everyone is okay. You provided a free waterpark, for goodness' sake. I see a bounce house and food. I also hear there's booze. You did good."

My hand finds his arm, my intention an innocent one meant to comfort, but it turns into something completely different when my fingers span his bicep and feel just how solid and thick it is. I drop my hand, my cheeks burning.

His amused eyes search mine. "Thank you. Lucy will be very happy to know you made it."

"I'm sure she won't even notice me with all her friends here. Or my present."

His eyes twinkle. "Just your presence is present enough."

A laugh bursts free as I grin at him. "You're so cheesy."

He shrugs. "I'm a dad. Dad jokes are supposed to be cheesy."

Biting down on my lip, I assess him once more, his beautiful green eyes illuminated by the sun and completely mesmerizing. "You have a good point."

He leans in closer, placing a hand on the curve of my waist while his beard tickles my cheek. "I'm happy you're here. That's all that matters, right?"

My heart leaps into my throat. Pinching a piece of his shirt fabric between my knuckles in a gesture to keep him close, I slowly shake my head. His beard scratches against my skin, and my pussy quivers with need. *Fuck me.*

"Lucy handed me the invitation. Not you," I tease.

Lincoln presses his lips to my ear. "Only because Officer Gabe was standing right there. I'm a patient man, Evie, but you should know I have very little restraint when I'm near you. It's only a matter of time."

"Is that another warning?"

He leans back, squeezing my waist before dropping his hand completely. "I'd say it's more like a promise."

After Lincoln and I part ways, it doesn't take long for Lucy to spot me. She darts over and wraps her arms around my legs, soaking the bottom of my swim cover-up with cold water. I laugh. Her excitement is infectious, her joy breathtaking. I lean down to give her a proper hug, happy the invitation warned of water activities.

"Thank you for inviting me to your party, Lucy. Are you having the best time?"

She nods eagerly before staring back at me with curious eyes. "Did you bring your swimsuit?"

"I did."

Popping onto her toes, she grabs my hand. "Let's go play!"

And so it begins, the four-year-old birthday party that I've now joined in every way, from tossing myself down the Slip 'N Slide to stomping around the splash pad to jumping in the bounce house. Unlike most of the other women at the party, I keep my cover-up on. No one else seems to mind, and the kids don't seem to care, but it feels slightly more appropriate than strutting around in a yellow bikini, the only bathing suit I own.

Even Lincoln takes his shirt off at some point to join in the fun, which slightly unsettles me for purely jealous reasons. There isn't a single shy eye in the yard as the women ogle his ripped body. He seems oblivious to the attention, his focus on Lucy with the occasional glance in my direction. He seems to always know where I am, our eyes connecting and holding for just long enough to awaken new flutters in my chest.

As the last hour of the party rolls around, the cake is served and Lucy dives into opening her presents, while Lincoln makes it a point to stick by my side. And when the first person makes a move to leave, I take it as my cue to go, too, but Lincoln looks me dead in the eye and mouths, "Stay."

It's a command, one I'm more than happy to oblige. I start helping Francine clean up, gathering empty cups, plates, plasticware, and wrapping paper from the backyard. Soon Lincoln and Lucy come out back to join us, but instead of cleaning, Lucy takes off for the kiddie pool, so Lincoln follows close behind.

I smile, watching them out of the corner of one eye while picking up random trash left in the yard. Francine piles a tray full of the leftovers, condiments, and unused plasticware, and takes it into the back door that leads to the kitchen.

"I'll get the rest of it," Lincoln calls out to me, waving a hand. "Grab a drink and join us." He grins, squinting from the sun.

As soon as I reach the cooler, Francine is beside me. I fish out three ice-cold seltzers and hand one to her, then we both head over to where Lucy and Lincoln are playing. We grab folding chairs and set them in front of the pool, sitting down and sticking our feet in.

Lucy squeals as Lincoln picks her up, flips her in the air, and plops her back into the water. Then he raises his arms, flexing them like he won some kind of championship, egging Lucy on. She hooks her entire body around his leg like a little monkey, trying to climb up, but he grabs her again, flips her, and flops her back down.

Giggles take over Lucy's whole body. She falls into the water, unable to control herself as she laughs at her daddy's antics.

Suddenly I realize I've never been more attracted to a man than I am to Lincoln when he's in full dad mode. It's the sexiest thing I've ever witnessed, which completely shocks me.

"Well." Francine sighs heavily. "You were right, Lincoln. That was a great party. Lucy got to invite all her friends, and everyone had fun. Great job."

He grins at her like there's some in-joke there. "Thank you, Francine. And thank you for all the help today." His focus shifts to me. "You, too, Evie. The kids had a blast with you."

Warmth spreads through me. "I had a good time too."

Francine pats my hand. "If you're hungry, there's plenty of food left over in the fridge."

I laugh and pat my tummy. "I already ate two burgers and a hot dog. Oh, and cake. I think I'm good until tomorrow." I grin up at Lincoln. "Didn't realize you were such a master of the grill."

"Then you don't come around enough," he teases. "Next time, I'll show you what I can really do."

I grin. "Okay. That's a deal."

As successfully as I've kept myself from taking in a good eyeful of Lincoln all day, I'm unable to stop myself now. His forest-green swim shorts nearly match the color of his eyes, and they are short enough to reveal the defined muscles in his thighs. The light covering of hair on his chest does nothing to hide his phenomenal build, from firm pecs to cut abs. I get lost in the shape of him, memorizing every inch. That is, until my gaze rises to his to witness him watching me right back.

Busted. The space between my thighs heats, and my nipples harden. I swear, the man doesn't even have to touch me for my body to come alive. "I should go," I blurt out, suddenly feeling an overwhelming need to get away from the one man I can't seem to control myself around.

"Stay," Lincoln pleads, disappointment and hope mixing in his expression.

"Yeah, Evie, stay!" Lucy leaps out of the pool, grabs my hand, and tugs.

Laughing, I let her lead me into the bounce house again. The hose to the slide has been turned off, so the inside of the inflatable is completely dry now. Maybe the cake has given Lucy a monster sugar rush, because Lucy goes a little crazy, jumping like she hasn't been active the entire day. At some point, Lincoln climbs in to join us.

Just when I'm starting to feel exhausted from the continuous bouncing, Francine pops her head in and holds her arms out for Lucy. "What do you say, birthday girl? Want to spend the night with Gammy?"

Lucy's eyes light up like Christmas morning. "Yes, yes!" We all laugh as she jumps up and down. "Can we watch a movie, too?"

Francine nods. "Yup, we can watch a movie, eat junk food." She grins at Lincoln. "I'll even let you get all showered and dressed in warm clothes first."

Lucy whoops with excitement, completely missing the psychological game her grandmother just played. "Bye,

Daddy! Bye, Evie!" She starts to flop around to get to the entrance, but Lincoln scoops her up and cradles her like a baby.

"Not so fast, my little birthday goose." He tickles her side, causing her to erupt in a deep belly laugh. "I'm going to need a better goodbye than that."

With that, he flips her back upright and earns a giant hug. Then he whispers something into her ear that I can't hear, but I assume it's something absolutely precious, since a look of warmth and love completely takes over her face. I can practically feel their deep connection tugging at my own heart like an invisible string.

Francine winks at us both when she finally takes Lucy in her arms, then they walk off toward the guesthouse together. Lincoln and I are silent as they head into the cottage, the silence so deafening, I'm sure he can hear the thrumming of my heart.

A faint click of a door sounds, and all at once, our eyes lock. The air seems to ignite, sizzling with electricity—and suddenly it becomes crystal clear that I'm in a whole lot of trouble.

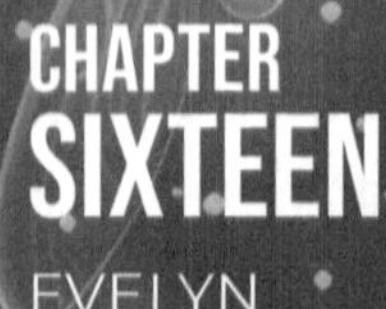

CHAPTER
SIXTEEN

EVELYN

Unable to handle the chaos of nerves zigzagging through me, I lie back and focus on the open sky above. The sun is preparing to set in the west, so all I see is a landscape of blue with a single white puffy cloud on a slow path to nowhere. It's shaped like a horse. Or maybe a puppy. No, definitely a unicorn.

Lincoln reclines beside me, our hands by our sides with our pinkies touching.

"You're a really good dad, Lincoln." The words come out before I even think about them first, but I don't have time to second-guess them. They're genuine—I've been thinking it all day long.

He turns his head, meeting my gaze. "I don't think you know how much it means to hear that."

"Well, it's true. Lucy is very lucky to have you."

The softness in his gaze tugs at my heart. Those beautiful eyes even appear to tear up slightly, but he looks away before I can confirm it.

"You were really great today," Lincoln says after a

moment. "Thanks for helping so much. I promise, that's not why you were invited."

I smile at his profile. "No problem at all. Helping was the least I could do, since you were so busy with your fan club."

He grins and turns his head back to me. "Good to know you were paying attention. You thinking about joining?"

I feel a deep blush spread through every pore of my body. "I'm not sure I meet the requirements." I hold up my fingers to count the ways. "I'm not married or rich and I don't have kids…" When I realize that's all there is, I shrug and twist my lips in mock disappointment. "Maybe Officer Gabe has a fan club I can look into."

Lincoln turns his body, propping his elbow near my head, then slips his fingers through mine while narrowing his gaze. "I think fucking not."

Amused, I regard him with wide eyes. His profanity should not turn me on even more, but it does. "Oh yeah?"

"Yeah." He looks so serious. The fire behind his eyes blazes bold and bright with zero fear. Zero hesitation.

How does he do it? How does he maintain such confidence when I'm such a mess of doubt?

"Do you want all that stuff?" he asks. "Marriage? Kids?" His nonchalant tone doesn't mask the depth of the question.

However, I have nothing to hide when it comes to this subject. "I haven't spent too much time thinking about it. I might be the only woman you know who hasn't created a Pinterest board for her future wedding." I smile. "That's not to say I wouldn't want to get married if I met the right person."

I can feel his eyes studying me as I watch the unicorn

cloud transform into something else. "If I marry, it will be for the right reasons—love as opposed to money, trust as opposed to fear, commitment as opposed to obligation." I don't dare to turn my head and meet his gaze. "Then maybe I can think about bringing a child into this world."

Lincoln's pinky hooks into mine. "Sounds like the responsible thing to do."

My chest tightens. "Families are all built differently, and sometimes the unexpected is the blessing we never knew we needed. I know all that. Lucy is the perfect example—what's meant to be, will be." I inhale deeply, considering my words. "I just really want to be a good mom, you know? My mom didn't exactly provide the best example."

His fingers slowly weave through mine. "You don't need an example, Evie. I watched you with those kids today. You're a natural."

It's a sweet compliment. "This is just one day." I finally turn to face him, smiling. "You can't tell me every day of parenting is like a walk in the waterpark."

He gives me a genuine smile. "Definitely not, but you're compassionate and caring, beautiful and driven. Just the fact that you care about bringing a child into this world the right way tells me everything I need to know. Just because your parents were shit doesn't mean you will be. You had your uncle. Plenty of kids out there aren't fortunate enough to have a Patrick they can run to."

"I know I'm lucky." I nod. "What about you? Would you ever want to have another child? Or marriage?"

He looks away, seeming to give the question some thought. "Would I? Yes. Lucy would have to give her stamp of approval, of course."

"Of course." I grin at his profile, loving his love for his daughter.

"And I suppose my wife would have to put up with my very demanding work schedule."

Realizing he's being sarcastic, I chuckle. "You mean your nine-to-five job that crosses into after-hours when you visit a certain bar manager?"

He turns to me, narrowing his eyes in consideration. "Good point. She'd also have to put up with my raging crush on a certain bar manager." He lowers his head, inching ever-so-slowly toward me, barely allowing his beard to tickle my lips.

My heart beats so fast that I can barely think straight. All I can focus on is how sexy Lincoln truly is, especially right now with his darkened gaze, his shirtless and perfectly sculpted body, and his powerful hands that slide around my waist in a secure grip.

"I've missed these lips," he murmurs before closing the gap.

As soon as his mouth lands on mine, all the air whooshes out of my body. Simultaneously, a groan rises from his chest, one so quiet that I might have imagined it, but when twin moans slip past our lips and into our mouths, I know it was real. We're in lockstep, vulnerable together and wholeheartedly savoring each other course by course. I can't wait to devour the whole damn meal.

"You have no idea how unbelievably sexy you are," he rasps between kisses. "I couldn't take my eyes off you today."

Desire burns through me as he wraps a leg around one of mine, pulling me closer until his hard length pushes against my center. *Fuck me.* At least, I hope he does. I can only imagine how we would fit together—his cock buried so deep inside of me that I would never be able to let him go. This is a man who knows how to fuck, I bet my life on it.

I'm blind with need as our kiss deepens, our tongues sliding in circles around each other's, and groans vibrate our bodies. At some point, I yank my mouth away, desperate for air. Throwing my head back, I suck in a deep breath, only to feel his mouth between my neck and shoulder, my sensitive skin buzzing to life.

Is this man for real? Single. A doctor. A damn good dad. A delectable kisser. And surely there's more, if that's even possible. I'm fucking ruined.

Lincoln's tongue darts out, swiping against my neck as he slips off the straps of my cover-up one at a time, never leaving my skin as it slides around my collar. Then he kisses a trail down my sternum, tugging the fabric of my dress as he goes, until his mouth is nestled between my heaving breasts.

"Your skin is so soft," he murmurs, his attention settling on my breasts. "So sweet."

His beard is rough on my skin, but the friction of it only adds to the pleasure building in my core. He manages to slip my cover-up completely off my body, so I'm left in nothing but my yellow bikini.

I nearly choke as he reaches for one of the triangles of my top then runs a long finger up and down the edge of the material as my nipples rise to attention. His mouth dips down so he's hovering there for a brief second before closing around me. He sucks the nipple into his mouth hard, soaking the material.

Pleasure shoots through me in a gasp, then he roughly yanks the triangle of fabric of my top to the side, takes one lingering look at my bare breast, then goes back to my nipple like a man on a mission.

A cry shoots up my throat at the intensity of his sucking. Just when I begin to feel a pinch of pain, he licks me there, soothing the ache before repeating the cycle over and over, then he moves to my other breast.

My bare breasts are completely exposed now as he feasts on me, an appetizer I swear he might not ever finish —until he moves back up to my mouth, lips latching to mine as his fingers slide down to my bikini bottoms.

"I've never wanted a man's fingers inside me so badly," I gasp.

He chuckles and slides his finger along the hem like he did my top. "Oh, Evie. When my fingers start fucking you, you'll never want another man to touch you ever again." He buries his mouth in my neck, baring his teeth and nipping my skin, causing me to jerk against his palm. He growls. "And I might just kill any man for trying."

As badly as I want him to rip off my bikini bottoms completely, I relent to his pace. I've already told him what I want, and there's no doubt he's going to give me what I want, but he's clearly a man who likes to tease and torture.

Lincoln slips a finger beneath the fabric, cursing under his breath when he reaches my center. He doesn't waste a second gliding over my slit, up and down, in achingly slow fashion. "So wet already," he groans, his fingers moving to my clit. "I bet you taste like absolute sin."

It takes everything in my power to not grab his hand and use it as my own personal sex toy. If he doesn't plunge those thick fingers inside me soon, I might just have to.

"Taste me and find out." I say it as a dare, like I'm brave enough to suffer the consequences. Like he wouldn't take me to a whole new level. Lincoln Reed won't just taste me. He'll eat my soul and spit out the pieces.

His mouth moves up to my ear, his breath hot. "Is that what you want, Evie? You want me to taste your sweet pussy?"

My whole body shudders at his dirty words and at the feel of his fingers tugging at the strings of my bottoms until they fall away, exposing me completely. "Y-yes," I manage.

He chuckles again then pushes himself onto his stomach until he's hovering over my center. His hands splay against my skin on the inside of my thighs, and he pushes them apart, spreading me wide and gazing down at me like I'm some kind of prize.

Then Lincoln looks up at me, his expression surprisingly serious. "Remember that day in my office when you told me you've never been able to have sex that involves an emotional connection?"

I nod, shivering at the memory and wondering why he would bring that up now.

"I'm not just going to make you come, Evie. I'm going to make you forget every other orgasm you've ever had."

Somehow, I don't doubt him.

"But I need to make sure this is more to you than just another casual experience." His eyes stare into mine. "Tell me you feel this connection between us. Tell me this is something more."

The desperation in his eyes, in his tone. I want to shout the answer he yearns to hear to the skies. I want to tell him I've never felt this intensity with anyone else. This isn't casual. I know that. He knows that. But I'm frozen, mute.

"Tell me, Evie," he repeats. "I need to hear you say it."

My heart is pounding, making words impossible.

He growls at my non-response before he dives down and laps at my center, his tongue so wet and warm. I groan as he wraps his lips around my aching clit then sucks my sensitive nub into his mouth while his fingers dart deep inside me, in and out until my body quivers at my pending release.

"You're good at that," I gasp out, aching for release, building to a height I've never reached before.

He rips his mouth away and glares up at me, a warning that this won't end well for me unless I do as he says. "You have no idea what I'm capable of doing to you." He breathes heavily against my clit as his fingers continue moving in and out of me. "Tell me this is casual, and I'll still let you come, but tell me this is more and you'll be handsomely rewarded." He curls his finger deep inside me. "I won't just fuck you with my tongue and fingers, Evie. I'll put you on my lap and bounce you on my cock until the moon and stars are all you see."

My insides coil as my orgasm threatens to unleash.

"Last chance," he warns.

When he latches his mouth back onto me, he pushes me closer to the brink. A little further and he won't be able to stop the orgasm aching to burst free.

Everything is different with Lincoln than with anyone else. He touches me, and I melt into him, wax to his flame. He talks dirty to me, and the vibrato of his baritone resonates deep inside me. He comes near me, and I'm engulfed by his cool evergreen scent. He goes down on me, and I feel worshiped by a man who knows how to pleasure a woman.

But I can't bring myself to say the words.

I'm almost gone, lost to the heavens in this journey he's

controlling, when he begs me again, but I hold back my reply. *Why am I so damn stubborn?*

Just when I think he might pull away completely and starve me from the release threatening to unravel at rip-roaring speed, he pushes a second finger inside, plummeting me over the edge.

My toes curl and my back arches, breath squeezing from my lungs as I ride out the endless waves that roll through my body. When my body calms, he slips his fingers from me then falls back on the floor of the bounce house.

I turn to face him, my eyes slipping to his tented shorts. Guilt eats away at me, and I want nothing more than to repay the favor. Sliding my hand down his chest and abs, I grip his hard length through his shorts. My mouth salivates at his size, and I begin to stroke him.

A strong hand lands on mine, stopping me midmotion. "I can't just be someone casual to you, Evie." He shakes his head. "I want more than that from this." He turns away, a single line denting his perfect forehead.

"I'm sorry," I whisper shakily as disappointment racks my body, pulling my hand away and lying back on the bounce-house floor.

Just when I feel like I've ruined what might be the most important relationship I've formed since I was a child, Lincoln's warm hand envelops mine. Then he says two words that rupture my already-bleeding heart.

"I'll wait."

Five days. That's how long it's been since I worshiped Evie and nearly deprived her of an orgasm. I'm not usually an arrogant man, but I saw the way she came alive at my touch, I felt the way she kissed me back, and I tasted her sweet juices as she opened up for me in that bounce house. No one could question the intensity of her reactions. I was so confident, in fact, that I was sure she would say the words I desperately needed to hear.

She didn't.

She isn't ready.

But like I told her that night, I'll wait.

It feels like I've already waited my entire life for her. For someone who gets me on a deeper level and who inspires me as much as she steals my focus. Such a contradiction, I know, but I wouldn't trade this feeling for the world.

There's something about her I just can't pull away from—beyond her intoxicating scent and transcendent eyes. She's gripped my soul and sank her teeth in, branding me hers for the rest of my days. Some might call it an unhealthy obsession—I just call it fate.

I'm not sure when or how to make my next move, knowing that things with her could have gone so much further that night. Both of us wanted it, and for once, we were completely alone with nothing but the stars staring down at us. But Evie isn't some woman I want to get my fill of and leave. She's someone I want to keep, as wrong as I know that is.

Wanting her is bad enough, but there's guilt there too. Guilt that I haven't been fully honest with her, that my move here wasn't entirely tied to J.D. leaving his practice. As much as I want to share everything with her, I can't— my hands are tied. And as much as I want to justify my lies, they're eating me away inside.

I push my laptop away, remove my glasses, and rub my eyes. Lucy fell asleep in the guesthouse with Francine, so I drove into town to the office with the intention to focus. So it's just me, lost in my thoughts, failing at the task at hand.

Firefly Effect

The title stares back at me like it's alive, taunting me. In a way, it is. I've been stuck for years, not for lack of inspiration—for some reason, the words just aren't flowing the way I thought they would.

What started out as a dissertation for my PsyD program at Duke in which I investigated and explored the Firefly Man serial murders became so much more after graduation. I blame the vast amount of research I conducted and all the rabbit holes I wandered down in the process of trying to stay on topic. With inspiration from author Dr.

Rohls, who became my mentor, I set out to create a short story that wove together the psyche of someone who could commit such heinous crimes, using fireflies to symbolize human life.

I skip to where I'm getting into the meat of my story, based on the philosophical take on truth and time and the idea that fireflies never truly die. It's a choice to live life as a guiding light for others or to stay masked in darkness. It's all one elaborate metaphor for how we can wield our knowledge as power for good or bad. The choice is up to us.

To dim our light is to close ourselves off to growth and opportunities, to choose ignorance.

Ugh. I close my laptop. It all feels wrong. Unfinished.

Moving to Bryson City, the location of the first Firefly Man murder, was supposed to inspire me so I could finally finish the allegory I began writing in college. Now it all just feels more complicated. Maybe I'm missing too many pieces of the puzzle.

I'm almost relieved when my phone lights up. I look down and see Evie's name flash across the screen. In record time, I've read the text.

> Evie: I'm outside your office. I saw your car.

I practically lunge out of my chair and run to jerk open the front door. Staring back at me is a fresh-faced Evie, glasses on over her beautiful blue eyes, wearing a black skirt and one of her favorite graphic shirts, this one burgundy. Her hair is wrapped up in a bun. *Damn.* She's gorgeous.

"Is everything okay?" I take her hand and pull her inside before closing the door and locking it behind us.

She stands in the waiting room, looking anywhere but at

me. "Everything is fine. I just…" She looks around as if to make sure she's not interrupting anything. "Is it okay that I'm here? I know you were upset with me last week, but—"

"Evie." I take her hand. "I'm not upset with you."

She locks eyes with me. "Okay." Her shoulders appear to relax a little. "I needed to talk to you. About something from that night Carley died."

An instant thunderstorm brews in my chest as I lead her into my office. I sit beside her on the leather couch, never letting go of her hand, and watch her for a moment, not wanting to break up whatever conversation she's having in her mind.

"It's been bothering me ever since Gabe brought it up, and I remembered what you said about repressed memories and how dangerous they can be."

I squeeze her hand, letting her know she can slow down, that I'm here and she's safe.

She takes a shaky breath and releases it before continuing. "Gabe started asking me about that night. About what happened after I left Carley and Foster to go get help. The detectives somehow figured out that an entire hour passed between me leaving the scene of the crime to when I found Patrick."

I widen my eyes slightly, but I'm not surprised at all. I've read those files. I've seen those interviews. In all the research I've done, that's a major piece of the puzzle that somehow got lost. Maybe I can help her locate it.

"I don't know why it took me so long." She stares off at nothing, shaking her head like she's desperate to remember something, anything, to help fill in the gap. "I don't think I would have gotten lost on my way to the campground. Unless I was just so devastated that I couldn't find my way."

I squeeze her hand again. "That's possible."

"Yeah, but unlikely." She frowns. "I just… I don't understand why I would have suppressed that part of the night, yet I can remember what Carley's body looked like in Foster's arms. And I don't know why I care now, other than the guilt I feel." She looks at me, tears gathering in her eyes. "What if whatever I'm forgetting is something that might help catch this psychopath? I could have stopped the killer a long time ago."

"Hey," I murmur. "None of this is your fault." A spark of anger rises from deep down in my gut. Evie taking on guilt about killings she bears no responsibility for makes me want to destroy this monster. "If you want to remember, I can help you—but don't force the memories. There's a reason your mind wants you to forget. It's protecting you from something."

She turns to me, eyes brimming with tears. "Or someone."

A chill prickles my skin. It's not that I haven't considered that the murderer could be someone Evie knows, but I hate that she's come to that conclusion too. "Anything is possible, I suppose." Frustration swirls alongside the anger. "What exactly did Gabe say to you?"

She frowns. "Just that I might be able to help them track down the killer once and for all. He wants to be the one who cracks this thing wide open."

Annoyance swirls into the mix. Of course, Officer Gabe is looking for a promotion, so he's willing to traumatize Evie to do it. "Interesting" is all I can mutter.

She faces me again, her gaze imploring. "You really think you can help me?"

Her pain is my pain, and my heart aches for what she's going through. I nod, my eyes searching hers. "I do."

Evie's entire body starts to quiver, so in a move I would never make with a patient, let alone any other human, on this same couch, I wrap my arm around her waist and gently tug her toward me. "C'mere."

She gives me such a helpless, desperate glance then moves toward me. She lets me guide her up onto my lap, her skirt bunching up with her legs on either side of mine. I fold her in my embrace, pulling her close until I feel her tension start to melt.

Relief seems to cascade over her entire body. I can see it in the way her shoulders loosen. I can feel it in the way her body relaxes on mine. I fucking love that I can do that for her.

"I've got you," I say, the words filled with emotion.

She sighs into my neck, her body shifting on my lap enough to catch the attention of a certain appendage. "I've missed you," she whispers.

My palms slide beneath her top and up the length of her slim back then down again. "I've missed you too." I just want to touch her, to show her how much I care. I want to give her anything and everything she needs, now and forever.

Her head lifts just enough to bring her mouth to mine. She kisses me first, her lips soft and plush and needy, and I groan as she moves against me again, awakening me until I'm at full attention and pressing into her core.

In a moment of weakness, I tear my lips away so I can look down at the inch of skin between her rumpled black skirt and burgundy top. I grip her thighs and pull her closer, managing to pull her skirt up around her waist. She's wearing pretty pink panties with yellow trim, the fabric so thin that I can see the shadow of her pussy. *So fucking hot.*

There's no professionalism. No control. There's just Evie and me in a whirlpool of desire versus self-control. One of those two things has to give—but even if she wants to give into desire with me, I still need to hear her say it.

I run my finger up and down her center, rubbing the cloth at her entrance and letting the damp fabric tease me with her arousal. A growl roars inside my chest, but I tamp it down to make my needs transparent. Evie needs to want this as much as I do, in the same way that I do. There's nothing casual about my feelings for Evelyn Vaughn.

She grinds against me, making my finger press deeper into her slit and gliding along the line in one slow sweep.

I look up just as she does, our gazes colliding. My finger lands on her swollen clit, and I leave it there, drawing slow circles while my other hand grips her neck and pulls her in.

Our mouths crash together with a force so powerful, it's instantly addicting. I want more. My tongue plunges into the depths of her mouth, tangling with hers before the hand slipping and sliding against her pussy moves around to grip her ass. I rock her into me, moving her just enough that my cock creates the right amount of friction.

She moans, and I know it's because she can feel me there, hard as a rock with wanting her. I move her ass, rocking her into me while I suck on her tongue then her bottom lip. I don't even need to move her anymore. She's taking control, grinding down like she's fucking me. The friction will be enough to get her off, but that's not what I want. Not before she tells me this is more than a casual thing.

"Tell me," I whisper between kisses. "Please, Evie." I

push up into her core, imagining every stitch of fabric melting away so I can plunge inside her. "Let me fuck you. Let me make you feel good. Just say it. You know what I want to hear."

Evie sighs, her hips still rubbing her pussy against me. "You know I want you, Lincoln."

Just those words drive me crazy enough to yank up her shirt, tug down her bra, and sweep my tongue around her nipple. "Want me?" I growl. "How?"

Her eyes roll and her teeth sink into her bottom lip. Her pleasure is mounting, and once again I'm aching for her to relinquish control.

"Tell me you're mine, Evie."

Her breath hitches, telling me she's close to her release. Fuck, I'm running out of time.

"Evie," I rasp, unwilling to relent until she tells me what I need to hear.

"I'm…" Her pace picks up, hips rocking into me at double the speed. "I'm…" she moans again.

This time, my eyes go wide, realizing what she's doing. *Fuck.*

"I'm…" A high-pitched screech.

My palms grip her waist, fingers digging into her ass to still her movements, but nothing can stop her now.

"I'm…" She wails the words, and I feel her convulsing above me as her orgasm rockets through her.

"Phone's for you!" shouts Armando as he slips around the bar.

I look up from where I'm reshelving books after the college group from earlier left them scattered all over the study desk. "You heading out to the street fair?"

Janessa and Kyle are already working the tent outside at yet another town event that Firefly sponsors. We're closing the bar, as we promised the city, to ensure all business stays with the vendors set up on Main Street.

"Yup. See you out there?"

Normally, I would say no, especially since I didn't sign up to work the Firefly tent, but Lincoln already told me he'll be there with Lucy, and he invited me to join them. "I'll be out there in a bit."

He leaves, and I walk over to the phone. "Firefly—this is Evie."

"Evie girl!"

I smile instantly at the sound of Uncle Patrick's voice. It

feels like he's been gone for months rather than weeks. "It's about time you called."

He chuckles. "I know, I know. You know how it is. I never slow down long enough to think about silly things like calling home." He pauses. "How's everything going? You surviving without me?"

"Barely," I tell him teasingly. "Gabe only had to kick Jimmy out once for me so far."

Patrick mutters something under his breath that sounds like "that shithead."

"Other than that, we've been keeping steady most days," I tell him. "Business is good. Your patrons are happy. But what about you? I want to hear about the trip."

In the back of my mind, I wonder if he knows about the recent murder, but the last thing I want to do is worry him while he's campground-hopping around the Appalachians.

"It's been great," he says. "The camper's been holding up pretty well during my great escape. I just left Elkmont last night. I think I'll just keep trucking along until I get bored."

Patrick has always been adventurous, always feeling restless at home. Hence all the different real estate proper-ties he's bought just to have something to occupy him when he wasn't at the bar. I'm glad he finally started taking off on longer trips.

"Who are you kidding?" I grin. "You'll never get bored. You might as well hand this bar over to me right now so I can get paid properly for running the joint."

He chuckles. "Hey, you get the paperwork together, and you've got yourself a deal. I was always planning to hand it down to you anyway. Why not now?"

My mouth hangs open, baffled by the seeming ease of acquiring a bar for zero dollars. Uncle Patrick must be high or something. "Do they sell those special mushrooms over there in Tennessee, or are you for real? Firefly is your baby."

"It's your baby now," he says. "I've been training you to run that bar since the day I bought it."

My heart swells. It's not the first time Patrick has told me this, but it's the first time I can actually feel like it will come true.

Then he says, "Hey, uh, speaking of Firefly…"

My heart sinks, knowing it's coming. "You heard?"

He lets out a heavy sigh. "I did." A few beats of silence linger. "You okay?"

I squeeze my eyes shut, hating that we've had to have this conversation so many times in the last ten years, after the killings restarted. "I think so. I just want it to end. This has been going on for far too long." I shudder.

"Fourteen years," Patrick says grimly.

"And the last two were so close to home." I chew on my bottom lip. "Maybe I'll talk to Gabe about putting warning signs at the campgrounds to warn people away from catching fireflies."

"That's never worked, Evie. People don't read those signs, and when they do, they don't heed them."

Guilt swarms my chest, knowing I was one of those people once upon a time. "It's worth a shot."

He's silent for a moment. "I suppose it's worth a shot. But it's been fourteen years since the first murder." He clears his throat, and I know it's because he's emotional. "Since Carley. Ten years since the second."

He has his math right, though I hate that I know every

detail of every killing. I know that after the fourth murder, the police began to string together the evidence that tied each of the killings to the Firefly Man.

"No matter how many murders there have been, they still think it's nothing but an old campfire tale," Patrick adds, sounding defeated.

We change the subject and talk for another few minutes so he can tell me about some of the interesting people he met on the road.

When we start to say our goodbyes, Patrick sounds concerned once again. "Call me if you need anything, Evie girl."

I smile a bit. "Will do."

After I hang up, I pick up my pace, putting the rest of the books away then rushing upstairs to change, opting for a shower once I get a whiff of stale beer after yanking off my top.

Thirty minutes later, I'm wearing my favorite yellow slip skirt with a slit that reaches the middle of my right thigh. I pair it with a matching stretch sleeveless tank with ruffle straps. As I slip into a pair of white sandals, I check my reflection, imagining what Lincoln might think when he sees me.

I would normally think myself ridiculous for fixating so much on my appearance, but I've never met a man who looked at me the way Lincoln does—like he sees straight past my eyes and deep into my soul. No matter how dark and empty I've felt on too many occasions, he doesn't see a broken woman. To him, I'm whole.

Taking a deep breath, I tear my eyes from the mirror and push the door to my room open. An unsettling sensation blasts through me the moment I step out to the balcony that overlooks the bar. It's been weeks since I've felt that nagging suspicion that someone's watching me like that night I walked to J.D.'s office to find Lincoln in his place. At one time, I was convinced the presence could be Carley, haunting me from her grave, warning me that danger was close—but danger never came.

I've learned ways to cope whenever that discomfort rises up. I take a long, deep breath, pulling air from deep in my lungs, then release it slowly. Eventually, the feeling starts to fade and my breath returns to normal, but my heart still thuds loudly in my chest.

Frowning, I step closer to the balcony rail, senses still on high alert. As I scan the bar below, my thoughts go to the pocketknife I always carry. Patrick gifted it to me when I first moved here in one of his many attempts to help me feel safe living in this town. It's not the deadliest weapon, but I've never left home without it.

Sighing, I almost begin to scold myself for being so paranoid. This is always how it goes. My panic spikes for nothing at all, every single time. But when I see the front door is ajar, my lungs instantly constrict. What the—

I look around the room frantically to identify anything else out of the ordinary. Everything appears just as I left it, save for the opened door, but Armando had rushed outside quickly. Maybe he didn't shut it all the way.

After another quick self-scolding, I rush downstairs, taking the steps two steps at a time. I jump from the last and rush for the door, closing and locking it behind me.

My eyes squeeze shut, and I lean back against the door, holding my breath to slow my heart rate. For the longest string of seconds, I'm stuck in a vacuum, my senses smothered by the tunnel I've successfully trapped myself in. It's where I go when my anxiety cripples me—when there's nowhere safe to go but inside my mind.

"Evie," a muffled voice calls.

My heart kicks in my chest, and my eyes flash open wide. Lincoln is standing there with a concerned expression. I don't know how long he's been calling my name, but thankfully his presence is the only antidote I need.

"Are you okay?" he asks.

I swallow and nod, then I look to his left to find Lucy beaming up at me with her beautiful smile.

"Hi," she says, her hand in her dad's and swinging his arm, completely oblivious of the panic attack her dad just pulled me out of.

"Hi, Lucy." My smile blooms easily, especially when I realize she's wearing the yellow dress I bought from one of the local shops as her birthday gift. "What a beautiful dress on a beautiful girl."

Lucy latches on to some of the fabric and fluffs it, letting it flow around her legs. "Thank you. It's yellow like the sun. Daddy says you like yellow."

Heat fills my cheeks, and my eyes dart over to find Lincoln's gaze already on me. "Look, Lucy. Evie's dress is yellow too."

Lucy squeals with excitement and takes my hand in hers. "We match, Evie."

I laugh. "We do, don't we? We must have good taste."

Lincoln sighs dramatically. "However am I going to handle two such lovely girls in two such pretty yellow dresses?"

"Oh, Daddy, you're a silly goose." Lucy swings his arm even harder.

He smiles down at her, love glowing in his eyes. I swear, this man couldn't be more attractive if he tried.

We walk down Main Street just like that, hand-in-hand, with Lucy swaying each of our arms at an uneven pace. I should feel ridiculous, especially with the eyes of the town on us. But there isn't a single thing about this situation that feels weird or awkward. It just feels… good.

The first stop we make is at the face-painting station. Doreen is surrounded by painting supplies, and she holds a brush in her hands, adding the final touch to a butterfly on another little girl's cheek.

Lincoln waves his hand over the board of face-painting options. "Which one do you want, Lucy?"

She taps a finger to her mouth a few times before her eyes light up, and she points at the bumblebee. "This one." Then she looks at me. "You too, Evie. We'll match!"

I was not at all prepared to get my face painted today, but there's no way I'm saying no to a good time. "Sounds like a great plan."

Lincoln smiles, his eyes crinkling around the corners. It's clear that anyone and anything that makes Lucy happy also makes him happy. That's not why I give in so easily to the little cutie, but it's a damn good bonus.

Lucy jumps in the chair first, so we wait for her at the entrance of the booth.

Lincoln's voice is soft when he says, "Thank you for always being so sweet to her."

I turn to him, surprised. "You don't have to thank me for that, Lincoln. Lucy makes it pretty easy."

He nods as his fingers brush mine. "She really does, doesn't she? You'd almost never know a whole parent was missing from her life."

I frown, hating that he and Lucy both bear the heavy weight of that statement. "Because she has a father who can do it all." I wink at him, hoping to lighten his mood.

His fingers sneak in among mine until he's fully holding my hand. "How are you holding up with everything?"

I know he's referring to the combination of our last encounter on his couch and the recent Firefly Man killing. "I'm okay. Actually," I say, perking up a bit. "Patrick called tonight. He's having the time of his life out there. He says he wants to hand the bar over to me, and I think he was dead serious."

Lincoln's eyes widen. "Really? That's a big deal."

I nod, excitement bubbling inside me. "It's what I've wanted since he bought the place—I just didn't think it could happen so soon."

"Well, you deserve it. You run the place like it's yours as it is. Everyone there respects you. Business is going well." He shrugs. "If Patrick is ready to retire, maybe the timing is just right."

I love how easy he makes it all sound and how much confidence he has in me to take over my uncle's business. Deep down, I've always wondered if I would ever feel any semblance of success in life, knowing how disappointed my parents were in me and my decisions. According to them, my future would amount to nothing, my happiness limited by the pennies I would make. I always hoped they were wrong, but now, I can look back and say without a single doubt in my mind that they were wrong—in every sense of the word.

"Evie, it's your turn!" Lucy hops off the chair and runs to us, painted face beaming, the most adorable bumblebee I've ever seen.

Lincoln squeezes my hand before releasing it so he can scoop Lucy into his arms.

I walk to the chair, smiling at Doreen as I sit down. "Make Lucy proud," I tell her.

She grins back. "I'll do my best."

I'm not surprised when Doreen begins to ask questions about my relationship with her boss. I don't give her much information, because I'm not sure at all what to tell her. I certainly can't tell her how I've fallen in love with his daughter, and she invited me to her birthday party where Lincoln went down on me in the bounce house after everyone went to bed. Or tell her how the last time I was in his office, I dry-humped him on his couch until an orgasm rocked my world.

"We're becoming good friends," I say, hoping to satisfy her with that alone.

A knowing smile plays on her face. "I'm rooting for you. If my old-woman senses are still as accurate as they once were, I'd say he's very much into you. More so than Lilith Thornefield, by a long shot." Annoyance radiates through her tone, then her eyes dart past me to where Lincoln and Lucy are standing.

I look over to find Lilith approaching Lincoln with a bright smile, her daughter Willow right beside her. That same spike of jealousy I felt at Lucy's birthday party hits me again, but it melts away instantly when I see Lincoln take a step backward from the woman when she gets too close. Lilith doesn't seem to notice, continuing to talk his ear off while Lucy wrinkles her face at Willow. And here I thought Lucy loved everyone.

Stifling a laugh, I decide to ignore the exchange.

Doreen shakes her head. "At least you had the common decency to turn away his professional care."

I frown. "Lilith is a client of Lincoln's?"

She blows out a sigh. "Oh dear. You know I can't divulge the details"—she looks around to make sure no one can hear her—"but yes. She's requested extra appointments, and you cannot tell me she gives an ounce for that husband of hers who just died. I warned him it's a conflict of interest, seeing as she just purchased the daycare Lucy goes to."

"She what?" I practically squeal the question, but no one seems to notice except Doreen.

She simply nods. "Yup. I'm telling you, Evie. I might be an old woman, but I know a thing or two about people. Lilith is after Lincoln—I'm sure of it."

Nodding, I look back at Lilith, who just happens to turn her focus away from Lincoln for a second to narrow her eyes at me. I could swear that I see realization dawn inside those dark little orbs as she realizes her plot to hook Dr. Lincoln Reed just got a whole lot more difficult.

I turn away, my eyes connecting with Lucy, who is squealing with joy as Doreen finishes my face paint.

A few minutes later, Lincoln is taking photos of Lucy and me, our bumblebee faces matching our attire so well that you would think we planned it. I'm thankful when I realize at some point that Lilith and Willow have disappeared into the crowd. I make a conscious choice not to bring her up to Lincoln. It's clear by his reaction to her proximity that he's a very smart man.

One food-truck stop and one temporary tattoo later, Lincoln stops in front of the ice cream stand to get Lucy a strawberry cone. Her eyes widen to capacity when he hands her the delicious treat, the bumblebee art beside her eye expanding too. It's clear why Lucy is so popular in her class. I've never seen a child filled with so much happiness. Lincoln must live for moments like these, when he can watch his little girl bask in the simple joys of life before the world begins to show its true darkness to her.

We walk another block toward a small stage, where a man is strumming his guitar and belting pop-rock hits. Moving her feet to the beat, Lucy tries aggressively to finish her ice cream cone until she can't stand it anymore. At the start of the next song, she thrusts the rest of her dripping cone at Lincoln and takes off for where a few people are dancing in front of the stage. Lucy moves in and dominates the space, letting her body take her in all kinds of directions.

Eventually, Lincoln goes out to the dance floor to scoop her up—and she embarks on the first tantrum I've ever seen her throw, her arms and legs swinging as Lincoln tries not to drop her. Her bumblebee face is all squished as she cries, "I wanna dance! I wanna dance!"

I watch how Lincoln handles it. There isn't a stitch of annoyance or discomfort on his face. Instead, he leans down and whispers something to her. At first, it seems like it's not going to work, and her whining intensifies until tears streak her cheeks and snot bubbles out her nose. But I take note of something that tugs at my heart and blankets me with emotion.

Lincoln only loves her harder through it.

After a few more whispered words from her dad, Lucy's tantrum quiets. Her face starts to dry, leaving tear stains behind, then Lucy throws her arms around his neck… and that's all it takes.

In that moment, I fall madly, deeply, unabashedly in love with Dr. Lincoln Reed.

Francine is ready and waiting as soon as I carry a sleepy Lucy inside. On our way home, I called and asked if she wouldn't mind watching Lucy for a bit while I said goodnight to Evie. Of course, she was more than eager to give me that time.

Francine waits by Lucy's bedroom door as I place my daughter on her bed then kiss her squishy, painted cheek. I'll clean her off tomorrow. "I love you, Lucy," I whisper.

"I love you, Daddy," she says with a yawn so big that tears begin to leak from the corners of her eyes.

I smile. "Today was so much fun."

She nods, her eyes still shut. "Best day ever." A smile lifts her cheeks, and she takes a deep breath, her chest rising and falling.

"That's what I love to hear." I pull the light-pink blanket up to her neck and tuck it around her. "Sleep tight, goose."

She yawns again, this time while saying, "Night-night."

I stand, giving her one more glance before I make a move to leave.

"Daddy?" Lucy asks, stopping me in my tracks.

I turn around to find her eyes still closed. "Yeah?"

She sighs with her entire body. "I'm so happy you're my daddy."

My chest and throat tighten with emotion, over-whelmed as I so often am by the amount of gratitude I feel for Lucy being mine. "I'm the lucky one, sweet girl. I'll see you in the morning."

When I walk back out into the hallway, Francine regards me with a smile. "Good night, I take it?"

I nod, fighting off a sleepy yawn of my own. I'm not about to call quits for the night just yet. "Great night. Thanks for watching her. I'm sorry I've been asking for so much lately."

Francine makes a face. "You barely ask for a single thing, Linc. Stop with the guilt already." She smiles. "Now, go get that pretty girl of yours home safely. I'll take the guest room tonight." She holds up the baby monitor to let me see that it's on and fully charged.

I wrap my arms around Francine. "You're an angel."

When I climb back into my car, I turn to Evie and smile. "Thanks for letting me kidnap you."

She laughs. "You're the worst kidnapper in the world, you know that?"

I shrug and raise my eyebrows. "I have you strapped into my car, don't I?"

She raises her brows in an amused challenge. "Is that what you call this?" Her finger glides down along the edge of the seatbelt. "I recall putting this bad boy on myself."

"Because you were afraid of what would happen to you if you didn't."

Her smile widens. "Maybe so. You should have seen me tonight before meeting up with you. Armando forgot to close the door completely when he left, and it gave me a bit of a scare when I noticed." She laughs. "Thought maybe Jimmy got desperate and broke in to get himself a drink."

The fact that I've only lived in this town a little over a month and have already heard about Jimmy's drunken reputation at Firefly says something. "Has he been back since Gabe tossed him that night?"

Evie's eyes widen. "Oh yeah. Are you kidding? Nothing can deter that man. He's a regular, through and through." Then she frowns. "I know he can act up from time to time, but that never happened before Lilith's mom left him. I think he's just having a hard time."

Ignoring that interesting fact about Lilith, I focus on how Evie can see the good in people even when they've been ugly to her. I love that. "Maybe so," I say, starting my car and backing down the driveway.

She sinks back in her seat, and her lips twist. "If you think about it, he's not getting any younger, and the odds of meeting someone new in a town this small is close to impossible."

Something about the way she says that makes me smile. "So you're saying there's a chance."

Evie laughs, music to my ears. "We're talking about Jimmy here."

I make a face, not hiding my sarcasm. "Of course." Biting down on my lip, I consider not adding to my thoughts, but I can't help myself. "Just because someone is going through a hard time doesn't excuse their behavior toward you. You don't have to accept it."

She blinks at me once, twice, and I wonder if I did, in fact, cross the line giving her unsolicited advice. "You're right." A smile blooms on her face. "I just know I could take him if things got heated again."

I chuckle and tilt my head. "Well, that is very true." My hand slides over the center console to her leg, a gesture that fills her cheeks with that perfect shade of pink I love.

We have to drive around Main Street to get to the small parking lot behind Firefly. I jog around the car to help Evie out and slip my hand in hers before walking her to the bar's entrance. Just like I do every single time we're together, I search my thoughts for any possible reason I can find to get more time with her.

"Thank you for driving me home," she says lightly, "even though I could have walked from the market."

Her teasing eyes linger on mine as she backs through the doorway to Firefly. I step forward, too, resting one hand on the open door and the other on the door frame. "What can I say? I prefer scenic detours."

She takes another step back, but it's too far. I lean forward and take her hand then pull her back to me. My arm slides around her waist to hold her as close as physically fucking possible as I crush my mouth to hers. A soft, sexy moan vibrates from her throat.

Evelyn Vaughn is the perfect match to my every need. She's intoxicating, imaginative, fiery, and resilient in the way she blazes through life despite all it has thrown at her. Goodness pours out of her, the brightest light in the darkest day. She's a firefly, through and through. My firefly. The only light I'll ever need in the dark, cruel world.

When I finally pull my lips from hers, my eyes are blurred, my head buzzing, and my resolve to leave dwindling. "How about a tour?"

My bold question is met with a look of shock, and I start to second-guess my confidence. This is all still so new. I don't want to fuck anything up.

"I'm not inviting myself in to… I mean—I was only curious, that's all." I take a shaky breath. "I always wanted a secret room as a kid."

Her lips curl into a smile. "Didn't we all?"

Her gaze burns into mine as she pulls me into the building. I lock the door behind us and follow her to the aluminum spiral staircase. She plants one foot on the second step, her ass stretching the soft fabric of her skirt. She looks over her shoulder, catching my inappropriate stare, and a smile teases her lips. "Follow me to my lair, Doctor Reed."

Losing all sense of control, my arm shoots forward, hooking around her middle. I pull her back, her height on the stairs now matching mine. I bury my face in her neck and take in her delicious scent. "You drive me so damn crazy, you know that? I've been wanting to hold you close all night."

She relaxes into me, her body warm. "Just imagine how close you can hold me when we get upstairs."

A growl rumbles in my chest, and I let her guide me the rest of the way. She turned out to have been joking about a secret book to pull to enter her apartment—instead, there's an actual door handle on one end of the bookshelf that she unlocks with a key.

When we're inside, she swings her arms up, gesturing to showcase her place. "Here it is. The infamous upstairs apartment." She smiles and turns around to catch my reaction.

I tear my eyes from her long enough to get a full view of the whole place. It's just one big room, for the most part. The bookcases from the outside flow naturally into the room, and a small brick fireplace takes up the same wall as her bed, with closet doors on the other side. There's a small kitchenette on the opposite wall with a pantry next to it, and on the other side of the door is a bathroom.

None of the decor matches, but somehow it all looks perfect together. The living quarters are small but cozy, and the vibe fits Evie perfectly—simple and rich with what I'm guessing is her favorite literature.

"Originally, this was just a nook in the upstairs library, but Patrick converted it to a bedroom while he was between homes. After he bought the house you're living in now, he turned this into an office, but he never used it. When I moved here for good, it became my home. He thought I should have a place of my own, and I was secretly so happy." She smiles proudly. "Is it silly that this is all I've ever dreamed of? To own this bar and live in this little apartment behind a hidden bookshelf?"

I shake my head, fascinated even more with the woman who has completely stolen my attention. I would have never thought I could possibly be even more into Evelyn Vaughn than I already was, but she's so far beyond that—she's the lifeline I never knew I needed.

When her hand slips into mine and she walks me to the edge of her bed, I almost can't believe it. I've taken my time, letting Evie warm up to me, hoping she will one day trust me, praying she will finally admit what I've already realized. I'm hers. She's mine. Not a single fucking thing on this Earth could be more certain.

So when she reaches for my shirt and starts to slip it up and over my arms, my dick instantly begins to harden.

She tosses my shirt onto the floor then starts on my jeans, never taking her eyes from mine. "Aren't you going to ask me to say it?"

My heart thunders in my chest, desperate for me not to fuck up. "Only if you're ready to." I swallow hard, hating my trickle of fear that she's messing with me right now, working me up to just let me down. I've been taking care of myself for years at this point, but the past month has been the fucking worst. I never knew my balls could ache for release like they do when I'm thinking about Evelyn Vaughn.

She's got me naked now, save for my green boxer briefs that leave little to the imagination. I'm hard as a rock, tent pitched and ready for the long night ahead.

Her hands move to my chest then slide down like she's examining every inch of my body's terrain, then she grips the elastic of my briefs and begins to tug. "What do you want to know, Lincoln?"

I growl at her teasing fingers as they slowly peel down my underwear. "Tell me you're mine," I say, and my cock springs free.

Her eyes open wide. "Oh my," she says, practically salivating. She's felt me before, but she's never seen me bare. Now she can witness firsthand how happy I can make her.

Her gaze flutters up to mine, her doe-eyed look only making me swell even bigger. But she doesn't respond. Instead, she continues peeling down my boxer briefs, kneeling as they hit the floor. Then she takes my cock in her small hands, pushes it up so it almost hits my stomach, and licks me from the base to the tip in one slow, confident move.

My cock jumps in her hands, making her bat her lashes up at me again. She's doing this on purpose. Teasing me. Tempting me while purposely not saying the words she knows I want to hear.

"Evie." Her name is a warning through gritted teeth.

A hint of a smile tilts her pretty pink lips before her tongue circles my tip, but when her mouth wraps around my crown and her eyes roll back into her head, I'm completely done for. There's no fucking way I'm stopping her now.

My jaw hangs open, watching it all play out, not wanting to pinch myself awake from this dream. I've almost forgotten the feeling of having a beautiful woman on her knees, worshipping me. Then again, there has never been a woman like Evelyn Vaughn.

"You have the sexiest mouth." I manage to squeeze out the words through my tightening throat.

As if in reward, she wraps my cock with her dainty fingers, surprising me with their strength. Then she strokes me slowly, rolling my skin toward her mouth as her lips stretch wider the deeper I go. Once she gets started, she's seemingly relentless in her mission to kill me, taking me toward the back of her throat until I feel the collision.

Her hands work my shaft, fast and furious, while she slides me in and out of her mouth. The closer she brings me to the peak, the more my brain fogs and my muscles tighten. As much as I want to throw her on the bed and fuck her raw right now, I'm terrified any sudden movement will ruin the entire thing. So I let her gag on my cock until my orgasm breaks free.

Evie releases me from her mouth as streams of liquid sex coat her lips, chin, and neck. I reach for her stretchy top and yank it down along with her bra, boosting her breasts. Then my other hand covers hers and guides my cock down to her heaving breasts, decorating her with every ounce of myself.

When I'm done, I reach for the back of her neck and help her to stand, then I crush her mouth with mine. Fuck, if I don't get inside this woman soon, I might just die.

"What are you doing to me?" I whisper against her lips.

Her body quivers. "I wanted to thank you."

I raise my brows, confused. "For?"

"For giving me an emotional connection I never thought I deserved."

She lets out a shaky breath, and I hold her tighter. When I find her lips again, I take my time sinking into them, appreciating them, committing the feel of them to memory.

Once I've worshiped her mouth enough, I slide my lips to her ear. "Get on the bed, Evie."

I'm still half delirious with pleasure, but there's no way I'm not repaying the favor. She obeys, getting on the bed and leaning back on her elbows, her beautiful nipples stiff with arousal.

Now it's my turn to get on my knees. I situate myself between her legs and reach for her skirt. As I peel it off and throw it to the floor, I take a long, appreciative look. Her pussy is already glistening, her arousal unmistakable, and I don't waste a second before I lean down to take a sweeping taste.

Landing on her clit, I flutter my tongue and wrap my arms around her legs. With a gentle push, I spread her wider, forcing her open in the most vulnerable position. My flicking pauses while I lap her up, and when I find her clit again, I suck it into my mouth. Her moan is soft but oh-so-guttural. I look up to find her lids half closed and her abs clenching, then her hips begin to move up and down, bringing her closer to my mouth.

She loves when I devour her. I learned that in the bounce house. And while I thought she was being timid then, those moans and that orgasm left a lasting impression. They kept me up late into the night while I pleasured myself to the memory. But that night had been dark, unlike now. Now, I get to witness her body come alive at my touch, and it's the best fucking thing in the world.

Her hands feather up her body and slide over her breasts. She plays with them roughly as her hips gyrate, her pussy slipping and sliding against my tongue. Her nipples are so hard that when she takes them between her fingers and pinches, my cock instantly begins to harden again.

"You're s-so g-good with your t-tongue," she moans through stuttered breaths.

If she only knew what that compliment just did to my cock. I cover as much of her pussy as I can with my mouth before flicking my tongue against it, licking her clit until her breaths become pants and her moans become groans. Then I flip my wrist and sink two fingers deep inside her, hooking inside in just the right spot to bring her to the edge.

Her hips buck and her palms flatten against her breasts. A half moan, half scream slips out into the air, making me wonder how much a full bar of patrons below would hear if Firefly were open at this hour. But I don't have much time to think about what-ifs before Evie's pussy pulses, tightening around my fingers so hard she just might leave bruises.

When she starts to relax, I slip my fingers out. My jaw drops when I see her fluids soaking my hand while more spreads out around her cunt. So fucking hot. And just when I'm thinking about how I can relieve this new ache between my legs, she sits up, grabs my hand, and tugs me onto the bed.

"I need you to fuck me now, Linc."

TWENTY

I just called him Linc when I've only ever heard Francine use that nickname, but it doesn't faze me. In the moment, it just felt right. The man is on a roll with these orgasms, his tongue so far proving to be the best weapon he wields. But I want more. I need him inside me. And I need to feel him completely bare.

"I love that you just called me Linc," he says, hovering over me, his elbows on each side of my shoulders and his knees pressed between my legs.

I smile while hooking my arms around his neck. "It kind of just slipped out."

He leans down and presses his lips against my neck. "How about I make it slip out of that pretty mouth of yours again?"

His hard length presses against my center, making me gasp just imagining that thing entering my body. He's practically twice the size of any man I've ever been with, and that's not an exaggeration. Maybe this was a bad idea.

He must notice the look on my face as I stare down at

where we're so close to being connected. "Hey," he says gently, "I'll go slow."

I swallow as my eyes stare into his. Somehow I believe him even when the logic of it all doesn't make sense. "H-how?"

He chuckles, his eyes crinkling at the edges and drawing me into his beautiful green gaze. "I'm a determined man when it comes to you, Evie. I thought you knew that by now."

Determined, persistent, phenomenal. He's all those things and so much more.

He takes hold of his cock and runs the tip up and down my entrance, coating it in my arousal. "Tell me you have condoms."

I shake my head slowly, watching disappointment mount in his expression. He bites down on his bottom lip, looking frustrated, like he's trying to stop himself from spewing expletives.

Spreading my knees farther, I invite him in, telling him it's okay. When he shakes his head, I smile. "Does it help that I'm on birth control? And I'm clean." I nod at the small desk on the other side of the room. "I have the test to prove it."

A smile curls his lips as he nudges his hard-on against my center. "That's great, but I failed to bring my own documentation. Is that a risk you really want to take?"

I glare back at him, realizing he's planning to draw this tease out for as long as possible—but I'm done waiting. In one quick move, I hook my legs around one of his and slip my arms around his torso, then I tug just enough in one direction to flip us over.

"What the—"

I cut him off with a kiss as I spread my knees and lift his heavy cock just enough for it to meet my entrance again.

If we're going to do this, I'm going to need all the leverage I can get.

His fingers grip my waist, and I can't tell if he's trying to stop me at first, but the moment I begin to sink down around him, his grip eases and a groan vibrates in his chest.

I try to breathe as I slide down, but my pace is so slow that I'm not sure if I'm moving at all. Looking down, I can see that I've barely made it past his crown, which doesn't surprise me. Fitting that thing inside my mouth was hard enough, but I was so turned on at the time that I would have unhinged my jaw just to give him the pleasure he deserved.

My eyes travel to his, curious if he's watching like I am, but his eyes are on mine, like they've been waiting for the connection.

"Can I help?" The way he asks is so sweet, it's almost dirty.

I nod, feeling a flush take over my entire body.

He grips my hips again and pulls me back up and off his cock, then he slides his fingers through my slit, gathering slickness as he goes. Once his hand is thoroughly soaked, he rolls it around his shaft, lubricating himself in slow and steady strokes.

"Now," he rasps darkly. "Try that again."

I press my palms to his chest as I lift my hips while he holds himself steady, then I sink down again. This time I can feel the glide, the stretch, until I'm so damn full.

"Breathe, baby. Take your time."

I shudder at his words in combination with the intensity of how he fills me. How my body makes room for this man like it's been waiting to welcome him since before I even knew he existed is a mystery I can't understand.

"That's it," he growls, lifting me slightly then bringing me down another couple of inches.

I cry out at the sensation, and I'm not even halfway down his cock. "Fuck, Linc. You're too big."

He grips my hips harder, holding me in place. "And you're fucking perfect." He jerks his hips, feeding me another inch. "So tight." He pulls me up to his tip and brings me back down. "That's right, baby," he groans. "We're made for each other, you'll see."

His words are such a turn-on that it makes me want to fight against my protesting limbs. My mouth hangs open wide with surprise as my body tries to accommodate him, but it's like my muscles are fighting me, trying to resist this god of a man who desperately wants me to be his.

"Does it hurt?" he asks, and something about his tone makes me wonder if he's aroused by the idea.

Just to test the theory, I nod.

His eyes flash with desire. "We'll get there. Together. Slowly. Just don't stop, baby. I know you can do it."

I push off his chest again, easing myself up to the crown before sliding lower, releasing a breath as I go. This time, I can feel my muscles relax just enough to take him deeper, so I do it again, rising and falling, gaining another solid inch.

"Yesss," he hisses between gritted teeth.

I love knowing the pleasure is hitting him just as hard.

"You're going to take all of me, aren't you?" His mouth parts just enough for him to lick his bottom lip as he watches my next descent, which finally brings me to his base. "That's a good girl."

Loving his praise, proud of myself, I lean down and capture his mouth with mine. His palms glide to my ass, squeezing as I begin to pick up my pace. Every ounce of pain I once felt disappears from my mind, replaced with a new, intense pleasure. The way he hits me so deep, right where I need him, is creating an addiction. I know I'll crave for the rest of my days.

I fuck him until my body starts to tire. It's been a long time since I've needed stamina like this to keep up with a lover—maybe I need to join Lincoln on his runs or use my gym membership.

He must feel me beginning to slow because he flips us until he's on top, pressing my thighs wide and slamming himself into me so hard the headboard crashes into the brick wall. Neither of us stop to assess the damage to the bed or wall, though I'm certain repairs will be required. Neither of us care.

He grips my wrists and holds them above my head with one hand while the other snakes under one of my knees and lifts it, giving him even more room to deepen his thrusts.

When I feel just how deep he can go, I scream, my head tilting back into the pillow and my back arching so high he might think me a contortionist. I'm anything but, hardly even flexible, but the way he's moving my body is making me question anything I've ever known about my whole life.

Lincoln picks up the pace, and everything inside comes alive. My bed continues to crash into the wall, the old frame squeaking with each thrust, the comforter gathering and twisting beneath us in all kinds of directions, while my orgasm builds to the top of the tallest rollercoaster ever made.

"Linc," I squeak out in warning.

His eyes flash in recognition. "Wait for me, Evie."

His command is almost futile, seeing as he's the one in control, but I somehow manage to hold myself off for several more seconds, desperate to feel his release in an epic collision with mine.

Just when I can't hold out anymore, when my body begins to rock forward, ready to plunge into release, he growls out, "Now," and I completely let go.

I give in to the freefall that takes me over the edge, trusting the journey even knowing it might just kill me. And I fall deeper in love with a man who has climbed so deeply into my soul, he might be trapped there for eternity.

I'm close to falling into a deep sleep when a groan wakes me up.

"I should go," Lincoln whispers.

Disappointment lances my heart. My arms are fully wrapped around his body, locking him to me like he's my lifeline. Maybe he is, considering I haven't felt this alive in… ever.

When he doesn't make an actual move to leave, I smile and let my eyes flutter closed again. "What time does Lucy wake up?"

"Seven," he says with a sigh. "I guess I could set an alarm and let Francine know."

The regret in his tone is enough to give me a change of heart. "Maybe just stay for a little bit longer. You should get home and get some sleep before Lucy wakes up."

His beard kisses me before he does, and my legs clench around his as I remember how that same facial hair felt on my pussy. Him carrying my scent when he kissed me only added to my arousal. This man can do no wrong, I swear it.

He proved that last night when he barged inside me like an intruder, then made himself a welcome guest. More than welcome, in fact.

The kiss is so soft and slow—my head goes dizzy, and my heart thrums violently in my chest. How does this man exist? How is he real? And how has it taken so long for us to find each other?

"Damn," he rasps when pulling away. "Is it too early to ask you to marry me?"

A giggle bubbles from my throat as my cheeks heat. "Probably, but I'm sure that won't stop you."

He grins and shakes his head. "You already know me so well."

Do I? My eyes search his while I chew on my bottom lip. "I feel like I do in some ways, but…"

He leans back on one elbow, regarding me curiously. "But what?"

I turn slightly to face him, bringing my fingers to his chest to draw slow circles there. "Why don't you ever talk about your family?"

Lincoln visibly tenses, and I wonder what nerve I've struck. "Honestly, Evie, it's not the happiest of stories."

Frowning, I press my hand to his chest and look up into his eyes. "I'm not going to judge you, Linc."

His tension eases a bit before he rests his head back on the pillow and tucks his hands behind his neck. "Okay, then. Buckle up."

I lay my head on my own pillow, keeping my focus on him.

"I don't remember much from my early childhood, but I know my home wasn't the ideal environment. It got so bad that CPS took me away from my parents when I was eight. They placed me in temporary homes until I was finally adopted by a good family when I was twelve."

Holy shit. Lincoln's story is not at all what I expected. "I'm so sorry."

He turns, laying on his side again and looking down at me, a frown creasing his beautiful brows. "Don't be," he says. "I'm grateful for what led me to my adoptive family." His eyes turn down as if in shame. "They were great."

Something doesn't seem to be adding up. If Lincoln has a great family somewhere out there, where are they now? Why aren't they part of Lucy's life like Francine? And why does he call Dr. Rohls the father he never had?

"Does your family live close by?"

I can sense the tension that radiates through his body at my question.

"No," he says, his tone sharper than before. He clears his throat. "We lost touch after I got into some trouble as a teen."

He sits up completely and starts to look for his clothes. I watch him, confused and a little hurt at this turn of events. I'm not sure if I should push him to talk more—the subject obviously hurts him. So I don't. Instead, I walk to my small closet and put on a long T-shirt before walking him downstairs to the door.

Once we get to the entrance, I almost expect him to just walk out without a word. The awkward silence is already intense. But he turns to me first, curves his hand around my neck, and brings my lips to his. It's another slow kiss, filled with all the pent-up emotion I feel like he wants to relay but for some reason can't. At least, that's what I'm choosing to believe after the best night of my life.

"I'm sorry I have to leave like this." He frowns, his

disappointment seeming to match mine. "Can I see you tomorrow?"

Relief floods me, and I don't know why. It's not like I doubted that he would want to see me again, but I guess I just needed to know we would be okay after this difficult conversation. "Of course." I smile. "You know where to find me."

He smiles back then kisses me again before finally stepping away. "Thanks for the tour."

I can't hold back a huge grin. "Anytime, Doctor Reed."

With one final mock glare followed by a wink, Lincoln leaves, and I lock up behind him, still with that ridiculous grin.

When I'm left all alone, I turn toward the bar. A neat shot of Tennessee Fire should help me get back to sleep.

I reach over the counter to grab the bottle and a glass, pausing when I notice an off-white envelope sitting next to the glasses behind the bar. "Evelyn" is written on the front in script, and a glob of red wax has been pressed on the back to seal it.

A strange feeling twists through my insides. I *know* I would have seen that envelope before I closed up earlier that night.

I reach for it with a trembling hand, thinking hard about who could have possibly dropped it off. Then I remember the Firefly booth was set up at the market with three of our employees working there—one of them could have easily slipped back inside.

But why would they?

I tear open the flap and pull out a white card, but I need my glasses to read the messy, loopy handwriting. Rushing back to my room, I lock the door behind me, my heart beating fast as I find my glasses. Sitting at the edge of my bed, I read the words scribbled on the card.

Run run as fast as you can,
you can't catch me,
I'm the Firefly Man.

I drop the card so fast, you would think it was on fire. When I look down at the envelope in my other hand, I realize something is imprinted on the wax seal. Against my better judgment, I hold it closer, re-seal the flap, and squint in an attempt to make out what's there.

A cry rips through my throat and tears fill my eyes. That isn't a design. Pressed into the wax is a tiny insect— red, black, and yellow with big beaded eyes, long slender legs, and wings.

I don't have to look closer to know with all certainty that these are the remains of a dead firefly, and the red wax is supposed to signify blood.

My entire body is shaking, and my heart is pounding. I race to find my phone.

Lincoln picks up on the first ring, surely sensing something is wrong for me to call him so soon. "Evie?"

I take a big gulp of air, trying to steady my heart rate, but it's impossible. "Lincoln, he was here."

"Who?" I can hear his panic. "Who was there?"

I squeeze my eyes shut, knowing how crazy this will sound. "The Firefly Man. I think he was in my bar tonight." I press my palm to my chest, hoping to calm my body's reactions, but nothing helps.

"Evie, I'm on my way back to you. But why do you think he was there?"

"He left me a note."

"What?" Lincoln booms. "He left you a note?"

I nod, even though he can't see me. "Behind the bar. When I left to go meet you and Lucy earlier, I thought it weird that the door to the bar was left wide open. I figured Armando just didn't close it all the way, but now…"

"It's okay, Evie. Are you in your room?"

"Y-yes." I let out a breath as the terror lessens, starting to feel a little ridiculous now that I'm talking to Lincoln. "I'm sure everything is fine. If he wanted to hurt me, he would have by now, right?"

Lincoln is quiet for too many seconds.

"Linc?"

"I'm sorry—I'm parking at the curb now. Stay on the phone with me, pack a quick bag, then head outside. You're coming home with me."

Work is the worst kind of torture this morning. Evie crashed on my couch the night before, since Francine was already asleep in the guest room. I insisted Evie take my bed, but she was terrified Lucy would wake up in the middle of the night and find her there, and she didn't want to take the cottage without Francine knowing. In the end, I had to allow it.

At six in the morning, I was able to head Francine off in the hallway to warn her about our guest. I told Francine the story, we called the police, then I rushed Evie back to Firefly, where Gabe was waiting for her. He did a sweep of the entire building, even checking closets, the attic, and anything that opened.

Unfortunately, Gabe didn't find any sign of forced entry or evidence of any person being there other than Evie. "What about that camera?" he asked Evie, pointing to it.

She frowned and shook her head. "Those haven't worked since Patrick left. He said he was going to send someone to fix them, but he might have forgotten."

What the hell? I didn't know Evie was living in a busy bar with no security cameras to back her up in case something happened.

Gabe promised to stay until Kyle got there for his shift, so I headed back to my place to start my routine, sans the run. I would have to work off the steam later.

Now I'm stuck in a session with Lilith, a woman who likes to treat our visits like a coffee date. She asks me just as many questions about myself as I ask her. It's inappropriate, seeing as she isn't Evelyn Vaughn—not even close.

I humor Lilith, understanding enough about my profession and the people who come here to know that she booked the session for a reason. However she chooses to use that time is up to her. All I can do is try to steer her in the right direction—to look deep within herself rather than to try to coax me into asking her out.

According to the file Jenkins had for her, Lilith has been in and out of therapy since she was a little girl. Apparently, she found her father dead in a blood-filled tub and has been traumatized ever since. She didn't speak for two entire years of her childhood, then she seemed to start overcompensating for it in her teen years. She was promiscuous, as Jenkins noted, welcoming sex as early as fourteen years old.

As much as I want to judge Lilith for the way she's presenting herself to me and using these sessions, I sympathize with the woman more than she'll ever know.

"And how is your daughter coping with the loss of her father?" I ask, hoping to get her off the subject of scheduling playdates for Lucy and Willow.

Lilith's eyes glaze over for a second, then she frowns. "If I'm completely honest... not great. I haven't been able to grieve for myself because I've been so busy making sure

Willow is okay." Lilith presses her shoulders back, raises her chin, and takes in a deep breath. "It's what my mom did for me when I lost my father. She showed me how strong a woman could be, how there's nothing we can't do. I looked up to her my whole life."

"Having a strong adult in our lives is very important. Your daughter is going to be just fine, Lilith. Please let me know if I can help in any way."

She smiles, her eyes filling with genuine warmth. "You've been wonderful, Lincoln." She lets out a light laugh. "I will say, I was a little wary of someone new taking over for J.D., but I'm glad I gave you a chance. I hope the others in town haven't given you too much of a hard time."

I shake my head, ruefully thinking that Evie was the only one who gave me a hard time. "Everyone has been great."

Lilith nods and purses her lips. "Speaking of J.D., you haven't heard from him by chance, have you?"

I shake my head. "I'm afraid I have not. Everything okay?"

"Just curious where he ran off to." She shrugs. "I've been in his care for so long—on and off, of course. It's not like him to just disappear."

"I hear he had some family things to attend to." I don't say more, not wanting to get any deeper into anyone else's business.

The alarm buzzes, alerting her that our time is up. I stand and give Lilith a friendly nod. "That was a great session today, Lilith."

Her smile spreads, and she walks forward, opening her arms for a hug. "Thank you, Lincoln." She wraps her arms around me, and I somewhat hesitantly pat her back in response.

"Same time next week?" I ask.

She nods and turns to grab her purse. "Absolutely." Then she looks back. "Willow wanted to have a few friends over this weekend. Maybe Lucy would want to come hang out? You can come, too, if you'd like to stay." Her brows raise as she awaits my reply.

I frown, conjuring up all the mock disappointment I can. "Lucy and I already have plans this weekend but thank you so much for the invitation."

Lilith's smile pinches tight. I can tell she's not pleased. "All right, Lincoln," she says, cocking her head. "Tell me the truth. Are you dating Evelyn Vaughn?"

Her bluntness surprises me. "Lilith, I really shouldn't be speaking to you about my personal life."

She gives me a sly smile. "Everyone is curious. That's what you get for moving to a small town."

I chuckle, still not sure what to say. "Well, don't go starting rumors until I figure things out for myself." I hope that will be enough to drive home that it's really none of her business.

She winks and struts toward the door, swinging her hips as she goes. "Well, I think it's a great thing, if it's true. Evie is a pretty girl." She frowns like something's just dawned on her. "Never seen her really with anyone, though. Well, except for Gabe, but we all know that was short-lived."

I walk toward the exit, passing her as I go. If she's not going to see herself out, then I'll help her. Smiling again, I open the office door for her. "Have a good night, Lilith. See you next week."

As soon as Lilith's gone, I tell Doreen she can go home,

then I text Evie to let her know I'm heading to Firefly to get her. She's coming to my office for a private session, but I don't feel comfortable letting her walk alone at night, considering recent events.

Fifteen minutes later, she slips out the Firefly door and regards me with flushed cheeks. Her shyness would almost make me think I hadn't just enjoyed the best sex of my life with her last night.

"Hey," I say, holding my hand out.

She slips her fingers through mine, her cheeks darkening. "Hi."

I squeeze her hand gently. "Work okay?"

She nods, batting her lashes up at me. I swear I've never witnessed Evie so nervous as I'm seeing her now. "Yeah," she says. "Thanks again for letting me crash on your couch last night. I'm sure it's safe enough to stay in my apartment again. Gabe did another sweep after you left and found zero evidence of anything out of the ordinary."

I want to tell her I don't trust Officer Gabe as far as I can throw him, but I force myself to consider her perspective. Gabe is her friend, creepy ex-boyfriend or not. They share a history I could never, and would never, take away. "I've already talked to Francine, and the guest room is all prepped and ready for you tonight. You can stay there as long as you need to."

She grimaces and shakes her head. "I can't, Lincoln. Lucy won't understand."

"Are you kidding?" I laugh. "Lucy will be ecstatic to have a live-in friend. Besides, I'll talk to her and tell her it's only temporary while your place gets cleaned. She won't find out what's really going on."

Doubt still shadows her eyes. "We'll see. Let's get this

whole repressed memories thing out of the way first. Maybe I'm more nervous about that."

I slip my hand out of hers to wrap my arm around her shoulders as we round the corner. "There's nothing to be worried about. It's just me."

She looks up at me, her features visibly relaxing. "Exactly." Her mouth curves a bit. "Maybe you're the reason I'm nervous. You're about to learn just how dark my life was at one point in time."

I hug her shoulders. "I happen to remember telling you some pretty dark details of my own last night. But what we uncover tonight is completely up to you. We'll go at your pace. We don't even have to get into anything specific if you don't want to. We can just talk."

Evie lets out a deep breath. "Okay."

It's one word, but it's acceptance, trust in something neither of us quite understands. The fact that she's trusting me at all is pretty fucking fantastic.

I unlock the door to my building and let her in then lock it behind me. Then I usher her into my office. She walks naturally to the couch and nestles into the corner, which seems to be her favorite spot.

Then she squares her shoulders and looks back at me. "Where do we start?"

I take a seat in the oversized chair across from her and lean back, ready to listen. "Wherever you want to begin."

here do I want to begin? Lincoln has already heard the gruesome details of that night fourteen years ago. Do I go back and explain the entire reason why I liked visiting my uncle in the summers so much or the details that led to me finding Carley's body in the woods?

"I have no idea where to start, Lincoln." I wring my hands together nervously.

"Why don't you start with Carley?" His voice is so gentle. "Tell me more about her."

As much as I want to smile, thinking about her, this entire conversation feels too heavy for that. I pull in a deep breath then exhale, releasing more built-up tension. "We were friends, but I'd just met her on that camping trip. Her family was visiting from out of town. We connected the very first day and became inseparable for the whole week. My uncle loved it—he could drink in peace with his friends while his friends' kids and I played."

I smile at the memory. It had all felt so joyous then.

"Every night after campfire stories, we'd go out to the trail to watch the fireflies during their mating ritual. It was so beautiful, Linc. And that night was special. There are different species of fireflies. One draws streaks through the sky with their blueish-white lights. We call those the blue ghosts. And the others are——"

"Synchronous fireflies."

I blink back at him. "You know about them?"

Lincoln frowns. "They made us study the Firefly Man killings in my criminology class, remember? We researched where the original campfire tale came from, the different fireflies. Anything that could help us piece together a profile of the killer."

I can't believe I've never asked him what he learned in that class. "Where did the original story come from?"

"It dates back to 1861, to the Confederate soldiers who fought in the Civil War. Some even say those glowing-blue fireflies are ghosts of the soldiers. Haunting, isn't it?"

I nod. Who would guess Lincoln knew more about fireflies than me? "What else did you learn about the killer?"

"Well," he says gently, like he's unsure how much he should tell me, "there's definitely a pattern in the killings. Each one seems to become more intricate as the killer gains confidence, which is usually the case in serial murders. Each one happened at or near a public campground, deep in the woods. And there seems to be a fascination with sneaking up on victims from behind and bludgeoning them to death."

I swallow. "What about the timing of all the kills? Is there a pattern to that? Or are there more possible victims, missing people whose bodies still haven't been found?"

Lincoln shakes his head. "Unfortunately, the likelihood

of there being more undiscovered victims is likely, and there definitely isn't a pattern to the timing of each kill. There are uneven stretches between victims as far as evidence shows, often years."

"But what about the sex of the victims? All of them were male except for one."

Lincoln's jaw clenches, and he adjusts his seat in his chair. I'm not sure why the conversation seems to be making him uncomfortable. "There are some stark differences between Carley's murder and the others. As far as I know, the reason why hasn't been uncovered."

I nod. "Maybe it's not the same murderer."

"There are still too many similarities between kills, namely the dead firefly pressed onto their bodies."

I gasp. "Wait. What? That's never been mentioned. How did I not know?"

Lincoln rubs his eyes with one hand. "Our class was privy to additional information to help them try to solve the case. But I probably shouldn't tell you any more."

Normally my curiosity would get the better of me and I would demand all the details he knows, but I'm not sure I want to hear anything else. It's been fourteen years, and I still get the same queasy stomach every time I think about seeing Carley lying there.

"We got off track. I'm sorry, Evie." He sighs. "Why don't we go back to your story? You were just getting to the part where you entered the woods to see the fireflies."

I take a deep breath and close my eyes, forcing myself back there. "Carley and her brother brought mason jars that night to trap the fireflies." Guilt radiates in my chest. "Foster handed me his jar, and I just… caved."

The memory stings just as much as it always has. I've

never stopped wondering what happened to Carley's wrongly accused brother. Other than that one damn poem I know he had to have written, I can't even find proof that he ever existed.

My cheeks flush as I hesitate to tell him about my silly childhood crush on Foster. For some reason, it feels invasive for him to know now. I was young and so damn naive to let one hot guy convince me to make a boatload of terrible decisions in one night. I will forever pay for those choices.

I wish it had been otherwise. Disobeying Patrick's orders wouldn't have changed Carley's fate. But at least I wouldn't have spent the rest of my life feeling responsible for everything that happened that night and after.

I continue with all the details that I can recall, from my uncle's warning to stay on the trail to the peer pressure that led me into the woods anyway. Then I get to our search for Carley, her scream, then…

I shudder and look back at Lincoln, more remorse compounding in my chest. "I'm sorry."

His forehead creases, and he leans forward. "Why? Why are you sorry, Evie?"

I blow out a breath, wracking my brain for an answer I'm not even sure is there. "I… I don't know. The details are disturbing, I know."

"But it's what you experienced." He gives me a sympathetic look. "You have nothing to be sorry about, you hear me?"

Something about his tone and his conviction makes me suck in a breath. "Yes."

My eyes dart between his, and in that split second, I get it. I get why Lincoln Reed does what he does. How he can help people put the ghosts of their pasts to rest. Because that's what it feels like I've been trying to do my entire life —put *my* ghost to rest. And while I always assumed that ghost was Carley, I'm wondering now if it has really been someone else. Someone who isn't a ghost at all, as far as I know.

Foster's disappearance has haunted me almost as much as Carley's death—for the sake of not having any type of closure, at the very least. I never got to talk to him about losing Carley. I never got to make sure he was okay after he was locked up for months while the authorities sorted out the details of the case. The fact that the justice system would even allow that is inexplicably heinous, in my eyes.

My only solace has been that he must be out there somewhere, if he can write poetry as beautiful as the one piece I found.

He must have changed his name. I've never thought of that before, but it's possible considering there's no other trace of his existence. Maybe he was worried the person who killed Carley would hunt him down. Maybe he saw something that night… after I left…

As this new realization dawns on me, I open my eyes with a gasp.

"Evie?" Lincoln is walking toward me, my blurred vision robbing me of the clarity of his perfect form. "Evie, are you okay?"

A heaviness presses down on me, forcing me to sink back into my memories from that night. It's the first time I've allowed myself to thoroughly rifle through these images from years ago, ones that used to fill me with dread. Now I feel nothing but safe as I make my way through the dark woods with fireflies dancing around me. In fact, with this whole new sense of clarity, I'm almost eager to go there.

I take in everything now, including the heavy, humid air and other compounding elements that add to my sensory experience. What may have been overload at the time is only a beautiful symphony. I stomp into the woods, unafraid, determined, the fear of losing my way or disappointing my uncle completely absent from my mind.

"Evie girl."

I hear the nickname given to me by my uncle, but I turn to find Foster there, his dreamy eyes filled with concern.

"We need to find her," he tells me, his voice sounding like he's underwater.

Everything goes into slow motion as Foster turns to dart back through the woods. I begin to run, and that's slow motion too. I can't keep up, my limbs struggling to move like I'm drunk off Tennessee Fire.

A streak of bluish-white light streaks past me, one of those damn ghost fireflies teasing me with its chase to find a mate. But this time, my eye follows the movement and widens at what it sees. The streak of light goes up, down, and back around, crossing over itself then curling in, before bouncing out and down into another shape.

It reminds me of the last Fourth of July, when my parents dropped me off at Uncle Patrick's on their way to a weekend-long party, and he and I played with sparklers all night long. We made up a game almost like charades, drawing words with the sparkling lights then making others guess them.

Only this time, there was no confusion over the words drawn in the air. One by one, the streaks of light spelled out a familiar phrase, a rhyme that I'd heard my friends recite whenever they went into the woods.

Run run as fast as you can, you can't catch me, I'm the Firefly Man.

A wheeze tears from my chest, lurching me forward. My eyes open wide with panic, and all I see is Lincoln's beautiful green gaze.

"Evie, say something. Please." There's fear in his tone and in his grip on my body as he pulls me into his arms. "I'm so sorry." He rocks me, acting like he's just hurt me in some way.

"I'm okay," I tell him before taking another deep breath. "Wow, that was…" I shake my head, trying to find the right word. "Hypnotic?" Then I look back at Lincoln, confused. "Did you just hypnotize me?"

He shakes his head violently, a genuine reaction convincing me it's the truth. "No, but it's not unheard of for someone with a traumatic past to attach deeply to their emotions in a session like this. It's what we want." He searches my eyes, still trying to assess if I'm okay. "This kind of thing can happen when bringing your suppressed memories to light, but you were in there too deep, Evie. It scared me."

His sweet, sympathetic care makes me fall even more deeply in love with him. "It felt like I was drugged… but happy. I wasn't scared at all."

He nods. "That's because you were locked in a cognitive trance. The type of emotions you feel about your past have the strength to lock you to them, in effect hypnotizing you."

"So it worked." After a moment, I blink at him. "What you were trying to do by bringing my memories back—it worked. Maybe if I had just stayed in it—"

"No," he declares with a growl. "We can find another

way to get you answers, Evie. I won't let you go back there again. That was…" He swallows hard instead of finishing, his Adam's apple bobbing.

There's something new written on Lincoln's features now, more than sympathy or concern. It's almost like he was right there with me, experiencing my every step, my every feeling—and he doesn't want me to get any closer to the truth.

I squeeze his hands and look deeply into his eyes. "I was fine. I knew I was safe the whole time."

He snorts in disbelief as his eyes close briefly. "You were shaking and crying. I had no idea what you were seeing or if you were coming back to me." He grips the back of my neck and brushes my cheek with a thumb. "I was so scared I was losing you."

His words don't make sense, but the emotions behind them do. I lean in, hugging his neck and never wanting to let go. "I'm okay, Linc." I pull away enough to kiss him softly, reassuring him that I'm here with him and I'm all right.

He frowns. "Let's stop."

I shake my head, desperate to continue. "No, please. I don't know what just happened, but I'm fine." I grip his thigh. "Let's keep going. Where did I leave off?"

He hesitates a few seconds longer before ultimately giving in and backing up a few inches, but he doesn't leave the couch. "You were telling me about Foster."

Oh shit. I nibble on my bottom lip, debating whether to tell him this next fun fact. "I kind of had a crush on him."

Lincoln's lips quirk up at one corner. "You had a crush on Foster? Your friend's brother?"

I can feel the intensity as my cheeks heat, and I know

they're an obvious shade of pink. "He was cute." I shrug. "And mysterious."

His eyes narrow slightly, and I swear he's just tucked that nugget away for future use as he leans back and nods. "Good to know."

I throw a glare his way. "Don't get any ideas."

He chuckles then nudges me gently. "Keep going."

Sighing, I search my brain. It's been such a long time since I've explained all the events of that night in one long retelling. "I followed him into the woods to where he thought he had found her earlier, a small beachfront at the lake, but she wasn't there. That was when we heard it." I swallow. "A scream. I knew it was Carley's scream, and it didn't sound normal. It sounded like she was in trouble. Scared."

I shiver and immediately feel a strong, warm arm wrap around my body. This time I lean into it, allowing Lincoln's comfort to get me through the rest. "We found her at the water's edge. Her jar of fireflies was on the ground, cracked, and the fireflies were escaping, their lights still blinking brightly. But Carley was already…"

Lincoln squeezes me. "Dead."

I nod, and he shudders, clearly affected by the visual I've painted for him.

"There was blood everywhere," I say quietly, slowly, in case he wants to stop me. "But her eyes were wide open. Foster went to her without even thinking. He tried to find her heartbeat, but his fingers were slipping too much because of the blood." Tears well up in my eyes. "He sat and lifted her into his arms while screaming for me to go get the police. Then he just cried and cried. Somehow, I was able to make my way back to camp." I sigh and look at Lincoln. "This is the part I've blacked out."

He nods, eyes soft. "That's okay, Evie. What do you remember next?"

Taking a deep breath, I sort through my memory and go to the last place I remember from that night. "I went straight to the first campsite and told them to call the police." I swipe the tears from my cheeks. "I don't think I was looking for anyone in particular. Not even my uncle. I just… wanted to save Carley even though I knew she was gone."

"What about Patrick? He must have been terrified when he saw you and heard your story."

I nod, feeling so much relief just thinking about how amazing Uncle Patrick was that night. "I don't know what I would have done without him. He helped me talk to the Pruitts and the cops. He knows the woods like the back of his hand, so he was able to help me retrace my steps just by my description of where she was."

At what comes next, a cloud overshadows my love for Patrick. "When we got back to the spot, the cops saw Foster covered in her blood." I blink at Lincoln, wondering what he thinks of this whole story, wondering if he thinks Foster could be guilty just like the cops thought back then.

"And they assumed he did it." Lincoln nods. He's finally realizing the guilt and worry I've carried for all these years.

"Yes. And he was arrested right there." I swipe at another tear. "After losing his sister. After trying to save her. He was still covered in her blood." I choke on the words, but I refuse to stop, my anger over Foster's jail time too much to bear. "And then he was interrogated for days. He didn't even ask for a lawyer because he knew he was innocent. He just wanted to help. But it was like they wanted to pin it all on him, as if he would murder his own sister."

I shake my head, disgusted all over again. "They had enough evidence to hold him, so they did for as long as they possibly could, but he was eventually let go. His prints weren't on the rock that bludgeoned Carley, and that alone was his saving grace."

"Sounds like it." His arm slips away, and he clasps his hands in his lap.

I let out a deep breath, finally able to relax after reliving it all. Well, all but the one part of the night I still can't seem to remember. "I'm so sorry to put all that on you."

Lincoln frowns, looking almost angry. "What did I tell you about your apologies? I don't want to hear them, Evie."

"It's just so dark. My past, my present." I start to tremble, my concern now settled in the fear that he might see me differently. "I wouldn't blame you if you wanted to walk away from this right now." I gesture at myself. "From me."

His brows crease again, but this time, what shadows his features isn't anger but sadness. "When are you going to understand? *You* are not the darkness. It's your light I would find in the pitch-black night. Out of the millions and millions of fireflies racing through the sky, you're the only one I see."

"Really?" I say, my heart beating fast. "Maybe you just haven't looked hard enough."

He smiles and leans toward me until his forehead touches mine. "Oh, Evie. I've been searching for you my whole damn life. I just needed some time to get to you."

Warmth blossoms in my chest. "Now here you are."

His lips brush mine, and he nods. "Here I am."

After leaving my office, Evie and I stop by Firefly so she can pack a bag. Kyle reassures her that he can close down the bar, so she comes home with me. Lucy is in the middle of the living room, dancing along to her favorite musical TV show, when we walk in.

"Daddy!" she squeals. She runs to me, throwing her arms around my neck in a giant hug.

"Oh wow," I say, picking her up. "That's the best hug ever."

I can feel Lucy's gasp when she sees Evie behind me.

"Evie!" Lucy exclaims, shooting her arms out.

I take a hint and lower Lucy to the floor so she can hug Evie too. It's the cutest exchange, one I know I shouldn't love as much as I do. Evie is a new person in Lucy's life, and I've always been careful about the amount of time she spends with other women. She could easily become attached, and I'm just not ready for that — or at least, I wasn't. Until Evie.

"Everyone hungry?" Francine asks, walking into the living room from the kitchen. She winks at Evie.

I gave Francine plenty of notice earlier that Evie would be coming back to stay with us. But this time, Francine will be in her cottage while Evie will be in the guest room.

"Me, me!" Lucy says, jumping up and down.

"Me, me, too," I say.

"I'm starved," Evie adds with a sigh.

Something about the honesty in her tone clutches at my chest. She must have been so nervous all day that she didn't even eat.

"You came to the right place, dear," Francine holds her hand out and drags Evie into the kitchen. "I made lemon chicken, but if you don't like that, there's plenty of Lucy's mac-and-cheese to go around."

Lucy and I follow behind them, entering the kitchen to find the round table set for four. Francine must have even deep-cleaned the kitchen. Everything looks better than when we moved in. Evie seems to be taking an appreciative glance around the room too.

I rest a hand on Evie's back in case she's at all uncomfortable. "Where do you want to sit?"

She shrugs and looks back at me while Lucy climbs into her booster seat. "Doesn't matter to me."

Lucy pats the spot to the right of her. "Sit by me, Evie."

I react dramatically. "That's *my* spot."

Evie grins and slips right into the seat. "Looks like it's my spot now, right, Luce?"

Lucy erupts into a fit of giggles. "Sorry, Daddy!"

Laughing, I head over to where Francine is dishing out the plates and shoo her away. "Go sit. I've got this."

Francine gives me an amused glare. There's no doubt

she's onto me. Francine has seen my crush on Evie since that day we picked sunflowers at the market. Even without knowing her that well then, Francine seems to have approved. Now I'm not the only one in love with Evie.

We spend the entire meal listening to Lucy's knock-knock jokes, most of which don't make any sense whatso-ever, but we laugh anyway. We laugh more because Lucy is so adorably confident in how she commands our attention. After dinner, I get Lucy bathed and ready for bed while Francine helps Evie get set up in the guest room.

Once I finish reading Lucy her favorite princess book, I shut off the light and sit beside her bed to tuck her in. "You comfy?"

She smiles and pulls her blanket up to her chin. "Yup." Then she tilts her head. "Is Evie going to live with us?"

Biting my tongue, I shake my head. "I'm afraid not, Lucy. She's just here for a short time while her apartment gets fixed."

Disappointment flashes in Lucy's eyes. "Oh. But I thought you liked Evie, Daddy."

My heart seizes. "I do, sweetie. Very much. But we can't just live with every single person we like, can we?"

Lucy's eyes widen as she thinks about it, then she shrugs. "Why not?"

I laugh and tousle her hair. "Our house isn't big enough."

Her brows lower in defiance. "It's big enough for Evie. And Evie can sleep in your bedroom, so someone else can move in too."

There's no arguing with this adorable four-year-old. Her big blue eyes get me every time. "Maybe Daddy should ask Evie out on a date first."

Lucy's entire face lights up. "And bring her flowers."

"Of course."

Lucy twists in her sheets to face me more fully. "And treat her like a princess. Like how you treat me."

Chuckling, I lean closer and nuzzle Lucy's cheek with my nose. "That's right. And all princesses need their sleep. Sweet dreams, goose."

She hugs my neck as she plants a sloppy kiss on my cheek. "Sweet dreams, Daddy."

Slipping out of the room, I turn toward the guest room and find Evie curled up on the bed with a book in her hand. Everything about the image feels like a dream I never want to wake up from. She looks so at peace in my home, and I know it's because she belongs here, just like she did back when she moved in with Patrick.

Evie looks up at me with a smile. "Hey."

"Hey. Your room okay?"

She nods. "More than okay. It's nice being back in this house."

"Even without the pink, blue, and purple flowers on the closet doors?"

"I mean, you could use a few upgrades in here, but it'll do." She grins.

I smile. "I'm glad you're coping with the complimentary amenities. If it were up to Lucy, I'd be moving you into my room, but I had to let her down."

Evie laughs. "Is Lucy trying to play matchmaker?"

I nod, eyes wide for emphasis. "Oh yes. From the moment she met you." Sinking my teeth into my bottom lip, I take in Evie's bedtime attire, a baggy white shirt and black cotton shorts. "Can't say I blame her. She happens to think you should be treated like a princess, and I can't disagree."

Evie's cheeks darken a shade. "Lucy is too kind."

"And me?"

She tilts her head. "You, Doctor Reed, are dangerous." A hint of a smile touches her lips.

"Dangerous enough to go on a date with? Say, Saturday night?"

Her cheeks darken another shade, and surprise lights up her eyes. "A date?"

I nod slowly, allowing my question to sink in.

She stares at nothing like she's ticking through a list in her head. "Okay." She smiles. "I'm sure I can find someone else to close down the bar for me that night."

"Lucy will be so happy."

Our eyes meet in a flirtatious glance, silence lingering between us. Meanwhile, I'm trying to keep from using any excuse to invite her into my bedroom.

"You should know," Evie says, "that I'm a bit of a night owl. It's probably from all the years of closing down the bar."

I shrug and lean against the door frame. "I'm the same. The house always gets so quiet once Lucy goes to bed and Francine is in her guest cottage. It's the perfect time to write."

Evie sits up straighter, tucking her book against her body. "You can write if you want. Just pretend I'm not here."

The nonchalance in her tone brings a smile to my face. "I'm afraid that will be impossible." Nerves fill my chest and throat. "I'm going to take a quick shower." The words *Join me if you want to* are on the tip of my tongue.

I'm not sure if it's wishful thinking or apt awareness when I see disappointment flicker in her eyes.

"Okay." She gives me a faint smile. "Have fun."

It's only two steps across the hall, but the journey to my bedroom feels like a walk of shame. How have I completely lost all sense of charm when it comes to Evelyn Vaughn? Every ounce of confidence I once had when it came to women seems to have completely diminished now when I'm with her.

I pause at my bedroom door, reminding myself that Evie's bedroom is right across the hall. Deciding to leave it wide open, I toss a look over my shoulder to find Evie's gaze on me. We make eye contact for only a moment, but it's long enough to extend a silent invitation.

Join me… if you dare.

CHAPTER
TWENTY-FIVE

EVELYN

The slowness of his steps, from my room to his, commands my complete attention. He doesn't even shut the door before he walks straight across to his bathroom, slips off his shirt, then heads in a bit farther to turn on the shower.

When he walks back toward the entrance to the bathroom, I fully expect him to catch me staring and slam the door shut, but he turns back to the mirror instead. He presses his hands into the edge of the counter, flexing his triceps and biceps and whatever other muscles that make up his masterpiece of a body. Even his back muscles expand in response to the way he's gripping the counter. Then he rolls his neck.

It's almost as if he's in deep thought. *Or maybe he's just waiting for me.* My heartbeat accelerates. As much as I try to convince myself it's all innocent, all I see is a slow striptease right in my line of sight.

It feels like an out-of-body experience, setting my book aside and swinging my bare feet to the wood floor. As I pad over to the door, I find him in the same position in front of the mirror, head down and jaw clenched. I haven't even considered the amount of stress he's been under, taking care of Lucy and Francine—and now me. Not to mention the number of clients he sees daily who pour out their hearts and deep, dark confessions to him. I don't know how he does it.

The hallway floor creaks, announcing my steps, making my heart thump even harder in my chest. Lincoln's house is so quiet. I'm starkly aware of the fact that Lucy is in the room down the hall while Francine is next door in the guesthouse.

When I enter Lincoln's bedroom for the first time, I shut the door behind me, far too nervous that Lucy might wake up and find me creeping into her father's bedroom.

I take a long, deep breath to clear the jitters, but it doesn't help. So I take the opportunity to scan his room for anything exciting. Porn on the nightstand? Nope. Women's underwear? Definitely not. Unmade bed? Not a chance. Dirty clothes strewn about the room? Never.

In fact, his room is rather boring. Besides the gold-post king-sized bed, the floor-to-ceiling mirror in the corner, and the long dresser, there's absolutely nothing to the room. No decor, no personality. It's like… a hotel room, at best. Nothing gives any indication that the Reeds are planning to stick around Bryson City.

I realize quickly that my rambling thoughts are a distraction to the mission at hand. Looking back toward the bathroom, Lincoln is still standing there, his back turned to me, his palms clutching the edge of the counter, but his eyes have shifted. Now, they're bold and blazing and focused on me.

Stopping in my tracks, I suck in a breath, but my hesitation only lasts a second. I've made it this far—I'm not stopping now. After taking another step forward, then another, then several more, I'm standing directly behind him and slipping my arms around his waist.

He groans. "It's about damn time you took a hint."

I smile and press my cheek into his back while letting my hands roam the terrain of his chest. "Is that what that was? I thought you just forgot to close your bedroom door before you started stripping for me."

He chuckles and places his hands over mine. "I didn't know how you'd feel about joining me for a shower."

"Then you should have asked."

He grips both my hands and moves them slowly down his chest. "But this was so much more fun. Now I know how desperate you are for me," he teases, bringing my hands to his washboard abs.

"That or I just wanted an excuse to check out your room."

"Oh yeah?" Lincoln chuckles. "And what have you found?"

My hands move perilously close to the elastic of his boxer briefs. "Your lack of decor, for one."

"Interior design isn't my thing. There's still a pile of unopened boxes in the garage too. I'll get to them one day." He smiles at me in the mirror, making me completely forget why I even noticed that his room looks less lived in than most vacation homes. Instead, I focus on the fact that he's just removed one of his hands from mine while slipping the other beneath his underwear.

He lifts his brows as if challenging me to take hold of him. "You want to know what I think?"

I nod, too nervous to speak with my heart practically beating inside my throat.

"I think you missed my cock." His raspy tone vibrates throughout my body as he pulls my hand down even farther and molds my fingers around his erection. "He missed you too."

My body shudders at the memory of his thick length sliding into me and the effort it took for my body to accept something of that magnitude—entering me, fucking me, owning me.

Lincoln's palms move back to the counter while I give in to the feel of him, appreciating his shaft with each long stroke, memorizing every ridge and contour like I might need to identify it by touch alone someday.

A moan tears from his throat. "If you had any fucking clue what you do to me." He spins around, sliding my hand from his boxer briefs, and he presses my belly against the counter. He takes hold of my chin and turns me so I'm staring back at him over my shoulder, then he crushes my lips with his.

As powerful and commanding as the kiss feels, there's a sweetness to it as well. Like every touch between us is careful not to cross some invisible line. Like he's holding back—but why?

When he slips a hand beneath my shirt and up to my bare breast, my negative thoughts flutter away.

His kiss engulfs me, his cock pressing insistently between my clothed ass cheeks as he takes a handful of my breast and squeezes. When his mouth slips from mine and he buries his sexy mouth in the crook of my neck, a pulse of electricity hums through my body.

"You smell so sweet," he murmurs. "Sweet, sweet Evie."

His free hand slips beneath my shorts and panties, all the way down to the wet evidence of my arousal. "I love that this is all for me." He sweeps a finger into my slit then immediately attacks my clit, teasing the bundle of nerves in a slow and steady circle.

It's me who's gripping the counter now, my focus bouncing back and forth between Lincoln's tongue and mouth kissing every inch of skin he can find and his hand in my shorts playing with me. He curses as his knuckle gets caught on the fabric of my panties, causing him to yank out his hand and immediately begin sliding off my clothes.

He whips off my shorts and panties first, followed by my shirt, then takes a long, thorough look at my reflection. He gazes at my naked breasts, his eyes dilating at the sight. His hands follow suit, the pad of one thumb brushing over one nipple before circling my sensitive peak while his other hand slips back down to tend to my pussy. Somehow, he knows just the right amount of pressure to make my eyes roll into the back of my head. *Fuck.*

My entire body is reacting to the way this man is touching me, teasing me. My legs quake, and my abs clench, all in preparation for an epic release. But just when I think my orgasm is building to release, Lincoln's hands slide down my body, until he's kneeling on the floor behind me.

Rough hands grip the backs of my thighs, wedging them apart. My eyes shoot open when I feel his wet tongue curl beneath my slit. With a single swipe, Lincoln licks me from clit to ass, a growl rumbling through him so intense that I can feel the vibration.

"Holy shit, Linc." I brace myself on the counter,

knowing nothing can prepare me for what he's about to do. "More," I beg.

Hands slide up my thighs to my ass cheeks. He spreads me so quickly that my eyes fly open at my reflection. My cheeks are stained red, my nipples so hard and tight they're aching for more of his touch. Then he tongues me again, this time tracing the outline of my pussy and ass, teasing each hole that he wants to drive his shaft into.

I press myself down onto the counter, cheek down, breasts flattened, then I lift my hips and move them against his face, needy for more. Two fingers plunge into my center, shocking my system as much as they turn me on. He pulls back just as quickly, then he stands, towering over me with his chest heaving and his mouth glistening with my juices.

I'm not sure if I should be afraid or aroused by the determination on Lincoln's face. He takes his cock in his hands and strokes it slowly while slipping it between my ass cheeks then teasing my entrance and ass, like he's not sure which one to push into. In this moment, my entire body flushed with excitement, I don't even care.

I watch in the mirror as his teeth sink deep into his bottom lip, then he settles on my entrance. He holds himself there for another minute while he strokes himself slowly, preparing himself for the hole he could barely squeeze into last time.

My stomach tightens, my center clenches, and I brace myself for the incoming bite of pain before the pleasure completely takes over. The anticipation is driving me mad. But I don't have to wait much longer. A second later, Lincoln's snaking one hand around my stomach to lift me, then he lines up his shaft and pushes inside.

"So fucking tight," he grits out, eyes rolling back in his head.

Unlike the first time, Lincoln doesn't stop to ease in and out of me. He takes one long dive down to the depths of my core, and he doesn't stop until we're locked together, base to base. From his wide-eyed expression, he's almost as shocked as I am.

"Are you okay?" His words are breathless as his cock twitches inside me, desperate for friction.

"Better than okay," I gasp, watching his expression transform from that of a concerned gentleman to a monstrous god of a man about to destroy me with the one-eyed beast between his legs.

I'm so ready.

The corners of his lips curl up, and he slides an arm up my stomach then crosses it over my breasts, hooking me to him. He lifts me so I'm standing as straight as I possibly can, my back arching past anything I knew I was capable of. His other arm slides around my middle. It's like he's fastening me to him so that he can have full control of our movements.

He moves his hips back then forward, driving in and out of me a few times before the real intensity begins. Soon enough, he's drilling into me from behind, fucking me so fast and hard that I know if it weren't for his embrace, I'd be bucked into oblivion.

His cheek moves to mine as the hand securing my breasts moves up to my neck. It's such a subtle move that I barely notice it until I'm locking eyes with his darkened gaze in the mirror, and I realize there's a wild side to this man that transcends anything I've ever experienced before.

Beads of sweat begin to escape my pores. My breathing

becomes labored, my limbs weakening by the second. As secure as Lincoln is making me feel, it takes every ounce of energy to keep me from turning into the rag doll I could so easily become.

Fuck this man. Fuck what he's done to me. And fuck him for making me love every dark moment like it's the brightest light in my universe.

"Linc," I warn in nothing more than a whispered rasp. "I'm going to come."

"I can't fucking wait," he growls, then he buries himself deeper inside me with his next thrust, quickening his movements until I'm nearly blinded by the force of him.

My orgasm spirals out of me from so deep that I swear every nerve ending in my body comes alive. Lincoln doesn't stop moving, making my orgasm last forever. By the time my brain is in a fog and my entire body is completely spent, he's still going, thrusting deeply, unrelenting as he brings himself closer to the edge.

When he yanks himself out and spins me around, I nearly drop to the floor with exhaustion, but Linc is right there to catch me. He lifts me onto the counter, spreads me wide, then buries his cock inside me again. With his arms locked around me and mouth locked against mine, he fucks me, this time at a much slower pace as his orgasm finally peaks. He erupts, warm fluids filling me, his grunts and groans pleasing my ears until there's nothing left for him to give.

Even when he's done and his muscles begin to quiver, he doesn't pull himself from me. Instead, he presses his lips to mine, kissing me like he never wants to let me go. All I can do is silently beg that he never will.

My fingers fly across the keyboard, the quick tapping sound, a symphony to my ears after weeks of writer's block. It's almost as if I've been building up all the things I wanted to say, and my brain is finally ready to let them loose. I must be three thousand words in when I see something move in my peripheral vision.

Looking over to the open door, I don't stop typing until I see my beautiful Evie smiling back at me, wearing nothing but an old Psi Chi shirt from my closet.

Just the sight of her has my heart revving to life. Francine took Lucy to Durham for the weekend to see some of their old friends. I took the day off work, and Evie doesn't have to be at the bar until this afternoon. We get the entire weekend together outside of the hours she has to work, but even then, I plan to hang out at Firefly with my laptop just to be close to her.

"Good morning, beautiful." I sit back in my chair, taking her in. From her long, wavy blonde hair to the black rimmed glasses she wears only in the mornings before she puts on her contacts, it's like she's right at home. After a full week of staying in my home, I would hope so.

"Good morning, yourself." She looks around. "What time did Francine and Lucy leave?"

I scrunch my nose. "Right after my run. Seven o'clock. Can you believe it? I guess they have a big weekend planned."

Evie takes a step into my home office, her eyes beginning to wander like that day she came into the office in town for her free consultation. I watch her perusal, fascinated by the books she chooses to pull off the shelves and the photos she stops to look at more closely. I made this office a bit more personal, so there is plenty of Lucy's art that she made for me at daycare and photos of her from all ages, some of which Francine gifted me after Becca passed.

"Come here," I say when she finally reaches my desk.

She sinks onto my lap, wrapping her arms around my neck. I kiss her slowly while snaking a hand beneath the soft fabric of her shirt. "This looks so much better on you than it ever did on me."

She smiles and looks down at her shirt. "What does it say?"

"Psi Chi. It's a student honors society I joined at Duke for psychology."

"Sounds prestigious."

I chuckle. "I'd say it is."

She smiles. "And here I thought it was a fraternity or something."

I slide my fingers up her bare leg and shake my head. "No, that wasn't my thing. I was very much buried between the pages of an academic book most of my school tenure."

She runs her fingers through my hair. "Nerds are so hot."

"And what makes me a nerd? Appreciating human minds and behavior?" My fingers draw circles on her skin.

"I love the way your brain works." Her cheeks flush with her sweet words. "The way you can explain things and completely change the way I've perceived things my entire life. You see the world in a multitude of angles, shapes, and colors." She shrugs. "It's smart, but it's more than that. It's empathetic, optimistic, and eye-opening. It brings peace and understanding to complicated, difficult things."

She searches my eyes, and I can't help but notice her nervous quiver. "You make me believe there's more for me out there than what exists in this small town."

A force squeezes my throat so powerfully that I'm not sure I can speak. I slip my hand out from under the shirt and cup the back of her neck while trying to find the right words. There's never been a woman in my life who could put my emotions in a vise the way Evie has. Not even I can comprehend what's happening to my heart. All I want to do is rip it out of my chest and give it to her, silver platter and all. I'm hers.

Still unable to speak, I pull her to me, meeting her with a kiss. It's not demanding, not lustful or filled with desire. It's love. Pure love.

She pulls back slowly, her eyes fluttering open then widening with a mixture of happiness and confusion. "Wow. What was that for?"

I close my eyes, resting my forehead to hers. "There's always been something about you, Evelyn Vaughn. Some-thing I couldn't ever explain." I open my eyes, pinning her with my gaze. "You love my brain? Well, I love your heart."

I swallow and slide my hand down to her chest. "I love your appreciation for the simplest things and your resilience even when life has dealt you some really shitty cards."

I bite down on the inside of my bottom lip, debating whether to say what's really on my mind, but I've already come this far. "I love the way you treat my family and the way you give without ever expecting to receive. I love the way you light up when Lucy runs to you or hands you a sunflower. I just… love you, Evie. It's like I've been looking for you my whole damn life, and now that you're here, all I want to do is keep you. Tell me I can keep you."

Evie's eyes fill with tears before she closes them and crushes her mouth to mine. She repositions herself on my lap so she's straddling me, her hands moving to each side of my face as she gives me all of herself.

Finally, she pulls away just enough to whisper against my lips, "I love you too. I'm yours, Lincoln. All yours."

A whoosh of breath escapes my lungs. I'm a firefly who's been starved of air for too damn long. My wings take me high into the sky, but it was Evie who set me free.

"I think you should stay here." My eyes search hers. "For good." When panic widens her eyes, I hurry to explain. "I know it sounds crazy and it's a big ask for all of us, but I still don't feel comfortable with you staying above the bar, especially when there's a murderer out there."

"There's been a murderer out there for fourteen years, Linc."

"But he's closer now. He's been in your fucking bar, Evie. I'm sorry, but I can't let you go back to living there."

She cocks her head. "It's not your choice."

Squeezing my eyes closed, I try to take a normal breath,

but it's impossible. "Evie, please don't be stubborn about this. You'll be safe here. With me. With us."

She wraps me in a hug and squeezes tight. "I have no doubt about that, but it's not right. Lucy wouldn't understand."

I frown, not wanting to admit that she's making sense. "Lucy adores you, Evie. She'd love to have you here permanently."

Sighing, Evie pulls back slightly and smiles. "I've already called to have the cameras fixed. If Patrick really is handing the bar over to me, then I need to take these matters into my own hands. And I'm adding alarms to all the windows too. I'll get better at using the system." Her resolute gaze bores into mine. "I've got this. I'll be fine."

Groaning, I bury my head in her chest. "I know. The problem is that I'm not." I look up, meeting her blue eyes. "I'm going to be a nervous wreck when you're not under this roof."

She ruffles my hair. "You've lived without me for the past thirty-one years. I think you can handle a few more."

I reel back in shock. "A few more *years*? Fuck that. I'm not waiting that long to make you my wife."

Her cheeks pinken, and laughter floats from her throat. "Lincoln, you're crazy."

"About you."

She rolls her eyes. "You really are one big cheeseball, aren't you?"

Revenge is the only thing on my mind as I laugh and pick her up off my lap. Sitting her on my desk, I roll my chair closer, wrap my arms around her ass, and plant my mouth on her cloth-covered nipple. It was easy enough, since her nipples have been hard as rocks for the past ten minutes.

I soak her shirt with my tongue, lapping at her, then finally pulling her into my mouth with one hard suck. She squirms against my attention, and I can feel the pleasure vibrate through her body when I bite down gently. Looking up, I see her hooded stare on me.

It's all I can do to not give her exactly what she wants. It would be so easy to yank my shirt away from her sexy body, yank her soaked panties to the side, and fuck her on my desk. It's what I want—and it's what she wants, which is precisely why I won't give it to her.

Curling my lips into a devilish smile, I drag my teeth against her hard nipple until I abandon it completely. Then I push back from my desk and stare back at her, knowing just how fucked-up I'm being right now.

"On second thought," I say, "since we'll be living apart and all, maybe we should behave ourselves."

Her jaw drops, eyes narrowing in a heated glare. "Is that so?"

I nod, fully confident that I have the upper hand. "That's so."

A flicker of mischief dances in her eyes. "Huh." Her legs close, and she slips down from my desk. "In that case, I should get ready for work."

My confidence falls away the moment I realize these games will not work on Evie. Not at all. I reach for her waist and pull her back down onto my lap. "Fine. Okay, you win." I groan, hating every second of my surrender.

She smiles and presses her mouth to mine for a lingering kiss before murmuring teasingly across my lips, "I always do."

Firefly is slammed by the time I get into work that afternoon. I have to call and beg Kyle to come in and help out. I can't remember the last time we had a full crew here working the bar, but it makes for an amusing night.

A group of out-of-towners staying at Deep Creek Campground have come in to celebrate one of their friends' birthdays. They've been piled at and around the bar since they arrived, getting plastered. If they hadn't taken a rideshare here, I would have kicked them out long ago, but I promise them one more round before closing out their tabs.

"C'mon, Evie," Lilith says, echoing the birthday boy, who she's been flirting with obsessively. "It's Billy's birthday."

Billy seems to be Lilith's type, or at least the types she's been here with lately—tall, bearded, handsome. I try not to dwell on how each one looks a little bit like Lincoln. Not nearly as striking in face, body, or mind, of course, but the similarities are alarming considering I know she'll stop at nothing to get what she wants.

"Sorry," I say to Lilith with a firm shake of my head. "Last call."

She rolls her eyes at me the same way she used to do when we were kids then goes right back to hanging on Billy. I fight against revealing my amusement and busy myself with delivering a Diet Coke to the man in the corner of the room. He wears a black hooded sweatshirt and doesn't even look up when I set the drink in front of him. Instead, he nods in acknowledgment but keeps his eyes glued to the book he's reading.

Something about the scene sends chills up my spine, but I'm not sure why. I realize I've seen this guy here before in the same closed-up hoodie, like he's trying to stay in the shadows. I back away slowly, my curiosity piquing when I see the small backpack on the seat beside him.

"You live around here or just passing through?" I try to make the question light, like I would with any other customer.

He shrugs, still not looking up. "Haven't decided yet."

I frown, confused by his answer. With no other choice, I walk back to the bar, determined to keep an eye on him for the rest of the night. But I don't get that chance. The man abruptly stands, gathers his things, and walks out of Firefly, leaving his Diet Coke sitting untouched at his table. *Weird.*

When Lincoln walks into Firefly a short while later, I almost regret that I asked him to come. Lilith spots him immediately and ditches Billy, worming her way onto a barstool near my man.

I don't even have to ask Lincoln's order, simply pouring him a Tennessee Fire neat and sliding it to him. He winks at me before swirling the amber liquid around his glass while half paying attention to whatever Lilith is rambling on about.

Sighing, I make my way down to the other end of the bar where Kyle and Armando seem to be trying to reason with the group of drunk campers. "What's going on?" I ask Janessa, who's watching the scene unfold with wide eyes.

"They're just wasted and refusing to leave," she says. "Armando's about to rearrange that one guy's face. Why are out-of-towners always so rude?"

"Beats me." I take out my phone and text Gabe. This scene is right up his alley. Then I step in front of Kyle to confront the group with a smile. "I'm going to do you all a favor, because I like you and really appreciate your business tonight." I nod toward the window. "You walk down that road two blocks, and you'll find a liquor store on the corner. It closes in twenty minutes. Pay your tab now, and you'll have just enough time to get there."

"What if we don't want to leave?" one guy demands.

I shrug, maintaining my smile. "I'm afraid you don't have a choice. You see, in five minutes or less, a police officer is going to walk into this bar and kick you all out for me. And if you give him trouble, you're going to spend the rest of your vacation in the shittiest little hole-in-the-wall jail cell you ever did see. You hear me?"

Billy puffs out his chest, drawing my eye to the beer stains on his shirt. "I hear you, bitch."

Before I can even react, a loud screech drags across the wooden floor, followed by the sound of a stool crashing to the floor. Then Billy's body gets jerked backward. "What did you just call her?" Lincoln roars before tossing him back into his group of friends, causing them all to collapse like dominos. "Get the fuck out of here!"

Kyle and Armando hop over the bar to hold back two of Billy's friends, who now want to take on Lincoln. Meanwhile, I make quick work of closing out the group's tabs and slide their cards over to the only one in the group who will make eye contact.

"Ah, what about our tips?" Janessa complains.

I give her a sympathetic smile. We don't have to deal with this kind of shit often, but when we do, it sucks for everyone. "I'll make it up to you," I tell her, and I mean it. She's already helped me more than anyone tonight by working a double.

The group staggers out of the bar, dragging their egos behind them. I should be surprised when Lilith goes with them, clutching Billy like he's just been wronged in some way, shape, or form, but I'm not. What does take me aback is something only I seem to catch—the subtle glance over her shoulder at Lincoln then a glare so heated he might have caught fire from it.

I move around the bar to Lincoln, who's helping Armando and Kyle clean up the fallen glasses, tables, and chairs. "Hey, you okay?"

By the scowl on his face, it's obvious he's still fired up. "I'm fine. Are you okay?"

Tilting my head, I nod. "I'm fine." I'm not sure if now is the time to tell him how turned on I am by the way he protected me just then, but I wrap my arms around his waist anyway. "I'm glad that didn't escalate into a brawl. I wouldn't know what to do if that pretty face of yours got messed up."

His nostrils flare. "It's not my face that would have

gotten all bent out of shape, babe. Billy Bob back there would have been on his way to the hospital. The nerve of that guy." He shakes his head and frowns down at me. "That incident didn't help your case for moving out of my place."

I bite down on my lip, amused. "I can't move out if I never moved in."

"I'm damn near ready to pack your shit up and move it into my house for you." He takes my face in his hands. "Why are you so stubborn?"

"I'm just being realistic. I've never lived with a guy before, Lincoln. What makes you think I'm going to move in with you after knowing you for, what, two months? That's insane."

"Yet it's the only thing that makes sense."

At his words, I'm like wax, his flame taking me down to the wick, leaving nothing left of me but a puddle of warm liquid that will harden and break if I'm away from him. "The fact that I've even considered your offer should be something."

A smile brightens his grumpy mouth. "I'll just have to keep holding back sex."

I narrow my eyes at him, feeling a challenge coming on. "I'd like to see you try."

His smile widens. "Are you sure you want to do this, Evie?"

My shrug should tell him all he needs to know. I'm not backing down.

"Is *this* why you called me in here?"

I swivel my head to find Officer Gabe, glaring between Lincoln and me. *Shit.* I turn around, instantly regretting calling him, especially when Lincoln's arms steal possessively around my waist from behind. Gabe's glare intensifies on him.

"No," I say quickly. "But we're all good now. Just a bunch of jerks celebrating a birthday and getting too rowdy."

Gabe nods, not taking his eyes off Lincoln. "Couldn't you lose your license for this?" He gestures at us. "Canoodling with one of your patients?"

Lincoln's arms stiffen around me. "It's none of your business, *officer*."

Gabe chuckles darkly. "Oh, but it is, *doctor*. Seeing as my job is to protect and serve. I should report you."

Jesus, this entire night is getting out of hand. I break Lincoln's hold and step into Gabe's space, glaring daggers up at him. "I'm not his patient, so lay off."

Gabe makes a disgusted sound in the back of his throat. "Don't lie, Evie. I've seen you sneak into his office late at night."

My cheeks heat with his words. "You've been spying on me?"

He frowns. "It's my job to notice things."

I plant a hand on his chest and push. "Get out of here, now. Actually…" I swivel around to locate the few people still left at the bar and cup my hands around my mouth. "Firefly is now closed. Everyone needs to go." I wave to Armando, Kyle, and Janessa. "You guys too. Everyone out."

Wide eyes greet this pronouncement, but I don't get any arguments. Everyone shuffles out except for Lincoln. I don't need to tell him to stay. Let's be honest—even if I did tell him to leave, he wouldn't.

I close the door behind Gabe, the last one to leave, then

I lock it, deadbolt and all. Lincoln helps me close all the blinds before we meet each other in the center of the room to take a breath.

"What now, Evie?" Lincoln obviously already has something devilish in mind.

I grin, because I do too. "How about that date?"

After ordering us a steak dinner and cheesecake to share from the nearby diner, I pour us both a glass of Tennessee Fire to sip on. I can't remember how or why we ended up on top of the bar, sitting cross-legged while he fills me in on all the changes in his life that came with becoming a father to Lucy. I hear about learning how to change a diaper, getting thrown up on too many times before he figured out that Lucy had an intolerance to sweet potatoes, and planning to be the most intimidating father alive to anyone she dares to bring home.

I shake my head. "You say that now, but she already has you wrapped around her finger."

He sets his glass down. "That she does, but that doesn't mean I have to go easy on her boyfriends. They need to know there's a loaded rifle waiting for them if they don't treat her right."

I smile and reach for his hand, squeezing it. "You're not going to need to do that, considering she's being raised by you, and any man she falls in love with will have to live up to the standards you've set—the way you treat her and how hard you love her."

Lincoln's eyes soften, and he leans in to kiss me softly. "Well, damn. Another reason you should move in. You just might save the lives of innocent men."

I laugh and pour us another glass of whiskey. "And how would you like it if Lucy moved in with a guy she knew for two months?"

Lincoln's lip curls in a snarl. "I'd kill hi—" He catches himself, and his mouth drops in horror. "That was fucked-up."

Laughing, I set my glass to my lips. "Just trying to make a point."

He waves a hand in the air. "It's not the same thing, and you know it."

I just smile, not wanting to argue.

"Was your father protective of you growing up?" he asks. "I know you said your parents were oblivious, but what about when it came to men?"

I shake my head. "I didn't date in high school. I had some crushes, but I was too riddled with anxiety after Carley's death to allow myself to feel much for anyone. Panic attacks were a frequent thing."

I bring my hands together and squeeze them. Just talking about my high school days triggers old feelings. "I was getting in so much trouble in school because of the anxiety. My teachers didn't know how to deal with me, and my parents didn't know what kind of help to get me. Or they didn't care. So I just kept going back to school, dealing with the same old shitty peers. This one girl would follow me and taunt me. One day, after I warned her several times to leave me alone, I ended up slamming her into the water fountain."

Cringing, I bring my eyes up to meet Lincoln's. He

looks to be in awe of my story, free of judgment, free of disgust. He's just… listening.

"I guess I snapped."

Lincoln scoots forward, lifting my legs so they wrap around him and I'm sitting in his lap. "Who could blame you for snapping, Evie? You'd never dealt with the trauma of Carley's death. You were expected to carry on like normal." His eyes dart between mine. "Like you were a firefly trapped in a jar, starved for air but continuing to flutter your wings. No one set you free, not even when your light was dimming."

Something about his analogy makes my throat tighten with emotion. "So I cracked the jar and escaped?"

Lincoln nods. "You escaped *and* you survived. You did what you had to do." His eyes are warm. "Whatever happened to that girl at school, anyway?"

I grimace. "She walked away with a bloody, broken nose, but her parents sued mine, and that's when my parents were done with me."

Lincoln's jaw clenches. "Sounds like you should be thanking that girl's parents for getting you out of there."

Smiling, I slide my arms up his chest and around his neck. "Trust me, that's the way I see it now. That incident was just proof of the help I wasn't getting at home." My thoughts spinning, I shake my head with a soft laugh. "Okay, enough serious talk. I'm too tipsy for that." I lean in, kissing his delectable lips, loving the scratch of his beard against my chin. "Hmm." The noise comes from the back of my throat when I taste his lips. "You taste like Fire."

He grins before kissing me back. "So do you." He hums against my mouth. "Who needs a shot when they can have you?"

It's not just the alcohol that has my head buzzing. It's my heart vibrating with happiness and my soul blossoming under his spell. I lose all sense of myself, clinging to him as I crush my lips to his. A low growl rumbles between us, and I take that as a positive sign. Especially when his teeth take hold of my bottom lip and my tongue lashes into his mouth like a weapon.

His hands become greedy, pulling at my top and lifting it over my head. I follow his lead, removing his shirt and tossing it to the floor. An intoxicating thrall envelops us in a haze of heat and passion. He fumbles a little with the clasp of my bra, only turning me on more. The fact that he doesn't have the pinch-and-twist down like he's in a race to win some kind of trophy is a total green flag.

I'm still dizzy when his lips slip from mine, and he shifts me off his lap then pushes himself off the counter. There's no time to wonder what he's doing, not when he swivels me to face him, spreads my legs, and presses himself against me with another soul-rending kiss.

He practically bruises my lips before ripping his mouth away and reaching for the bottle of Fire. "Take a shot."

I let out a startled laugh. "What?"

He holds the bottle up to me. "Take a shot. I can't taste the whiskey on your lips anymore."

Still confused, I do as he says, tipping the bottle to my lips and letting the cinnamon-flavored liquor set fire to the back of my throat. When I pull the bottle away and my eyes catch on Lincoln's, his tongue darts out to wet his bottom lip, then he reaches for my skirt and tugs. I lift my hips to help him slide the fabric down around my ass then my legs. He takes my panties too, leaving me completely bare.

His heated gaze scrolls the length of my body in one slow sweep. His hands move to my ass as his lips find the space between my breasts, and he kisses me there before lifting his head to kiss my whiskey-coated lips.

"That's better," he murmurs against my mouth. "My turn."

He pulls away as I lift the bottle to his mouth, but he shakes his head with a wicked gleam in his eyes. "Not like that. I want to taste it *on you*." He lowers his body onto a stool then frames himself between my open legs. "Here." He grips my hand around the label and pulls it down before twisting my wrist, pointing the bottle down so reddish-brown liquid starts to slide out and down onto my belly.

A gasp slips past my throat as the cool liquid pools in my belly button. I try to tip the bottle back to stop the endless waterfall, but Lincoln's grip is too strong. Soon, the whiskey overflows in every direction, and his tongue is there, too, saving the liquid from reaching my clit. He licks each streak of liquid then sucks the pool in my belly button, making me shiver.

With one devilish glance up at me, he slides his mouth back down, this time flicking his whiskey-covered tongue over my clit. He laps me once, twice, then places both lips around my sensitive bud and begins to flick his tongue while sucking me hard. The cool buzz of sensation on my clit is overwhelming, thanks to the cinnamon liquor that adds to my pleasure.

My insides coil tightly as he moves my hand to set down the bottle and places both of his hands on either of my thighs. The pleasure has my head spinning and my muscles tense, the force of his mouth enough to make my body convulse. The bottle drops from my hands and lands on the counter with a thud, and my palms slam onto the bar top behind me as an orgasm lights me up from the inside, illuminating my release and sending me straight into a free fall. Like a firefly producing light to seek a mate, I know without a doubt that I've found mine.

My orgasm is already ebbing when Lincoln pushes two fingers deep inside me. "Y-yes." I wheeze the words, feeling the way my walls pulse around him.

His eyes roll with his groan. "Fuck, you're so wet, Evie. I should be inside you for this."

"What are you waiting for?"

"I want to memorize every inch of you to keep me company late at night." He rolls my sensitive clit with the pad of his thumb, like I'm not already revving up for a second release. "You know, since you won't move in with me."

His fingers enter me again, deeper this time.

"Keep that up," I moan, "and I just might."

His eyes widen, and he flexes his fingers, flicking them rapidly. It's like he's punishing me with pleasure, milking me for all I have to give. At least he's nice enough to let me come again before sweeping me off the bar and heading for the stairs to my apartment.

TWENTY-EIGHT

LINCOLN

Someone forgot to close the blinds.

Squeezing my lids tighter, I groan and roll over, expecting to bump into the petite bed hog who kept me up all night with her constant movements, every single one triggering me to tighten my hold on her. So when I realize there's nothing to hold onto, my heavy eyelids fly open. My heart rate instantly triples as I look around the small apartment in one full sweep but don't find her.

I rip the comforter away, ready to leap off the bed, when I hear the flush of a toilet and the squeal of the faucet followed by the sound of shower water hitting the porcelain tub. *Chill, dude.*

Everything seems to have me on high alert these days, between the recent murders, the break-in at the bar, then last night's fight. I just need to know Evie is safe. Knowing Francine and Lucy have been far away from this place is one thing I haven't had to stress about.

I consider joining Evie in her shower, but every muscle in my body is screaming with pain. *Why the hell am I so sore?*

I quickly think back to the events of last night—the fight with Billy, dinner on the bar, body shots, carrying Evie up the spiral staircase, and then a marathon of sex. With every give, there was a take followed by another give. Everything about being with Evie feels so new, like we're randy teenagers. I'd never tried so many different positions in one night, but we couldn't get enough of each other. I certainly couldn't get enough of *her.* I never will.

Stretching, I glance around the room, smiling at just how perfectly the entire vibe of the room matches Evie. The simplicity. The coziness. The mismatched color palette that makes no sense but somehow works well. And the rows upon rows of colorful book spines.

When I finally get the strength to slide from bed, I head to the kitchen and start the coffee pot. I'm going to need several cups to make it through the day. Lucy and Francine will be home in a few hours, and then it's daddy-daughter day—a time when I commit to doing anything and everything Lucy asks me to do to show her how much I missed her this weekend.

While waiting on the coffee, I peruse Evie's bookshelf the way she'd explored mine in both of my offices. She's such a book lover that it's interesting to see what she has in her personal collection. I had assumed I would find classic literature, like the book she was reading at the Deep Creek picnic area, but no. Evie's collection consists of a mixture of genres and subgenres.

I do a double take when I get to an empty spot on the shelf. At first, I assume it's just missing a section of books until I look deeper and find a framed piece of paper pushed to the very back. I'm not wearing my reading glasses, so I can't make out the words.

I reach for the frame and pull it toward me, confirming what I've already suspected. A familiar poem in familiar font. But how did Evie find it? Swallowing my surprise, I read the words I already know by heart.

A Flicker of Light
By Foster Pruitt

What happens when a light burns out?

Does it spark back to life or die?

That night, I heard a terrified shout

When a flicker lit up her cries

She died under a pale-blue moon

Bioluminescence bled her path

With blood-soaked hair and lake-shone shoes

Weapon placed in a moonlit bath

A final breath squeezed between bones

Her small body, so limp, now serene

A moment too late, her light flown

Yet somehow, I knew she was free

I didn't even notice the shower had stopped until the door to the bathroom creaks open. Evie walks out wearing one of her favorite yellow graphic tees paired with white cotton shorts. Her hair is still damp, and she's wearing her glasses. Completely transfixed by her, I almost forget what I'm holding until her gaze drops to my hands.

"You found my dirty little secret." She stands beside me and takes the frame delicately from my hands. "Foster wrote this." Her eyes find mine. "Carley's brother. I found it one day while scouring the internet for information on him. This was all I found, and I guess it brought me peace to know he was still alive out there somewhere."

My heart beats hard in my chest. "Your dirty little secret, huh?"

She smiles and sets the poem back on the shelf. "Isn't it a little weird that I obsessed over finding him then framed the only proof of his existence?"

I take her hand in mine, loving the way her cheeks go a shade darker. "After what you went through, I think it's perfectly acceptable, Evie. I'd think it would be weird if you didn't try to track him down."

She tilts her head, offering me a grateful smile. "You're not the least bit jealous that I'm keeping something from my first-ever crush?"

Chuckling, I shake my head. "After last night? No." I wink, and she blushes even more. "I'm sure the opposite is true too. I'm sure Foster looked you up."

She frowns, a glimmer of anger flashing in her eyes. "He's had fourteen years to find me. Trust me—that never happened." Then she shrugs. "It's not like I even really knew the guy. It was a little-girl crush for reasons I can't even remember. I just want to know that he's okay."

Wrapping her in a hug, I try to ignore the wild stampede in my chest. If there's one thing worse than going through tragedy, it's coming out of it alone. Evie has been so strong for so damn long, and I want her to know she doesn't have to carry the weight of that night alone anymore. I'll be here for her however she needs me to be.

"I better get going. I'll call you tonight after Lucy goes to bed. Maybe we can stop by Firefly tomorrow night for dinner?"

She slides her arms around my back. "I would love that."

I leave her with a slow kiss and a smile. "Me, too, Evie girl."

As I turn away, my eyes catch on the poem one last time before I walk out her apartment door, down the spiral staircase, and through the front door of the bar. All the while, the words from the poem spin round and round in my head like a record.

I was nineteen when I wrote that poem. It just came to life one day when I was sitting in the library, studying the biological makeup of fireflies. There was something about my studies when paired with the inspiration of Dr. Rohls's *Waterfall Effect* story and my yearning to stay connected to Carley, somehow, some way.

During my education, my thirst for knowledge grew, and putting pen to paper to let my thoughts pour out became increasingly therapeutic. Fast-forward to the Doctor of Psychology program at Duke where I spent three years writing a dissertation on human life in comparison to that of a firefly, and my obsession only became magnified, not dispelled.

I wanted to do more with my work, but I could never figure out what. I was sure moving to this town with all its history for me and my family would inspire words to come faster. While it has, distractions from a certain someone consume my mind.

The first dose of that inspiration came when I was seventeen years old. It was one week of camping, five nights of campfires, and several trips into the woods where we were all mesmerized by the synchronous fireflies. My family had driven in from a few towns over, so we'd seen the occasional flashes of light in the woods, but nothing like the magical show that lit the woods each night at Deep Creek Campground. It was a true phenomenon, one that lit up my little sister like nothing I'd seen before.

Until her light was put out by a monster.

And the worst part—that monster got away with it.

He's still out there, lurking in the Appalachian woods.

Stealing lives, one light at a time.

A predator now known as the Firefly Man.

I knew he would come back to this town.

The trail he's taken to claim his victims has led him straight back to his very first kill. And this time… I'm going to catch him.

e, too, Evie girl.

The door to my apartment clicks closed, but I'm frozen in place. My heartbeat takes off in a race, creating a heaviness in my chest. My breath goes shallow, and my mind hazes with a dizziness I haven't felt in years. I'm back there, lost in my past, fighting against the thoughts that scream into an abyss of my own creation.

Evie girl.

I don't believe in coincidences. There have only been two people in my life who have ever used that nickname. Patrick and…

Foster Pruitt.

Just thinking his name catapults my heart rate into a rapid flutter. I can't stop it. I want to ignore the panic working its way through every nerve ending. Breathing is hard, like sipping air through a straw. I can't get enough. My eyesight begins to darken.

Fuck. Not this feeling again. Panic attacks are my past. But suddenly I feel like a teenager again, unable to sleep, through a single night without seeing a dead body in the woods.

Somehow, I force my legs to move. I find my way to the bathroom and the medicine cabinet, and I search for my anxiety meds, finding only expired cyclobenzaprine, but I'm desperate. I swallow one down dry, then I slip back into bed, wrap myself in the covers, and focus on one slow breath at a time.

I try to ignore the scent of Lincoln's pillow as I squeeze my eyelids closed. While usually every reminder of Lincoln is welcome, it only worsens my anxiety now. Because I realize, as my heart begins to crumble, that I've fallen in love with a man I may not know at all.

Twenty-four hours. That's how long I allow myself to stay in the darkness of my thoughts before finally throwing clothes on and heading downstairs. The bar stayed closed on Sunday, and I had nowhere I needed to be. Lincoln tried calling and texting late that night, but I simply told him I was exhausted and was heading to bed.

That wasn't a lie. I woke up only to go to the bathroom and grab water. Otherwise, I let myself slip back into a sleep that I knew would turn into a nightmare before jolting me back awake. Another familiar pattern I remember from my teen years. After Carley's death, nothing ever felt normal, steady, *okay*. I was on edge, riddled with anxiety, and alone.

At some point in the middle of the night, I allow myself

to think about what produced my panic attack. Not that anything needs to cause an attack—they can come at random moments in the day—but this time, there was a clear trigger.

Evie girl.

The way Lincoln let that nickname slip out… It was like he had used it before, and now I'm certain that he has. Over time, I piece together every memory I have of Lincoln since his arrival in Bryson City and to try to understand how he could possibly be Foster Pruitt.

Did he change his name?

Did he stop talking to his family after Carley's death?

Did he write that poem?

My questions just keep coming, spiraling out of control to the point that they threaten to kick off another anxiety attack. But at the same time as I accept the fact that all the answers could be yes, I'm also finding reasons why all the answers could be no.

Every time my combative thoughts reject the notion that Lincoln is Foster, I picture Lincoln's face, specifically his eyes. Those forest-green irises with the golden swirl. While I had only been up close and personal once when we were in the dark woods of Deep Creek, I'll never forget the safety I found in his gaze. It's the same sense of safety I've felt with Lincoln. How did I not see the connection before?

Is there a connection?

I'm still hesitant to accept it, which is why I need to just confront Lincoln.

I rush down the staircase and out the door, locking it behind me. Then I march down the street, and I don't stop until I'm standing at the front door of Lincoln's office building.

Doreen is typing something on her computer, so she doesn't see me right away. When she does, she freezes completely then her brows bunch with confusion. "Evelyn, I don't believe we're expecting you this morning."

"I didn't make an appointment," I blurt. "I'm not a client of Doctor Reed's. I'm here for… personal matters. I need to talk to him."

Doreen's forehead smooths a bit, but she looks more disturbed now than confused. Lincoln has told me about the women who have made appointments to see him for less-than-honest reasons, and I know Doreen has taken notice of that as well, judging from what she told me in the face-painting booth. She probably thinks I'm one of them.

"I'm sorry, dear, but his first appointment isn't until ten o'clock, so he stepped out to run some errands."

Frustrated, I debate my next move. Do I try to track him down or stay here? "I can just wait in his office," I suggest. "He won't mind, I promise." I cringe when she hesitates. "Call him if you're not sure."

Her hesitation lingers a few moments longer before she sighs and picks up the phone. I listen closely, trying to make out his voice on the other end, but it's just a deep murmur.

Once she hangs up, she gestures to Lincoln's office. "Doctor Reed will be back shortly. You may go in."

I exhale my relief and enter his office, lightly closing the door behind me. At first, I don't know what to do with myself. It's one big, empty room without Lincoln in it. The shades are pulled up, revealing the view of the river and the morning foot traffic.

Looking around the familiar space, it's like I'm seeing everything for the first time, trying to place the boy I knew long ago behind the big gray desk, typing away on his sturdy laptop.

As hard as I try, I just can't see it, probably because I didn't really know that boy. Foster was just a crush, a stranger with gorgeous eyes and a love for his sister that made me completely obsess over him for one week. One week. That was the length of our time together, and it all ended so tragically. How could I have possibly known he was the man who was supposed to be my new therapist?

And the timing of it all…

My stomach knots when I think about J.D. and his sudden disappearance. His wife won't even talk about his whereabouts. Why? Is any of this connected at all? My thoughts churn, and my spine tingles. Nothing makes any sense, but I'm scared to learn what it all might mean.

Unable to sit still, I peruse his bookshelf, this time looking for anything and everything that can tell me who Dr. Lincoln Reed really is. So far, there's one thing that begins to coalesce—a connection that drives me closer to an answer I'm still not sure I want to accept.

Foster Pruitt seems to have disappeared at the exact same time that Lincoln Reed came into being—at least, as far as anything I could find online.

His bookshelf brings me no answers. Frustrated, I pull out the chair to his desk and sit. When I see his laptop sitting there, temptation overwhelms me. It seems he's always typing something on that thing. Maybe that's where I can find answers.

I don't even hesitate to open the laptop, though I get to the password screen and know it's a dead end. Sure, I could try to hack it by stringing together likely passwords, but that just feels like a waste of time.

More determined than ever, I yank open the center drawer, instantly scouring it for hidden passwords. Nothing. I move to the large drawer to my right that's labeled "Patients." Lo and behold, there's a stack of patient files. They're alphabetized by last name, but after Thornefield, the next file is Zimmerman. Vaughn is nowhere to be found.

I'm not sure if I'm relieved or frustrated by him not having a file on me. I guess that makes sense, considering I was never technically his patient. Still, it's frustrating to come up with nothing. I'm beginning to feel like a complete psychopath, rooting around his things.

That doesn't stop me from moving to the next drawer on the opposite side of his desk, but it's completely empty. Not even a speck of dust. I shut the door with more force than I mean to, causing it to slam. Cringing with guilt, I hear the rattle of books then the thud of something falling to the floor.

Panic squeezes my chest, and I look down to find the source of the sound, though it's deathly quiet now. Opening the drawer again, I look but see nothing—until I notice the back wall is shorter than the length of the drawer.

"What the—"

My heart begins to quicken as I push against the back wall of the drawer. It moves slightly, but I have to peer down to see if there's a way to remove it. At the very top, I find a small hole. I stick my pinky through it and pull, revealing a variety of spiral notebooks and a black hard case.

My hand shakes as I reach for the items, knowing whatever I'm about to see will change my entire life. After a long, deep breath, I let it out slowly and open the notebook that sits at the top of the pile. I don't expect the first thing I see to smack me right in the face.

It's my name scribbled in Lincoln's handwriting.

Evelyn Vaughn was always entranced by the synchronized fireflies.

What the fuck? The notebook shakes in my hands.

She believed their light to be something magical in her normally mundane existence. She looked at the fireflies as a symbol of hope—hope that she would one day escape the glass jar that contained her past, present, and future. At least that's what it felt like, living with parents who cared more about their social status than their daughter's existence.

The night her jar of fireflies broke in the dark woods of Deep Creek Campground, Evelyn watched how the fireflies escaped one by one into the night—and she knew that's what it would take for her to escape as well. She too felt trapped.

For a millisecond, I consider closing the notebook. It feels... personal, like a journal of some sort, but it has nothing to do with Lincoln. It's about me. It's everything I've told him about why I moved here. Like watching a train wreck, I can't look away.

After that tragic night at the campground, Evelyn

became haunted with what she witnessed as well as
the mystery that remained. Someone murdered Carley
Pruitt in those woods. Experts said the body was still
warm when they got to her. Rumors pointed to her
brother as the main suspect, but there wasn't
enough evidence to convict, which meant a murderer
was still on the loose. Because of this, Evelyn couldn't
seem to get a grip on her anxiety. Panic attacks and
paranoia led to her unleashing on a bully in high
school.

That was all it took to finally crack the jar.

I'm riveted by the story—my story—told through
Lincoln's perspective. The question is *why* is he writing it?
Maybe it's habit for him to write every little detail down.
Maybe he's just trying to make sense of the traumatic chaos
that brought me here.

My eyes slam shut, and I shake my head, chastising
myself for giving Lincoln excuses when I know now he's
hiding so much from me. I keep reading.

Evelyn was expelled from school, alienated from
friends, and kicked out of her house. She was sent to
live with Uncle Patrick, the only adult who had ever
seen any good in her. Under the care of a therapist,
Jenkins Wright, she took a job at her uncle's bar,
finished high school online, and found solace in her
new life.

I pause to take a breath. It's like he's writing a synopsis of my life in all its highlights. Is this why he came to Bryson City in the first place? Because he's Foster, and he's trying to find his sister's killer? He did mention that he became obsessed with the murders in college. Maybe there's much more to it than that. I focus back on the notebook.

Fourteen years later, Evelyn Vaughn is now a woman driven by routine, casual relationships, and a thirst for knowledge she can never seem to quench. She doesn't like change, and she's wary of strangers, yet she dreams of a life she's been conditioned to believe she will never have.

My knuckles whiten as my grip tightens on the notebook. What am I supposed to make of any of this? He's been studying me and summarizing my life like I'm the synopsis of his next fucking book.

Firefly Effect.

A gasp escapes at the realization. He had mentioned something about being inspired by his old mentor at Duke, Dr. Rohls, and how he wanted to take his dissertation and expand it to write something similar, based on the Firefly Man serial murders.

Setting the notebook aside with shaky hands, I reach for the rectangular black case. My chest is still heavy, making it hard to pull in a deep breath. That's all I want—for my lungs to expand so I can release some of this built-up tension. I'm afraid it's only going to get worse.

And it does.

Sitting in the open case is a stack of newspaper articles

paperclipped together. Articles that detail each Firefly Man killing. Beneath that are police reports from every incident, a map pinpointing each location, but it's the photos of the crime scenes that have me immediately slamming the case closed as tears begin to stream down my face.

What the fuck is going on? This can't all be from Lincoln's college research. Why would he have it stored in his desk? There are too many coincidences—too many flashing lights.

And with fireflies, the lights they carry aren't always used to find a mate.

Sometimes, they're used to send warning signals… in case of a threat.

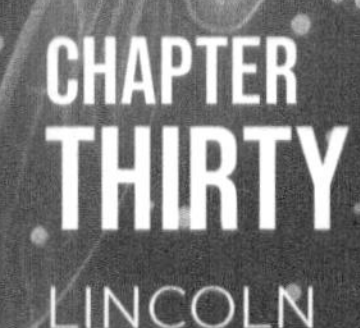

CHAPTER
THIRTY

LINCOLN

I'm in a rush leaving Lucy's school, knowing Evie is waiting for me at my office. She never answered her phone last night, so now my mind is going wild with the reasons she came to see me. I imagine her propped up on my desk with her stretchy maroon skirt and gray tee, her perfectly pink lips plumped and ready for me. A quickie before work. I can get behind that, considering I couldn't get her out of my mind as I was falling asleep last night.

A bunch of parents volunteered to bring breakfast to the classrooms as a coordinated act of kindness, and I didn't want to miss it. I'm so appreciative that Lucy has a great place to spend her days while I'm working and while Francine is off doing Francine things, but breakfast has been over for a solid hour.

It seems like every time I start to leave, someone tries to stop me to talk to me about the upcoming field trip to Deep Creek Campground. The school is organizing a nature day there on Friday where they take the kids to picnic, swim, and check out the wildlife, which is bad enough, but they're also trying to organize a community firefly walk that same night.

"We're all going to be chaperoning, Lincoln. We'll all keep an eye on Lucy," one of the moms says with encouragement. "She can stay and watch the fireflies with us too. She would love it."

Lucy hears this and clings to me with adorable puppy-dog eyes. "Please, Daddy. I want to see the fireflies."

I shake my head, hating that I must disappoint my daughter. "We'll go another time, Lucy."

"But I want to go with my friends." She frowns, eyes brimming with disappointment. "All my friends get to go."

Lilith comes up beside us and places a hand on Lucy's back. "You heard your daddy. He'll take you another time, sweetheart."

I give Lilith a grateful smile, but it doesn't help with Lucy's obvious sadness over the whole ordeal. She pouts even harder, folds her arms, and stomps away from all of us.

Sighing, I thank Lilith and wave to everyone else before jetting out the door.

Given this town's history with Deep Creek Campground and firefly walks, allowing Lucy to join in the festivities and even get tempted to join in the nighttime activities is a definite *no*. I can't help but question the daycare's judgment with continuing to plan for this field trip. Then again, I've come to realize that while the people of Bryson City are not desensitized to the fact that the Firefly Man *has* murdered here, they seem to make a concerted effort to not let it impact their lives and choices. Just because the Firefly Man never returns to the same place to kill, doesn't mean he won't.

I shiver thinking about the day Evie and I went tubing

by *the* campground and Evie completely froze. Just seeing the way she reacted to the memories of finding Carley continues to haunt me. If I could have told her who I was then, I would have. Sooner than that, even. She deserves to know. She deserves to find peace after all this time.

To avoid any further conversation about Lucy's field trip, I crumple up the permission slip and shove it into my pocket as I make my way out of the building. I don't even want to talk to Francine about it. If she doesn't see the permission slip, then she won't ask.

Francine doesn't know about Carley or my ties to that fateful night. No one in my life does, and that was always the plan. I was sworn to secrecy—something I didn't hesitate promising in hopes of finally catching my sister's killer.

"Lincoln," Lilith calls after opening the door to the building behind me. "Willow was asking for a playdate with Lucy this weekend. I know you're against the field trip, and that's completely fine, but what if I brought Lucy to our house after daycare on Friday? Then maybe she won't feel so terrible about missing the field trip with her friends. I'll make the girls my famous spaghetti." She gestures to me, as if in afterthought. "And you're welcome to come too."

Her suggestive eyes are blatant, and I try not to let my annoyance show. "Aren't you going on the firefly walk after the field trip?"

She shrugs. "We don't have to."

Then I frown, figuring I might as well ask the question that's been on my mind. "Why Deep Creek Campground? You could take the kids anywhere. Why that awful place?"

Lilith crosses her arms, her expression telling me she's considering my concern. "Deep Creek Campground itself isn't an awful place, Lincoln. If these kids grow up in fear because of something that happened fourteen years ago, then we are doing them a disservice. Why not teach them how to feel comfortable with nature and defend themselves rather than avoid something that will never happen to them."

"You don't know that," I snap. She flinches like I've just slapped her, causing guilt to swarm my chest. "I'm sorry, Lilith."

She shakes her head, her hand landing on my arm. "Don't be. I completely understand your concern, but I hate that you think I'm making a reckless choice with these kids. Their safety is my number one concern. Most of the parents will be there, so we'll have one chaperone for every two kids, at the very least. Besides. The Firefly Man has never killed in the same place before. I would think Deep Creek Campground is the safest place of all."

I want to chuckle at her logic, but there are too many other emotions swarming my chest. "Alright, well I appreciate you inviting Lucy over after daycare, but we already have plans." I pinch out a smile. "Sorry to cut this short, I really need to get back to the office."

I ignore her disappointed stare as I leave. Lilith is the least of my concerns right now.

As soon as I cross the parking lot, I take longer, faster strides. The distance between Lucy's school and my office is only six blocks, but I'm wishing I had brought my car now that I'm in a hurry. I pick up my pace to a light jog.

Doreen greets me at Calm Waters with a warm smile. "How was your daughter's event?"

I return her smile. "Oh, you know. All the kids fought over the chocolate-frosted donuts with sprinkles. Same old, same old."

She chuckles. "I'm sure the kids just loved getting a celebration for no reason."

"That is correct." I point to my office. "Evie in there?"

Doreen nods. "Waiting patiently."

A sigh of relief whooshes through me. "Great. Thank you, Doreen." Then I stop and stick my hand in my pocket, fishing around for my wallet, then I hand it to her. "Why don't you head next door for some coffee on me?" I wink. "For being so great."

Doreen's eyes widen, and she takes my wallet from my hands. "Thank you, Doctor. That's so sweet of you. Can I get you anything?"

I pat my belly. "Just ate. Thank you."

I wait for Doreen to leave and then walk the rest of the way to my office. At least now Evie and I will have complete privacy. Grinning, I open the door, my eyes aimed at my desk where I already fantasized she would be sitting.

And that's exactly where she is. What I'm not expecting is to find her with tears streaming down her face, my desk covered with my personal notebooks and the hard case filled with documentation of the Firefly Man killings.

Her accusing stare bores into mine. "What is this, Lincoln?" Her eyes narrow into a glare. "Or should I call you Foster?"

Fuck fuck fuck.

I rush forward, eyes wide as fear fills every pore in my body. "Evie, that's not…" I stop myself before I can lie to her. It's probably exactly what she thinks it is. So instead, I say the only thing I can think of. "I can explain."

She chokes out a laugh. "Explain what? That you've been lying to me for months?" She stands, her knuckles turning white against the pressure of her fists as they press into my desk. "That you've known who I was from the very first day I sat on that fucking couch?"

I stop a few feet away from my desk, now terrified to come any closer. Squeezing my eyes closed, I try to give her some time to realize that it's just me. That I'm not the threat.

"What is all of this? What does it mean?" She swipes at her eyes with the back of her hand. "Is it you? Are you the killer?" She picks up the stack of newspaper clippings and drops them back down on my desk. "Are these your souvenirs?"

A ball of anger bursts in my chest at her accusation. "You think I did that to Carley? To any of them?" It's my turn to glare. "No, Evie. I'm not the fucking killer. I'm just a broken man who lost his sister in the most horrific way possible—who then got locked away for nothing. I couldn't do anything for nearly a year. I was helpless. On top of that, I lost everything. My home, my family, my fucking sanity."

I draw in a deep breath to settle my emotions as much as possible. "By the time I was released, I knew what I had to do. I've been trying to track down Carley's killer ever since." I hesitate to tell her this next bit even though she's already figured it out. "That's why I came back here."

"But you brought your daughter here."

That comment is a punch in the gut I know I deserve. I fight the urge to jump to my own defense, knowing that once again, I need to be careful. "Lucy is safe."

Evie's jaw drops, her eyes flaring in anger. "How can you possibly know that, Lincoln?"

I hate the way I feel right now. Guilt stirs again, but this time it's mixed with anger. My eyes close tightly as a hiss of breath streams between my teeth. "I just know, okay?"

"Because she doesn't match the victim's profile? I hope that's not what you're thinking, because Carley didn't match the profile, either."

"Stop," I say, unable to take any more. "Lucy is safe." I open my mouth then close it again, debating my next words. "There's someone watching over her, okay? Someone I trust. I just…" I search her eyes. "I can't say more than that. I'm sorry."

I see the pain spread from her eyes to her entire expression. I'm not the man she thought she fell in love with, I know. But I'm still the man that's loved her for far longer than she can ever imagine.

"Did you think, in some sick, twisted way, that being my therapist could help you?" she asks. "Is that why you wanted me to remember more about that night?"

More guilt riddles my insides. "Initially, yes, my plan was to get to know you as my patient, and to uncover details about that night that no one but you knows. But Evie… I wasn't expecting to fall in love with you. That was never part of the plan."

Seconds turn into minutes until the flame of her anger begins to die down. Now, she seems more like a rain shower of curiosity. "Why didn't you just tell me who you were? I would have understood. I would have…" She sucks in a deep breath. "I told you that I'd been searching for you. I told you I had a *crush* on you way back then."

Her chin quivers, and she swipes at another tear. I can't stop myself from walking around my desk and wrapping my arms around her. When she doesn't push me away, I bury my face in her neck. "Evie, I'm so sorry. I couldn't say anything." This is the part when I might just lose her. "There's much more to this. But you need to know my feelings for you are very real."

She trembles in my embrace before placing her palms on my chest and pushing me away. "I don't know how I can possibly believe you now. I… I don't even know what to call you anymore. Are you Lincoln? Are you Foster?" She shakes her head.

Another dose of guilt injects my veins. "Lincoln is my name. It always has been. Foster was a nickname."

Evie's forehead wrinkles at the center. "What?"

I swallow hard. There's so much I've never told another soul, but here I am spilling my guts to the one person who might just hate me for it. "I told you about how I moved from foster family to foster family. That was the truth. When I came to live with the Pruitts, Carley started calling me 'Foster,' as in her *foster brother*, and it just caught on. When it came time for the adoption, the Pruitts changed my entire name."

She blinks at me, unbelieving. "Then you changed it back?"

My jaw clenches, and I nod, the pain bringing me right back to the day I found out I would never have a relationship with my adoptive family again.

"I didn't have a choice. My adoptive parents didn't want me anymore after Carley died." I sigh. "They filed for separation of my adoption while I was in jail, and the paperwork was finalized the day I walked out of there, leaving me without a home, without a place to go. Without a family."

Evie's gaze exudes a sympathy I don't deserve. "The Pruitts thought you did it."

My jaw tenses again. "The entire world thought I did it. Some still think so. Even you questioned it."

Evie tilts her head then shakes it as another teardrop falls down her cheek. "I know you didn't. I just didn't understand why you felt the need to lie to me about all of this. I still don't. Especially after we…" She blinks hard before pushing out a huge breath. "How could you expect for us to have a relationship when you were hiding your identity the entire time? Would you have *ever* told me?"

I hesitate, hating the pain that lances through her eyes. "I… I don't know. I couldn't risk you knowing any of this, Evie, especially if I was going to help you regain your memories. You need to understand—I did this for Carley."

Evie's shaking hands cover her face briefly before she lets them slip away. "But you were writing about me. In there." She points.

I look down at the familiar notebooks and nod. "I was."

"Why?" The anger in her voice tells me she's sick of asking questions.

"I told you about writing my dissertation on the Firefly Man killings. I've wanted to elaborate on it for years. It wasn't until I got here that I felt… inspired."

Her eyes widen, and I jump to say more.

"I would have never published it without your permission. Hell, I probably would have never published it anyway. As much as I always looked up to Dr. Rohls, I'm not him."

Tension squeezes my head, and I bring my hands up to massage my skull. "I've always used writing to cope with what happened that night. Living in a jail cell for months, not knowing when I'd ever get out, gave me a lot of free time to think. I had to get the feelings out somehow.

Between the poem, my journal entries, and my dissertation, it's *my* therapy. It's all I know."

Evie's anger seems to have faded. Her cheeks are stained with dried tears, and her eyes have even softened, but I don't mistake any of that for forgiveness. How can she forgive me when I'm only sorry that she found out about my lie?

"You said you came back to track down the Firefly Man." She squints. "Why here?"

I cringe, knowing this is where I need to be very careful. "I've been pulling together clues over the years. Studying the path of his killings, the details of the… act." I swallow, knowing I'm already passing my own boundary lines. "I can show you if you want."

Her eyes search mine before she nods.

I pull out my chair and gesture for her to sit. After she does, I open my laptop and enter the password. "If this gets to be too much, you have to let me know."

She looks from my screen to me then nods. "I will."

I reach forward and click around with the mouse to find the electronic whiteboard I've been working on for years. The file has multiple pages, revealing maps of the Smoky Mountains that point out all the locations of each killing. It contains details of each crime, each victim, and every single documented person in the nearby vicinity at the time of the murders.

"I've been looking for common threads. Patterns. Suspicious activity in and around the area before, during, and after the crimes were committed."

Evie seems to be scanning the documents I'm clicking through, her eyes shifting around rapidly. "The media has already called out some of the links," she points out. "Like the force of the attacks, the positioning of the bodies after the murders, and the fact that they've all taken place at or near campgrounds in the Appalachians—specifically in and around the Smoky Mountains." She lifts her eyes to meet mine. "Is there more?"

Nodding, I reach over her to zoom in on one part of the whiteboard. "Did you know my sister was the only female victim? She was also the youngest. But look at this." I illuminate a section that highlights the demographics of the murders. "Look at the ages of the victims in the order of the killings."

Evie looks closer for a second before her eyes widen. "They get older."

"By the same number of years between events."

She shakes her head before looking back at me. "What do you think that means?"

"I can't be sure, but I believe that means the killer likes his victims at or around his age. He also likes the element of surprise. He sneaks up on them and bashes them in the skull before they even have a chance to fight. In most cases, the one strike does the trick."

"But Carley screamed," Evie points out.

Another fact that's haunted me. "She must have seen him before the attack. Reports say she must have taken off and started running, then she was attacked from behind after she screamed."

Evie shudders, and I wish I could wrap my arms around her and tell her everything is going to be okay. I'm going to find the Firefly Man if it's the last thing I do. Then, just maybe, Evie can forgive me for the lies.

"You still haven't said what brought you back here, Lincoln. We haven't had a murder here since Carley."

I nod, knowing this might be the secret that makes her hate me the most. "I wanted to revisit the original murder, spend time here, with some of the people who were there that night. I thought maybe I could uncover some details that were missed back when they only had their eye on me."

She frowns. "That's true. They weren't even investigating anyone else. They probably missed so much."

Anger rumbles through me again. "They absolutely did." Again, I reach over to click through the documents pulled up on my website to get to the map of the Appalachians, zoomed in on the Great Smoky Mountain National Park—this one overlayed with dots and lines that showcase the Firefly Man's path. It's not a perfect route, and at first, it just looks like a bunch of curved and straight lines with no sequence whatsoever.

Until I pull up the next semi-transparent layer with a firefly drawn on top that perfectly connects the dots.

A gasp is wrenched from deep in her throat, and she leans closer, placing her finger on the last connected dot. Then she drags that finger right back to where the connections begin—on Carley Pruitt. She frowns, dragging back to the last kill location. "If you've been tracking this then why weren't you able to stop the last murder?"

"Evie..." My heart pounds furiously in my chest, despite the weight crushing it. "Tracking the killer to his next kill spot has proved to be impossible. There are dozens of campgrounds and miles of woods in all these areas. But this map does give me an idea of the direction he's heading next."

Her eyes go back to the map where her finger is, then her finger slowly draws a line down to finish the firefly symbol, landing on the original site of the killings. All the color drains from her face. "He's going to kill here again?"

"It's possible, but this town is shit at heeding any type of warning. Not even the media can instill the fear necessary to keep people out of the woods."

She leans back slightly. "Do you think it was the Firefly Man who left that note in my bar?"

"Whoever wrote it certainly wanted you to think so." There's no point in lying now. I search her eyes, worried what this next bit of information might do to her. "Which leads me to wonder…"

Evie looks pale as she begins to realize what I'm saying. "W-what?"

"If the killer wrote that note and that firefly map is accurately assuming the killer is returning to the original kill site, maybe the Firefly Man isn't just returning here… maybe he lives right here in Bryson City."

The next week is a whirlwind. I'm a robot before, during, and after work. My staff, somehow, just knows to pick up the pieces. They don't ask too many questions, and part of me wonders if they assume Lincoln and I broke up—not that we were ever officially together.

He hasn't come by like he used to, thanks to my request that he give me some time. That doesn't mean he hasn't parked his car outside of Firefly after Lucy goes to bed, all to watch over my building until five in the morning. Then he returns home, gets Lucy ready for school, works, and comes back for his nighttime shift.

I refuse to let him in. I'm still grappling with his lie. Still trying to make sense of the fact that he—*Foster*—has been out there the whole time while I've been scouring the internet for any sign of him. In a way, I'm angry that he's let fourteen years go by without confronting me. Maybe a little embarrassed too. I was the closest link he had to Carley after his family rejected him, yet he never came to check on me. Never wanted to know how I was doing.

Foster and Lincoln are beginning to blur into the same person, making the man I fell for so hard and fast into a complete stranger. How does that happen? And how do I get past this? Or worse, *do I* get past this? I have so many questions but no one to help me find the answers. I won't go to Lincoln, and I still can't get ahold of J.D.

Frustration rushes through me as I look at the time, knowing what I must do. It's four in the evening on Thursday. That's three hours until Kyle's shift ends, giving me just enough time.

After letting Kyle know I'll be back, I skip out the front door and quickly tap into my rideshare app. Ten minutes later, I pull up to J.D.'s driveway, but no cars are parked in the drive. I let my driver leave anyway, determined to wait as long as I need to. I'm not leaving until I speak to him.

I approach the front door. When I raise my fist to knock, I stop myself, knowing that I'm risking a repeat of the events of last time, that Gena will open the door and turn me away. There needs to be another way to get to J.D.

"Come to the back," a male voice whispers.

My heart catches in my throat and I look around, trying to find the owner of the voice.

"J.D.?" I ask, still searching the open space around me.

"He's watching you." Another whisper, this one more haunting than the first.

I look behind me and notice the same faded black car across the street. *Holy shit, someone is watching me.*

"We don't have much time," the voice says.

Tearing my eyes from the black car, my heart begins to beat fast. I should run—just take off at a sprint and get the hell out of here. But while I know spending one more second here is only sending me into a deep end when I've never learned to swim, I'm so desperate for a chance to speak with J.D. that I don't listen to my own warnings.

A stone path circles the house, overgrowth sticking up between the rocks. I follow it blindly, my mission to see J.D. surpassing any regard for my safety.

At the back of the house, nothing is fenced in. It's just an acre or so of land and woods surrounding it. A chill snakes up my spine as I turn back to the house.

"He can't know we're talking," whispers the same voice from the front of the house. It seems to be coming from a screened window.

The lump in my throat is leaving little room to swallow. "W-who?" As if I need confirmation. He could only be talking about one person.

"Why are you here, Evelyn?"

I squeeze my eyes shut, finally recognizing the famil-iarity of the voice, even in a whisper. J.D. was my only comfort for so many years, besides Patrick. "I need to talk to you," I whisper back. "There's no one who understands me like you do."

"What about Doctor Reed?"

I let out a shaky breath. "You mean Foster Pruitt?"

Silence fills the air. "I'm sorry, what?" J.D.'s voice rises slightly.

I nod, looking in the direction of the window. Now that I can finally place it, I can see an outline of a figure behind the screen. "Foster Pruitt *is* Doctor Lincoln Reed. The Pruitts were his adoptive family, but when he went to jail, they reversed the adoption. He's been tracking his sister's killer from campground to campground since he started to connect the dots. He thinks the Firefly Man lives *here*. In Bryson City."

More silence fills the air, and chills explode all over my body.

"I think he might be right," J.D. says.

I balk, confused how he could know such a thing. "What? Why would you say that?"

J.D. pauses again, and now I know he's just trying to choose his words carefully. "Because… I fear the killer is one of my patients."

Fear seizes me—the killer is so close and possibly someone I know. Even worse, it's someone who has sat on the same couch as I have with J.D. and even possibly Lincoln. But my fear turns into dread, then into anger.

I ball up my fists, tired of the game being played by the two men I've trusted most in my life. "Tell me what's going on. Please."

"I can't, Evelyn," J.D. says. I can hear his desperation. "Just be careful. Please. You're not safe. No one is. Not until the Firefly Man is caught."

I squeeze my lids together, confused at what to do with this information. "If you think the killer is one of your patients, can you at least tell me who?"

Several beats pass before he speaks again. "He's coming." The rushed whisper makes all the hair on the back of my neck stand on end. "Go, Evie! Leave now."

The image behind the screen disappears, and I'm left with panic beating at the walls of my chest.

All I can do is run.

"You sure you don't need me to help?" Janessa asks when she swings by to get her paycheck later that evening.

I'm trying so hard to not show the jitters I still feel long after leaving J.D.'s house. I raise my hand to wave while my head stays down as I wash the remaining dishes. "I've got it. Have a good night, and thank you for everything this week."

Janessa grins and walks out the door. I turn off the hot water and wipe my hands, intending to lock up behind her. Before I can make it halfway to the door, Lincoln slips inside and pushes his back against the door.

I halt in my tracks.

He raises his hands in instant defense. "Please, Evie. Can we just talk for a minute?"

Everything J.D. said earlier rushes back, my chest swarming with conflicting emotions. "I'm not ready, Linc." Even his nickname feels foreign to me now. "I'm still so confused."

He lets out a breath and nods. "I know. And I'm sorry I'm the reason for it all. I don't deserve your forgiveness. I don't deserve your understanding. What I feel for you is real, Evie, and while I don't expect you to see that after everything I've told you, I do need your help to find Carley's killer."

His eyes plead with mine. "Please, Evie. Let me help you remember."

After everything I've learned in the past twenty-four

hours, I didn't expect for him to ask for my help. At the same time, I'm relieved he asked. "I do want to remember."

His eyes widen, illuminating the forest green I love so much. "So you'll let me help you?"

I let out a breath and nod. "On one condition."

He nods. "Anything."

I search his eyes, building the courage to ask for what I really, truly want. "Tell me who you really are. Tell me everything. No more secrets."

CHAPTER
THIRTY-TWO

LINCOLN

"Evie, I…" I stop talking when she starts to shake her head.

"Tell me the truth, Lincoln. The whole truth. Or you can turn around and leave."

She has me. She doesn't know how or why, but she found her bargaining chip and isn't afraid to use it. I consider my options.

I could tell her what I'm hiding and relieve myself of all secrets, but who does that put at risk?

I could turn around and walk back out that door, but then I lose Evie and my chance of digging further into her memory for answers.

Sighing, I nod. "Okay." I look around the empty bar. "But not down here."

Her eyes are still narrowed on me. "Wait here while I shut down, then we can go upstairs."

I pull out my phone to send Francine a warning that I might be home very late. She assures me she's got it.

Then I send another, more troubling text.

Lincoln: I have to tell her.

Dylan: I warned you this would happen, man. This is why you never should have gotten involved.

Lincoln: You know I didn't have a choice.

Dylan: Yeah, but you're comprising the whole operation.

Lincoln: How? She agreed to help me if I tell her what I'm hiding.

Dylan: Jenkins probably said something to her.

I dwell on that thought for a second, knowing Dylan had seen her go around to the back of Jenkins's home. Just as Dylan was coming to scare her away, she ran away like a crazy person.

Lincoln: If he did, she'll tell me. This needs to happen.

Lincoln: I need you to keep an eye on my house. I've got things covered here for the night.

Dylan: All right, man. You got it. Good luck.

After I stick the phone in my back pocket, I look up to find a rattled-looking Evie. She does a half-assed job of cleaning before she tosses the towel onto the nearest table. Then she locks up behind me and walks straight up the spiral staircase to her bedroom behind the wall of books.

It's not until we're both inside with the door closed that she turns and speaks to me. "You should know, I went to see

J.D. today." She stares me down like she's waiting for my reaction, but I have none. I already knew.

"Did you talk to him?"

Her eyes narrow at me, and for a second, I think she might know a hell of a lot more than I've let on. "What do you think?"

It's my turn to narrow my eyes. "I think… if you expect honesty from me, then you need to be honest with me too."

She blinks, her brow creasing slightly. "That's fair. But why do I get the feeling you already know the answer to your question?"

I let out a heavy breath. "Because I do."

Anger flashes in her eyes. "What the hell, Lincoln? You followed me to his house, didn't you?"

"No. I didn't follow you."

"But someone did."

The silence is enough to answer her question.

"Who?" she asks.

I shake my head. "Evie, I promised to tell you everything, and I will. As long as I have your word that you'll help me in return."

A flicker of pain flashes through her eyes. "You want my memories."

I step closer, desperate to hold her, but stop in my tracks when she flinches. "I want everything." My voice cracks with emotion. "All of you. Your memories included."

"Why is J.D. hiding in his house? What is he afraid of?"

I take a long, deep breath, giving me time to reframe my thoughts to start at the beginning of my transfer to Bryson City. "Three years ago, I joined the FBI as a special agent. Dr. Rohls connected us. With my clinical-psychology expertise, my connection to the original victim, and my dissertation on the Firefly Man killings, the Bureau was interested in tapping into my knowledge to help build a theoretical profile on the killer."

Evie's delayed reaction makes me nervous, but when realization hits her, I see the color start to drain from her face. Her mouth parts ever-so-slowly, and her next blink is more like a flutter. "You're in the FBI?"

I suck in a breath, hoping this confession allows me to feel relief at some point. "I've only been contracted to join the BAU for this job."

Evie frowns. "The what?"

Cringing, I shake my head. "Sorry. The behavioral analysis unit. They investigate violent crimes. I'm a forensic psychologist on a task force. Anyway, until Lucy came into the picture, I had been traveling all over the Smoky Mountains with my partner, Dylan. You might have seen him lurking around."

Evie sucks in a breath. "The man in the hoodie?"

I cringe again, hating how much I've had to keep from her. "Yes."

"Was he the one who followed me to J.D.'s house?"

Taking a deep breath, I nod. "That's him. We follow the crimes, investigate each murder, profile the people there, then move on. We were never in one town for more than a few months."

"And when Lucy was born, you… what? Just stopped traveling?"

"Basically," I admit. "I went on leave, and honestly, Evie, I wasn't planning to ever return. Lucy was my number one focus. I had a new purpose. I was working on letting go of my past and everything I had been holding onto for so many years."

Evie's eyes search mine like her brain is working over-time to catch up. "Then that man was murdered three months ago a few towns away from here."

Emotion swims in my chest. "That's when I started to pick up on the pattern. It was the first time we were able to start looking at the Firefly Man's hometown versus focusing on locations of upcoming killings—which are random, to an extent," I explain. "He might choose a city, but it would be damn-near impossible to guess which campsite and which piece of land he will go to. After I offered up my theory of where he most likely lived, they asked me to rejoin the task force. We were able to confirm that the deceased man was a Smoky Mountain hiker who had passed through Bryson City not long before his death. That's when we started talking to Jenkins."

Evie's frown deepens. "You were here in town before you moved here?"

I grimace. "Yes. Only because we were interviewing Jenkins. At first we were just talking to him about the hiker and the profile of the killer we had put together by then. We wanted to see if anything matched any of his patients."

Evie's eyes widen. "Did he identify anyone?"

Tilting my head, I tense. "I can't tell you that."

"Why not?"

"Evie," I say, frustrated now. "I'm telling you everything I absolutely can without compromising the work we've done. You shouldn't be involved at all."

She glares at me, her chin quivering. "I've been involved ever since I found Carley dead. Her death is a part of me, too, Lincoln."

A breath rushes out of me as my eyes close. "I know. Please don't take this as me discounting your part in all of this. I'm just trying to keep you safe." I hope she can see the plea in my eyes and hear the desperation in my tone.

"Safe from whom, Lincoln? If it's someone close to me, I should know. Especially after the break-in. You can't sleep outside the bar every night."

Anger mixed with possession and love rages in my chest. "I'd rather you just move in with me, but we both know I already tried that."

She scowls. "I can't even trust you. Why the hell would I move in with you?"

My chest burns like she touched a torch to it. I deserve her anger. I deserve these words. "Fine. Hate me if you want, but that won't keep me from loving the hell out of you. Until this evil son of a bitch is caught, I'll do whatever is necessary to keep you safe. If I don't have my eyes on you, then someone else does."

I step forward again, closing the gap between us so I can stare down into the depths of her eyes, shining like swirling sapphires. "And when this is all over, I won't stop until I make you understand why it all had to happen this way. Why I had to move here. Why I had to get close to you. Why I had to get you to talk to me. And why I couldn't help falling madly in love with you."

Evie flinches. "You can't tell me you love me. Not right now. I'm too mad at you, Lincoln."

My hand moves to cup the back of her head. "Be mad at me all you want. You have every right. But I still love you."

"You took over for J.D. so you could interview his clients," she accuses.

My nod comes slowly, the fear of her pushing me right back out that door a definite possibility. "Yes."

"But I wouldn't take the consultation, so you sought me out."

Again, I nod.

This time, the pain in her expression is accompanied by tears. "I opened up to you."

A force strangles my heart at just the sight of her misery. My hands instinctively reach up to cradle her cheek. "Exactly, Evie. You opened up to me. We weren't in a session. You weren't under my care. You opened up to me as a friend, and I listened. That day tubing with you is one of the reasons I started falling in love with you."

She squeezes her eyes shut again like she's trying to stop more tears from falling, but they seep out anyway. "How can you say that when your reasons for getting to know me were all based on a lie?"

I growl and lean my forehead on hers. "This is so much more complicated than that. I came here for my sister, but I'm staying for you. You, Lucy, Francine—you're my fucking world, and I refuse to let you think anything else. I never stopped thinking about you after Carley died, and not just because of her death."

I pause, thinking back. "I remember how scared you were to go against Patrick's rules. I remember how you giggled all day long with my sister. I remember the joy that lit up your face every time we watched the fireflies. I never stopped thinking about the way you looked at me. And even though it was so fucking wrong, considering how young you were back then, I was looking at you too."

She grips my shirt as new streams of tears slip down her cheeks. "Stop," she whispers. "You're making it impossible for me to hate you."

Hope ignites in my belly, illuminating the darkness we

share like the single flash of a firefly's light. "Because you don't hate me. You can't hate me, Evie. We're connected, you and me. We'll get through this, okay?" I brush her cheeks with the pads of my thumb, drying her tears. "I promise I'll tell you everything I can."

She opens her watery eyes. "Is Jenkins a suspect?"

I frown. "Everyone is a suspect at this point, but he's been complying."

"How?"

"By allowing me to take over his practice and disappearing to make it all believable." My hands move from her face to her hips. "If my suspicions are accurate, then whoever we're dealing with isn't a stranger. In fact, it might even be someone very close to you. We think the killer is one of Jenkins's patients and was at Deep Creek with us during Carley's murder. Most of the campers there that trip lived in Bryson City. My family—the Pruitts," I correct myself, "were the only out-of-towners. None of the Firefly Man's victims live in the same town where they were killed."

Her shoulders sag. "But you have leads?"

I nod. "Yes."

"Who?"

"I can't tell you that, Evie. I'm sorry."

She searches my eyes again. "Does Francine know about your job? About your past?"

"No." I swallow the quickly forming lump in my throat. "She knows nothing."

Evie's eyes widen. "Does Lucy know about Carley?"

I shake my head, and my reply comes out in a guilty whisper. "No." I squeeze my eyelids shut then open them again. "One day, I'll tell Lucy about her Aunt Carley, but the undercover work I'm doing needs to stay between us for now."

She blinks at me a few times, seeming to process everything I've just told her. "So, now what?"

My entire body softens, wanting nothing more than to wrap her in my arms until this whole mess is over. "We can try to jog your memory."

She shudders. "I'm scared, Lincoln."

My heart swells. "I know, but I'm here, and I'm not letting anything happen to you."

She waits a few beats like she's trying to psych herself up, then she pushes back with a nod and a lifted chin. "Okay. I think I'm ready."

Relief blows out of me in a rush of air, relaxing my shoulders. I reach my hand out to hers. "Why don't you lie down and get comfortable? Then we'll get started."

Evie sits back on the bed and takes a deep breath before lying back. I turn off the big overhead lights and take my time coming back to her, giving her a moment to relax.

I sit down in the oversized chair near her bed and lean back, admiring Evie while praying that this time, we can bring out more memories.

"I'm not going to take you as deeply as I did last time. Can you pick up where we left off last?" I speak slowly, calmly, providing a safe environment in which her brain can roam free. "Picture yourself back in those woods, leaving Carley and me to go get help."

She flinches slightly at my words. "I still can't believe you're Foster."

I reach toward her and squeeze her hand. "I know. If it helps, try to avoid the connection right now. The boy is Foster, and he's holding his sister, thinking of any possible way to bring her back to life and kill the monster who did this to her."

She squeezes my hand, causing the same sensation in my heart. "I can do that." Her voice is so soft and empathetic despite her being mad as hell at me for all my secrets.

Silence fills the room, creating a heaviness that weighs us both down—but sometimes that's how waiting feels. I allow her to explore her thoughts without interjecting, until a gasp rises her chest.

"There's someone else in the woods."

The critical knee-jerk reaction in me wants to remind her that there were many people in the woods that night, but I refrain.

"Someone's running. It's so dark. I can't see who, but they're running away from me." She balls her fist in frustration. "I follow them. I'm screaming for help, but… they're running faster." She frowns, her eyes closing tighter. "Someone grabs me. I scream again." Her face twists. "He's covering my mouth, whispering for me to be quiet."

Suddenly, Evie's entire body freezes, and color fades from her cheeks.

"What is it, Evie? What do you see?"

She shakes her head. "It's not what I can see. It's what the man says next."

My chest tightens. "What does he say?"

She gasps. "Be quiet, or you're next."

I freeze. "Was it him? The Firefly Man"

Lines crease her forehead. "I don't think so," she whispers, then she sucks in a stuttered breath. "He held me to him for a long time, like he was buying time for someone to get away. I was so scared." She quakes with those words.

"Did he hurt you?"

Evie shakes her head. "No." She frowns again. "It was almost like he was trying to calm me down and protect me."

Relief tries to knead at my tense shoulders. "Did he say anything else, Evie?" I try to hold back my desperation to get inside her head, to see what she's seeing, to hear what she's hearing.

She nods. "He kept saying it was an accident and that he felt so awful. He failed someone, but he didn't say who. He didn't know it would come to this."

I catalog every detail of what she's telling me into the buckets of evidence I've created in my mind. There's not much to her story, but the smallest elements are what create and place the final puzzle pieces in my mind.

There's just one more detail I need her to try to remember.

"Who was the man holding you, Evie?"

She shakes her head. "I don't know. I couldn't see him, and he was whispering so I couldn't place his voice."

"That's okay. Try to think about other details. His height, his build, his scent."

She squeezes her eyes closed again. "I'm trying. Everyone seemed taller to me back then. I was a short little thing."

"Think about the men who were there that night and try to place him that way. Jimmy, Jenkins… Patrick?" I hesitate on the last name, knowing she's not ready to consider her uncle a possible suspect.

She jerks, her eyes flying open. "There's no way Patrick is involved. I would know if that was my uncle behind me. It wasn't."

I move to the bed, hating that I've upset her. "I'm not

saying he did anything, but whoever this man is, it sounds like he's covering for the killer. I wasn't counting Patrick out, but you're right, you would know if it was him."

Her eyes are pleading for understanding. "It wasn't Patrick." She sits up like she's remembering something else. "After the man finally let me go, I ran straight to Jimmy's campsite. They were both there, drinking beers."

"Okay." I lean forward as more puzzle pieces click together. "What else did you see at the campground? Was anyone acting suspicious?"

"I remember feeling… confused and disoriented, and I didn't know what to say about the man who had just held me captive in the woods. So I told them about Carley. We called the cops together."

She pauses and shakes her head. "The rest you know. The cops came, and I led them to Carley. And the next thing I knew, you were being handcuffed by the cops." Tears slide down her cheeks again. "I tried to tell them you had nothing to do with it, but they didn't want to hear what I had to say until I came down to the station. I did everything they asked, Linc. I told them every single detail, I begged them to listen, but they kept getting caught up in the fact that you and I got separated for as long as we did."

Frustration rummages through my chest as old feelings surface. "But she was attacked before we got to her. I didn't even see her when we got separated." I try not to beat myself up for the millionth time over letting her take off without me in the first place.

Evie's frown deepens. "She was wearing your black sweatshirt when we found her dead, Lincoln."

The reminder of that small fact crushes me. "When I got to the lake and didn't see her, I was worried. It gets chilly at night, especially down by the water, so I dropped my sweatshirt there, knowing she would grab it if she got cold."

She blinks like she's remembering something. "That night *was* especially chilly." She looks at me. "Is any of this helping you?"

She has no idea. "Yes and no. We were still looking into Patrick and Jimmy, even though your testimony stated they were at the campsite during the murder. We couldn't be certain that you weren't just protecting your uncle and his friend. That hour missing from your alibi was critical. We still have work to do to narrow down our list of suspects."

My heart throbs when I see her face fall with disappointment. I squeeze her hand. "We're close, Evie. So close. It's been fourteen years. Remember that, okay? We're going to catch this guy."

She slips the hand I'm not holding to my shirt, clutching it like she loves to do. It makes my chest fill with warmth, knowing I can provide her a smidgen of safety in our fucked-up situation.

"I can't even imagine anyone in this town wanting to hurt all those innocent people," she says. "It doesn't make any sense."

I reach for a strand of hair draped over her shoulder and brush it back. "Of course it doesn't make sense. You're good to the core."

But she's so deep in her thoughts, it's like she doesn't even hear me. "Is the campfire story true? Is the killer really going after people who hurt fireflies?"

"Ahh, I see you haven't read my dissertation."

She cocks her head, a hint of a smile teasing her lips. "Maybe if you published it, I would."

"Touché. I guess I can give you the CliffsNotes version." I place my hand on her silky thigh, waiting to see if she will remove it, but she doesn't. "We are all fireflies," I say, starting the same way my dissertation starts, "roaming through the sky. We seek a mate to call our own, until the day we die. Our sparkling light shines ever-so-bright in a nighttime serenade."

Evie blinks back at me, her entire body softening with my words. "That's beautiful, Lincoln. Is that another poem?"

My cheeks heat. "An unfinished one, but yes. My theory started a long time ago, right after Carley's murder. Up until her death, the campfire tale was just that. Hers was the first, so I think the killer used the story to justify their actions."

"That makes sense," she says. "Like a copycat in a way."

"Exactly."

She shudders. "How are you going to track him down?"

I don't want to give Evie any more details than she already has. Knowing her, she'll hunt down the Firefly Man herself. "I think we've done enough detective work for the night." I slide from the bed to stand. "Get some rest, Evie. I'll be outside until morning."

Something flashes in her eyes that I have trouble interpreting. Fear? Disappointment? Anger? I'm not sure.

"Can't you stay?" she asks, and it jolts me like a bolt of electricity.

"Really?"

Her whole body sags with her next exhale. "You're already here."

I move back toward the bed so fast, it's like I never left at all. "You don't have to ask me twice."

She scoots over and slips under the sheets, not bothering to change into something more comfortable, so I follow her lead. I climb under the sheets and wrap my arms around her waist, pulling her back to my front and sighing into her hair.

She melts into the pillow as her eyes flutter closed. I watch her drift away in the comfort of my arms, waiting until she's fully asleep to speak.

"I love you, Evie girl."

I felt Lincoln leave at some point in the early morning, and I opened my eyes just enough to see that the sky was still dark outside. Other than that disappointing loss, I strangely had the most restful sleep.

When my eyes fully open, I stretch and roll to Lincoln's side of the bed, inhaling the scent that he left in his wake and sighing.

At one point, I thought I might never forgive him for lying, but that was fleeting. Somehow, deep down, I knew Lincoln has been doing what he must do, and for good reasons. I can't even say I would make a different decision in his shoes, which is why I had truly forgiven him before he'd even stepped into Firefly last night. Before I knew there was something holding him back more than just his need for secrecy.

He's part of the fucking FBI.

I thought I needed time to process it all, but I realized last night that I could process the situation *with* him rather than without him, and that's exactly what I plan to do.

from here on out. At the end of the day, the only thing that matters is finding the Firefly Man and bringing justice to the lives of his innocent victims and their families.

Somehow, I manage to be more like myself when my morning shift begins. By the time the night shift comes, I let the distractions of work take over my mind.

It's a busy night, so Janessa is helping me behind the bar while Armando and Kyle wait on the tables. It almost feels like old times, when the Firefly Man was dormant and worries about a fresh death weren't the hot topic around the Smoky Mountains.

I half expect Lincoln and Francine to walk into Firefly with Lucy around five o'clock. I never expected to miss that little girl so much, but it's been over a week since I saw her last, thanks to recent revelations.

Frowning, I turn away from the bar and pluck my phone from my back pocket. Lincoln hasn't texted in a few hours, which isn't abnormal with how busy he's become at work, but something makes me uneasy after our conversation last night.

Chalking my discomfort up to the unearthing of suppressed memories, I tuck my phone back into my pocket and turn to help the next customer. My whole body lurches with surprise when I see Uncle Patrick staring back at me with a grin.

"Patrick!" I squeal before leaping over the bar to throw my arms around him.

"Whoa," he says with his familiar chuckle. "I knew we should have put you into gymnastics when you were younger."

"Ha." I squeeze him tight. "We both know I would have

failed miserably, thanks to the lack of coordination bestowed upon us Vaughns."

"Speak for yourself." He pulls back before shimmying his shoulders. "This old man's got moves for days."

I smile as my chest swells with emotion. "I've missed you."

He tilts his head. "I've missed you too, Evie girl. So, what do you say? Want to pour your favorite uncle his favorite drink? I'm a paying customer tonight."

I laugh and walk back behind the bar to serve him. He tells me all the interesting details of his travels and how he's already planning another trip around the Smokies. A knot begins to form in my chest. "Are you sure that's a smart idea?"

Patrick tenses slightly, but his voice is light. "The Firefly Man hasn't yet stopped me from doing what I love most. He's not going to stop me now."

I wouldn't be so sure of that. But according to Lincoln, the killer only goes after men his own age, which puts Patrick out of the risk zone. Then again, Carley didn't match up to that profile.

"Evie, you okay?"

I look up to find my uncle in mid sip, staring back at me with a frown.

"I'm fine. Sorry, just spaced out."

Realization dawns on his face. "The murders are closer to home than they have been in fourteen years," he says.

I nod, knowing I can't tell him a shred of information that I know. "They are, and Carley's been heavy on my mind because of it."

He lifts his tumbler in the air. "To Carley. May her soul be resting where the Firefly man can't reach her."

I pour myself a shot and toast with him. The liquid burns down the back of my throat, sending a chill through my body. "I think I needed that."

Patrick grins. "You sure did. So, what's been going on with you?"

"Oh, you know," I say, cleaning off the counter to avoid his gaze. "Just trying to keep things afloat." When he doesn't respond, I begin to think I'm in the clear.

"And how are things with my new tenants? Doctor Reed taking care of the place?"

I shrug, trying to give him my best nonchalant attitude. "Yeah, I think everything is all good over there."

I finally look up to find one of Patrick's brows raised. "You think?"

Cringing inside, I smile as widely as possible. "I helped them with the furnace in the guesthouse. Lucy, Lincoln's little girl, loves my old room. I think they're really enjoying it here."

Patrick sits back, seemingly satisfied. "Great. Sounds like you're handling everything really well. Thank you, Evie."

Relief floods me now that we've entered a new topic. "You're welcome, Patrick. Glad I could hold down the fort while you were away. When do you think you'll head back out?"

"In about a week or so. I want to get some maintenance done on the RV and check on my rental properties before we head out for a longer period of time. And..." He bestows on me a bigger smile. "I want to officially hand the bar over to you."

My jaw drops. "R-really? I mean, I know you've been talking about it, but so soon? Are you sure?"

Patrick brushes his hands together in two claps, gesturing that he's washing his hands on the place. "This isn't my dream anymore, Evie. It's yours." He looks around proudly. "You've earned this, you know? From the first day you stepped foot in this space as a kid, when it was nothing but concrete floors and bare-brick walls. You may not be getting the Vaughn fortune from your parents, but you're getting something that means a little bit more to the both of us."

Emotion clogs my throat. "That means a lot to me, Patrick. Thank you."

We exchange smiles, the sentiments running deep. I don't know what would have happened to me if Patrick wasn't there to step into the role as parent when I needed one so desperately. He hasn't missed a single milestone in my life, and for that, I'll be eternally grateful.

I hold up the bottle of scotch. "Another?"

He sticks out his glass. "You need not ask. It's a keep-em-coming kind of night."

Laughing, I finally feel some sense of normalcy, and I'm grateful for that. Weight feels like it's been lifted off my chest. For once in a very long time, everything seems like it just might be okay. At least, that's how it feels until Officer Gabe walks in with a sour look on his face.

He walks straight up to the bar and sits down next to Patrick. He doesn't even look at Patrick when he claps him on the back. "Nice to see you home, old man."

Patrick elbows him in the side, causing Gabe to wince. "Watch yourself, son. I've got more powerful pistols than that one in your holster."

Gabe chuckles. "Only you would threaten an officer."

"And only you would be stupid enough to fuck things up with my niece here." Patrick winks at me.

Gabe turns his amused eyes on me. "Oh, you haven't heard? Our little Evie is spoken for."

Patrick's face twists in confusion. "What?"

Gabe leans back in his chair and raises his brows at me. "Well, go on, Evie. Tell your uncle what you've been up to while he's been gone."

I roll my eyes and shake my head, wishing I could ignore him. "Shut up, Gabe."

Patrick leans toward me. "You hiding something from me?"

Groaning, I turn away to help the customer next to Gabe, but that doesn't stop me from listening.

"Evie and her therapist have entered into a rather illegal affair."

Patrick snaps his head back in my direction. "What?"

I slam down the bottle I'm holding and glare at Gabe. "For the last time, he is *not* my therapist."

"Is that true, Evie? Are you dating Doctor Reed?"

My face heats, and I know I'm turning bright red.

Apparently, my non-answer is enough, because Patrick chuckles and lifts his tumbler to his lips. "Well done, Evie girl. I'll drink to that."

Gabe's frown deepens when he doesn't get a reaction out of Patrick. "Don't drink that too fast. He's only renting out your house, Pat. He's not planning to stick around."

I open my mouth, ready to tell off Gabe, but Patrick beats me to it.

"Actually," Patrick says, "Lincoln asked for the rent-to-own agreement that I offered him. Looks like he has intentions to stick around. For whatever reason."

Warmth blooms in my chest before the sight of Gabe's scowl annoys me all over again. "What are you doing here, Gabe? Drinking on the job, or just paying Patrick a visit?"

He tilts his head at me, a challenge in his stare. "Neither, actually. Remember that guy Billy from last week? The guy you kicked out of here?"

I nod, feeling Patrick's focus shifting between the two of us. "Yeah, what about him?"

"He and his friends were planning on leaving Deep Creek a few days ago, but they haven't been able to find Billy. Have you seen him again since that night?"

I shake my head, not needing to think about it. "No, not at all. I figured that group left town after the weekend."

Gabe studies me for a second longer then looks around the room before leaning in like he wants to tell Patrick and me a secret. "The story is that Billy and his friends went into the woods on Tuesday night, and Billy didn't come back out. No one noticed until the next morning, but they didn't start panicking until Thursday. That's when they called me."

Dread fills every inch of my body. "Are you sure none of them saw him? Or maybe he passed out somewhere in the woods and got lost?"

Gabe shakes his head. "I don't know. We sent our K-9 unit into a section of the woods earlier today and came up empty. We're going to try again tomorrow. We've already interviewed that entire group, but I wanted to check with you, just in case I was missing something."

Something clicks in my brain as I think back to that night. The fact that Lilith was with them didn't faze me that night, but it does now.

"Lilith left with them from here, hanging on Billy. Maybe you should talk to her."

Gabe's brows raise. "Right." He checks his watch. "She should be back from the field trip with her kid. I'll give her a call." He taps the bar and tips his head to me. "Thank you, Evie. See you around, Patrick."

Gabe takes off, but I can't stop thinking about what he just said. *Field trip.* Maybe that's where Lincoln has been all day. If so, then he's been with Lilith all day.

Annoyance rumbles in my chest. I hate that she bothers me so much, but it's not like she's ever tried to make friends with me. I reach for my phone to text Lincoln, curiosity taking the reins.

> Evie: Did Lucy have a field trip today?

I'm surprised by how quickly he responds.

> Lincoln: No. I mean yes, but she didn't go.

> Evie: Oh, okay. Hey, did you hear that drunk from the bar went missing?

I help several customers before he finally responds.

> Lincoln: Billy. Yeah. Just found out.

> Evie: Gabe just stopped in and gave us the news. Wanted to know if we'd seen him. So strange. I hope he's okay. Anyway, I reminded Gabe that Lilith left with them that night, so maybe she can help.

My phone buzzes in my hands, Lincoln's face popping

onto the screen. I turn away from the bar and answer it. "Hey."

"Hi," he says, sounding distracted. "Where's Gabe now?"

I frown at this unexpected question. "He just left to go track Lilith down. He said her daughter's class went on a field trip, so I figured you might be there too."

Lincoln makes a noise in the back of his throat. "No fucking way. They were going to spend the day at Deep Creek Campground, so I refused to sign the permission slip." I hear noises from the other end. "Hold on, Evie. I'm picking up Lucy now."

I wait nervously, then loud, muffled voices come through the line, and I try to listen closer. It's Lincoln, raising his voice, but why?

A few minutes later, Lincoln gets back on the phone. "I need to go."

Panic claws through me. "Wait. What's wrong?"

It sounds like he's walking to his car. "Francine found out about the field trip and picked Lucy up from daycare to take her to the campground. She knew Lucy would want to play with her friends." His car door opens and shuts.

"That doesn't sound too terrible. I know Deep Creek is an awful place, but she's safe with Francine."

"Right, but there's a firefly walk tonight at the campground. Lucy is bound to hear about that, and she'll beg Francine to take her. A bunch of Lucy's friends' parents were begging me to hang back at camp with them to take the walk and see the fireflies."

My blood goes cold. "Okay," I say slowly. "But again, she's with Francine. She'll be okay, Lincoln. Are you heading there now?"

"Yes." He sounds completely panicked and stressed, and I don't blame him one bit.

"It's not Francine's fault. You haven't told her anything."

"I know," he says with a sigh. "I'm going to call her before I freak out any more."

"Good idea. Call me back."

"I will." A click as he ends the call.

I'm shaking as I wander around the bar like a zombie, wondering if I should be more worried than I am. With everything going on, the last thing Lincoln should be dealing with is Lucy roaming around Deep Creek Campground and checking out the fireflies.

The thought of Lucy, Francine, and Lincoln being there doesn't sit right with me. I can't focus on anything else, and I know I won't be able to until I hear from Lincoln.

Then again, why do I need to wait for a call when I know he's already headed to Deep Creek?

Without saying anything, without even taking off my apron, I head out the front door and stop when I realize I have no way to get to Deep Creek campground fast enough.

Patrick comes blowing out of the building behind me. "What's going on?" he asks, a look of concern on his face.

"I need you to take me to Deep Creek Campground."

Patrick looks at me like I just grew two heads. "What? Why?"

I grit my teeth. "Just please take me there. I'll explain on the way."

I'm flooring it through town as I hang up with Evie and call Francine. Her phone rings and rings, but she never picks up. I try her a few more times before growling and slamming my hand into the dashboard.

Finally, I call Dylan. He picks up on the first ring. "Please tell me you have eyes on my daughter?" I demand, knowing I sound exactly how I feel.

"What? No, I had eyes on Evie like we planned. I was just about to call you."

Shit shit shit. I pinch my eyes closed but only for a second. I need to concentrate on driving and getting to the campground. I rush to catch Dylan up with everything Evie and I talked about, finishing just as I pull into the parking lot.

"Hmm," Dylan says, sounding distracted. "Evie and Patrick Vaughn just left Firefly. It looked like they were in a hurry."

"Wait." I replay what he just said. "Patrick Vaughn is back?"

"Yeah, just arrived tonight. He went straight to Firefly to see your girl."

Well, that's interesting. "Haven't we been tracking Patrick? How did we not know he was coming home today?"

"Must have been planned. He doesn't have any more campground reservations for another week."

What the fuck is going on tonight? Everything feels like it's unraveling. Billy is missing. Francine took Lucy to Deep Creek Campground to see the fireflies without even telling me. Patrick Vaughn is mysteriously back in town. Jenkins is going rogue while on house arrest.

And I'm about to lose my damn mind.

"What's the plan?" I ask. Dylan is always the one with the plan—I've just been helping him narrow down his suspect list. But now that my daughter is involved, I need him to tell me the fucking plan.

"I'll follow them, see what they're up to, then I'll meet you at Deep Creek to help you find your daughter." He pauses, and silence lingers on the line. "She's going to be okay, Linc."

Nothing seems to be working right—my brain, my heart, my senses. I'm blindly following the only information I have on the whereabouts of my daughter and hoping it's enough.

"Hey," Dylan adds gently. "Wait for me before you do anything reckless. I'll call Gabe and get us some backup. Call me if you find Lucy."

I take in the deepest breath I can manage, trying to control my heart rate. "Thanks, man. I will."

After we hang up the phone, I reach over to retrieve my

gun from the glove compartment then call Francine one more time, just in case.

"Hello?"

I want to cry with relief when Francine's voice comes on the line. My head falls back against the seat. "Thank god, Francine."

She laughs like she doesn't have a care in the world. "Oh my, I've never known you to be so happy to hear from me."

Gritting my teeth, I try to hold back my anger. She has no idea what's going on. "I've been trying to get ahold of you. Why didn't you tell me you were taking Lucy to Deep Creek?"

"Oh," she tsks. "That's what this is about. You forgot to sign her permission slip, and the daycare called me telling me she was sobbing because all her friends were on the field trip except for her. So I took her."

Again, being angry at Francine is completely wrong. She doesn't know. She loves Lucy. She's only trying to do the right thing by Lucy.

"And I didn't think I had to tell you. Lilith said she'd call you."

I freeze, my relief short-lived as horror washes through me. "Lilith hasn't called me, Francine. Why would she call me?"

"Because Lucy wanted to stay at the campground with Willow. She wanted to go on that firefly walk tonight. The bugs were biting me like crazy, so Lilith offered to watch Lucy. She was going to call you and see if you wanted to join them."

My chest constricts, and I'm not sure I'm capable of breathing right away. My worst nightmare has just come true—my daughter will be among the fireflies in the same place where my sister was killed. With a killer on the loose.

"Lincoln, are you okay?"

I don't respond. I'm not sure how to. Instead, I hang up the phone and call Lilith next. It rings, but no one picks up, so I try one more time, already mapping out my search route in my head as I wait for her to pick up the phone. When it goes to voicemail again, I grab the gun and shove it in the back pocket of my jeans.

Just then, a loud banging comes from the passenger window. I jump and look over to find a completely disheveled Lilith. Her hair is wild like she's been running a marathon in a windstorm, her eye makeup is smeared in black streaks around her face, and her eyes are bloodshot like she's been crying.

"I'm so sorry," she shouts. "I'm so so sorry."

Anxiety winds through me. Somehow, I already know why she's sorry. Yanking open my door, I step out of the car and come around it to face her. "Where's my daughter, Lilith?" I don't even try to hide my accusatory tone.

Her eyes plead with mine for forgiveness. "I don't know."

"What?" I boom, causing her to jump.

She shakes her head. "The girls ran off when I went to the restroom, and I've been searching for them ever since. I was about to check the trail, but I saw you coming. I thought I could find them before you got here."

I narrow my eyes, wondering if I should remind her that she was supposed to call me and tell me Lucy stayed at camp with her. "How do you know they went into the woods?"

"They kept trying to dart off in that direction earlier,

but I was able to stop them." She covers her face with her hands and begins to tremble. "I'm so sorry. If he has them, I will never forgive myself."

My worst nightmare is coming to fruition. "What do you mean *if he has them?*" I ask through gritted teeth. "Who?"

"The Firefly Man." She looks up, seemingly terrified. "He's back, isn't he? That's what everyone is saying. I just heard Billy went missing." Her whole body starts to shake. "I would have never brought the kids here today if I thought the killer would come back here to this camp."

"Why are you so sure Billy went missing because of the Firefly Man?"

She stares at me, eyes wide. "I'm not, but that night I came back here with him and his buddies, he was drunk and making fun of the Firefly Man story. Just to prove it was all one big joke, he went out into the woods and brought back a jar of dead fireflies." She lets out a breath. "And now he's missing." Her eyes snap to mine.

I glare back at her, unable to hide how delusional I think she is. "Yet there have been murders nearby recently, and you still wanted to bring the kids here?"

She flinches, and I wonder if she just realized her lies don't add up. "But I thought he was long gone, Lincoln. I swear. I would never put our girls in danger."

I don't waste another breath talking to Lilith before sprinting toward the campground, heading straight for the same entrance to the woods that Evie, Carley, and I entered fourteen years ago.

"Lucy!" I yell as I slow to a walk and head down the trail, trying to keep my voice calm even though I feel anything but. "Lucy, it's Daddy! Time to go home, sweetie."

My feet pound the path as I continue calling for my daughter, desperate to hear her voice in return. Too many minutes go by, but I'm losing track of time as I strain to pick up any sign of my daughter.

"Wait up, Lincoln. You're too fast."

I grit my teeth when I hear Lilith's voice behind me. The woman has some nerve to take my kid and lose her in the one place I would have never allowed her to go. Then to try and fail to keep up with me as I desperately search the woods?

I'll deal with her later.

"Lincoln," Lilith calls again. "I think I see them."

Slowing to a walk, I spin around and sprint in her direction, just in time to see Lilith dart into the woods. I hesitate for only a moment before taking off after her, knowing I have no other choice.

"Lucy!" My voice has become a deep croak after straining for so long. "Yell if you can hear me, sweetie!"

While Lilith takes over calling for the girls, I slip my phone out of my pocket to see if anyone has tried to get ahold of me. When I tap my screen a few times, I realize my phone is completely dead. *Shit.*

Anger snakes its way through me as I'm forced to continue on a mission to find my daughter and nothing is sitting right with me. Everything about the trip into the woods to find two little girls, who must be scared out of their minds, seems like a flashlight illuminating a new piece of the puzzle, one I've been missing.

Now I'm almost *too* focused on Lilith and her every move, my distrust chaining me to her like a prisoner. Lilith is leading me on a wild goose chase, I just know it. But why? What's in it for her other than to get me alone?

It's not like she's hidden the fact that she's interested in me. Even Doreen has noticed the frequency of her visits to the office once I took over for Jenkins. And I'm still not sure what troubles Lilith, when all she's doing is brag about her perfect life, her perfect daughter, and her endless charitable contributions, despite her husband's death.

"Maybe we should try to call the park ranger or Gabe. The more people out here helping us search, the better. Can I use your phone?" I ask her.

Lilith stops and reaches for her back pocket, but she just pats around the area. "Shit. I forgot my phone. Can we use yours?"

I want to fucking scream. "It's dead."

Something flickers in her eyes—a hint of amusement? Again, nothing is making sense.

"Tell me the truth, Lilith," I suddenly demand. "Did you really lose the girls? Or are we out here for a different reason?"

Her eyes go wide. "What? No, Lincoln. I told you, I don't—"

A loud crunch of leaves steals our attention. We both turn toward the noise just in time to see Jenkins spring out of a thick of branches. There's no time to react before he raises a gold cane in the air then swings it, full force, into the side of Lilith's head.

The crack reverberates through the air, and Lilith falls to the ground, her hand immediately moving to the site of impact as her face contorts in pain.

I'm stunned for a second as Jenkins looms over Lilith like a predator, staring her down like he's daring her to make a move. When he lifts his cane over his head again, I don't think before reacting. I rush toward him, leaping over Lilith's body and body-slamming him to the ground.

He half yells, half moans at the impact, and I know I must have done some damage to his already brittle, aging bones. I'm too angry to care. I keep my hold on him as he tries to fight back.

Jenkins is the Firefly Man.

Jenkins, who's been helping Dylan and me put together profiles of suspects.

Jenkins, whom Evie and Lilith have trusted for years. A man they both considered to be a friend.

After he began complying with us, he plummeted to the bottom of our suspect list. With all the evidence gathered, we had no reason to suspect him, especially since his age didn't match the pattern of the other victims. Jenkins is an older man but strong, seeing as he's wrestling with me now and putting up a good fight. Still, I'm stronger.

"Let go of me, you idiot," Jenkins sputters. "I'm not the bad guy here. She's going to kill us both."

A multitude of feelings come over me next—anger, confusion, shock. Then I turn to see Lilith slowly getting to her feet, an evil gleam in her eyes.

Blood runs down the side of her face, and a large rock is raised above her head.

I've had it all wrong.

In fact, I'm not sure I ever had it right.

The Firefly Man isn't a man at all. It's *Lilith*.

But the realization comes too late, and there's no time to stop her before she's bringing her arms down and smashing the rock onto Jenkins's skull.

"I think his phone is dead."

An overwhelming sense of helplessness nearly knocks me to the ground, but Patrick is there with his hand holding mine, supporting me. In the five-minute ride to Deep Creek Campground, I filled him in as much as I possibly could, leaving out the bits and pieces I promised Lincoln I would keep confidential—like the fact that he's a profiler for the FBaI.

Patrick winces, the worry lines on his face deepening as we pull in beside Lincoln's car. "I have a bad feeling about this, Evie."

I could laugh at that sentiment if I weren't focused on finding Lucy. He was always the one who would encourage me to explore the woods, even late at night, as long as I followed his one rule. *Stay on the path.*

My stomach sinks when I replay the exact moment I decided to break that rule all those years ago. Foster had come back to get me. He didn't want to stop searching for Carley, but he didn't want to leave me behind, either. For years, I wondered if the reason he never tried to find me was because he hated me. I had been so stubborn about staying on the trail. Maybe if I had just gone with him the first time, we would have found Carley before she was killed.

Shaking off my dark thoughts, I head toward the entrance of the campground. We make it all the way to the same campsite that strangles me with nostalgia. It's so easy to remember the first time I saw Foster Pruitt and his moody scowl as he was forced to listen to the same campfire tale over and over.

I'm almost lost in my memories when a voice calls my name.

"Evie!"

I snap my head to find the man in the black hoodie jogging toward me.

He speaks.

At least now, thanks to Lincoln's confessions, I know the man is his partner, Dylan.

"What are you doing here?" Dylan demands. "You need to leave."

Narrowing my eyes at the near-stranger, I shake my head. "I'm not leaving until I know Lucy is okay."

Patrick is glaring at the man too. "Who the hell are you?"

Dylan sighs and pulls down his hoodie to reveal a head of shaggy strawberry-blonde curls and crystal-blue eyes. They must only hire Abercrombie models in the FBI. I guess that was the point of him keeping his features covered, considering he was hiding in plain sight from me, spying on me for Lincoln.

"This is Dylan," I tell Patrick, trying to calm him so we can focus on the mission at hand. "He's Lincoln's friend."

"You both should go," Dylan says. "Lincoln wouldn't want you anywhere near this place."

"No offense," I snap, "but I don't really care what Lincoln wants. I'm staying."

Dylan tilts his head and challenges me with a look that tells me he knows a hell of a lot more about me longer than I know about him. "You sure about that? I tracked his phone before he lost signal. He's in the woods, Evie."

"Why would he be there?" But the answer dawns on me a second later. "Is Lucy in the woods?"

Dylan's expression and tone soften. "I can only guess that's why Lincoln went in there." He sighs. "I know this goes against everything you want to do, but if you won't leave, maybe you should at least wait here. If he is in there looking for Lucy, then you can be here waiting if she comes out."

"I'll go with Dylan to search," Patrick says, his eyes steady on mine. "Everything will be okay."

"She doesn't know you, Patrick." My heart is breaking at the mere thought of not being out there, searching for her myself.

Even Dylan does a double take between us. "Which is why you should be here in case she finds her way out." When Dylan seems to realize that his words aren't convincing me, he tries again. "She knows me. Patrick and I will stay close together."

I open my mouth to argue, but I quickly realize how much time is being wasted. "Just go already. Go find her." I throw my arms out, showing them that I've given up. They win. "Go!" I yell.

They jolt into action and run in the direction of the trailhead. I pace for what seems like forever but is probably five whole minutes before I get too frustrated to stand by and do nothing to help.

I take a few steps toward the trailhead, looking desperately for any sign of activity through the trees. There's still a good two hours left of daylight, so the chances of Lucy being found are good. I let that thought calm me a bit, then I pick up my phone again and search for Francine's number.

She answers on the first ring. "Evie," she says, sounding breathless. "Are you with Lincoln?"

Dread fills me. "I was hoping you were. He went to Deep Creek to find you guys. He was so worried Lucy would want to go on that firefly walk and…" I pause, not wanting to give any details he hasn't given her yet. "I just got here to make sure everything was okay. Are you here?"

"Oh dear," Francine says. "I was there earlier, but Lucy desperately wanted to play with Willow and see the fireflies, so I left. Lilith said she would take care of Lucy, but she was supposed to call Lincoln to tell him. I guess that didn't happen. Now I can't reach Lincoln or Lilith." Her voice has begun to shake. "Oh, Evie, I think I made a terrible mistake."

I pull in a deep breath, not wanting Francine to sense my worry. She's frightened enough as it is. "You didn't know. I think Linc's phone is dead or he's lost signal. It last pinged in the woods, so he might be in there with Lucy." I try to give her an optimistic outcome. "Maybe they went to see the fireflies." I cringe, knowing without a doubt it is not the truth.

"Maybe so." Francine already sounds calmer.

"Dylan and my uncle Patrick are out there looking too. Everything is going to be okay, Francine."

Even as I say those words, I know I have no right to. Carley didn't make it out of the woods alive fourteen years ago, nor did the other eleven victims—possibly twelve, if Billy counts. What makes me think anyone would be safe now?

After ending the call, I take another two steps toward the woods, not sure how much more patient I can be. So I make rounds at the campsite, asking every single person there if they've seen a little blonde girl. I show them Lucy's picture. Some saw her with the group of kids from earlier, but no one saw her walking alone.

Then I reach one of the last campsites and see a group of kids roasting marshmallows by the fire, along with several adults who are helping them.

The moment I spot a giggling Lucy holding a flaming marshmallow on a long stick, I want to burst into tears. Willow and her other school friends are holding sticks too. No one seems to understand that utter madness has broken out in the woods.

Lucy's eyes widen when she sees me, and she leaps to her feet. One of the moms takes the stick from her before she sprints over and tosses her entire body into my open arms.

I inhale her sweet strawberry-shortcake scent then pull back. "Hey, Lucy." It takes everything to keep the emotion out of my voice. "I didn't know you were camping tonight."

She nods excitedly. "Did you come with Daddy? He's supposed to pick me up."

More red flags abound in my thoughts. "I'm meeting him here too," I tell her. Then I look up to one of the moms who's approaching. I've seen her around town. "Hi," I say. "Have you seen Lilith or Lincoln anywhere?"

The woman, who I now recognize as Julie, the owner of a retail shop on Main Street, shakes her head. "Lilith got a terrible migraine earlier, so she went home, but the girls were desperate to see the fireflies, so I said I'd watch them. I'm supposed to take Willow home later. I was told Lincoln would be picking up Lucy."

Julie is mid-sentence when a series of suspicions wrap my heart like a coiled snake. My blood goes cold as I begin sorting pieces of an entirely new puzzle, one I never thought to put together until now.

Lilith is taking care of Lucy without Lincoln's knowledge or permission.

Lilith is taking Lucy to see the fireflies, of all things.

Lilith lives in Bryson City, the suspected hometown of the killer.

Lilith was with Billy before he went missing.

Lilith is a patient of J.D.'s and now Lincoln's.

Lilith was there on the night of Carley's murder.

Lilith.

My heartbeat triples, and I immediately turn back toward the woods.

I'm not sure how much more evidence I needed to put the last piece in the puzzle, but I'm not sure I can believe it even though it's staring me right in the face.

Lilith can't be the Firefly Man. No fucking way. If she were, that would mean…

That would mean *she* killed Carley fourteen years ago and continued killing long afterward.

Julie tilts her head as if she's picking up on my panic. "Is everything okay?"

I force the best smile I can manage, not wanting to cause anyone else to worry. "Yes, of course. I'm just trying to track Lincoln down, that's all."

I look over in the direction of the trailhead, knowing what I need to do next.

Lucy tugs on my hand. "You'll find my daddy, Evie?"

Sinking to my knees, eye to eye with my favorite little bumblebee, I give her the most encouraging smile I can muster. "I will, Lucy. Stay here while I go get him, okay? I'll be right back."

I hate that I have doubts that I will be back, and worse, that I will find Lincoln alive. Losing Carley was one tragedy too many in my lifetime. I won't allow that to happen again.

She nods, and I squeeze her hand before determination floods me.

I pick myself up off the ground and move straight into the woods. I should have learned my lesson about listening to Uncle Patrick the first time, but I'm disobeying him once again. Then again, somehow I know deep down that whatever decision I make is one he'll understand.

As if I need his encouragement, I imagine Patrick with a raised chin and a gleam of pride twinkling in his blue eyes, freeing me to do what I need to do. Something my parents would have never agreed with.

It's so easy to remember why I found safety in Patrick's presence throughout my life. He was always there for me. Never judging me. Always showing me the options but never deciding my direction. Just like Carley, Patrick was a firefly, helping me find my way through life when my parents had abandoned me.

Now it's my turn to light my own path.

Explosions go off in my brain, and my hands are burning with a wet, sticky substance. I try to shake my head to clear the brain fog, but that only makes everything hurt more. I try to move, but no luck. My body won't budge.

What happened to me?

I sort through my choppy memories until I recall following Lilith into the woods to find Lucy. My heartbeat quickens as the turn of events begin to unfold from the point when I first suspected Lilith was up to no good to Jenkins leaping from the bushes and bashing Lilith's head with his cane and finally to my failed heroics when I tackled Jenkins and brought him down to the ground, only to look up to see Lilith bring down a boulder on his skull.

All my bones and muscles ache at once when I remember how I shielded Jenkins from the blow by throwing my body on top of him. Lilith's rock landed on my shoulder with a loud crack. Pain lanced through my right side, but I wasn't going to let that stop me. I pushed through the pain and began rolling over, but that's when the gold cane came down—once onto Jenkins's head, and next onto mine.

Everything went black after that.

Groaning, I force my eyes open, which isn't easy considering the weight of them. Everything is fuzzy as I look around. The sky has darkened considerably since I was last conscious, but I see familiar flashes of blue, yellow, and green lights that make my chest ache with thoughts of Carley.

"Run, run as fast as you can," a singsong voice taunts from several feet away. "You can't catch me." A swoosh of air rushes past my skin. "I'm the Firefly Man."

Lilith.

My brain hisses her name as all the events that led to this moment play out in my mind. I turn my head, searching for Jenkins yet coming up empty in the near-darkness. I'm about to turn away when I spot a figure propped up against a nearby tree. I blink, attempting to make my vision less fuzzy, and vaguely make out the gray slacks and black cotton shirt Jenkins was wearing.

"Don't worry," Lilith says with a devious cackle. "He's just resting to give us some alone time."

Resting? As in… I gasp. "You killed Jenkins?"

Lilith gasps in dramatic fashion. "Kill the man who spent the last fourteen years protecting my secrets? I think not."

Confusion grows in my brain. "The man who just lunged at you and tackled you to the ground? Are we talking about the same person?"

Lilith waves a hand like the scuffle was no big deal. "Oh, he'll pay for that." She winks and raises his gold cane, the one she'd just used to knock us both out. "He always felt guilty for what happened to your sister. I was his patient, and he somehow convinced himself her death was his fault. So he continued to work with me."

She pauses thoughtfully. "Of course he was right, but of course I denied having anything to do with the rest of the murders over the years. Deep down, I knew he must have been suspicious." She looks over at him and sighs. "Never thought he'd turn his back on me like that, but..." She shrugs. "I suppose the FBI will finally have someone to blame for all these unfortunate lives."

It doesn't take a genius to figure out that what she's insinuating. She's going to set Jenkins up for murder. Mine and all the others. That's when I notice the black leather gloves she managed to slip onto her hands at some point while I was unconscious.

"Where's Lucy?" I can't stop my voice from trembling.

Lilith chuckles. "Your daughter is perfectly safe—hanging back at camp, roasting s'mores, listening to tales of the Firefly Man, and starting her venture at the trailhead to look at the fireflies. Like father, like daughter, right, *Foster Pruitt?*"

I freeze, my aching body molding me to the ground. "How long have you known?"

She chuckles again, this time it's airy and free. "How long have I known that Doctor Lincoln Reed is Foster Pruitt?" She holds up my wallet and tosses me the worn picture of Carley and me I've kept there. "That was quite the little twist in our story, I must say. I am pleasantly surprised. It's like I'm getting two for the price of one."

"What the hell is that supposed to mean?" I mutter angrily.

"Let's just say, I don't take rejection very well. Just ask my dead father. It was so easy to make it look like he killed himself after he passed out in that bathtub. As I got older, I fantasized about doing something just like it to all the men who wronged me over the years." She gives me a half smile. "So I did, but it was all supposed to start with you."

Anger continues to brew in my chest like an inevitable storm, clouds gathering before the first strike of lightning. "Then what about Carley? How did she fit into your little revenge plot?"

Lilith's face twists into something resembling annoyance. "It was dark. She was wearing your fucking sweatshirt. I thought she was you until she turned around, but she'd already seen me coming for her." Her mouth curls into an evil smirk. "I even considered pretending it was all a stupid joke, but then that little bitch screamed, and something just came over me. She was only able to run a few feet before I caught up to her and bashed her pretty little skull in." She tsks. "Poor thing."

I lunge to my feet—at least, I try—but my muscles scream with pain as loud as I do. "I will kill you," I roar as I fumble, trying to get up.

A laugh escapes from somewhere deep in her chest. "You've had fourteen years to try," she taunts. "You failed, but you've come pretty damn close, haven't you?" She paces around me in a wide and slow circle. "That's right. I've known that you've been stalking me, you and that FBI friend of yours. I'd say it's been a few years now, and I'm still five steps ahead of you. Did you think I wouldn't recognize you in and out of all the same towns I visited? Did you think I wouldn't realize what happened to my long-time therapist?"

She lets out another low laugh. "At first, I thought you already knew it was me. When you replaced J.D. at Calm Waters and you wanted to have that free consultation, I thought the cuffs would be snapped around my wrists then." Her pace picks up. "But no. Which begs to ask the question… why did you move here and replace J.D. if you didn't have a clue who the Firefly Man was?"

I shrug. "To re-investigate the original murder. I replaced Jenkins to get up close and personal with the locals. Somewhere in there, I hypothesized that the ascending age of the male victims could match the age of the killer too, which means you would have been fifteen at the time of Carley's death. And there weren't any fifteen-year-olds visiting from out of town that week, aside from Evie and my family. And then there was the firefly map… "

Lilith's eyes brighten like I've just made her day. "Clever, wasn't it?"

"Not exactly what I would call it," I tell her, dryly.

After a few more attempts to move, I look down at my feet to find the reason I'm not gaining an inch. A rope has been pulled tightly across both of my ankles, and each end is secured to a boulder, pinning me to the ground. Desperate now, eyes wide, I look to my right then left, confirming my arms are tied down too.

Panic clutches my chest, my desperation to break free as intense as my search to find Lucy. Just because Lilith says she's okay doesn't make it true.

"Since when do you tie your victims down, Lilith?" Distracting her is all I can think to do as I wiggle my feet against the rope. "Seems out of character for you."

She stops pacing and moves toward me, the moonlight casting an eerie halo around her head. "It's not every day your first intended victim reappears in your life with a whole new identity *and* FBI credentials. Call me curious."

That makes two of us. "What do you want to know?"

She narrows her eyes. "Let's start with this. Why Evie?"

"Does it matter?" I know through our therapy sessions that Lilith hates when I answer a question with a question. "A *femme fatale* isn't in it for a lasting relationship."

Her lips curl at one corner, her eyes flashing wider with excitement. I can practically see every ounce of her delighted by the connection I just made.

"So you're familiar with my favorite species of fireflies?"

How had I never made this connection before? With all my research, with all the time spent on my investigation, I completely overlooked this one, interesting fact about a certain species of female fireflies.

"You mean the species that trick males, signaling to lure them in just to kill them and eat them?"

Lilith's amused smirk transitions into an expression of mock innocence. "Only to acquire defensive steroids to ward off their enemies."

Anger blasts through me. "Except you've got one thing wrong in your attempt at symbolism."

Her eyes narrow, challenging me. "And that is?"

"In order to lure a mate, the male needs to show interest in you first. Did Billy reject you too?"

She breathes in and out deeply while keeping her slitted eyes laser-focused on me. "As a matter of fact, Billy had a girlfriend back home that he didn't mind cheating on. I did her a favor."

"Ah, so you're a mission-oriented killer now? And here Dylan and I thought this entire time that you were just plain hedonistic. Thrill-seeking. Possibly just into the power and control of it all."

Lilith steps forward again, this time placing one foot between my legs and the other to my side so she's towering over me. "I kill because I want to. Call it a charitable contribution to the world by ridding it of men like you."

"Oh, you mean men with high standards?"

Her foot kicks me hard, hitting square in the balls with so much force that I wish I could keel over to attempt to ward off the pain that's about to wash over me. Instantly, everything goes numb and my stomach clenches, and I just know the pain will be more intense than anything I've ever experienced before.

"Don't worry," she jeers before stepping to the side to reach for her pet rock—the one she tried to smash Jenkins with earlier. "When I'm done with you, you're not going to need any of that to work anyway." She picks up the rock, looking at it like she's in some dreamlike trance as she rotates it in her hand. "I'm going to squish you like a little bug."

I can't even focus on her words as I groan through the swelling pain that only seems to be getting worse. I'm nauseous and in agony, knowing I don't have much time to figure my way out of these ropes but physically incapable of doing a damn thing.

Sucking in a strangled breath, I reopen my eyes to find Lilith still there, admiring her rock. In the distance, I see Jenkins stir against the tree, and hope blooms in my chest. He doesn't seem to be tied down.

It's like I'm watching a movie in slow motion as Jenkins slowly, stealthily pulls himself away from the tree and takes several unsteady steps to reach his cane. He continues toward Lilith from behind, maintaining his slow pace while raising the cane above his head.

The sound of crunching leaves nearby steals all our attention. Lilith, Jenkins, and I look in the direction of the noise. I panic, not wanting anything to distract Jenkins from his intended mission.

"Now!" I yell.

Lilith whips her head back toward me just as Jenkins sends his cane down on her head. But this time, Lilith is too fast. She turns and drops the rock, shooting her hand up to grip the cane before it strikes her.

A laugh booms from her chest as she yanks the cane from him. "Nice try, old man."

My heart sinks, but it only lasts a moment before a figure bursts into view, coming from the direction of the earlier noises.

"Everybody freeze!" Gabe yells.

Just like that, Lilith's evil laughter transitions into a cry of fright so real, I almost believe her.

"Thank god!" She points the cane at Jenkins. "He's trying to kill us!"

Gabe glares back at Lilith. "Cut the shit and put your hands up, Lilith. We already heard everything."

We?

Two more figures come out from the same section of woods Gabe just stepped out from.

First is Dylan, who raises his gun and aims it for her head. "Hands up, Lilith. You're under arrest for the attempted murder of Billy McDouglas, for starters."

Attempted murder?

I'm not sure what to make of all that yet, but I'm too shocked by the sight of the third figure walking toward me. Evie looks just as shocked, confused, and scared as me.

She darts immediately over to me. "Are you okay?" she asks, tears brimming in her eyes. "I was so scared, Lincoln." She yanks away the rope at my feet then moves to my hands. "Lucy's okay," she tells me in a rush as she unknots my hands. "I'm so glad we got to you in time."

As much as I want to kiss Evie senseless, I'm not letting Gabe and Dylan take over this arrest without me. I leap to my feet, ignoring my body's screams of pain. Then I reach for my back pocket and pull out my gun.

That's three guns pointed at Lilith, but she refuses to put up her hands. She doesn't even look phased as she looks down the barrel of each one.

"Well, shit," is all she says.

My body won't stop shaking, not after the hour-long search through the woods. Before finally finding Lincoln, Lilith, and Jenkins in the small clearing, I wasn't sure what we would stumble upon. Too much time had been passing, and I kept flashing back to our awful discovery of Carley fourteen years ago.

Anxiety had whittled away at my emotions like a fickle beast. The relief at finally reaching Lincoln and untying his bruised and battered body, almost too much to handle. My only relief in any of it was when I ran into Patrick on the trail. He had his arms around Billy, who was caked in dried blood down the side of his head.

"That crazy bitch," he muttered, when I'd asked him what happened. "She tried to kill me."

That was all the confirmation I needed to know exactly who he was talking about. I sent Patrick back to camp with strict orders to get Billy help then find Lucy and stay with her until I made it back out with Lincoln. In turn, he told me the direction Dylan started searching. Seeing as that direction led toward the same section of woods we found Carley in years ago, that's where I went.

Just when I thought I heard someone talking past a thick of bushes, a hand wrapped around my mouth from behind, just like fourteen years ago. This time, I knew who had me in his grip. As confirmation, I looked up to find Dylan there, his eyes wide, and a finger pressed to his lips, gesturing for me to be quiet.

"It's just me," Gabe whispered. "Do not move another step. And don't make a sound." He slowly started to release his hand. "Listen."

My heart was racing when I started to tune into the sound of Lilith's conversation with Lincoln.

Now, as Lincoln, Dylan, and Gabe all take steps toward a completely fucked Lilith, I can almost sense the silent agreement between them that the moment she starts to run, they'll take her out. No hesitation. No questions.

Even I know that the cane in her hand and the boulder at her feet are enough to lock her away for several crimes, not just the ones Dylan mentioned.

Meanwhile, I make my way to J.D., whose chin is quivering as he watches his oldest client get arrested for a series of murders he surely feels is his fault. We all heard what Lilith said. He knew she killed Carley. He knew and helped cover for her by buying her time.

It was J.D. who had grabbed me that night when I was on my way to get help for Carley. *He* was the one who had placed his hand over my mouth. *He* was the one who whispered for me to be quiet or I would be next. *He* was buying her time by holding me back from getting help.

Emotion climbs up my throat as I stare at the man I

trusted for so many years. "You deserve to go to jail for what you knew. You could have saved so many lives."

He doesn't even look at me. He can't. As much as he's helped me through the years, the guilt must be eating him alive.

Tears begin to stream down his face, and he just keeps nodding, accepting his fate. "I'm so sorry, Evie. I thought I could help her. I thought I did help her. But I was just in denial." He bows his head in shame. "Lilith called me. Told me she was having thoughts of hurting people again. She told me to meet her here. I should have known she was trying to set me up."

We both watch as Lilith drops J.D.'s gold cane and lifts her hands, finally surrendering herself to the arrest. Gabe is right there to cuff her, then he reads her rights while Dylan makes his way over to us. He stands in front of J.D., eyes narrowed. It's clear just how betrayed he feels by a man who was supposed to be an informant.

"Maybe we can find you a cell next door to your friend." He raises his chin. "Turn around and put your hands behind your back."

J.D. does what he's told without a fight. It's not until both Lilith and J.D. are locked in cuffs, with Dylan and Gabe leading them out of the woods, that I run to Lincoln and throw my arms around him.

He winces in pain but hugs me so tightly, I think I might break from the desperation of it.

"It's over," I tell him, reassuring us both. "Lilith will never hurt another person ever again."

Lincoln leans back and nods, his eyes locked on mine, fourteen years of pent-up emotions behind them. "She's a *femme fatale.*"

My next breath is shaky as I remember their entire conversation. "A black widow in the firefly world."

"I completely overlooked that rare species in all my studies. I never would have thought the killer was a woman." He shakes his head. "I had completely forgotten she was even there that night because she wasn't even staying at the campground. Her mom would just bring her to hang out every day."

Even I had forgotten that, but he's right. Lilith's mom would have never gone camping, not even when she started dating Jimmy.

"She's disturbed, Lincoln," I tell him. "But she's going to jail where she belongs. She won't be able to hurt anyone else, and that's all that matters." I tilt my head, hoping he can get past the fact that he wasn't able to figure this one out on his own. "And Lucy's safe. The most important fact of all." My throat tightens. "She asked me to come find you and bring you back." I smile. "She has no idea anything is wrong."

He blows out a heavy breath. "That's a relief. I was so worried." He frowns. "I don't understand how Lilith thinks she would have gotten away with hurting me without anyone figuring out it was her. You all would have known she set up the entire thing."

I shrug tightly. "I don't know, Lincoln. I didn't realize Lilith had anything to do with it until I talked to Francine. But Lilith told the rest of the group that she had a headache and went home. I'm sure that's because she didn't want to get placed at the scene. It was clever, but I don't think she was expecting the search party that came after her tonight."

He leans against me and shudders.

"We should head back," I tell him. "You should probably get checked out by a doctor." I pull back and try to assess his injuries. He's clearly in pain, but I can't see where the wounds are.

"I'm fine," he says with a brief shake of his head. "She bashed that rock into my shoulder then followed it up with a blow to the head with Jenkins's cane. She knocked me out for a bit, but what hurt the most was where she nailed me between the legs." He winces as if the memory alone triggers more pain.

I cup his face with my hand. "I'm so glad you're okay." Emotion trembles in my voice. "I've never been so afraid in my entire life. As soon as I knew Lucy was fine, my mind went wild with where you could be and what could have happened to you. I was so afraid I would lose you again."

He takes my face in his hands, too, bringing his forehead to mine. "Never again. I'm right here."

I sigh, my entire being filled with a new sense of calm I didn't even know I'd been craving. "You know what I realized when I was alone in the woods searching for you?"

"What?"

I take in a deep breath and smile. "As afraid as I was to lose you, I never felt alone or afraid of the woods themselves." I look around at the tiny sparkles of light surrounding us. "Carley is with us, Lincoln. I can feel her. Her light will never die."

He nods and holds me tighter. "And that, Evie girl, is what I like to call the firefly effect. A firefly truly never dies —it always leaves a piece of itself behind so that the cycle of life can continue." He smiles gently. "The question is how do we want to leave the world? As a guiding light, or something dark and deceitful? Whatever it may be, that is our legacy."

A smile curves into my cheeks, and I love that he can take our worst tragedy and turn it into something so incredibly beautiful. "Carley's legacy is pretty damn great."

Lincoln nods. "And ours will be too."

I raise my head to his as my chest explodes with love. "So what's next, Doctor Reed?"

His gaze sweeps around us, and he gestures to the symphony of lights. "Well, I guess now it's time for you to pick your mate. Who will it be, Evie? The choice is yours."

My heart beats faster as our eyes connect again. All I see in his beautiful green eyes now is an endless forest filled with sparkles of hope.

I touch his nose with mine. "I made my choice fourteen years ago, Linc. And my life has been so dark for so long. I've just been waiting for you to find me."

His eyes close, and he presses his lips to mine. "I'm sorry it took me so long to get here, Evie girl."

"**D**addy!" Lucy squeals before breaking free from Patrick and the rest of the campers. She sprints several yards to get to Lincoln before tossing herself into his arms.

He doesn't even wince, though I know the weight of impact must have been painful. It's not just his shoulder that hurts from the large rock Lilith struck him with, but there's a giant golf ball-sized bump on his head from where she hit him with the cane. Instead of showing his pain, his eyes squeeze tight as he clutches his little girl in his arms like he'll never let her go.

My heart swells, my throat tightens, and my eyes spring a pool of water. I realize the significance of this moment. Fourteen years ago, his sister died in the very woods he just stepped out of. That time, he came out wearing handcuffs, and he never even got to properly grieve over the person he loved most in this whole world. He also spent months paying for a crime he didn't commit. Now…the tables have completely turned in the best possible way. This time, the true killer exited the Deep Creek Campground woods wearing handcuffs, and Lincoln got to walk out a free man to the girl he loves most in the whole world.

Lucy clings to Lincoln just as hard as he's clinging to her. It's almost like she knows that he needs that hug more than she does. The innocence of it all has my watery eyes leaking tears of happiness for their love. For the slightest second, I find myself wishing I knew what that kind of love felt like from a parent. And then a warm arm wraps around my shoulders, the firmness of it causing a cry to lift from my throat.

I turn to Patrick and wrap my arms around him. It's like he could hear my thoughts. Maybe he could sense them, at the very least. Either way, the hug is proof that I have always had a parent by my side, even if it's not my biological mom and dad. Uncle Patrick is everything I've ever needed and more as far as a parental figure goes. He's been my rock, my shoulder to cry on, my lifeline. And I'll never be able to thank him enough for giving me such a beautiful life.

"I'm so glad you're okay." He sighs. "I saw Lilith and J.D. get hauled out of there and I nearly lost my mind waiting for you to come out too. Lilith killed all those people?"

I shudder. "I still haven't grasped it all, but she admitted to it all."

Patrick squeezes me again, and I know it's an effort to comfort me.

"Gabe was able to fill us in a bit, but he had to get to the station," he says.

"It was awful," I tell him, honestly. A tremble follows my words, and it feels more like a release of all the stress I'd been carrying. "Lilith used Lucy to lure Lincoln and J.D. into the woods. She was planning to kill Lincoln and then pin it on J.D."

His body tenses. "Geez. Who knew Lilith was capable of something so awful?" He shakes his head. "She was always a little off, but I would have never pegged her to be a serial killer. Even though…"

I lean back from Patrick and narrow my eyes, my heart beating faster, sensing that he knows something that I don't. "Even though what, Patrick?"

He hesitates for a second before continuing. "I was just going to say…even though Lilith always made these strange comments to me that if the Firefly Man story ever came true, it would be a blessing, because he would end the lives of bad people only."

A chill shoots up my spine. "It's like she thought she was some sort of vigilante, ridding the world of men that reminded her of her father."

Patrick twists his expression into something resembling agreeable. "That would make sense. J.D. did tell me once that Lilith's upbringing wasn't the best."

I'm sure the shock is plainly evident on my face. "He broke client-patient confidentiality to tell you that?"

Patrick shrugs. "He told me a lot that he probably shouldn't have." He frowns. "That was shitty of him, but I still can't believe he was covering for Lilith for all these years. That's sickening." He shakes his head. "I wish I would have caught on somehow."

"Yeah, well, he managed to keep that secret from every-one. Don't feel bad."

When I look back over at Lincoln and Lucy, I'm surprised to find Francine there too.

I regard Patrick with a tilt of my head. "When did Francine get here?"

He turns to look at where my eyes are focused. "Right after you went into the woods," he says. "She was worried sick about Lucy. I didn't know she was in the dark about everything. I might have said too much."

I cringe, knowing what that means. "What did you tell her?"

He shrugs. "Everything, I think."

My eyes widen incredulously on him.

"I didn't have a choice," he says, defensively. "She didn't understand all the fuss. Now that she knows, she's probably beating herself up for leaving Lucy with a madwoman."

"Probably, but everyone is safe now. That's what we should be focusing on." I assess the warm embrace Lincoln has Francine in and I know whatever guilt she feels won't last long. Lincoln won't allow it. Besides, Francine was left in the dark for a reason. It's not her fault. Not one bit.

"Daddy, look!"

Lucy's excitement is so infectious, we all look in the direction of her focus. She holds out her little hand and a firefly lands on her finger, lighting up her soft pink skin.

"Oh wow, Lucy. That's good luck."

She squeals when the firefly's abdomen flashes. "It twin-kles," she says through her giggle.

Lincoln's smile is the biggest I've ever seen as he kisses Lucy's sweet head. "Make a wish, Goose. Maybe your firefly will make it come true."

Lucy squeezes her eyes shut so tight and then blows on her finger, so hard the firefly instantly flies away. When she opens her eyes, it's gone, and her grin gets even bigger. "He took my wish away." Lucy turns to look at me and then back to her dad. "Will it come true now? Will you and Evie get married, Daddy?" She tilts her head like she's trying to reason with him. "Then Evie can be my Mommy and you can be my Daddy."

My heart jolts into my throat before it beats a million miles an hour in my chest. As much as I'm expecting Lincoln to reject the sentiment altogether, he looks at me instead and winks, then he leans down to whisper something in Lucy's ear. Whatever that something is makes her smile so bright that her cheeks flush with a different kind of happiness—one that tells me he's just made one of her fairytales come true.

He ignores my glare, and instead turns back to look at the fireflies with Lucy.

"Hey, Lucy. Do you know who else loved fireflies so much?"

My breath catches in my throat. Meanwhile, Francine's eyes begin to glisten, and I know it's because this news is nearly as new to her as it is to Lucy.

"Who?" Lucy's giant eyes show her innocent curiosity.

Lincoln smiles. "Your aunt Carley, Daddy's sister."

Lucy's little gasp squeezes my heart.

"You have a sister? Have I met her?"

Lincoln shakes his head, maintaining his smile. "No, sweetie. Carley had to go away a long time ago."

Lucy frowns. "Where did she go?"

Lincoln nods toward the synchronous lights. "Well, I'm not really sure, but sometimes I like to imagine she's one of the fireflies, lighting up the sky like she never even left at all."

It takes a few seconds, and I can almost hear Lucy's brain trying to imagine exactly what her dad is trying to say, and then a new smile blooms on her face. "I think I see her, Daddy." She wiggles in his hold until he sets her down, then she sinks to a crouching position and extends her hand to point to a tall blade of grass just as a firefly flashes its light. "Right here," she whispers. "This is Carley."

Lincoln sinks down with her to examine the little beetle. "You know, I think you're right. That is her."

Lucy clutches his leg. "Can we keep her?"

Lincoln shakes his head slowly. "But then she wouldn't be able to fly."

Lucy tilts her head like she's thinking carefully. "Then maybe we can just come back to see her?"

Lincoln's arm wraps around Lucy's body as he nods. "Now that is a perfect idea my little Goose."

I don't argue with Lincoln when he says he's taking me back to his place. Dylan and Gabe agreed to hold off on any questioning until the next day, so we could get home and get some rest.

Lincoln lets Lucy stay up a little bit longer so we can all have a late-night snack, then he gives her a quick wash before tucking her into bed. I'm almost surprised when he walks out of her bedroom and into the kitchen five minutes later, chuckling that she fell asleep mid-sentence.

I look over my shoulder from washing the dishes and smile. "Do you blame her? She had quite the eventful day."

Lincoln comes up behind me, wraps his arms around my body and nuzzles his mouth in the crook of my neck.

"No fucking kidding. A kidnapping, roasting s'mores, firefly watching."

"Learning about her aunt Carley," I add.

"Nearly losing her dad to a deranged serial killer."

I shudder. "Yeah, let's not add that one to the list. You'll make me drop a dish."

He reaches for the plate I'm holding and sets it back in the sink. "Those can wait. You must be exhausted."

Surprisingly, I'm not tired at all. "Wide awake." I swivel around and wrap my arms around his neck. "I could desperately use a shower, though."

Lincoln quirks a lip. "By all means, use mine." He kisses me softly. "With me in it." He kisses me again. "And me inside you."

This time, his mouth stays on mine as he pulls me backward, out of the kitchen, past the living room and den, then down the hall to the bedrooms. I giggle against him when he shuts the door to his room and fumbles for the baby monitor on his nightstand.

There's something about the fact that Lucy is four years old and he still feels the need to check on her breathing throughout the night that makes me fall so much deeper in love with him than the moment before.

His lips continue to claim mine as we stumble our way into the bathroom. He doesn't even pull away from me when he reaches behind him to start the shower. The desperation in his hold and in the way his mouth practically suctions to mine is the equivalent of reaching deep down into my soul and stealing it to be his for eternity.

I will happily give it.

Lincoln strips me bare, then he removes all his clothes until our naked bodies are colliding as steam fills the room. When we finally step under the water, I almost expect him to hitch my leg up and take me right then and there. I wouldn't complain a bit. Apparently, he has other ideas.

He breaks the kiss, causing us both to gasp for air. He's fully under the water, the stream cascading over him while he fills his hands with soap and proceeds to lather up my chest. He makes excruciatingly slow work over my breasts, kneading them, pinching my nipples, then starts on my back, continuing to my ass, and finally to the space between my thighs.

"So beautiful," he murmurs when my back is to him. His cock is hard against my back as his tongue darts out against my ear. "Every inch of you." He snakes his fingers between my legs again, this time with a soap-free hand and begins to toy with my clit. "I just got the shit beat out of me and I don't feel a single fucking thing when I get to touch you like this."

My abdomen tightens as I feel him sink to his knees. "Be careful," I warn, clearly caring more about his injuries than him. "We don't have to do this now."

He growls as two fingers push deep inside me. "The fuck we don't." Then his tongue darts out against my ass, causing me to jerk, but his fingers have me locked in place as he works me faster. "I almost died tonight," he reminds me before sliding his tongue to where his hand is. "I want to feel more alive than ever right now, baby girl. Making you come alive right before my very eyes is about to be my salvation."

Between his tongue and fingers and his dirty words, I'm plummeting to my first orgasm with barely any effort on his part at all. I've been so wound up all night that it didn't take much for Lincoln to unravel me. But he doesn't stop with one. He never does.

"Hang on to the ledge," he demands before spreading my legs apart and covering my pussy with his entire mouth.

I swear the man is trying to devour me like I'm his last meal. He's sucking and slurping, licking and flicking. There's no pattern to his madness, just constant attention to my clit before a moan escapes me. My next orgasm is more intense, electrifying my nerves and causing my muscles to weaken.

"Linc, I think you might end up killing me tonight if you keep this up."

He stands, pressing his body against mine and teasing his lips with mine. "Don't worry, baby, I'll revive you."

Before I can react, he picks me up into his arms and he walks us out of the shower. I'm not even sure how he manages to turn it off on the way out, but the water squeals to a halt. The next thing I know, I'm getting placed on a firm mattress, my body and hair soaked from our shower.

He doesn't seem to care one bit as he crawls on top of me, lifts one of my knees and presses it toward me, and then pushes his cock inside of me so fast I gasp from the shocking feel of him.

Nothing will ever prepare me for his size, yet nothing could fill me so perfectly, so fully. The man was made for me, and I will never take that for granted.

"I want to fuck you," I beg him, knowing if he keeps this up, I'll be on my third orgasm before I could ever repay him. "Will it hurt if I get on top?"

He slows his hips from rocking into me as his teeth scrape his bottom lip. "No, not if I sit up."

I'm nearly in tears when he slips out of me, but it's not

long until he's pulling me onto his lap and I'm sinking back down around him.

"Ah, yes," I groan as my muscles clench against his thick shaft. I can feel him so deep from this angle that I'm surprised it doesn't hurt.

"Tell me how I feel." His eyes are hooded, and his words come out so low and gravelly that a chill snakes up my spine.

I grab hold of my breasts so I can pick up the pace. "Too good to be true," I gasp. "I love the way you fill me, so completely." Then I lean forward, because I want him to know that he fills me in more than one way. My heart is the fullest it's been my whole entire life, and it's all thanks to him.

I kiss him slowly as my hips pick up the pace. His fingers dig into my hips like he's trying to steady me, but I'm not sure if that's possible. I'm chasing another orgasm, but first, I need to make sure he's with me.

"Come with me?"

He nods against my mouth. "You couldn't stop me if you tried. I'm with you, babe."

We're frantic now, our slick skin slapping together as he drives into me as deep as he could possibly go. Just when I feel my orgasm begin to take control, a sexy groan releases from his throat, telling me he's just as close. That's when I let go. The jar cracks, we both escape, and then we're flying, soaring, lighting up the night sky, our souls now conjoined into one.

Our bodies slow as our breathing grasps for control. We hold each other tight, still connected, his arousal seeping out from where we're connected.

"I'm going to spend the rest of my life worshiping you,

Evelyn Vaughn." His promise comes with a kiss to my chest, right above my heart. "Loving you..." He kisses me again. "Chasing fireflies with you." Another kiss.

My throat tightens with emotion. "Linc," I try, but my voice is just a feigned attempt.

"All I want is to make you so damn happy," he says, this time looking up and deeply into my eyes.

"You already do, Linc." I swallow over the lump in my throat. "I love you so much." I place my hands on both of his cheeks. "More than fifteen-year-old me could have ever imagined. I chose you then, you know?" Then I smile, loving that he told me he would spend his life chasing fireflies with me. "Of all the fireflies in the sky, I knew it then. You're my one and only."

His cheeks lift and his nose brushes mine. "I guess that means you're finally moving in. You heard Lucy earlier." He grins. "She thinks we should get married and everything. I know how you hate disappointing her."

I bite down on my smile, but I can't contain it long. "You're evil."

He chuckles and shakes his head. "Just trying to make my two favorite girls happy." His gaze softens, a seriousness radiating from them now that causes my heart to kick. "Marry me, Evie."

I open my mouth in surprise, ready to tell him he's crazy, but he's not done talking.

"I don't have a ring. I didn't plan this at all." He shakes his head. "But if there's anything I've learned since losing Carley, it's that time is the most precious thing we have. I don't want to waste another second when I already know you're my forever." His eyes search mine. "Marry me," he says again, this time a whisper. "Evelyn Beatrice Vaughn."

Seconds pass, only because it's hard for me to speak with this damn lump lodged in my throat. I'm not sure I ever told Lincoln my middle name, but I remember telling his sister fourteen years ago.

I swallow over my building emotions and sip in as much air as humanly possible while my heart orchestrates an entire symphony in my chest. "Yes," I finally say.

Lincoln's eyes widen but he doesn't say a word.

"Yes," I echo, this time with a slow smile spreading across my face. "I'll marry you." Pressing my lips to his, I can feel my eyes burning with a fresh set of tears. "Dr. Lincoln Reed."

He grins, and I can practically feel our chests exploding together.

"So, what's next?" I tease, since the answer is completely obvious as he grows hard again between my legs.

"Well," he says, placing his hands back on my hips. "For one, we can get you off birth control, so we can give Lucy a sibling. That was what she wished for tonight, you know?"

My heart melts. "I don't think you're supposed to tell me that. It might not come true now."

Lincoln's brows raise and he flips me over, so I'm flat on my back and his mouth slides to my ear. "Oh, it's going to come true." He presses himself deeply inside of me. "I'll make sure of it, Evie Girl."

EPILOGUE

EVELYN REED, ONE YEAR LATER

We Are All Fireflies

by Foster Pruitt

We are all fireflies

roaming through the sky

We seek a mate to call our own

until the day we die

Our sparkling light

shining ever so bright

in a nighttime serenade

All except the femme fatale

whose clever plan, a charade

She's a black widow

of the firefly world

who returns a mating call

With a deceptive glance

she holds her stance,

in a plan to lure her prey

With a flashing light

it's then she strikes

entrapping him to die

We are all fireflies, you see

but there is only one who lies

My heart catches in my throat as I read the final words of the poem. This is what Lincoln has been working on for the past year while he finalized his novel, submitted it to multiple agents, and then began preparations for publishing. After everything we've been through, after all his studies, his research, and his work with the FBI, Lincoln's philosophical theory is finally complete.

After reading the first complete draft, my mind was completely blown. While Lincoln had rattled off bits and pieces of his work to me, it never quite made sense until I read through it all myself.

Firefly Effect is a philosophical concept rooted in existentialism, the uniqueness of human beings, and how we are wired to find our own paths toward a higher purpose. The theoretical novel is layered in truths, allegories about the Firefly Man, poems, and hypothetical ponderings. It's brilliant in every way, and my heart swells with pride for my husband as I stare across the room at him.

He's currently standing near the bar engaged in conversation with an older man I've never met before and a beautiful brunette woman with a soft smile and eyes so stunning, I can see their depth from where I'm hanging out by the kids' section of Firefly.

We're having a private party for Lincoln to celebrate his massive achievement. A book release. Who would have thought fifteen years of life would surmount to something we're both so incredibly proud of. But it's his dedication that puts a chokehold on me after reading it for the first time.

To Carley, you blazed a trail so we all could finally see. Thank you for sharing your light. Love you forever, sis.

I close the novel and smile down at the cover, an illustration of a jar of fireflies. The glass is cracked and the fireflies are escaping into the night. I used to think of that cracked jar as the reason for Carley's demise, but I know better now. That jar doesn't represent death or loss. It represents freedom—freedom from darkness, freedom from pain.

On the opposite end of the spectrum—confinement, which is Lilith Thornefield's new reality. Locked away for life for twelve counts of murder as the Firefly Man. And the attempted murders of Billy and Lincoln. It's safe to say, Lilith will never dim the light of another innocent soul again.

Lilith's daughter, Willow, was placed into the care of her grandmother. Not the most ideal of situations, but it's the best one she's got. At least Willow will have family and friends in town looking out for her as she tries to deal with her new life. As young as she is, Lincoln believes Willow can learn to accept who her mother is, what she's done, and find a way to live a good life, unlike her mother.

As for why Lilith chose to murder under the Firefly Man alias—she gave no finite reason other than that she was inspired by the campfire tale and made it her own.

A shiver shoots through my body just thinking about the deceit of a woman so many trusted with their children.

Kyle hands me a glass of water from his tray with a wink and I smile back, grateful to him for choosing to work the event today when he was invited to attend as a guest. He, Armando, and Janessa decided to tag team the event so that they could enjoy the best of both worlds.

I slip through the crowd to get to Lincoln, then slide my arm through his, not wanting to interrupt his conversation. He tugs me closer and trails off mid-sentence anyway. "Evie, I want to introduce you to the man I've spoken so highly about. This is Doctor Rohls, my mentor from back in my Duke days."

The surprise in my gasp is completely genuine. While I

knew Dr. Rohls had been given an invitation, he never RSVP'd. We weren't expecting him. "It's so nice to meet you, Doctor. I suppose I should thank you for inspiring my husband."

His weathered smile reveals deep lines on his face, especially beside his eyes. "Oh, he was already putting in the work, my dear. I just encouraged him a little, I suppose. But I hear it's you who's the true inspiration."

My cheeks heat. "I wish I could take credit for such a brilliant mind, but I just provide the drinks." I grin and gesture around the bar.

Dr. Rohls lifts his glass. "Cheers to that."

Lincoln leans down to kiss my head. "Dr. Rohls brought a friend with him today, too. Meet Aurora June."

It takes everything in my being not to gasp at the familiarity of the woman's name. The woman is practically a celebrity in the Appalachians thanks to her abduction in a string of serial murders. Lincoln had told me that Dr. Rohls was once her therapist, helping her through the trauma. His published work, *Waterfall Effect,* was inspired by her.

"From Balsam Grove," I say, extending my hand out to shake hers. "I recognize the name."

She nods, her gray eyes even more stunning from up close. "The one and only."

"I hear you lived to tell your own tale," I say.

She smiles. "As did you."

"Hey now," Lincoln says, lifting his own glass of Tennessee Whiskey. "Let's cheers to that. To those who live to tell the tale."

We all grin and lift our glasses, and I catch the look in Aurora's eyes when she sees my water. I wink at her, answering the question I know she wants to ask. *Yes, I'm pregnant,* my wink tells her, but since I'm only two months into my pregnancy, no one besides Lincoln and I know.

We're so excited to tell Lucy and Francine next month, and we're already thinking of all the adorable ways we can spill the news that Lucy will be a big sister. She'll be an amazing one too, considering her new favorite thing to do is carry her own plastic baby around with her.

"We'll let you mingle," Dr. Rohls says after setting down his glass. "Enjoy your moment, Linc. You deserve it." He wraps Lincoln in a hug, causing a new lump to form in my throat. "I'm proud of you, son."

Geez, we're only an hour into this event and my eyes have watered more than they did when I found out we were pregnant.

"How are you feeling," Lincoln asks as soon as Dr. Rohls and Aurora walk away.

Poor Lincoln has had to hold my hair back too many times during morning sickness that, funnily, is not just contained to morning hours. Everything makes me nauseous lately. But I smile up at him, not wanting him to worry about me for a second. "I'm perfect. How are you?"

He looks around nodding. "Besides the awkward elephants in the room, namely your parents and the Pruitts who look to be in deep conversation, I'm doing good."

I snap my head to another corner of the room where my mom and dad are, in fact, engaged in what looks to be an engrossing conversation with Lincoln's former adoptive family.

My parents managed to slip back into my life when they found out about the wedding. They came to town and all but demanded to meet my fiancé, the doctor. I allowed it, knowing that it didn't matter if they approved or not. Their opinions can't affect me anymore. So, we deal with them in small doses.

The Pruitts were deeply apologetic to Lincoln after Lilith's arrest and the facts of her case were made public. Lincoln, too, was able to accept an apology and make a little bit of room for their presence in our lives.

The relationships aren't perfect, and they are far from ever being repaired. That simply isn't possible. But we are more than okay with moving on from the darkness that came with our past in every way we possibly can.

We're still watching the Vaughns and Pruitts as they break into a fit of laughter, causing Lincoln and I to sigh together.

Lincoln turns his focus to me. "What do you say, Mrs. Reed?" He sticks out his elbow. "Ready to continue making our rounds?"

"Yes, but I'll need you to do one thing first, *Doctor*."

He narrows his eyes at me then smiles. "Anything."

Smiling, I hold out my copy of *Firefly Effect* along with a black marker. "Can I please have your autograph?"

He accepts the book and pen with a grin. "I thought you'd never ask."

Evie Girl,

Thank you for making all my dreams come true.
Love, your mate for eternity.

Linc

THE END

CONNECT WITH K.K.

I hope you enjoyed Evie and Linc's story! If you have a few minutes to spare, please consider leaving a review on Amazon, BookBub, and/or Goodreads. Reviews and sharing your love for our stories mean the world to an author. You can also connect with me on social media and sign up for my mail list to be sure and never miss a new release, event, or sale!

Subscribe: https://geni.us/KKAllenNewsletter
Instagram: Instagram.com/KKAllen_Author
Facebook: Facebook.com/AuthorKKAllen
TikTok: Tiktok.com/@k.k.allen
Website: www.KKAllen.com

Join Forever Young
Enjoy special sneak peeks, exclusive giveaways, enter to win ARCs, and chat it up with K.K. and special guests.
Facebook.com/groups/foreveryoungwithkk

ACKNOWLEDGMENTS

THANK YOU for reading. From the depths of my heart, I am so grateful that you chose to pick up and read *Firefly Effect* when I know you have an endless amount of choices. If you're here because you loved *Waterfall Effect*, thank you for wanting more in this world. If you're new to me, thank you for taking a chance! Here's hoping I took you on a ride you'll never forget.

Evelyn and Lincoln were two characters that came to me easily. They guided this story in a way that felt so right to follow. After taking over a year off publishing, I did not expect that to happen. There was a time I was terrified I might never write again. Life got hard. My heart was broken. My entire world changed so drastically, I had no idea how I would come out of it on the other side. But here I am—the happiest, healthiest, and strongest I've been in a long time. I was even able to pump out a novel out in the process. Even better, it might just be my favorite novel I've ever written.

To my family for supporting me through life and work

and all the transitions. I wouldn't have been able to write any of these words without you. Jagger, thank you for letting me read the prologue of Firefly Effect out loud so we could talk about the story. You have an incredibly creative mind. I can't wait to see what you do with it. Dad, Sheryl, and Corey—I'll never forget seeing my first firefly with you all in Texas. I like to think that night was the first seed in many that were planted for this story to bloom.

Lindsey, Cyndi, and Patricia, thank you will never be enough. You brainstormed with me and encouraged me with every draft. I love you all to the moon and back.

Sammie, Erica, and Kristie! Boss babes all the way. I'm so grateful for your time and support. Thank you for helping me get *Firefly Effect* as perfect as it can possibly be.

To all the bloggers and bookstagrammers who have supported this release, THANK YOU. You all do so much for this community and ask for nothing in exchange. I'm honored you chose to read and support this one.

While I've had *Firefly Effect* on the brain for years, the details of the story were explored and researched as time went on. A quick shoutout to my beautiful friend, Kristine, who let me bug her with random questions about the legal stuff.

An extra shoutout to my bestie, PA, and all-around boss, Lindsey. You just keep upping your own game day after day. I don't know what I'd do without you. Don't make me ever find out.

To Mary from Red Adept Editing. THANK YOU for working with my crazy schedule, for the phone call that saved this book, and for giving *Firefly Effect* your time and energy to make it the best it could possibly be.

To my amazing reader group, FOREVER YOUNG,

who is still cheering me on, even during my hiatus. Thank you for reminding me how good it feels to share bits and pieces of myself with the world.

To my Angsters <3—my street team who stuck around even after I disappeared for a year. All the heart emojis.

To Roxie and Jen with Wordsmith, it's so fun to think about how our friendship started in 2016. You took a chance on *Up in the Treehouse* and then encouraged me to publish a very steamy rockstar romance that I had put under a different pen name. Wolf and Lyric thank you, and so do I. <3

Last but not least, to the Elite 9 crew and porch hang mommas (and dads). Peggy, Steffy, Kim, Melissa, Sarah, Tonya, Kristine, Michelle, Kelli, Heidi, Stephanie. You were there for me during some really tough times, though you probably didn't even realize it. You keep me busy and laughing constantly. I love you all the pieces.

To everyone, I hope you loved Evie and Linc's story. Thank you so much for reading!

Much Love,

A BRIDGE BETWEEN US (EXCERPT)

AVAILABLE IN KINDLE UNLIMITED

PROLOGUE

I had always known he wasn't mine to keep, but that didn't change the way I loved him—quietly, gently, and from afar.

As the seasons changed, the corn stalks grew strong, and the grapevines flourished with hope. But none of it mattered, not when the soil at our feet bound us in a century-old rivalry. We'd never even had a chance.

They said life flashed before your eyes on the way to death, but on that night, after my final scream burst from my throat and my world started to fade to black, I only thought of him and his sweet chocolate eyes, his desperately cautious stare, and his silence that carried more weight than gold.

I should have died that night. Instead, I crossed the moonlit bridge and never returned. I let rivalry win. If only that had been enough to keep us all safe. If only we didn't have a bridge between us.

CHAPTER 1 - THE PAST (CAMILA)

The dark barrel of the shotgun stared back at me, halting me in my tracks. My heart should have been pounding like a gavel, but I suspected the boy on the other end of the trigger was no threat. He was just scared.

His hands shook, though he was desperately trying to steady the weapon. Beads of sweat formed around his mouth, and his dark-brown hair stuck to his forehead. I was a stranger to him, but even with a scowl and dirt from a long day's work on the farm coating his face, he wasn't a stranger to me.

I'd seen him just the day before when my parents were setting up their wine-tasting booth at the farmer's market in downtown Telluride. I was sitting on the tailgate of our truck, restlessly swinging my legs, when my gaze caught on an older boy carrying crates to one of the produce booths —back and forth, back and forth, like a pendulum. His eyes were cast in front of him, his hair was disheveled, his lips were flattened in a line, and he carried himself in a way that made it all look effortless.

In a small town like ours, it was easy to spot the newcomers because of the clear difference between the residents, the snowbirds, and the tourists. That boy was none of the above.

Curious, I kept my eyes glued to him as he tried to angle the corn bins onto the display and failed miserably as they rolled down and around his feet. I giggled at the show, finding it fascinating how a strong boy could seem so flustered at a simple task. I didn't know why, but I wanted to know everything about him, including why he had come to Telluride, of all places.

A moment later, one of my questions was answered when Harold Cross, an older man with a long, full beard and a plaid button-down shirt over jeans, approached the boy with a disapproving frown and a shake of his head. He mumbled something to the boy, but I couldn't read his lips. Clearly, Harold was displeased, which didn't surprise me. The farmer was known as the town grump, always walking around with a chip on his shoulder.

Two prominent farmlands featured in the red rocky mountain land that bordered the southeastern side of Telluride, Colorado—the Cross Farm and Ranch and the Bell Family Vineyard and Winery. Harold owned the farm-land across from our family's vineyard, though we rarely came into contact with him. Our lands were separated by an area of dense woods and a strip of acreage as long as our land was wide, so it felt silly to call ourselves neighbors. In fact, it was forbidden.

When my parents walked back to the tailgate of the truck, my curiosity grew even more. "Papa, why haven't I seen Farmer Cross at the market before today?"

My papa's eyes widened in surprise as he registered my words, then he took a quick look over his shoulder. The way his back stiffened told me all I needed to know. The surprise wasn't pleasant.

"Must be a mistake," he said, clearly miffed by Farmer Cross's presence. "Cross has been on the vendor waitlist for years."

He and Farmer Cross would never be friends. The whole town was privy to the famous Bell and Cross feud that went back over a century. The feud had started with land, became fueled with money, hastened with greed, and ultimately ended in power. My papa held that power, thanks to his prime social standing in the community, and he would do anything to keep it.

I'd just opened my mouth to change the subject when my papa whipped his head toward my mama. "He brought that boy here, Selena. I'm going to say something to Bill."

My mama leaned in and narrowed her eyes. "You will not get the town manager involved in this, Patrick. Harold Cross and his son have just as much right to be here as we do."

"His son?" I asked, the question slipping from my mouth more quickly than I could catch it. "I've never seen him be—"

My papa huffed and gave me a warning look. "That boy is trouble. You're not to go anywhere near him. You understand me, Camila?"

"You're speaking nonsense," my mother hissed. "He's just a fifteen-year-old boy."

Only two years older than me. Hope sparked in my chest.

My papa shook his head. "No. He's a Cross. Therefore, he's trouble. If he's not now, then he will be soon enough. Just you wait." He leaned forward, his face reddening like it always did when he got worked up. "The boy's a Ute, I'll have you know." He whispered that part, telling me it was something bad.

Everyone around there knew the Ute people were the first indigenous inhabitants of Western Colorado. The Ute Mountain reservation was just across the San Juan Mountains, nearly a two-hour drive away. Our teachers talked about it in school, and the various landmarks in and around town pointed to their history. But my knowledge was clearly vague, according to my papa's anger.

"What's wrong with being a Ute, Papa?"

"Those *Indians* think this land is still theirs, and that makes them trouble," he snapped. "My ancestors worked hard to purchase the plots we live and work on, and no one will make me feel different." His indignant huff could be felt for miles. "And that's that."

"You mean *Native American*. And the boy has a name," my mama said, her eyes filled with anger. "It's *Ridge*."

"How do you know?" my papa shot back.

Every time my parents argued, their cultures spewed out like pent-up lava. With my papa's Spanish roots and my mama's Brazilian roots, they shared passionate dynamics that worked for them in love but against them at a crossroads.

"Harold brought him by the country club for a round of golf the other day."

My papa's face twisted in confusion. "Harold *golfs?*"

Mama rolled her eyes. "I don't know, Patrick. Maybe he was just showing his son around town. The boy seems so quiet and sweet."

"Who wouldn't become a mute if their mother went missing one day and never came home? Doesn't mean the boy's sweet. Don't be so naive, Selena. It's the quiet ones you need to watch out for."

My throat closed at the thought of Ridge losing his mother. *Missing?*

As if detecting my sadness, my mama turned toward me with a sympathetic expression then wrapped an arm around my shoulders and planted a kiss on my cheek. "Don't worry, *mija*. A mother's love never goes away. I'm sure she will turn up."

Then she faced my papa with sharpened daggers in her eyes. "This conversation is over."

I hoped what she'd said was true. Though I hoped Ridge was okay, I didn't know how he could be. To lose a parent in that way and never know if you would ever see them again—I didn't even want to imagine such a thing.

I'd chosen to say nothing more about Ridge or Farmer Cross that day. I'd heard my papa's warning loud and clear. *Stay away or else.* But that didn't mean I had any intentions of listening.

Hence why the boy was standing in front of his property, aiming a shotgun between my eyes.

It was my second time seeing the boy, and I couldn't stop my pulse from racing at just how good looking he actually was. With high cheekbones that kissed the sun, almond-shaped chocolate eyes that looked lost, smooth skin that clearly spent time outdoors, and a strong angled nose that gave him a distinctly different appearance from anyone else I'd ever known, the new boy in town was utterly fascinating, so much that I ignored the flags and whistles that blew with our first meeting.

I propped my hands on my hips and leaned forward so that my small voice would carry over the bridge. "You can put the gun down, Farm Boy. I'm not leaving."

My papa had taught me to stand my ground in the presence of a bully. He told me that in most cases, the one doing the threatening was the real coward. My mama, on the other hand, had warned my papa that he was making me too confident for my own good. I wasn't afraid to test both theories.

The boy clenched his jaw then shook his head before jabbing the gun in my direction.

I tilted my head and squinted, trying to determine whether everything my papa had told me about the boy was true. "You're Ridge Cross," I said finally. I was confident in the statement, but it irked me that the boy didn't even flinch at the fact that I knew who he was.

According to my papa's rant, which had seemed to last the good part of the previous day, the boy didn't speak—ever—but I wasn't convinced it was because he *couldn't*. "Are you really a mute?"

The boy's eyes flashed with anger.

Blood raced through my veins. "It's fine, you know, if you don't want to talk. I don't mind. My parents tell me I talk enough for everyone else, anyway." Daring a step forward, I cautioned him with my eyes. "I just want to come a little closer and introduce myself. Is that okay?"

I didn't wait for his permission again. After a series of long strides over the center of the forty-foot-long bridge, I slowed to assess the situation. Ridge still hadn't moved an inch as he spied me with curious brown eyes and a stiffened frame. And he hadn't taken his barrel off me.

"I'm your neighbor. I live right through there." I pointed behind me at a thick patch of forest that separated a section of landlocked public property from my parents' vineyard. "Where the grapevines grow?" I said the last part as a question to see if I would get any sort of response from him. Even a simple nod would have appeased me.

Again, he didn't shift an inch, causing me to sigh as I took another step forward. Annoyance was starting to twist its way through me. I didn't like to be ignored.

"I'm standing on public property. You shoot me now, you go to jail." I pointed toward a large spruce tree marked with red spray paint by my papa. "Your property is past that red *X*."

That time, the boy looked, following the direction I'd

pointed to, and I took it as an opportunity. I marched the rest of the way to him then wrapped my fist around the barrel of his gun and shoved it away from my face.

His head snapped back to mine, and my lips curled into a smile.

I stuck out my other hand. "Camila Bell. Nice to meet you."

His face bunched into a deeper scowl as he glanced at my hand then back to my face. He didn't shake my hand in return or speak. Instead, he blew out a breath and yanked his shotgun from my grip before setting it against a nearby tree. I chose to believe it was a truce of sorts.

I nodded past him again, gesturing to the plot of land his father owned, where the cornfields grew tall over the summer. "Wanna run with me?"

Confusion replaced his scowl.

"I like to run through the cornfields. It's fun. You'll see." I reached for his hand, but before I could even touch it, he yanked it away.

Shock and annoyance rippling through me, I stumbled back. Not only was I curious, but I was also determined. "Okay, fine. Whatever." Holding up my hands, I rolled my eyes. "I was just trying to be nice."

With a glare, I turned to make it look like I was leaving, but then I pivoted and made a dash for the tree that held his gun and turned the barrel on him.

His eyes flashed with surprise as I started forward, causing him to have to walk backward. "You think you're some tough guy, huh? Pointing this shotgun at me like it gives you power? Well, it doesn't. The most powerful weapon you possess is your tongue, Farm Boy, and it appears you don't like to use yours much. So, tell me, who has the power now?"

I stepped forward one more time, and it was enough. Ridge took a final step back, his foot caught on the edge of the creek, and he fell back into the water. The shock on his face was priceless as water soaked through his white shirt and dark jeans.

I laughed a little too hard and pulled the gun back to check the safety. As soon as I confirmed my suspicions, I grinned. "Surprise, surprise. Safety's on, Farm Boy." Then I inspected the chamber and laughed even harder when I saw that it was empty. "I knew it." I threw the gun to the side and backed toward his land while he pulled himself out of the creek.

He shook his head so adamantly at me that it made me laugh.

"What is it, boy? You don't want me to trespass?"

He nodded just as viciously as he'd shaken his head.

"Well, that's too bad." I took another step back, crossing the red X on the tree. "I've been running through the fields for years. Besides, it's the easiest way to get where I'm going." I shrugged. "So come with me or don't. But you sure as heck ain't stoppin' me."

With that, I turned and took off through the woods and into the cornfields.

CHAPTER 2 - THE HUNTER

Through the scope of his binoculars, the hunter tracked their movements at the bridge and through the woods then lost them when they tore through the cornfields. He didn't bother chasing them there. He'd followed the girl enough to know exactly where they were headed and would take another path.

Twigs snapped and leaves crunched beneath his heavy boots as he worked his way along the creek toward the hilltop, not even bothering to be quiet. No one dared to walk that route. Not only was it inaccessible to the public, but it was dangerous terrain, just a narrow piece of land above a steep slope. The bed of water below widened and rushed faster where it got deeper and colder—which was why the girl preferred the forbidden route through the corn.

With each step, annoyance swirled inside the hunter like it did every time the girl broke the rules. Camila Bell was beginning to become a problem. Her papa was too blind and stupid to see the trouble behind his little girl's eyes, but the hunter saw her for the mischievous little brat she was and would always be. Something would have to be done. A lesson would need to be taught.

The hunter emerged from the woods and stepped into the tall dried grass, which just reached his eyes. His heavy breathing slowed as he paused and scanned his surroundings. A second later, he saw her again, just as he knew he would.

She was trudging across his line of vision a safe distance away from spotting him when she stopped and glanced over her shoulder to see if the boy was still following her. He was, begrudgingly so, but his presence only added to the hunter's frustration. Besides the fact that she had wandered too far, her dad would have her head if he ever found out *who* she was hanging around with.

Camila had only ever traveled to the hilltop alone, and she had already gotten too close for comfort. She had no business traipsing around land she didn't own, especially when her father owned plenty.

That land belonged to the hunter. And he would do whatever it took to keep it.

Want to keep reading? Grab this **EPIC** love story **HERE**. Read it **FREE** with Kindle Unlimited!

MORE K.K. ALLEN BOOKS

Up in the Treehouse

Haunted by the past, Chloe and Gavin are forced to come to terms with all that has transpired to find the peace they deserve. Except they can't seem to get near each other without combatting an intense emotional connection that brings them right back to where it all started… their childhood treehouse.

Under the Bleachers

Fun and flirty Monica Stevens lives for food, fashion, and boys… in that order. The last thing she wants to take seriously is dating. When a night of flirty banter with Seattle's hottest NFL quarterback turns passionate, her care-free life could be at risk.

Through the Lens

When Maggie moves to Seattle for a fresh start, she's presented with an unavoidable obstacle—namely, the cocky chef with a talent for photography and getting under her skin. Can they learn to get along for the sake of the ones they love?

Over the Moon

Silver Livingston has spent the past eight years hiding from her past when the NFL God, Kingston Scott, steps off the bus to mentor a football camp for kids. Kingston wants to be anywhere but at Camp Dakota… until he sees her. The intoxicating woman with the silver moon eyes, the reserved smile, and the past she's determined to keep hidden.

Weight of Regret

Hope Davies has loved Anderson Bexley since the moment she first spotted him on that rickety camp dock. It took her years to finally confess her feelings, only to get rejected at the start of, what she thought, was their happily ever. A year after his heartbreaking rejection, an unexpected reunion forces them to reevaluate their feelings.

Moments In Time

Single mom, Violet Hart, will do anything for her little boy. Even if that means moonlighting as a dancer in disguise to make ends-meet. After a surprise encounter with her childhood best friend, Jamison Bexley, her secret is threatened… along with her heart.

Heart of Stone

Benson Bexley is back in his hometown with the same heart of stone he left with ten years ago. When a new art venture takes him on an unexpected journey, his instructor, Brooklyn Kennedy, is there to challenge him every step of the way.

Blanket of Stars

Cayson Bexley always wanted to fly, until a near-fatal accident clipped his wings. Now, he's back in his hometown of Orcas Island, looking for a new purpose. He never expected to meet Olivia Jade, a local musician who's as flirtatious as she is challenging. She's also the one woman he can't have.

A Stolen Melody Duet

Lyric Cassidy knows a thing or two about bad boy rock stars with raspy vocals. In fact, her heart was just played by one. So when she takes an assignment as road manager for the world famous rock star, Wolf, she's prepared to take him on, full suit of heart-armor intact.

British Bachelor

Runaway British Bachelor contestant, Liam Colborn, is on the run from the media. When he gets to Providence to stay with his late brother's best friend, all he wants is a little time to regroup from his time on a failed reality show. That is, until he meets the redheaded bombshell nanny who lives in the pool house.

Fired Up

Meadow Matthews isn't a woman who needs saving, but she just might save me. As a single mom to an adorable little boy, she leaves little time for play. Which is why, when I approach her with a fun opportunity, she instantly declines. Unfortunately, snapping photos of greased-up firefighters for a calendar isn't her thing. Lucky for us, she fires me up just enough to convince her otherwise.

Waterfall Effect

Lost in the shadows of a tragedy that stripped Aurora of everything she once loved, she's back in the small town of Balsam Grove, ready to face all she's kept locked away for seven years. Or so she thinks.

Firefly Effect

Evelyn is nothing more than a shell of her former self. Her life moves like a clock, from one moment to the next, never a surprise. Gone are the days of chasing fireflies through the woods. Until her therapist goes missing and he's replaced with someone new. Dr. Lincoln Reed. A devastatingly handsome single dad with an intensity behind his evergreen eyes that jolts her back to life.

A Bridge Between Us

With a century-old feud between neighboring families with only a bridge to separate them, Camila and Ridge find themselves wanting to rewrite the future. It all starts with an innocent friendship and quickly builds to so much more in this epic second chance coming of age romance.

Center of Gravity (Gravity, #1)

Lex was athleticism and grace, precision and passion, and she had a stage presence Theo couldn't tear my eyes from. He wanted her...on his team, in his bed. There was only one problem... He couldn't have both.

Falling From Gravity (Gravity, #1.5)

Amelia was nothing like Tobias had expected. Even after all the years—of living so close to her, of listening to her giggle with his sister in the bedroom next to his—he hadn't given much thought to his sister's best friend, until a secret spring break trip to Big Sur changed everything.

Defying Gravity (Gravity, #2)

The ball is in Amelia's court, but Tobias isn't below stealing —her power, her resolve, her heart. When he wants a second chance to reignite their connection, the answer is simple. They can't. Not unless they defy the rules their dreams were built on and risk everything.

The Trouble With Gravity (Gravity, #3)

When Sebastian makes Kai an offer she can't afford to refuse, she learns taking the job will mean facing the tragedy she's worked so hard to shut out. He says she can trust him to keep her safe, but is her heart safe too?

Find them all here: www.kkallen.com

Shop EXCLUSIVE

* Signed Books
* Book Boxes
* Book Inspired Drinkware
* Collectors Items & Swag

FREE
Shipping
on orders over
$100

www.KKAllen.com/Shop

ABOUT K.K. ALLEN

K.K. Allen is a *USA Today* bestselling and award-winning author who writes heartfelt and inspirational contemporary romance stories. K.K. is a Hawaiian girl who graduated from the University of Washington with an Interdisciplinary Arts and Sciences degree and currently resides in central Florida with her ridiculously handsome little dude who owns her heart.

K.K.'s publishing journey began in June 2014 with a young adult contemporary fantasy trilogy. In 2016, she published her first contemporary romance, *Up in the Treehouse*, which went on to win the Romantic Times 2016 Reviewers' Choice Award for Best New Adult Book of the Year.

With K.K.'s love for inspirational and coming of age stories involving heartfelt narratives and honest emotions, you can be assured to always be surprised by what K.K. releases next.

www.ingramcontent.com/pod-product-compliance
Lightning Source LLC
Chambersburg PA
CBHW031828310726
48972CB00005B/1202